SILVER VALLEY UNIVERSITY

# Hidden Secrets

## ALISHA WILLIAMS

Book cover design: Alisha Williams

Editor: Foxtale Editing

Formatting: Dez Purington with Pretty in Ink Creations

*I'd like to dedicate this book to someone who came to me as a reader but turned into a best friend. Nikki, thank you for working with me side by side and helping me make Ellie's story real. Thank you for the hours of voice messages, bouncing ideas off each other, and for just loving my characters so much to be so invested. I don't think this book would be what it is if it wasn't for your help. I can't wait to see what we do for the rest of the series. Love you, girl.*

## Author's Note

Please be advised. This is a reverse harem/why choose romance, meaning the heroine of this story does not have to pick between her love interests.

This book contains explicitly described sexual content and the excessive use of swear words. This is a dark-themed book and contains a lot of things that may trigger some readers. It is not for the faint of heart, so please read the trigger warnings before you dive in.

# *Trigger Warning*

This book contains one rape scene in slight detail. This book, as well as this series, plays a big part around that tragic incident.

There is also bullying that takes place. Please go into this book with an open mind. You have been warned.

# Playlist

*FMRN* by Lilyisthatyou
*Hey, Mama* by David Guetta featuring Nicki Minaj and Bebe Rexha
*Shout Out To My Ex* by Little Mix
*Hands To Myself* by Selena Gomez
*Guys My Age* by Hey Violet
*Never Forget You* by Zara Larsson and MNEK
*Abcdefu* by GAYLE

# *Prologue*

## ELLIE

"YOU LOOK STUNNING, BABY," Rain whispers against my neck, making me shiver as she looks at me in the mirror. Her fiery red hair, which matches her personality perfectly, hangs over my shoulder. She's dressed in her graduation gown, but I still have yet to put mine on over my dress.

"Thank you." I blush. Rain is a very outspoken person. She says what's on her mind with little to no care about what other people think, and her boldness always affects me in the best way possible.

Sometimes her mouth gets her in trouble, but that will never stop her. She won't change for anyone, and that's one of the many things I love about her.

Her hands skim down my sides, then up to cup my breasts through my strapless white flowy dress. I suck in a breath, and my eyes flutter close but not before I see the wicked glint in her eyes. She loves being able to light up my body with a simple touch.

She slowly peppers kisses on my neck and behind my ear while kneading my breasts as I get lost in the sensations.

"Enough of that, you two, or we will never make it across that stage."

Chase's voice snaps me out of my lust-filled haze. "Party pooper," she growls against my neck before giving me one last kiss. "I'll see you downstairs, beautiful. The dickhead does have a point." She wiggles her eyebrows at me.

Turning in my chair, I watch as she makes her way over to Chase.

"Who are you calling a dickhead?" Chase asks with a raised brow.

"You, dickhead," Rain taunts, then reaches up to mess with Chase's platinum blond strands that are slicked back.

"You little shit!" He gawks at her, and she gives him a wide grin.

"Oops," she shrugs, still smiling. Chase narrows his eyes at her and attacks, lunging for her. He gets her in a headlock and starts giving her a noogie. She screams in protest, but I know it's all fun and games with them.

When I moved here in fourth grade, I was this shy little girl at a new school starting all over, yet again. This was my fifth school. My dad always moved around for work, but thankfully, this was our last stop. I didn't know that at the time, so I did what I always did and avoided people. I always knew I'd have to leave anyone I made friends with, so what was the point of even trying?

One day, I was sitting on the grass by the playground, reading one of my *Nancy Drew* books, when a soccer ball came out of nowhere and sent my book flying. When I looked around to see where it came from, this pretty girl with auburn hair towered over me. She told me her name was Rain and that she was sorry. When I looked behind her, I saw three boys. She introduced me to Jax, the one with black hair, Brody with the brown hair, and Chase, who had the whitest hair I'd ever seen. Jax and Chase were the jokesters and just as friendly as Rain, but Brody was quiet. Not because he was shy, but because he was always on guard, observing every situation. *Mr. Serious.*

The 'not wanting to make friends' idea? That went out the

window when Rain started hounding me every day to hang out with her and the guys. After a few weeks, I gave in. She was relentless, and because of that, Rain always got her way. As the year went on, we all became good friends.

By seventh grade, I had the biggest crush on the guys. Puberty hit, and they were all I could think about. I thought Rain had feelings for them too, but later discovered that she didn't like guys at all. Shortly after that, she let it be known that she actually had feelings for me. That's who Rain is. When she wants something, she goes for it, and she wanted me. When she told me, I was surprised, but the more I thought about it, the more I realized that maybe the feelings I had for her were more than what best friends felt for each other. Maybe that's why I was always staring at her boobs and wondering what it would feel like to touch them or why I had the urge to be in her arms during sleepovers.

At that point, I was officially screwed. I had feelings for my three best guy friends *and* her. The summer before eighth grade, I had a break-down. I cried in Rain's arms, telling her everything because it was all too much to hold in. Rain promised me that she was cool with me liking the guys too, as long as she got to be with me as well. I thought she was crazy because the guys were for sure going to make me choose. I asked her to keep it between us, but when Rain asked if we could be official, I couldn't help but say yes. That changed things within our group. The guys started acting weird for a while. We were still close, but the guys got into sports more, and they made a bunch of guy friends.

In ninth grade, Rain and I caught Chase making out with a girl at our first party. It broke my heart and made me cry. So Rain marched right up to him and clocked him in the face, catching the attention of everyone in our little group. The two of them got into a screaming match, and that's when Rain revealed my feelings for him as well as the other guys. The look in their eyes told me they had *no* clue.

Turns out, they thought I was only into girls because Rain and I were dating. It's understandable they would have thought that. They all confessed they had feelings for me too and that they had made a pact to all date me or no one would, but that was abandoned when Rain and I had gotten together.

Apparently, they were heartbroken, but they didn't want it to change our friendship, so they chose to move on. Or so they thought. We left the party and spent the rest of the night hanging out at the park, talking everything over.

Well, Rain did most of the talking because that girl knows me better than anyone. I was too nervous about what to say and do. By the end, we all decided to give it a try.

Things weren't much different from before. We were still best friends, but with added affection. It took a while to get used to intimate touches and to go from friends to lovers, but now we're all a close-knit family.

We spent years growing closer and surviving high school with each other for support when we needed it. We've never kept our relationship a secret. Rain and the guys are proud to be with me, so we never hide our feelings. All of our parents have been surprisingly supportive of our unique relationship.

The guys are popular. All three were on the football team, and they all got scholarships to Silver Valley University to play on a more professional level. Rain was a cheerleader and also got a spot on the SVU cheer squad, but she will attend as a paid student like me.

I, by default, am popular; but being my shy, awkward self, I only go to parties because the others want to. I'm always happy to just relax at home with an excellent book while being cuddled in one of their arms.

Today is the last day of this part of our lives and the first of a whole new one. I can't wait to experience everything with my loves.

"Come on, Ellie-Belly, let's go!" Chase says, excitement

shining brightly on his face. He's always had the energy of a puppy.

Laughing, I put a few finishing touches on my makeup and slip on my graduation gown, smoothing out any remaining wrinkles.

"Fuck me, baby, you look amazing," Chase groans, and I smile, blushing slightly. These guys have seen, touched, and tasted every inch of my body many times over, but I still tend to blush at their random appreciation of me. To me, I've always felt plain. A typical blonde, basic girl, but Rain and the guys have always had a way of making me feel like a goddess, and I love them for that.

"Come on, you, we're gonna be late." I laugh, grabbing a hold of his hand, and drag him out of the room. He groans like it's the biggest inconvenience to him.

"But can't we just stay here and fuck all night?" he whines. "It would be so much more fun than sitting in a hard plastic seat for hours on end."

"You're such a big baby," I smile. "I'll make it worth the time, I promise."

His face goes from pouty to wicked. "Oh, really? And what do you have in mind?"

I give him a grin of my own. "You're just gonna have to wait and see." He lets out another groan, but this one is due to him imagining every which way he's gonna fuck me tonight, and I can't wait.

When we get to the bottom of the stairs, Jax and Brody look up from their conversation. Jax gives me a heated look like he's thinking along the same lines as Chase, and Brody gives me a thorough once over, his eyes consuming my body. I flush under his gaze and feel a heat growing in my lower belly from his intense stare.

"Damn, baby girl, look at you!" Jax praises, scooping me up and spinning me around, making me giggle. He places a kiss on my cheek, not wanting to mess up my lipstick, and sets me down in front of Brody.

"So...?" I say, biting the inside of my cheek, waiting for him to say something.

He tucks a strand of hair behind my ear and gives me a half, yet still meaningful, smile.

"You look radiant, sweet girl." His deep, smooth whiskey voice makes me shiver. He pulls me to him and places a tender kiss on my forehead, making me sigh in contentment.

"Alright, pictures!" my mom cheers as she enters the foyer from the kitchen.

The guys groan, and Rain hooks arms with me. We spend a good twenty minutes ensuring we have a million different photos before piling into two different vehicles. Rain and I go with my parents, and the guys go in Jax's jeep.

We meet the other parents at the school and get even more photos.

We spend the next few hours listening to speeches. I give my valedictorian speech while trying not to puke. I hate crowds, and I've never done well being amongst them. One time, we had a talent show and I tried to sing, but I ended up puking all over the stage from nerves. After that, I never sang around anyone again, not even Rain and the guys.

We cheer for each other as we walk across the stage, each of us proud of the other. Afterwards, we go out to eat with our families.

After saying goodbye to our parents, we head to one of the guys' teammate's house for a post-graduation party.

I'm not normally one to drink because I'm a lightweight, but I don't want to put a damper on everyone's night and be the reason why no one can really enjoy the party without worrying about me.

I'm two coolers in when I decide I don't want to drink anymore. The guys have been playing beer pong with the team while Rain is singing her little drunk heart out and hogging the karaoke machine. I love that girl like crazy, but she can't sing worth shit. Think of cats getting their tails pulled, badly. But she doesn't care and has this confidence about herself that I envy. She is comfortable with her body, and although she doesn't fully flaunt it, she is not afraid to show it off. I'm okay with that because it's who she is, and I'm okay with how people look but don't touch. She's never been shy around the guys in the bedroom, either. She's joined us in group sex more than once and hasn't cared if they see her naked as long as they don't lay a hand on her.

I'm just chilling against the wall, waiting until the others are ready to go and trying to avoid Tim, a guy from the swim team. It seems he's made it his mission tonight to hang out with me, but every time he spots me, I move on to a new location. I'm too polite to tell him to go away, and he doesn't seem to be that bad of a guy, but I'm never really interested in anything he talks about.

He's been trying to be my friend for the past year. The guys don't like it, and honestly, I'm not looking for any friends, especially not guys. But even after the guys told him to back off—more than once—he's still found ways to talk to me when they aren't around.

"When are you gonna tell that guy to fuck off?" Brody says, surprising me as he comes to stand next to me.

"He's harmless, B. He's just telling me about his plans for after the summer," I say, sipping my drink.

He grunts. "You're too nice. This guy has been sniffing around you all year, and we've been nice about it, at least to you, because you're too good of a person to tell him to go away, but I don't like it."

"Look, I'll never see this guy again after tonight. It's not gonna hurt to play nice for a little longer. I'm sure he will find some girl and forget all about me." I smile, trying to calm his drunk, grumpy ass down. Brody is usually all put together, but he likes to drink, sometimes a little too much. I'm normally his babysitter once he gets mouthy with anyone who's within hearing range. He's the only one of us with a shitty home life, and although he's good at keeping that part of himself hidden, he uses parties and drinking to forget about everything and drown his pain.

I tried talking to him about it, but he just shuts down, so I always make sure he knows I'm here for him whenever he needs me.

"Well," he slurs, "I'm going to get another drink."

"I think you've had enough," I say, grabbing his hand.

"And I don't remember asking for your opinion," he snaps back, making me flinch at his harsh tone. I'm not used to this Brody.

"Fine," I say, letting go of his hand. "If you want to be a fucking dick, then I'm going to find a quiet spot to sit and read on my Kindle app. I know when I have had enough to drink and when to stop," I say, sighing as he glowers at me. Then he stalks off.

This isn't him; this isn't the guy I love, and it's best to just leave him be when he's like this.

I walk around the house looking for a quiet spot to sit when I start to feel dizzy. My vision blurs, and my body sways.

"There you are. I've been looking for you," a voice says, but it sounds muffled and far away. I feel arms wrap around my waist. "Let's find a place for you to lie down."

I feel my body move, but I don't know if it's me or who is holding me. *Who is this? Where am I? What's going on?*

My body is met with a soft surface. I try to open my eyes, to speak, but nothing. I can vaguely hear things happening around me, but my body has shut down. I start to panic, causing a whimper to slip past my lips.

"Shhh, you're okay. You must be burning up. Let's get this dress off you." Hands rake over my body, but they're not any I recognize. Although, the voice sounds familiar.

"Beautiful," they whisper. "Do you know how much I

dream about this body? About touching it, tasting it with my own two lips?" I feel a warm breath against my neck before they kiss me. I don't know who this is, and when I try to use my brain to figure it out, the hazier it gets, no matter how hard I try.

"I tried to get your attention, but Rain and those guys always get in my way. Now they are too drunk or distracted, so I can finally have my chance to be alone with you."

His hands wander over my body as he continues to kiss everywhere his fingers touch. I don't want this. I want it to stop. I may not be able to pinpoint who this is, but I know it's not one of my guys.

I feel sick. I try to scream, fight, move...anything, but nothing works. My limbs don't cooperate.

I feel tears pooling in my eyes as I realize what's about to happen when I feel my panties being pulled down.

Whoever it is keeps talking and touching, but I block it out. When I feel my legs part and he enters me, I pray for death because I don't think I can live my life after what's happening to me.

## BRODY

I down my beer and stagger over to the guys. "Where's Ellie?" I say with a bit of a slur.

Chase and Jax look around. "I don't know. She was hanging out against the wall over there not too long ago," Chase says.

The guys on the team call Jax and Chase over for another round of beer pong.

"I'm going to go find her," I say.

"When you do, come back here so we can find Rain and go. I'm done for the night after this round," Jax says.

I nod and start my search. After looking everywhere on the first floor, I stumble my way up to the second. I remember her saying something about finding a quiet place.

I make my way down the hall when the sounds of grunting stop me. Just as I'm about to turn around and look elsewhere, I hear whoever is behind that door moaning Ellie's name.

My heart stops, and my stomach bottoms out. There's gotta be another Ellie here because it can't be mine. Needing to know for sure, I open the door, not giving a fuck.

There, grunting like a fucking pig, is Tim. Looking down, I see blonde hair fanning out over the pillow. When Tim shifts to the side, I see exactly who this fucker is plowing into. Ellie's half-lidded eyes are locked on Tim. I hear whimpers of pleasure from her, and my entire world comes crashing down.

Fury fills my veins, and I'm ready to kill every fucker in this place.

I do my best to storm out of the house, even though I'm pretty drunk. But I'm not too drunk to be mistaken about what I just saw.

She's cheating on us. I thought she fucking loved us! I thought she was happy! But she's just like my mother. Nothing is ever good enough. I always felt like she thought she was too good for us. Us being just a bunch of jocks while she's the smartest fucking student in the school.

Maybe she just stayed with us out of guilt for ruining our friendship.

"What the fuck is wrong with you?" Chase asks, rushing after me as I burst out the front door with Jax close behind.

"Where's Ellie?" Rain asks, looking around as she follows the guys out.

"Where's Ellie?" I laugh a humorless laugh. "Oh, she's just upstairs getting railed by Tim."

Rain's eyes go wide, and the guys shake their heads.

"What the fuck are you talking about? I think you've had way too much to drink," Jax says.

"Ellie would never do that!" Rain growls.

"Oh yeah? Well, I'm pretty sure I know what our girlfriend looks like, and that was her laying on that bed getting fucked good and hard by that piece of shit Tim who's been sniffing around her all year. Makes sense why she never told him to fuck off. God knows how long she's been fucking him behind our backs," I scoff.

"Stop!" Chase shouts. "You're drunk. You must have mistaken her for someone else."

"Go look for yourself, I'm sure they are still going at it. Third door on the right. Second floor," I yell, slinging an arm out at the house.

I ignore their shouts as I turn around and start walking down the street. As of this very moment, Eleanor Tatum is dead to me.

## CHASE

"He's wrong," Rain says, panic setting in. "He's lying."

"Only one way to find out," Jax says, then races back into the house, and we follow. We push past the party goers, heading right to the bedroom Brody directed us to.

We burst into the room and immediately stop dead in our tracks. Laying there on the bed, looking freshly fucked and satiated, is a sleeping Ellie.

I feel sick. My mind is going a mile a minute. No, this can't be happening. Why? Why would she do this? She told us she loved us.

Rain is crying, and Jax's chest is heaving. A door to the left opens, and out walks the sack-of-shit Tim. His eyes go wide as he looks from us to Ellie and then back to us. "Fuck," he whispers.

"You're dead!" Jax roars. He rushes Tim, taking him to the ground hard, and gets to work smashing his face in.

Some guys from the swim team push past us and pull Jax off a bloody Tim.

"Look dude, just because your girlfriend likes to share, doesn't mean you can beat the shit out of Tim. Sorry to burst your bubble but you're not the only group she likes to be fucked by," some dumb fuck says.

"Are you saying you fucked her too?" Rain says in a soft, numb voice.

"Sorry to break it to you, but you're not that special. She's been fucking us all for the past few months. All the times she's at the library? More like at one of our houses getting what she doesn't get from you lot."

I'm gonna kill him. But there's five of them and only two of us.

"Come on guys, let's go," Rain says, pulling at my arm. The guys shove Jax toward the door. We're too drunk to be dealing with this right now, and these guys seem sober. We don't stand a chance.

Jax takes off in a fit of rage, cussing up a storm as he leaves. Rain takes one look at Ellie and I don't know if she's disgusted and gonna puke, or cry. Maybe both.

We leave the house numb and broken because the love of our life just ripped out our hearts like it was no big deal. Sometimes you think you know someone, but I guess we really didn't know Ellie as well as we thought we did. I'll never make that mistake again.

# *Chapter One*

## ELLIE

"ELLIE, hunny, there's something in the mail here for you!" Mom shouts from the bottom of the stairs.

"Coming!" I shout back as I try to wrangle a three-year-old into a frilly pink dress. "Lilly, baby, can you please just let Mommy put this on you? Then you can go to daycare and see Callie," I say, throwing her best friend's name out there, knowing she can't resist seeing her.

"Callie! Okay," she says in her adorable little voice. Lilly is three and her vocabulary is amazing for her age. She can use full sentences, but sometimes you can't always make out a word.

After I get Lilly dressed, she tries to dart past me, heading to the stairs, but I scoop her up, making her giggle. "Not so fast, Lillypad. You know you're not allowed on the stairs by yourself. Mommy doesn't want you to fall and get hurt."

Once I'm at the bottom of the stairs, I let the little Tasmanian Devil loose on the rest of the house while I head to the kitchen to see what came in the mail.

"It's on the table," Mom says without even looking at me. She's making Lilly some pancakes.

Picking up the pile of letters, I look through until I find a thick letter addressed to me. It's from SVU. My heart paces and my hands grow clammy. I've been waiting for this letter since I reapplied last month.

Silver Valley University is one of the most prestigious schools in the country. It's located in Silver Valley, the town I grew up in from fourth grade up until we moved a few years ago.

They accepted me with high honors, and I was all set to go after I graduated from high school, but with my father's company going belly up, we didn't have the money to pay for tuition anymore.

Not that I'd wanted to stay there and go to the same school as *them* anyway. Not after how they handled the situation, how they were so quick to kick me out of their lives and treat me like shit.

Just thinking about them makes me sick to my stomach. The horrible things the guys said to me, the dejected look Rain gave me as she cut all ties with me.

When I left, I didn't know I'd be leaving with a piece of them. No matter how shitty that time in my life was, I got the best little thing out of it. Lilly is my entire world.

When we got here, I spent the whole summer thinking I had some bad flu, when it was actually morning sickness. My mom finally took me to the doctor, and they told me I was four months pregnant. I had no idea. I wasn't gaining any weight. A few months later, I gave birth to a beautiful little girl. My whole life became about her, and I know I'd do anything for her.

My parents were and still are amazing when it comes to taking care of Lilly. After I got the okay from my doctor, I got a job. My parents worked with me to arrange their schedule to fit with mine so that someone was always home to care for Lilly. A few months ago, I started making enough to put her into daycare because my parents were finding it harder to make things work as their jobs got busier. My mom is a trauma nurse but she's also going to night school to become a doctor. I didn't feel right getting in the way of that since she's already done so much for me.

My father has his law degree and did something with it after his company went under.

Seeing my parents work hard to provide for me and my daughter made me want to be like them. I want to give Lilly the best life she can have, so that means going back to school. It also means going to the best school in the country if I could get in again. I was valedictorian of my graduation class, so I hoped that it would be enough to get a scholarship and get in.

If I do, that would mean packing up Lilly and moving back to the only town that ever really felt like home, leaving my parents behind, and truly being on my own.

I have money saved up, and the school has an amazing child care program that's included in the scholarship I applied for.

With the money I've saved, I could put the first three months rent and a damage deposit on a one-bedroom apartment. If I worked right away, I could afford a babysitter. It will leave very little time with Lilly, but I need to do this for both of us.

Putting on my big girl panties, with shaking hands, I rip open the letter.

I don't bother reading the whole thing, just the first few lines. When I read the word 'accepted', my heart stops. I'm sure I fainted or am I dreaming?

"Well, what does it say?" Mom asks, with hope lacing her voice.

I turn to her with tears welling in my eyes. "I got in," I whisper, my face splitting into a big smile. "I got in!!!" I shout louder. My mom cheers, almost sending the plate of pancakes flying, before setting them down and wrapping me in a big hug. She jumps around and squeals with excitement. Lilly runs into the room and starts clapping her little hands, cheering along with us, even though she has no idea what's going on.

I laugh and gather her into my arms, spinning her around and making her giggle in delight.

*It's me and you, baby girl. Mama's gonna do whatever it takes so you never want for anything in your little life. You will always be loved and cared for. I won't let anyone or anything get in my way.*

---

Driving across the country in a U-Haul was a bitch. Trying to keep a toddler occupied while operating a big as fuck truck was even harder.

But I have to give it to her. With an iPad, some snacks, and a lot of breaks, we made it to Silver Valley in just under a week.

I found a place online pretty fast, and my mom bought me a used car from one of her old friends who she grew up with. I tried to tell her I'd pay her back, but she wasn't having any of it. She said I needed some form of transportation to get to and from school and work.

She was right. There were no apartments within walking distance to the school, so I needed something to get around.

The new school year is starting in just a few days, so we made it just in time to settle in before our new life truly starts.

I feel bad for taking Lilly away from her Nana and Poppy and her friends, but she will make new friends, and Mom and Dad plan to come and visit for holidays if they can.

"Mama, where my room?" Lilly asks, looking around at all the boxes. We had dropped off the truck and took a cab home. I just got done ordering pizza. We don't have much—just the old couches from my parents' basement, a small table, and everything from our rooms back home. I plan to get as much as I can from the Dollar Tree tomorrow.

"You're gonna share a room with Mama. Is that okay?" I ask, squatting down, taking her little hands in mine and swaying them back and forth.

Her big blue eyes light up. "Really? Sleepover!" she cheers, and runs to the bedroom. I chuckle, following after her. I brought most of Lilly's stuff with us, but ended up having to leave some behind.

There's no room for her bed, so she will be sleeping with me. Not like it matters because the little turkey has been sneaking into my bed since she's been able to walk.

It has wooden pallets as a bed frame, so it's off the ground but not too high if Lilly falls off, or wants to get on. I have it pushed up to the wall, so she will be sleeping on the inside anyways.

I was able to bring her little dresser, as well as my own, some bedside tables, lamps, toys, and clothes. Oh, and all of my books. I could never leave those behind.

Silver Valley University offers a wide range of classes so you can become just about anything you want. I'm sticking with a business degree for now. I want to open up my very own book store and be able to have time for Lilly.

Lilly helps me take some things out of the boxes and puts them away. She doesn't do too bad of a job either. I only have to help her a few times.

The buzzer to our apartment rings, and I hurry out to let the pizza man in. When the door knocks, I find a man around my age. "That will be $24.50 please," the man says. He looks familiar, but I can't put my finger on it.

He looks up and his eyes go wide. "Ellie?" he asks, then his face splits into a big smile. "Ellie Tatum, is that you?"

"Yes..." I say, wondering who the hell this guy is and how he knows my name. He must be someone I went to school with.

"Wow, this is unbelievable," he laughs. "Wait until they find out," he whispers to himself. He hands me over the pizza and I give him the money.

"Do I know you?" I ask, before he turns to leave.

He shakes his head. "No, but I know all about you. We went to the same high school. I wanted to ask you out, but you know, you were with the Silver Knights, so I knew I had no chance in hell," he shrugs. "Are you back in town for school?" he asks, and I nod, not really feeling hungry anymore at the mention of the guys and the silly name that they went by.

"Well, good luck with that. The Silver Knights and Lady Rain rule that school. Rumor has it, you're still a sore spot for them." He cringes. "Anyways, gotta go. Bye!" He waves as he walks away.

He leaves me standing there bewildered. So Rain and the guys are still in school. I guess it makes sense that they're not finished with university yet. I mean, it all depends on what you're going here for. The guys were coming here on a football scholarship, and Rain wanted to become a child therapist, so it's not surprising they are still here. I knew there is a chance I'd run into them, but I guess I never knew how much of a reality it was until now.

*I'm going to the same university they are. Apparently, the one they rule. And from what that guy said, they still hate me.*

It sucks and I'd be foolish to think they will just ignore me and pretend I'm not there. I know the moment they lay eyes on me, it's not gonna be good.

Hopefully, because we are in different years and with the campus being as big as it is, I'll be able to dodge them for a while. It's not like I'll be hanging there all day. I'll go to my class, pick up Lilly, meet the sitter at home, then work and come home.

Lilly and I eat our supper and watch some Netflix on the iPad. The cable people won't be here until Monday. Thankfully, we downloaded some shows and movies when we had Wi-fi.

After we're done, I give Lilly a bath, then put her to bed. Laying there with my little girl in my arms, I think about everything I'm blessed with. Amazing parents, a smart, funny little girl, and now I have this opportunity to take the first step in making our lives better in the long run.

I'll do whatever I can to keep my baby girl safe, and if that means keeping her from her father, whoever it might be, then I will. For as long as I have to.

## *Chapter Two*

### ELLIE

THE WEEKEND WAS BUSY, but I found Lilly a highly recommended nanny, who is also in college and looking for a job. I love that my mother has so many friends. There's always someone here willing to help in some way.

Being a single mom on a fixed income, it helps a lot. I've turned in my application to a few restaurants and clubs around town. I need something that offers a night shift so that I can go to school, spend a few hours with Lilly, then go to work. I'm hoping to get at least a few days off work so that she's not always in someone else's care.

"Mama, can we go now?" Lilly asks as she comes running into the room, both legs in the same hole of her shorts.

I can't help but laugh. "Lillypad, did you dress yourself?"

"Yup." She beams up at me, her bright blue eyes shining, extremely proud of herself.

"And you did an awesome job," I say crouching down in front of her. "But I think one leg goes in here." I tug on the side that's sticking out.

She looks down and pouts. "Hey, it's okay, sweet girl. You did good. But sometimes we need help and that's okay, too," I tell her, giving her a hug. I dress her properly and lather her up in some sunscreen before checking to see if my blue striped sundress looks good. Once I have our picnic basket in hand, we take off for the park.

I'm glad there's one just down the street. I have a feeling that until the snow comes, we will be spending a lot of time there.

I sit on a bench and watch her run around, not afraid to take on the jungle gym on her own, saying 'excuse me' to all the bigger kids who hog some of the equipment.

After a while, I look around and see there are a lot of mothers here, but no fathers. I can't help but wonder if they are single mothers like me? Or if coming to the park just isn't their husband's thing. From what I can see, I seem to be the only younger mom here.

"Which one is yours?" a masculine voice comes from behind me. Startled, I jump a little and look to the other side of the bench. A man with dark brown hair, glasses, and a short beard smiles at me, waiting for my answer.

"Umm..." I blank. *Damn, he's cute.* Shaking my head to get my thoughts together, I start over. "The little blonde one in the sand-pit," I say, pointing her out. *What the fuck, Ellie?! You just showed which child is yours to some random man. What is wrong with you?!*

"Oh, nice. She's playing with my son." He smiles as he watches Lilly get up and chase around a little boy with shaggy brown hair. Thank God he has a kid here or this would be creepy.

I sit there awkwardly. He's cute, a dad, and seems nice. But I don't know if he's single, so I don't want to say something to embarrass myself. I haven't gone on a date in years. I tried after Lilly was born, but not many guys want to date a young mom. At least none I've come across.

"Are you new here? I haven't seen you around," he asks. Thankfully, he keeps this conversation going because that ship was sinking fast.

"I grew up here. My family and I left a few years ago for my father's new job. I wanted to come back to school. Anything to give Lilly a better life," I shrug and smile.

"I think that's amazing," he smiles.

We both watch the kids play a little more.

"My name is Theo, by the way."

"Nice to meet you." I give his outstretched hand a shake. "Ellie."

"Ellie. That's a beautiful name."

I huff out a laugh. "My full name is Eleanor, but I never really liked it. So I make everyone call me Ellie."

He chuckles, making me blush.

We talk for a little while. Turns out, he's a widower. He lost her shortly after she gave birth to their son. She had breast cancer, but refused to terminate the pregnancy, so she gave her life up for her son's. I almost cried when he told me. He actually did a little.

After about half an hour, Lilly comes running over to me. "Mama! I made a friend." She smiles.

"I see that, Bug. And what is your name, young man?" I smile down at the adorable little boy who's standing next to his dad.

"Toby!" he shouts.

"Not so loud, buddy," Theo laughs.

"Sorry," Toby says, lowering his voice.

"Can they eat too?" Lilly asks with hopeful eyes.

I look down at the basket. I did pack more than enough. I shrug and look over at Theo. "You up for some peanut butter and jelly sandwiches with juice boxes?" I ask.

"My favorite," he smiles back.

We all sit and eat. The kids talk about their favorite toys, while Theo and I keep our conversation going.

"Alright, little lady. Time to get you home," I say as I start to put everything away.

"Aww," she pouts.

"I'm sure we will see them again soon," I say, looking over at Theo.

"For sure. Here..." he says, taking out his phone. I put my number in and we say our goodbyes.

Lilly and I hold hands as we walk back to the apartment. When I look behind me, I see Theo and Toby walking in the same direction as us.

Feeling a little off, I pick up my pace. When we get to the apartment building, I see them walking across the parking lot, right toward us. *Did I forget something?* He hasn't tried to get my attention.

Not wanting to find out, I scoop Lilly up into my arms and start heading up the stairs to the top floor, where we live. Not too long after, I hear footsteps and voices. Is he following me? God, I knew he was too cute to be true.

"Mama, what's wrong?" Lilly asks, bouncing in my arms as I quickly walk down the hall.

"Mama just really needs to pee," I lie.

When we get to our door, I set Lilly down and fight with my keys, trying to find the right one to put in the lock.

"Look, Daddy, they are our neighbours!" a little boy says from behind me. I freeze and slowly turn around.

Four apartments down is Theo and Toby. Theo has the door of the apartment open and is looking at me with a big, amused grin. I feel the blush that takes over my face.

*God, Ellie, they live here, you dumbass.* I didn't even think about that possibility. My past has me so fucked up. It's also played a big part in why I could never have a genuine relationship.

I turn around quickly and unlock the door. Lilly goes inside first, yelling something about needing to pee before me. I go to close the door and see Theo still looking at me with a goofy smile. "Night," I squeak and shut the door behind me.

After giving Lilly a bath, she cuddles in for a story, but before long, she passes out. Right as I'm about to join her, my phone beeps. It's a text from Theo. My belly flutters a little as I read the text.

*Theo: You're cute, you know? :) Have dinner with me this weekend?*

I bite my lip, not knowing what to say back. He's cute, a single dad and a good one, from what I can see. We have a lot in common and can hold a conversation well. Why not? My therapist says that I can't let what happened to me control my life. I think it's time to take it back.

Before I lose the nerve, I text him back.

*Ellie: Alright. Where to?*

*Theo: I know this little place downtown that I've been dying to go to, but didn't want to go alone.*

*Ellie: What kind of food? Not that it matters. I'll eat anything.*

Great, that makes me sound like a pig.

*Theo: A woman who loves food. I like that. ;)*

I let out a sigh of relief.

*Ellie: I'll find someone to watch Lilly.*

*Theo: Sounds good. I'll pick you up at 6pm Saturday.*

*Ellie: Should I wear anything fancy?*

*Theo: Whatever you feel comfortable in. I know you would look gorgeous in anything.*

I grin and play with my lip.

*Ellie: Goodnight. :)*

*Theo: Goodnight :)*

Feeling light and happy, I snuggle into Lilly and fall asleep. Maybe life is starting to look up.

Still sleeping, a tiny hand smacks me in the face, making me jolt awake. Groggily, I sit up and rub my eyes. Sun shines through the window, and I can hear cars zooming past on the street next to the building. *What time is it?*

Reaching over to the nightstand, I check the lock screen on my phone and see that it's 9:15 a.m. and my economics class starts at 10. Dammit! We're going to be late.

Jumping up out of bed, I scramble around to get ready. I quickly brush my hair, and throw it up into a ponytail. I dig through a box for some clothes. We've been here for a few days, but with looking for a job and getting everything set up for Lilly and school, I haven't had the time to unpack anything.

I quickly change into clean panties and a bra, and throw on some jeans and a white sweater.

"Lillypad, wake up, my love," I mumble around my tooth-brush as I give myself a quick brush.

Lilly blinks her eyes open slowly. "What's wrong, Mama?" she asks, her voice slow and sleepy.

"Mama forgot to set the alarm, you're gonna be late for your first day at daycare," I say, running to the bathroom sink to spit. I dig out some clothes for Lilly and find her in the bathroom playing in the sink. "Mama's gotta put this on you." I throw on a summer dress and some shorts, and brush her hair and teeth.

Thankfully, I already have her things packed for today as well as my own stuff. Grabbing our bags, we slip on our shoes and rush to the car.

When we get to the campus, I'm ready to lose my shit. Why didn't I come here for orientation? Right. Lilly. I had no one to watch her. Dammit. I have no idea how to read this map.

Not wanting to waste any time, I ask a guard in passing, through my car window. He directs me to the other side of campus. After twenty minutes, I finally find the daycare.

Knocking on the door, a woman in a long jean skirt and white blouse opens the door.

"Hi," I say, a little out of breath. "I'm so sorry we are late. This is Lillianna Tatum."

"Hi. You're just in time." She smiles and crouches down until she's eye level with Lilly. "Hi. My name is Miss Macy. It's nice to meet you," she says.

"Hi, I Lilly," Lilly beams. She's not shy and loves making friends with everyone. If only it was that easy for me.

Knowing Lilly is in excellent hands, we say our goodbyes and I set out to find where the hell I need to go.

The guard said that all my classes are on this side of campus, but there are so many buildings, I don't know what order they go in.

Taking another look at the map, I see building D is not too far from where I am. When I lay eyes on it, I let out a sigh of relief. With five minutes to spare, I quickly grab a coffee from the cart outside the building.

I find the auditorium I'm meant to be in and open the door. Everyone is sitting, but class hasn't started yet. I search around for an empty seat. The only one available is up front. Great.

"Shit," I hiss when I spill a little coffee on my white sweater as I struggle to sit down with everything in my hands.

"Late on the first day, eh?" the girl next to me comments. I look over and see her smiling at me.

"Yes." I huff out a laugh. "And a hot mess, too." I gesture at my shirt. Thankfully, I have a black tank top underneath.

"It's my first day, too. I was so nervous about being late, I set about seven alarms," she giggles.

"I got distracted and forgot to set mine," I huff, setting my coffee down to take off my sweater.

"Oh, staying up late talking to your boyfriend?" She wiggles her eyebrows and I laugh.

"No. But it was a guy," I smile, thinking about Theo and his cute dimples when he smiles wide. He's thirty, but he has a boyish charm to him.

"I'm Tabitha Brigs by the way." She smiles, tucking her long black hair behind her ear.

"Ellie Tatum." I smile back. Her eyes go wide for a moment, and I raise a brow at her reaction. She schools her features quickly.

"Nice to meet you," she says.

The professor comes into the room and starts the lesson. I try to pay attention, but I can't help but think about *them*. Do any of them have this class? Probably not. They have been here for a few years already. But I also don't want to look around to find out. I don't know how I'd react to seeing them after all this time.

Class goes by faster than I expected and I don't retain anything the professor said.

"What class do you have next?" Tabitha asks, following me out of the building. I look at my schedule. I only have two classes on Mondays, Wednesdays, and Fridays, and three on Tuesdays and Thursdays. I wanted to keep my course load as light as I could so that I'm not overworked with school, work, and home life.

"My marketing class does not start until 1."

"Perfect," Tabitha chirps as she hooks her arm into mine. "We have time to eat and get to know each other." I say nothing and smile as she drags me along with her, chatting about everything and anything.

"This is the campus food court. It has a booth for most of the fast-food places around town. What are you in the mood for?" she asks as we get to what looks like a mini indoor mall.

I'm overwhelmed by the size of this place. Silver Valley itself is a small town, but the school is one of the biggest and best in the country.

Looking around, I find a little shop selling nachos. We both grab something to eat and sit down at an empty table nearby.

We're chatting and eating when two girls take a seat on either side of Tabitha. "Is it true?" the girl in a pink bob asks.

"Please, tell me it's true," the other girl, the one with long curly brown hair, says.

"I'm sorry, what?" I ask, confused on what the heck they are talking about.

"I'm so sorry about my friends. This is Val," Tabitha says,

looking at the girl with the pink bob. "And this is Lexie," pointing to the girl with brown hair.

"Sooo, is it?" Val asks with excitement.

"Is what?" I ask.

"Are you really *the* Ellie Tatum?" Lexie asks.

"Well, if you're asking if my name is Ellie Tatum, then yes."

"So you're the Ellie who dated the Silver Knights?" Lexie asks.

"Don't forget Lady Rain," Val giggles, but it's more like she's swooning.

That self proclaimed title they gave themselves has my stomach dropping. I used to think it was hot because they were all so popular and I was in love. But now it just sounds stupid. They are no better than anyone else.

"If you don't mind me asking, how do you know them or me and my past relationship with them?" I ask no one in particular.

"You're kidding right?" Lexie asks.

"Not at all." I raise a brow and Tabitha groans.

"Well, after you left that party on graduation night, the news spread like wildfire. By the end of the week, everyone knew your name and what you did."

I'm gonna be sick. That night flashes into my mind and I want to run, go get Lilly, and leave town. But I can't. I close my eyes and take a deep breath.

"I don't know what that rumor is, but I can tell you, none of it was true," I say, picking up a chip and forcing myself to take a nibble.

"So you didn't have an orgy with a bunch of guys who were not your boyfriends?" Val asks.

"No!" I growl.

"So why did you leave?" Lexie asks.

"Look. That's none of your business. I don't know you and I don't owe you, or anyone else, an explanation," I snap, picking up my tray and moving to another spot.

If I didn't have another class soon, I'd go home right now.

"I'm sorry about those two," Tabitha cringes as she cautiously sits at the new table with me. "I told them you were here, and well, they're nosy."

"So it's true, everyone here knows who I am. Or, at least, once they put my name to the face, they will."

"Yeah. The guys and Rain really did a number on your reputation."

Great. Just what I need. People are talking about me and judging me before I even really start school.

Just as I'm about to say something more, cheering has me looking to the food court door. In walk the Silver Knights. The only three men who can make me weak in the knees and cum like a river. *Fuck*. I'm so not ready to face them.

They all look the same, yet completely different. The guys are wearing silver football jackets. Jax is taller, more buff but still has jet black hair, only it's shaved almost to his skull. He has an arm around a girl who clings to him as if the sun shines out his ass. My stomach does a flip, a dead, unenthusiastic flip.

Chase is joking around with some football buddies as he takes a tray. His platinum blond hair is longer at the top and shorter on the sides. He's still as fit as ever. Behind them, Brody walks in and, just by entering a room, he commands everyone's attention without even trying. His once short brown hair is now shaggy. I never imagined him with longer hair, but *fuck* it looks good.

Then, the one person I've been dreading seeing the most saunters in. Rain. She's in a skimpy cheerleading uniform that has a similar design and color scheme as the guys.

Her long red hair flows down her back as she laughs at something one of the other cheerleaders said.

They all sit down at a table on the opposite side of the room. Jax pulls the girl he's with down onto his lap and immediately starts ramming his tongue down her throat.

Chase smacks the ass of a girl who's in line to get something to eat, as he walks by and shamelessly checks her out. And she doesn't seem to mind.

Let's get something straight. I won't be denying my feelings. I never fell out of love with the guys and Rain; that's what made moving on and raising Lilly, as well as dealing with my trauma, so fucking hard. It's the kind of love that attaches to your soul and feeds off it's life force until you're nothing but a shell of your old self. You become so entwined with that person that they become a part of you. That's not something someone can ever truly get over.

And the sad thing is, if they had loved me enough and trusted that love like I did, we would still be together. All they had to do was talk to me and ask. But they believed the lies of strangers. And that was their downfall.

"Rain is the head cheerleader. She's pretty good too. We have won a few competitions since she came here. Chase is our running back. Jax is our left tackle and Brody is our quarterback."

All the same positions they had in high school.

"You still love them, don't you?" Tabitha asks with pity. I huff out a laugh.

"What gave it away?"

"The look of heartache and longing." She gives me a half grin.

Awesome. How pathetic.

"If it makes you feel any better, they don't have any girl-friends," Tabitha says, taking one of my chips.

"But Jax has a girl in his lap..." I challenge her statement.

Tabitha laughs. "That's just the new notch on his belt. He has one every week pretty much."

I'm not hungry anymore. The idea of the guys, who used to tell me I was their everything, sticking their dicks in random girls all the time is soul destroying.

"And Rain," Tabitha laughs. "Yeah, she collects pussy like a crazy cat lady."

Just as she says that, I see Rain straddle some girl and they start to make out. I can't take it anymore. I need to leave.

"I gotta go," I say, holding back tears. I rush out of the food court as the room fills with catcalls and wolf whistles as they watch whatever show Rain and that girl are putting on.

My heart feels like someone ripped it out, ran it over, and then stomped on it for fun.

In my last class, I can't concentrate at all. I feel numb. Maybe coming back here was a mistake.

After class, I pick Lilly up from daycare.

"Mama why you crying?" she asks from her car seat as we drive home. I wipe my eyes and nose.

"Mama is just having a bad day, sweet girl." She doesn't say anything else.

We eat, have a bath, and watch a movie. When it's bedtime, I tuck her in.

"Here," she says, handing me her favorite stuffed dog. "Mr. Doggie makes me feel better when I sad," she says, and I'm ready to burst into tears at her kindness.

"Thank you, my sweet Lillypad." I kiss her cheek and cuddle into her, bringing her to my chest.

Once she's asleep, I sit at the window and cry, holding her dog tight to my chest. It's the dog Chase won me at a fair in 10th grade. I never had the heart to get rid of anything they gave me. So when Lilly found it when she was one, she took a hold of it and never really let it go.

Just like they took my heart, body, and soul, and never really let them go.

## Chapter Three

### ELLIE

STANDING in front of my bathroom mirror, I fix my hair and makeup for the hundredth time. Nerves swarm in my belly at the thought of my date with Theo. This will be the first real date I've been on in years.

The doorbell rings, causing my head to snap up, getting my attention. "I get it," Lilly calls from the living room.

"Oh no, you don't!" I say, racing out of the bathroom as Lilly runs toward the door. Giggling, her little feet pitter-pattering across the floor. I catch her right before she reaches the door, scooping her up into my arms. "You little monkey," I laugh as she giggles.

Setting her down on the floor, I crouch down so that we are eye level. "Baby, you know you can't answer the door. You don't know who is on the other side, and even if you did, you still can't answer the door. Mama just wants to keep you safe, okay?" I smooth her hair down, giving her a kiss on the forehead.

"Okay, Mama. Sorry," she says, then looks at the door. "Who is it?"

"I don't know. Let's see," I say, standing up and looking through the peephole on the door. Smiling when I see who it is, I look down at Lilly. "Katie is here."

Her eyes light up. "Katie!" Lilly cheers.

Katie is the nanny I've hired. She's been by to see Lilly, spending time with her to get to know her before she officially starts next Friday, my first day of work. I got a call back from one of the places I applied to, a little club called Dynamite. The top half is pub style and there is a club in the basement. They offered me Thursday to Sunday nights. The pay is minimum wage, but apparently the tips are supposed to be good. I guess drunk rich college students love to throw their money around.

"Thank you so much for watching Lilly tonight," I say after letting her in.

"No problem. Lilly and I always have a good time, isn't that right, little one?" Katie says, smiling down at Lilly, while ruffling up her hair.

Lilly glares at Katie, putting her hands on her hips. "I'm not little. I a big girl."

I bite my lip, holding back the smile threatening to take over as I watch my feisty daughter.

"You know what? You are very right. I'm sorry," Katie apologizes, holding back a smile of her own.

Lilly gives her a nod of approval, and smiles again. "Come on, Katie, let's play dollies!" Lilly grabs Katie's hand, and drags her toward the living room where Lilly has all her toys set up.

Smiling, with a shake of my head, I go back to the bathroom. Taking a look at myself, yet again, I'm not happy with what I picked out. I know he said to wear something I'm comfortable in, but this is a first date. I don't want to be too casual. Taking off the black dress shorts and blouse, I open my closet and search for something that catches my eye. Finally, after looking at almost everything I own, I find a little red dress. Smiling, I take it out and hold it up. It's one of my nicer dresses, but nothing too flashy. A simple fit with a flowy bottom. Also doesn't hurt that it does wonders for my breasts.

Glancing at the clock, I see that I have ten minutes before Theo said he would pick me up. I quickly change into the dress, feeling beautiful as I do a little spin. It's been a while since I've had a reason to dress up, so I think I deserve to spend a little extra time on myself.

Wiping off the nude lipstick I put on earlier, I replace it with a crimson shade. That, with my smokey eye, makes my bright blue eyes pop. Fixing my beach curls, making sure everything looks good, I give myself a confident smile.

"Wow," Lilly breathes as I enter the living room. "Mama, you look like a princess."

"Thank you, baby," I smile.

"Where you goin'?" she asks as I slip on my black heels and grab my matching clutch off the counter.

"Mama is gonna go out with a friend for supper. Katie is gonna watch you for a bit."

"Oh."

"I won't be long. Then we can snuggle and read before bed, how does that sound?"

She beams up at me. "Can I pick?"

"Of course."

"Yay!"

There's a knock at the door, and I know it's Theo. My stomach drops as my nerves take over again. *I think I'm gonna be sick.*

Closing my eyes, I take a few calming breaths. I have nothing to be worried about. Theo is a nice man. He makes me laugh and smile more than I have in a long time. I can't hide from my past and be alone forever. That only gives my demons power over me. And I don't let them control my life anymore. I deserve happiness.

But what if I run into them? What if they happen to be at the same place we are, and ruin everything? *No, no, I can't think that way.* We may not have any of the same classes this semester, but that doesn't mean we won't in the future. I will have to deal with them at some point, I'm sure, but tonight won't be that night. *I hope.*

"Wow," Theo says, his voice saturated in awe as I open the door. "You look amazing."

My cheeks flush as a flutter in my belly takes over. The way he's looking at me is something I'm not used to. Men look at me with attraction, sure, but no one has looked at me like I'm the only girl in the room worth the attention. Not since *them*.

"Thank you. I hope it's not too much for where we're going?" I ask.

"No. It's perfect," he smiles.

"Mama, you have a playdate with Toby's daddy?" Lilly asks, coming up next to me.

"Umm..." I look up at Theo who's smiling at Lilly, then back down to her. "Kinda? Theo and I are friends. So we are going to go out and have something to eat."

I say goodbye to Lilly, giving her a hug and kiss, leaving a red lipstick print on her cheek. I wonder how long it will take before she notices, or even cares.

Following Theo to his car, my mind is wild with all the things that could go wrong, but when he turns to me, looking at me with his hazel eyes, all my worries fade away.

"You really do look beautiful, Ellie," he smiles, stopping next to his car.

"Thank you. You look handsome tonight," I say with a smile, blushing a little when his eyes light up at the compliment. Handsome is an understatement. He looks fucking edible. He chose to go with a more dressed up style—a hard navy blue suit with a sky blue dress shirt. His brown hair is styled back with a freshly shaved beard. I hope I'm not drooling, because this man makes me feel things I forgot I could feel. Horny and hopeful. My life is complicated like that.

As we drive to the restaurant, I tell him about the first week of classes. He doesn't comment much, like he's unsure of how to respond, but he listens patiently as I ramble on.

"Sorry. I've been talking about my week this whole ride." I laugh nervously, getting out of the car.

"I don't mind. I like listening to you talk. You have a nice voice." He grins as we start walking across the parking lot to the building. It's a nice little brick place. I can smell a variety of different foods, and they all smell so delicious, it makes my mouth water.

Theo smiles at the hostess, but passes right by her, bringing me to a booth in the back as we seat ourselves. I look over my shoulder in time to see the woman greet another couple before leading them to a table.

"So I have a bit of a confession," Theo says after we slide into the booth facing each other.

"Oh?" I ask. *Oh god, is this where he tells me he has some kind of secret fetish? I hope it has nothing to do with feet.* I try to suppress a shudder at the thought. I knew he was too good to be true.

"I've kind of been here before. I know I said I've been dying to come here, but I just didn't want you to think I always bring my dates here when I tell you what I'm about to."

He looks so cute when he's nervous. He adjusts his glasses before tapping his fingers on the table.

"Okay," I smile.

"I own this restaurant," Theo says. My eyes go wide. I was not expecting him to say that. "Well, not me, but my parents."

"Really?" I ask, my smile brightens as my nerves go away. I look around, really getting a good look at the place. It's cute and homey. It has a 'real person' feel to it. Nothing like chain restaurants.

"I...I've never brought anyone here on a date, mostly because this is the first date I've been on since my wife died. But when I asked you out, this was the place I wanted to bring you. It means something to me. And I had a feeling I'd be really nervous. So I thought maybe being in a place I'm familiar with would ease my nerves." He gives me a panicked look as his cheeks stain pink. "And here I am blabbing on and making a fool of myself. I'm sorry, like I said before, this is my first date in years."

"It's okay." I give him a light hearted laugh, letting him know I'm not at all bothered by his little bit of rambling. Actually, I find it kind of cute. "This is my first date in a long time too. I don't get out much between work, school, and taking care of Lilly." I lean in closer like I'm going to tell him a secret. "To be honest, Lilly is more fun than any man I've met so far."

Theo gives me a husky chuckle, sending a shiver down my spine. I love how my body reacts to him. "You do have a point. Toby is so much fun to hang out with. He's my best friend. But sometimes you need an adult to talk to though, someone who knows more than Paw Patrol and Peppa Pig."

I groan. "Tell me about it. I know every word to all the Frozen songs."

He gives me another chuckle. "Well, I can assure you, I can offer you more of an intellectual conversation."

We sit and talk for a while, ordering our meal when our waiter comes by. I can see how at home he is here. He seems to know everyone, always saying 'hi', or waving when he makes eye contact.

Over time, my nerves start to lessen as well, and we fall into an easy conversation.

"So, what do you do for work?" I ask, taking a sip of water, before taking a bite of my pasta.

"I'm a teacher," he says. "Started as an elementary school teacher about eight years ago."

"Oh, that sounds like fun," I beam.

He smiles and nods. "So, what are you going to school for?"

"Business. I want to open up my own little book store."

"So you like to read?" He smiles. "So do I. What kind of books?"

My heart picks up it's pace a little. I hate when people ask this question. How do you tell someone you enjoy reading books about one girl falling in love with multiple people? Then tell them that your favorite books are when she's getting railed by all of them at once?

"Romance," I say. It's the safest bet. "What about you?"

"I like thrillers. Horror is good too. And who doesn't like a mystery here and there?"

"Theo," someone calls from across the room. Theo's body goes stiff as a panicked look overtakes his face. "Theo, hunny."

"I am so sorry for this. I thought she had the night off," he sighs, his eyes pleading with me not to think less of him for whatever is about to happen. "Hi, Mom." He looks over to the woman who is now next to our table.

"You didn't tell me you were going to stop by." She smiles at her son before turning to me. Her eyes light up a little and she smiles. "And you brought a lady friend."

"Hi," I say, giving a little awkward wave.

"Mom, this is Ellie."

"Ellie. So nice to meet you."

"I thought you weren't going to be in tonight," Theo says, looking like he wishes his mother would go away.

"Peggy called in sick, so I offered to take her shift. Bless her soul, poor girl got the flu, can't keep anything down."

I look at my food, cringing to myself before pushing it away, not really hungry anymore as that image flashes through my mind.

"Mom, please..." Theo groans.

"You know, you must be a special lady. He never brings anyone *here*," his mother addresses me.

"Because I don't date, Mom. And you know it." Theo sighs, realizing he's not getting rid of his mom anytime soon.

"I've offered to watch Toby. Speaking of Toby, who's watching him while you're here?"

"He's with the babysitter."

"Well, why didn't you call me?" she asks, offended.

"What does it matter? You ended up needing to work," Theo cocks a brow.

She ignores his answer and looks at me. "He has a son. Did he tell you that?"

"Yes, ma'am," I smile.

"Do you like kids?" Oh boy, it seems like this is turning into an integration. And on the first date, too.

"I love them. I have a three-year-old daughter."

She seems to like that answer.

"Mom. Please. This is our first date. And you're kind of imposing."

"It's okay. I don't mind," I say. I really don't; she seems like a really sweet woman who loves her son and grandson.

My phone rings. Looking down, I see it's Katie calling. "I'm going to need to take this. Excuse me." I slide out of the booth and head into the bathroom, answering the call as I go. "Hi, Katie, is everything okay?"

"Hi, Ellie. I'm so sorry to call. But Lilly ate a little too much sweets, and she has a belly ache. She got sick, and I cleaned it up, but she just wants her mommy."

"Of course. Tell her I'm on my way home now."

I hang up and head back to my table. When I get there, his mother is no longer there. "I hate to do this, but Lilly isn't feeling the best."

"Of course. She comes first," Theo says, getting up and standing in front of me. "I hope you'll let me take you out again to make up for tonight." He smiles down at me, making my belly flutter. There's something about him that makes me feel giddy and nervous, like I'm afraid to do or say something stupid and embarrass myself.

"I-I'd like that," I smile back at him.

Theo excuses himself to talk to someone at the bar before coming back over to me. "Everything is taken care of with the bill. Perks of knowing the owner." He winks at me, making me giggle.

With his hand on my lower back, he leads me out of the

restaurant and to his car, before opening the door for me. "Thank you. Always the gentleman," I say, getting into the car.

"I try," he laughs. "But for you, Miss Tatum, always."

He shuts the door, making his way around to his side. I sit there, fiddling with my fingers. I know I've only known Theo for a week, but I already find myself liking him more than anyone I've gotten to know since...well, since the others.

He makes my heart race and I laugh so much that my face hurts from smiling all the time. It terrifies me. Last time I allowed myself to feel something for someone, I got burned, times four.

I need to remember what my therapist said. Not everyone is out to hurt me. Not everyone is going to let me down, and I could miss out on something amazing by letting my past dictate my future. I need to stop overthinking everything. Theo and I are friends. Our kids are friends, and if it leads to something more, would it be so bad?

When we get to the apartment building, Theo is quick to get out and race to the other side to open my door. I bite my lip, holding back a smile at how sweet he is. "Thank you," I say, getting out.

"You're very welcome." He smiles at me. We walk inside and to our floor in silence. We look at each other a few times, smiling and softly laughing when we catch the other.

"Well, here's your stop," Theo says, scratching the back of his neck.

"Yup," I say. He's so cute.

"I'll text you with plans for our makeup date, I mean, if that's okay?"

"Sounds good. Thanks for taking me out tonight. Supper was amazing, and your parents' restaurant is wonderful."

He lets out a groan. "I'm so sorry about my mom. She's not a bad person, I swear. She just got a little excited. I'm an only child, and she adores Toby. She just wants what's best for us.

Seeing as how I don't really date, and you're the first person I've gone out with since my wife died, it was a surprise to her."

"Really, Theo, it's fine. She seems like a nice person. And I love that she cares for you so much."

"I just don't want you thinking I'm some mama's boy or something," he cringes and sighs. "I'm probably making a fool of myself. I'm just gonna go. Bye." He turns to race away, but I grab his arm, stopping him from leaving.

"You're cute," I laugh. He looks at me, shocked.

"I am? You don't think I'm some weirdo?"

"No. I think you're kind, a good dad, a good friend, and I really look forward to getting to know you more."

"Really?"

"Yes," I smile, shaking my head. "Goodnight, Theo." I lean up and give him a kiss on his cheek. He gives me a bright smile, and God if that doesn't have me crushing on him even more than I already am.

"Goodnight, Ellie," he says softly before turning around and heading to his own door.

Putting the key into the lock, I look back over my shoulder finding him doing the same thing. With one last smile, we disappear into our separate homes.

Katie tells me that Lilly fell asleep, and that she feels bad for pulling me from my date so soon. I thank her for watching Lilly and pay her, telling her it's no problem.

Sighing, I look around the quiet apartment. The place is spotless, which makes me love Katie even more for going above and beyond what I'd asked of her. Slipping off my heels, I pick them up and carry them into the room, quietly trying not to wake my sleeping beauty who's passed out in our bed. After putting my shoes back in the closet, I take my dress off and hang it in the bathroom to be dry cleaned.

I look in the mirror, getting ready to take my makeup off from the night and smile as I replay the better parts of the date.

The damaged part of me wants to block Theo, ignore him

and hide, because it's scared to get close to him, have him get close to Lilly, and ultimately break our hearts. But the other part of me is excited at this new chapter of my life. I didn't expect it to be anyone but Lilly and me, but these newcomers don't seem all too bad.

Now, what to do about the Silver Knights and Lady Rain.

# Chapter Four

## ELLIE

I WAKE up Monday morning with a pep in my step and a grin so wide that when my face eventually starts to hurt, I don't even care.

Yesterday, Theo and Toby stopped by to check on Lilly. I swooned when I saw that he brought over chicken soup in case Lilly was still feeling ill. She was fine by morning, running around like nothing happened, but I invited them to stay over and enjoy the meal with us. It tasted so delicious that I even let out a moan of pleasure while eating and my cheeks were stained pink from the look of interest Theo gave me.

We ended up watching movies all day with the kids singing every song that came on. My eyes kept drifting to Theo, checking him out when he wasn't looking. I was itching to make the space between us disappear, but this is all so new, and we are just getting to know each other. In front of the kids, I want to keep things friendly. I've never brought a man into Lilly's life, and I don't want her getting too attached to Theo too soon.

When they left, we spent the whole night texting each other, sending funny videos back and forth until I fell asleep with my phone still in my hand.

Is this what it feels like to have a crush for the first time? I was best friends with Rain and the guys before developing feelings for them. Everything kind of just flowed from friendship to something more.

So what I have with Theo, it's new and exciting.

"Mama!" Lilly yells from the bathroom as I pack up her lunch for daycare.

"What's wrong, Lillypad?" I shout back, putting the lunch bag in her backpack before grabbing my own.

"I peed!" she says, running out of the bathroom with her Pull-Up around her knees.

I snort out a laugh, taking in the sight of my silly little girl. We've been working on and off with potty training, and because of the big move here, away from the comfort of the only home she knew, it set her back a little. So her doing this on her own now tells me she's starting to feel comfortable in our new surroundings. My smile is for a completely new reason now.

"That's awesome, baby. I'm so proud of you!" I say, placing the bags down and moving her Pull-Up back into place. Picking her up, I spin her around, making her giggle as I kiss all over her face. "I think that calls for ice cream after daycare, what do you think?" I ask, putting her down to put her pants back on.

"Yay! Can Toby come?" she asks with big, hopeful, blue eyes.

"I don't know, I can ask his daddy, how about that?"

"Okay." She nods and runs back into the bathroom. I hear the toilet flush, and the sink turn on. God, she's growing up way too fast, and she's so damn smart. I love that little girl more than life itself.

⸻

"How was your weekend?" Tabitha asks, wiggling her eyebrows after taking her seat next to me in our Economics class.

"It was good," I smile. "We had to cut the date short, but he's going to take me out again soon to make up for it."

I haven't told her or the other girls about Lilly yet. I want to make sure I can trust them to keep that information to themselves. It's not that I'm ashamed to have anyone know that I have a kid, but I don't need that getting back to the guys and Rain. I'm not ready to deal with *that* right now.

"Did he kiss you goodnight?" She grins.

"Kinda," I laugh.

"What do you mean, kinda?" she huffs out with a laugh.

"I...I kissed him on the cheek. He's really sweet."

"Aw. That is pretty cute."

The professor walks in, causing Tabitha and I to go quiet. I get lost in the lesson plan for the day and before I know it, the class is over.

"Wanna eat with us today?" Tabitha asks, slipping her backpack on.

"You know I do," I laugh.

After the not-so-good first impression of Tabitha's friends last week, she convinced me to give them another chance. So I did, and they turned out to be not as bad as I originally thought. Val is a little more hyper than what I'm used to. She kind of reminds me of Lilly on sugar. Lexie, on the other hand, is a little too nosy for her own good, but Tabitha isn't afraid to put them in their place.

"Soooo...Are you going?" Val asks after taking a bite of her pizza.

"Going where?" I ask, leaning back into my seat.

"Homecoming, silly." Lexie rolls her eyes.

"Oh," I say, putting down my fry.

"Yeah, it's a pretty big deal here. Since Brody, Chase, and Jax started at the school, the team has won more games than all past teams combined. We don't win them all, but enough to be one of the best teams on this side of the country."

Great. That's just what they need, a week of the whole

school praising them like they are some kind of Gods. It's not like they don't get enough of that already.

Since seeing them in the cafeteria, I have gone out of my way to avoid them. We started eating outside in the courtyard, but soon, it's going to be too cold and if I want to eat while I'm here, I'll have to suck it up sooner or later. *I've chosen the 'later' option.*

I know I can't let them control my life but is it wrong of me to want to enjoy every little bit of peace and quiet I can get before everything comes crashing down? It's not like I can avoid it forever.

"If you're worried about them, don't be. There's thousands of people in this school, and with the exception of the cafe, it's highly unlikely they will see you. From what you've said, they don't have any of your classes this term, and this place is big," Tabitha says. "Come on, it's gonna be fun. We can watch the game, enjoy some time away from our studies, and there's tons of parties to choose from after."

I mull over the idea as I nibble on my lip. I could see if Katie is available to watch Lilly. Plus, with me starting work this weekend, I don't see myself having an opportunity to enjoy time out like this again, at least not for a while. No way am I asking for a night off after just getting hired.

Looking at the three girls staring back at me with big puppy dog eyes, I sigh in defeat. "Alright, I'll go."

"Yay!" Val squeals, making me wince at the high pitch noise. "This is going to be so much fun! You're going to love it!"

"I'm not sure I wanna go to any party though." What if they are there? It's one thing being in the same school as them, but being in the same house, or even room as them? I don't know about that.

"They always go to Benson Fletcher's parties after. So, as long as we avoid that party, we should be good," Lexie informs me.

We talk some more before parting ways, each of us heading

to our next classes. I'm starting to really enjoy marketing. Everything I learn here brings me one step closer to being able to open my bookstore, and give Lilly the life she deserves.

---

"Mama!" Lilly cheers as she runs into my open arms. "I missed you," she says into my neck.

"I missed you too, bug. How was your day?" I ask, kissing her cheek and placing her feet back on the ground.

"So much fun! I play with dollies and colored. Ruby took my dolly, so I licked her hand to make her let go." She gives me this evil grin and I have to hold back my giggles. I can't let her think that was okay, but damn, this kid is always surprising me.

"That's not what we do, Lilly. If someone's not being nice, we tell Miss Macy, right?" The fact that kids are nasty little things covered in germs doesn't even cross her mind but I shudder just thinking of where that kid's hands could have been.

"I know," she pouts. "Miss Macy make me say sorry."

"That's good. Did Ruby say sorry back?"

"Yeah," she smiles. "We friends again."

I laugh and shake my head. Kids have it so easy. You can scream and yell at each other, and the next moment, it's like nothing happened. If only it was that easy all the time.

"Mama, we get ice cream now?" she asks, looking up at me with her big blue eyes.

"Yes, sweetie. We can go grab some as a snack before supper," I laugh. Of course she remembers ice cream.

"Toby come too?"

Shit, I forgot to text Theo and ask. I take my phone out of my pocket and send a quick text to Theo.

"I don't know, sweetie, we will see," I say, scooping her up into my arms and heading out to the car.

When I get Lilly all strapped into her car seat, my phone pings, telling me I got a text message.

*Theo: We would love to. Meet you there :)*

Smiling at the phone, I get a rush of excitement at the thought of getting to see him.

"Good news, Theo and Toby are going to meet us there," I tell her as I start up the car.

"Yay!"

Biting my lip, I smile at how happy Lilly is. I was so worried about this move, but meeting Toby and adjusting to daycare has helped her so much.

When we get to the ice cream shop, Lilly races to the display window. "I want that kind! And that one! And that one!" she exclaims, pointing to every flavor.

"Wow, slow down there, little sugar bunny. You can have two scoops, each one a different kind, but that's it. You still have to eat your supper in an hour," I tell her.

"Okay," she says and turns back around and looks at all the different kinds again. I grin down at her little thinking face as she tries to decide.

"I want that one and that one," she says, pointing to the one labeled 'cotton candy' and another one noted as 'bubble gum'.

"Good choice. Mama likes those kinds too."

"They pretty," she explains, then runs over to a table by the big bay window.

Following her over, I take a seat on the chair next to her. Lilly tells me all about her day while we eat and wait for Theo and Toby to come.

A little bell on the door has my attention shifting in that direction. I can't help the smile that makes its way across my face when I see my tall, handsome neighbor. He gives me a heart-fluttering smile that has me sweating.

"Looks like we happened upon two pretty ladies, Toby," Theo says, as they make their way over to us.

"Where?" Toby asks, looking around.

I snort out a laugh, shaking my head. Theo does the same. "Over there," Theo points to us. Toby looks over and his face lights up. "Lilly!"

Lilly jumps up and rushes over, dragging Toby to look at all the different kinds of ice cream.

"Hi," I say softly when Theo's gaze turns to me.

"Hi," he smiles. "You look beautiful today."

I don't. I know I don't. I'm in a pair of sweatpants and a school hoodie. My hair is tossed up in a messy bun and I have no makeup on. I didn't think I was going to see him until I was already leaving my house and I have no one to impress at school. I don't always look like a hot mess, but sometimes I can't help but just say 'fuck it'. With taking care of Lilly, school, and homework, sometimes I just don't have it in me.

But I thank him anyway. The guys get their ice cream and we all sit and eat.

The way Theo's eyes follow my tongue as I lick my cone has me shifting in my seat. When he notices me watching, he quickly looks away, a slight blush taking over his cheeks. God, he's so cute. It's a nice break from all the meat heads full of themselves and alpha assholes who used to hit on me at work or whenever I went out.

Theo is a sweet, kind, and gentle soul. He's what one might call a sexy geek, and I can't help but wonder if he has any muscles under that dress shirt he always seems to be wearing. From the way the sleeves hug his arms when he takes off his jacket, I don't think I would be disappointed.

"So, how was your day?" Theo asks.

"Not bad. Classes were good. Hung out with the girls before going to my second class of the day. They asked if I was going to go to the homecoming game this Friday," I say, taking another lick.

"That sounds like fun. Are you going to go? It might be nice to get out with some friends. And with your new job starting up this weekend, who knows when you might get the chance," he says before his eyes go wide. "Oh God, I'm sorry. Please don't think I'm telling you what to do."

I laugh. "I don't." He relaxes a little. "I want to, but Katie is going also, so I don't have anyone to watch Lilly." I shrug.

"I don't mind watching her," Theo says. "I mean, if you want. I understand if you're not comfortable with it, but the kids are already best friends, and it's not like we would have to go far."

I really do want to go. Life is short, and I haven't really let loose in...well, since Lilly was born. I might have only known Theo for a week, but when I'm with him, I feel safe and wanted. He looks at me like I'm the only girl in the world and fuck, if that doesn't make me swoon.

Also, I had my father do a background check on him and it came back clear. I don't plan on telling him that, but I wanted to know I was safe before I got too close. He is squeaky clean. No arrests, nothing that would send red flags, and the fact that he is an elementary school teacher helps. There is also the fact that Lilly does seem to feel comfortable around them.

"Really?" I ask. "Are you sure? I don't want you to feel obligated or anything."

"Nonsense. I would love to. Lilly and Toby can play. We will even come over to your place, if you're alright with it, and that way if she falls asleep, we don't have to wake her."

"Thank you," I smile.

"You're welcome," he smiles back.

Laughing and shouting outside gets my attention. Across the street is a group of students and with them, my guys and Rain. *Not my guys anymore. Haven't been for years.*

I'm quickly reminded of that when I notice Chase with

some blonde floozy clinging to his side like a leech, her fake laugh standing out among the others.

Brody and Jax don't have anyone with them. They walk, talking to each other with giant smiles on their faces. *What are they talking about? What has them smiling like that?*

Doesn't matter, Ellie. They don't matter.

Rain runs up behind Chase, jumping on his back, making the girl stuck to his side stumble back. The girl stops and crosses her arms as she shoots daggers at Rain, jealousy shining bright in her eyes.

Chase laughs as he stumbles forward a bit. When Rain gets off, he puts her in a headlock, messing up her hair. She squeals as she struggles to get free. He lets her go with a little push and a laugh. Rain walks backwards, flipping Chase off with both middle fingers before turning around to catch up with the rest of the group.

My heart hurts now after watching that. Seeing how close they still are after all this time. They were best friends before me, why wouldn't they be after me? I was the late addition. What they have is unbreakable. Something I used to think I had with them too, but I was oh so wrong about that.

"People you know?" Theo asks as I watch them completely disappear from view. My head snaps over to Theo.

"Oh, umm, yeah, I guess you could say that," I mumble, nibbling on my cone, the fun of enjoying ice cream long gone.

Theo looks at me with a raised brow.

Sighing, I decide to give him some information. "I grew up in this town. Well, at least from fourth grade. Something happened after graduation, and apparently, I'm the talk of the town. Even after almost four years. Gossip and rumors are hard to let die in small towns."

His brows furrow, a million questions wanting to be asked.

"I'll tell you...someday." I give him a forced smile.

"Of course." I'm grateful he doesn't push.

God, that was close. Sometimes I forget that even though I

haven't seen them since the first day of school, they still live around here and the next time I see them, it might not just be in passing. I'm bound to bump into them at some point. They have to at least already know I'm back.

Theo and I chat while the kids finish their cups of ice cream.

"I think it's time to go," I say as I look at my very dirty daughter. Her face is covered in pink and blue ice cream. Toby looks the same but with green from his mint chocolate chip.

"I agree. I see two messy little monkeys in need of a bath," Theo chuckles when he gets a good look at them both.

Heading over to the counter, I grab a handful of napkins but as I'm turning around, I bump into Theo. "Sorry," I apologize. Looking up, I find him towering over me.

"You have a little something here," he says, his voice low and smooth. My lower belly flutters. My heart skips a beat and my breath hitches as he lifts his hand and wipes something from the corner of my mouth. Pulling back, I see a little bit of ice cream. His eyes bore into mine as he brings his thumb up, putting it into his mouth, and sucking off the ice cream.

Holy shit. There go my panties. I try really fucking hard to hold back a whimper. God, he's so fucking sexy, and the way he's looking at me makes me wish he would throw me up on the counter to lick and suck me like that. Is it weird that I really wish a certain body part of mine was his thumb?

He gives me a devilish smirk as he pulls his thumb out of his mouth. It's like he knows what he just did has an effect on me.

Then, my neglected lady bits dry up fast as reality comes crashing back in. "Mama, my hands dirty," Lilly states, shoving her hands in my face.

"That they are. Let's clean you up," I say with a shaky laugh. I hand a few napkins to Theo. He takes them from me, his fingers lingering on mine as he does, before going to clean up his son.

This isn't the Theo I expected to see today. He is definitely not the one who dropped me off after our date.

Just now, he was all confident, hot as fuck, and a little dirty.

There seems to be two different sides of my sexy neighbor, and I think I'm going to like one just as much as the other.

# Chapter Five

## ELLIE

"OKAY, I'm gonna say it. We look hot," Val says, checking herself out in the mirror.

I do have to admit, we kind of do. We're all decked out in silver and blue. We have Silver Valley University sweaters on, along with blue and silver war paint on our cheeks. My hair is in long flowy curls, and for the second time in a week, I took the time to really put work into my makeup.

It's nice to get away and act my age for once. This is college and I know my main priority is Lilly and bettering my life for her, but having a night out to myself here and there is healthy.

Then why does a part of me feel guilty for leaving her tonight?

Shaking myself out of the negative thoughts, I decide I'm gonna do what my therapist said, and take some 'me time'. It's just been Lilly and me for so long that having friends is a nice change.

"Okay, so the game starts in thirty minutes. If we leave now, we can grab a bite to eat at the concession stand and find some good seats before kick off," Lexie says as we all file out of her bathroom.

Lexie's parents live just down the street from the school, so she spends most of her time here while her parents are at work, even though, technically, she has a dorm room with Val. So, since every girl in their dorm will be getting ready for the game there, Lexie suggested we get ready at her house.

After dropping Lilly off at Theo's, I met the girls here. We drank a little, laughed, and gossiped while we got ready. At first, I felt a little awkward, but hanging out with these girls outside of school is different. They were pleasant and funny, making me feel included while I sat there quietly. I feel bad that I was quick to judge Val and Lexie before getting to know them, even though their first impression wasn't the best.

I also learn that everyone seems to know who I am. Could have fooled me because I feel invisible in this place, not that I care. I enjoy not having people gawk at me like I thought was going to happen when the girls found out who I am.

But apparently, everyone is focused and waiting on the Silver Knights tonight. They know I'm here and that thought has my stomach sinking. They haven't sought me out, so maybe if I keep avoiding them, I can get through this year, drama free.

*Ha, don't go kidding yourself, Ellie. Life isn't that easy.*

We grab our purses and head out into the crisp, September air. It might be nice during the day, but it is much colder at night. Perfect sweater weather.

We walk down the road, the wind blowing a few falling leaves around my feet. I smile as the girls joke around; a warm content feeling takes over me. As we get closer to the school, more and more groups of students seize up all the available space as we head in the same direction until we are all squished into one big crowd.

Once we get to the stadium, I can hear the chatter of the crowd as the noise from drums in the band echo throughout the night air.

My heartbeat starts to race as my body flushes with sweat. I don't like big crowds much, but I don't want my fear to hold me back from having a good time.

Grabbing onto the back of Tabitha's sweater so I don't get lost, I'm led by her to the concession stands.

"What do you want? My treat for your first official college football game," Tabitha grins over at me.

I look over the menu board. I already ate supper with Lilly, and my nerves are causing my appetite to disappear. "I'll take a large popcorn and a tropical spritzer."

Maybe I just need some liquid courage.

After getting our food, we make our way to find some seats. As we pass down the narrow walkway and into the open space of the stadium, my eyes go wide. The field is lit up with big lights, setting the whole place alight. The opposing team sits on the sideline waiting for the game to start. The place is already crowded and from the looks of it, there doesn't seem to be any empty seats.

"Where are we gonna sit?" I ask Tabitha, yelling over the chaos of the stands.

"I asked one of my friends to save us some spots!" she yells back.

The girls lead us through the crowd, excusing ourselves as we go. It feels like forever before we stop.

"Hey, Matt. Thanks for saving us some seats," Tabitha says, taking a seat next to a guy with brown curly hair. He looks up at her like she is the light of his life, and I bite back a smile.

"No problem. But I'm glad you ladies got here, I thought I was going to have to start fighting people off," he laughs.

I take a seat next to Tabitha and the other girls take the two free ones on the other side of Matt.

I can see why people would be fighting to get these seats. They are amazing—only a few rows up from where the team will be sitting.

"Ladies and gentlemen. Thank you for coming here tonight

for one of the most important games of the year! Let's welcome our Silver Knights cheerleading squad."

The crowd loses their shit. Deafening cheers erupt across the crowd. The cheerleaders get off the bench and make their way onto the field. I hadn't even noticed that they were there amongst the craziness.

Reality kicks in as I watch Rain turn around as her team takes up formation. The song starts and the girls perform an amazing routine. There's so much going on that normally it would be hard to focus on one thing and my eyes would be trying to take over the whole group as they cheer, but not this time. My eyes are firmly on Rain. Her bright and cheerful smile as she does each move flawlessly. The way her silver crop top and shorts form to her body, showing off her large breasts and tight ass. Her bright red hair sets her apart from everyone else. She's gorgeous.

They do a few more songs, each captivating me more than the next. The girls make their way back over to the bench. Rain waves to the crowd with a megawatt smile on her face. She genuinely looks happy. That is until her eyes find mine. My stomach drops as my body starts to sweat. I feel like I'm going to be sick.

She stares at me like she's seen a ghost, her eyes wide in shock, but it doesn't take long before she narrows her eyes at me with pure venom.

I blink rapidly as my breathing starts to pick up but that's when she breaks eye contact to go sit with the other girls.

My throat feels like it's closing, and my ears are ringing. Closing my eyes, I take a deep breath, trying to calm myself down before a panic attack is triggered.

"You okay?" Tabitha asks, bringing me out of my inner thoughts.

"Yeah," I smile back. "Not really good with big crowds." I huff out a laugh.

"Oh, shit. I'm sorry. If I knew, we wouldn't have bugged you to come," she says, her eyes fill with guilt.

"No, it's okay, really. I'll be fine."

Before she has the chance to respond, the announcer comes back on. "Now let's make some noise for our boys—the Silver Valley Knights!"

The crowd goes wild. Louder than before, if that's even possible. A moment later, the team busts through the paper banner. One after the other, the guys make their way onto the field, waving and fist pumping to the crowd. The guys are led across the field by Brody. His brown hair is wet from a shower. Looks like some things never change.

Back when he played for the high school team, Brody would take a cold shower before each game to cool his body down, so he did not get overheated. I used to laugh because he would just end up having to shower again afterwards.

Following behind him is Jax, his black hair slightly curly and sitting across his forehead, and Chase, his platinum blond hair so bright I could pick him out of any crowd.

They jog over to the bench where their coach is waiting. Rain gets up and goes over to the guys, waiting until the coach is done talking to them. They huddle together for a moment before all four of them turn. Rain finds me right away, already knowing where I'm at, but it takes a few seconds for the others to follow. When they do, I'm met with looks I never thought I would ever see from them.

Mixes of hurt, rage, and disgust hit me like a punch to the gut.

My mind flashes back to that night. To the night that changed everything.

I woke up the next morning, sore and confused. Everything came rushing back and I started to cry. I quickly gathered up my clothes, thankful no one else was in the room with me, and rushed home with tears streaming down my face the whole way home. I felt so broken and lost.

For the next two days, I was numb. I laid in bed, staring at the wall. I didn't eat, and when I got up to use the bathroom, it was like I was a zombie going through the motions.

My mom and dad gave me space at first, but when I didn't come out of my room, they got worried. They came to check on me, and all it took was one look at my mom's concerned face for me to break down and tell her everything. They held me as I cried, demanding to know who did it. I lied and said I couldn't remember the details, just that it happened. I was afraid that if I did say something and they took him to court, it would all be for nothing, costing my family more than we had. With my father losing his job, the cost of court fees and lawyers was more than they had at the time. He could have represented me, himself, but I couldn't put him through that. Knowing all the details would have destroyed him.

Tim's family was far better off than ours, and would have drained us dry in the fight.

When they finally left my room, I looked at my phone, desperate to hear from my lovers, to have them hold me and tell me everything was alright. They had to have been worried about me, not hearing from me for two days.

But when I looked at my phone, the only thing I saw was a missed call that went to voicemail. It was dated the night of the party. With shaking hands, I pressed play and was met with Brody's voice. I sat there, sobbing as he told me how much of a whore I was. How I was a monster for cheating on them, that they were all done with me, and that they never wanted to see me again.

When the voicemail ended, I felt like my soul was dying. They didn't see the truth. They didn't see that a part of me was dying every second that it was happening to me. How could they think I would do that to them? They didn't trust that I loved them with my whole heart. That I would never cheat on them.

I was raped, and they thought I cheated on them. From

what Brody said, he read the scene wrong, and with what he said Tim and the others said to them, he chose to believe them over me.

After that, I just wanted to go far away from this town, from them. So I let the school know that I wouldn't be attending and left with my parents when they moved. I deactivated all my social media and changed my number, wanting to put this place and everyone in it behind me.

The blow of a whistle snaps me out of my past, bringing me to the present. My eyes flick to the guys running out to the field. The game starts and I try to get into it, cheer along with the others, but I can't.

It's official. They know I'm here, saw me with their own eyes. And from the looks of it, they don't like that I'm here and in their school.

Something tells me they aren't going to take it lying down and this is only the beginning of one hell of a first year at college.

"They are normally a lot better than this," Val says as the other team gets another point. Brody gets pissed off, ripping his helmet off, and tosses it to the ground as they come back over to the bench during half time. The coach starts yelling at them, telling them to do better and demanding to know what's gotten into them, causing them to play so badly so soon. After a few more harsh words, the guys get drinks and take a seat.

"Yeah, I think they might be off because of me."

"What makes you say that?" Tabitha asks.

"Well, from the looks they gave me earlier, they are not happy to see me."

"Oh."

The game starts up again. They make a comeback, playing the last half of the game smoothly. By the end of it, we win and the stadium loses their shit yet again.

"That was awesome! I was getting worried there for a bit,

but they came back full force," Lexie says as we all get up and follow the crowd out to the parking lot.

"Ready?" Val asks with a big smile.

Am I ready to go to a party? Before getting here, I was ready to ditch the party early and go home to snuggle with Lilly. But I can really use a few drinks, with music blasting from the speakers, and to just let loose.

# *Chapter Six*

## BRODY

"JUST OUR LUCK that the first real party of the year gets shut down by the cops," Rain mutters as she gets out of the car, slamming the door shut.

"Hey!" Chase shouts in protest as he gets out too. "You mind not doing that? I'd like the door to stay on the hinges, you know."

Rain repeats Chase's words but in a mocking tone and I fight to hold back a snort of laughter. Those two are more like siblings than best friends most days.

"You suck," he huffs, heading toward the house with the blaring music seeping out of it. The lawn is covered in people, some even passed out, and there are cups everywhere.

"Nah, I lick, they suck," Rain says with a cheeky grin, pointing to Jax and I. A slight blush takes over his face as he avoids eye contact with her.

"Why don't you say it a little louder? I don't think the people in the backyard heard you," I growl, getting into her face.

"Oh, chill out, big boy! No one heard anything. Your secret is perfectly safe," she says, rolling her eyes. She steps away from me, walking up behind Chase, who is surveying the house, and slaps him on the ass.

"Ouch!" Chase jumps and Rain bursts out laughing while taking off toward the house. "Get back here, you little shit," he calls after her. Once they walk through the open door, cheers from within the house ring out in greeting.

"You good?" I ask Jax, who's oddly quiet.

"Yeah, why wouldn't I be?" he asks, giving me a side eye.

"No reason." I say, my gaze lingers on him for a moment before I look back at the house. "So whose place is this anyways?"

"No fucking clue." Jax huffs out a laugh. "Someone on the cheer squad's cousin's house or some shit I think." He shrugs.

"Alright, I need to get fucking smashed. Tonight took a nose dive and our whole world just got fucking flipped upside down."

He gives me a dark look before nodding.

I woke up buzzing with excited energy for our first game, pumped to kick some ass on the field. I mean, we did, but it was a rough start. After seeing her with our own eyes, the face of the only woman who destroyed all of our hearts, well...for the guys and I, it fucked with our concentration.

We knew she was here, at OUR school, but with the place being so big, and none of us having the same classes as her, we hadn't actually seen her. Until tonight.

She looks so different now. She went from the beautiful girl we grew up with to a stunning woman. And that hurts more than it should.

All the hurt and pain from that night came crashing back at that moment. As I ran across the field, flashes of her being fucked by that pig clouded my vision. When we got to half-time, Rain reminded me she's not worth it. She's a part of my past. She doesn't matter anymore, and Rain's right. I'm not gonna let that bitch fuck with my life any more than she already has.

After that night, we didn't hear from her. She didn't call back crying and begging for forgiveness like someone who felt like they did wrong and was sorry. No, she moved away, blocked everyone, and started over like we meant nothing. Like she never loved us.

She's just as bad, if not worse, than my fucking mother.

No, no one's worse than that sorry excuse of a parent.

"Come on, let's get drunk then," Jax says, heading toward the house and I follow him.

When we get inside, we are greeted with the same response as the others. I nod as people say hello and congratulate us on our win. Most of the people who were at the party that got shut down found their way here too.

This house is ten minutes out of town, with no other houses for miles. Perfect for a college party.

"I'll grab us some beers, you find the others," Jax says, breaking off into the crowd of people.

Weaving my way through a sea of people, careful to avoid drunk assholes, I find Rain and Chase sitting on a couch in the back room.

"Move," I bark at the guy who's sitting on the far end watching Rain and some chick make out while looking like he's ready to whip out his dick and jack off at just the sight of them.

The guy jumps up and fucks off, but not before I get an eye full of his hard on.

"Pervert," I scoff, taking his seat on the couch.

"What, girl on girl doesn't turn you on?" Rain asks with a smirk as she breaks apart from her make-out marathon. I give her a blank look in response. Her lips are swollen and hair is a little messy from the girl's hands that were tangled in it, but are now groping Rain's breasts.

"No," I deadpan. "It fucking doesn't and you know it," I growl. Girl on girl doesn't appeal to me in the way that it does to most guys. When Rain and Ellie were together, what got me hard was watching how much my best friend loved her. How much her touch made her feel good, but it was the same with Chase and Jax. I just loved seeing my girl be loved and cherished.

*She's not my girl now. And apparently what we offered her wasn't good enough.*

"Why don't you go get us something to drink," Rain says, rubbing the girl's thighs. The girl gives Rain one last kiss before getting up and taking off.

"Make room," Jax says, handing me his beer. Rain gets up, then plops down on Chase's lap, getting a pained grunt out of him in return as Jax takes her seat.

"Well, hello there," Rain grins up at Chase. "What do we have here?" She wiggles in his lap, making him groan.

"Don't do that!" Chase says, pushing Rain off him and into Jax's lap. "It's fucking weird! You're like my sister." Chase shudders.

"Well, you're the one with a boner from watching me and that girl," Rain laughs.

"Look, I'm a guy and I'm horny. Also, she is fucking hot and her tits are pretty much hanging out of her dress. It wasn't what she was doing with you, just the noises she was making. I'm only human."

Laughing catches my attention, drawing my eyes toward the crowd where I heard the sound.

"Fucking great," Rain growls, shooting venom at the bane of our collective existence as she staggers onto the homemade dance floor with a couple of girls.

"There's twenty other fucking parties happening tonight and we just happen to end up at the same one she's at?" Jax mutters, taking a sip of his beer.

Chase says nothing as he watches her dance with her friends.

"We need to do something about her. She sure as fuck has big enough balls to come back here, waltzing into our school as if nothing happened. I want her gone!" Rain snaps, her eyes glued to the girl's hand that's gripping Ellie's hips as they dance to the beat of the music.

"Why the fuck is she back here anyway?" I ask.

"Umm, to go to school," Chase says, cocking an eyebrow at me as he takes a swig of his beer. "Like the rest of us."

"From what I heard, she moved to the other side of the damn country. Why not go to some place closer to where she lived? Why come all the way back here?" Rain counters.

"Look, this might sound like I'm defending her, but I'm not," he says, in a tone bordering caution and defensiveness, "This is one of the best schools in the country. And she was the smartest kid in our whole school. It makes sense why she would choose to come here."

"But why now? Why almost four years later?" Jax asks.

"I don't know, but thank fuck this is our last year so we don't have to spend a long time being forced to look at her," I say.

"Or, I say we just make her life a living hell until she drops out and runs back to wherever the hell she came from." Rain grins like she just came up with the best plan ever. Rain might come off as a bitch sometimes because of how strong she is and how she handles herself in most situations, but she is honestly one of the nicest people I know. Unless you hurt someone she cares about. That doesn't happen too often because most people don't fuck with us and we never let anyone get close enough to hurt us. Not after Ellie.

Any girls that Rain and the guys allow in their lives are nothing more than a quick fling and then they are on to the next one. The women know this going in. Although sometimes, they get a few clingers that they have to deal with.

Me, I don't fuck around. Meaningless sex just isn't my thing.

"Rain, we all know you're a bad ass bitch, but making her life a living hell? I thought we got over this. I thought we all moved on and decided not to let her ruin our lives. This? This is the exact opposite. I know you, Rain. You're gonna fixate on this. You, too," Chase says, looking at me.

"So what? We just let her walk around like she did nothing to us?" I ask, raising my voice, growing more angry by the second.

"I'm not saying that, but come on man, we have one year left before we start the rest of our lives. Together. Like we've always planned. You really want to let some girl we dated in high school come between something we've built since we were babies? We were a family before her and we are one after."

"It's not that easy." I turn to face him. "We loved her with every ounce of our being. So much so that we shared her so that we could all be happy. Then she fucked the whole damn swim team and ruined our lives!" My breathing is heavy now. I've been drinking on and off all night, even before we came to this party, and when I've had this much, I can be a little unpredictable. And with how Chase is acting, like we should just forget about it, is pissing me the fuck off.

"Calm down," Jax says, stepping up behind me, placing his hand on my shoulder. My body relaxes slightly at his touch. Jax is always my anchor when I get like this.

"Look, if it means that much to you, do what you need to. But leave me out of it."

"So you're taking her side?" I hiss.

His eyes flash with hurt, then frustration. "No! I'm not taking her fucking side! I'm on yours, always. It's just not in me to seek out to specifically hurt someone."

"But she cheated on us," I growl.

"And I got over it," he shrugs.

Rain starts to laugh, the sound making me worry about her a little. "Bull-fucking-shit, dick face. None of us got over that and you fucking know it."

"Whatever. I'm going to get something to drink," Chase mutters, dismissing this conversation. But it's not over, not by a long shot.

"What about you?" I ask, turning around to face Jax, his hand slipping off my shoulder. "Where do you stand in all this?" I lick my lips and his eyes follow the motion.

His gaze snaps up to mine. "With you. You know that," he says and I know he means it.

Taking a deep breath, I sigh and nod my head. "Good."

*FMRN* by Lilyisthatyou starts blasting through the speakers and my eyes find her. But now, she's not only dancing with some girl, she has Cooper from the football team behind her. He has his arms wrapped around her waist, holding her in place, as he grinds his dick into her ass. Her arms are wrapped around his neck with her eyes closed as she moves her hips along to the music. A blissed out smile takes over her face and the girl's hands skim her sides, lust blazing in her eyes.

Pure fucking rage takes over. I have no fucking idea why, but I wanna go over there and smash Cooper's face in for touching her. For laying a hand on what's mine. *Only...she's not mine. Not anymore.*

Rain lets out a low growl of fury, her nostrils flaring. Guess I'm not the only one who doesn't enjoy the little show Ellie is putting on. We stand there, watching them. The song seems pretty damn fitting seeing how she's practically fucking them on the dance floor.

By the end of the song, we've had just about enough of this.

"Here's your drink, babe." The girl from before holds out a red Solo cup to Rain, giving her a sultry look.

"About damn time!" Rain snaps, snatching the cup out of her hand. Some of the drink splashes out and over the rim. Rain takes off, heading toward Ellie. Jax and I follow. *What is she about to do?*

Without stopping, Rain takes the drink and chucks it into Ellie's face. Ellie lets out a gasp, her hands rushing to her face to wipe it out of her eyes.

"What the fuck was that for?" Ellie shouts, her eyes wide as she registers who it is that hit her with the drink.

"My bad. Thought you needed something to water you down with, you know, with you flopping around like a fish out of water," Rain sneers.

"You giving out free shows? Is live porn your thing now? No one wants to see that shit," I say, looking her over in disgust.

The whole party starts to laugh, gathering around to watch the show.

"What the hell is your problem?" the girl who was dancing with Ellie asks in shock.

"Me? I don't have a problem." Rain shrugs. "Well, not with you anyways. *Her*—" She points to Ellie who looks like a drowned rat with her hair all sticky and make-up smeared, "On the other hand, I do have a problem with."

"With what?" Ellie asks, her voice sounds like she's holding back a sob. "I haven't seen you in years, Rain. Why are you starting shit?"

Rain makes an unstable laugh again. I think she might have had too much to drink tonight, but who am I to judge? I've probably drank more.

"Are you kidding me? No, you're right, we haven't seen each other in years. But don't you remember the last time we *did* see each other? Because, I sure as hell do. It was the same night you had a fucking gang bang with half the fucking swim team, cheating on your fucking boyfriends and ME!" she roars in Ellie's face. Jax grabs Rain by the arm, pulling her a step back. Rain's chest is heaving, and she looks two seconds away from beating the shit out of the next person to look at her the wrong way. "Then you come back here, to *our* school, acting like nothing happened, dancing like a slut, and dry humping two people at once for all to see. I guess you're still into sharing." Rain looks at the people Ellie was dancing with. "Watch yourself with this one. She will end up fucking all your friends behind your back. Probably best not to bring her home to Mommy and Daddy. She would probably end up screwing them too."

Ellie's eyes fill with fear, and a sick look takes over her face as she lets out an anguished sob before pushing past us, racing through the crowd.

She has no right to cry like a little bitch. She knew what she did was wrong, and it's about fucking time she owns up to it.

"That was fucked up, man," Cooper says, shaking his head as he walks away. Ellie's little friend takes off after her.

"Listen up," I shout. "That little slut you just saw run out of here, that's Ellie Tatum. From now on, you are to treat her like the dirty slut she is. She isn't good enough for this school, and it's our job to make her see that. The sooner, the better." The crowd erupts into cheer.

"Come on. Let's get the fuck out of here. This party sucks and I'm over tonight. Leave it to the bitch to ruin our first win," I say, heading out of the house, Rain and Jax on my heels.

"Where's Chase?" Jax asks as Rain gets into the car, slamming the door behind her.

"For fuck sakes, take it easy on the damn door!" Chase shouts as he jogs across the lawn over to us, doing up his pants as he goes. I raise a brow at him and he just gives me a dirty smirk, shrugging. "What? When a hot chick practically begs you to let her suck your dick, you would be an asshole to say no and not give the girl what she wants."

Grinning, I laugh and shake my head. "Let's go home."

"From what I heard, in the bits and pieces I gathered as I ran out here to find you guys before you left without me, something went down with Ellie?"

We get into the car, and Rain hands Chase her phone. "Why don't you see for yourself?" She grins.

We press play and a video of everything that just happened from the moment Rain grabbed the drink from the girl she was with, to us walking out of the house plays on repeat.

"Damn," Chase says, shaking his head, handing the phone back to Rain. "You guys went hard, fast."

"She deserved every bit of it," Rain defends.

"If you say so."

With that, I blast the music on the radio and drive home, done talking about tonight.

*Hope you sleep well tonight, Ellie. Because we have only just begun.*

## *Chapter Seven*

### ELLIE

I KNEW RUNNING into them wasn't going to be fun. I knew they hated me then, but a small part of me hoped they would have moved on. It's been four years, surely they would have. *Right?*

But seeing their looks of pure hatred and venom on the field took away that little bit of hope that I was holding onto real fast.

The girls told me Rain and the guys would be at a different party, that they never went to the ones they go to. *So why were they there tonight?*

I was having so much fun—drinking, dancing, laughing. For a little bit, I forgot about earlier. Forgot about the fact that the four people I love the most in the world, aside from Lilly, hated me with a burning passion. I got to simply enjoy being twenty-two and let loose.

I was reminded just how much they hated me the moment that drink met my face.

Their words were like a dagger to the heart. It all became so real. That night came rushing back, yet again, at Rain's cruel comments. Brody's voice caused the memory of that voicemail to play all over again in my head.

I wanted to defend myself, to yell that they had it all wrong, that everything they thought I did was lies.

But why should I have to? They didn't trust me back then, they sure as hell wouldn't believe me now. They would just accuse me of lying. I know what happened that night. I've relived it more than I wish to. I don't need to justify myself. And after what they just did, they sure as shit don't deserve an explanation.

Shivering, I run my hands up and down my arms, trying to keep myself warm in this cool night air. My shirt is wet and sticky from whatever was in the cup Rain tossed at me. My sweater is back at the party somewhere. I took it off after getting overheated from one too many drinks.

My teeth chatter as I hiccup on a sob. How could she be so fucking cruel? The Rain I knew would never have done something like that. She would have punched anyone who dared to do that to another person.

But, then again, this isn't the Rain I knew and loved. At least, not when it comes to me. This is someone so damaged by hurt and pain that they should have never experienced to begin with. A miscommunication that changed all of us and from the looks of it, for the worse.

I want to go home. I want to shower and cuddle with my Lillypad. To wrap my arms around the one person who would never hurt me.

The sound of a car's engine has me looking over my shoulder. *Please don't be them.* I have had all I can handle from them tonight and I'm too drunk for any more of their bullshit.

The car slows, pulling up next to me. The window rolls down and I see the guy who I was dancing with at the party. He's cute—blond, shaggy hair, and a flashy white smile. When he asked if he could dance with me, I saw the football jacket. I was ready to say no thanks, but he seemed nice enough and I was having a good time.

"Hey. Do you need a ride?" he asks, his face showing concern as he takes in my appearance.

My first instinct is to say no. Being alone in a car with a guy I don't know, the first thing my mind thinks is 'what if he's like Tim?' But I push those thoughts to the back of my mind because I have no clue where I am or how to get home. All I know is that I am in the country, somewhere outside of town. I had no clue what direction I went, I just ran out of the house and kept going.

"Umm..." I say, gnawing on my lip. "Yeah. That would be great actually." I make my way around the back of the car to the passenger side, wiping my eyes with the heels of my hands, trying to rid myself of any evidence of my tears.

*Kind of pointless seeing as how you probably look like a raccoon hooker.* Looking down at my hands in the moonlight, I see black make-up smeared on my hands.

Fuck, I have to look like a total hot mess right now, but I don't care. I just want to go home.

Getting into the car, I'm silent as I buckle my seatbelt, aiming my body toward the door. I look out the window so I don't have to make eye contact with him while also trying to avoid him seeing me look like a mess.

"Thanks," I whisper, sniffling as my body tries to calm down from crying so hard.

"No problem," he says, as he speeds down the road. We say nothing as we head closer to town. When we see the lights of the little town ahead, he speaks. "Look, what they did was totally fucked up. They had no right to treat you like that."

I bite my lip, trying to hold back more tears. "They seem to think so."

"I'm not gonna lie, when they mentioned your name before I left, I knew who you were. I mean, I don't know the whole story and I didn't grow up here, but even if the rumors are true, it doesn't matter to me. That was years ago and they should be adult enough to move on with their lives."

He says nothing more when I don't respond. Once we get into town, he lets out an awkward laugh. "I just remembered, I don't know where you live. Where would you like me to drop you off at?"

Looking up and out of the front windshield of the car, I see that we are only a few blocks away from my apartment. "You can just drop me off here," I say, not wanting him to know where I live.

"Are you sure?" he asks, slowing down and pulling over to the sidewalk.

"Yes. It's not too far from here. I already took up enough of your night. It's fine."

"Okay, if you're sure. I'm just glad I could help you. I was having fun, up until those assholes fucked it up."

"Aren't you on the team with the guys?" I point out.

"I mean, yeah, but surprisingly I'm not friends with many people on the team." He shrugs. "We don't have a lot in common except for the game. I'm only on the team for the scholarship to this amazing school." *Well, he just earned bonus points in my book.* "My name is Cooper, by the way. Thanks for dancing with me tonight." He gives me a genuine smile.

"It was fun...until it wasn't." I smile, getting out of the car. "Oh and Cooper..." I dip my head so I can see him.

"What's up?"

"It's not true."

"What's not true?" he asks, his brows pinching in confusion.

"The rumors," I say, before shutting the door. He stays there for a moment before taking off, leaving me on the sidewalk in almost complete darkness with only the streetlight on the other side of the road casting a little illumination.

I start heading toward my apartment, quickening my pace as my mind runs wild with all the worst possible things that could happen to a girl alone and drunk at night.

When I get to my building, my stomach turns, the events of

the night getting to me, as well as everything I drank. I race up the stairs, passing Theo's apartment, only briefly thinking about how Lilly is before frantically trying to get my door unlocked. When I do, I head straight to the bathroom just in time to heave my stomach contents into the toilet.

After I know I'm done, I flush it with a groan, a headache already setting in. Fuck, I have school tomorrow. And I start my new job. What a good first impression. Looking like death always gives off hospitality vibes.

Stripping out of my clothes, I set the shower temperature as hot as I can get it before climbing into it. After my sad attempt at a relaxing shower, I don't bother to get dressed. I just climb into bed, wet and naked.

I have never felt the need to get drunk in the past. The idea of a hangover has never appealed to me and seeing Rain and the guys while they were hungover didn't look like fun at all.

The only time that I've ever come close to how I'm feeling right now is *that* night, when I was drugged. Only that was much worse than this feeling. I would take this right now over how I felt that night any day.

Closing my eyes, I will my mind to shut down. Thankfully, I'm drunk and tired enough to fall asleep right away.

I have a feeling tomorrow's going to be hell, and not just because of the hangover I'm sure to have when I wake up.

## THEO

Giggling and the feeling of something on my face has me slowly blinking awake. When I open my eyes, I see Toby and Lilly leaning over me. Their eyes go wide while jumping back. "Uh oh," Lilly whispers, tossing the marker that's in her hand to the floor.

"Run!" Toby shouts, also tossing his as he scrambles off the bed. Lilly hops down and runs after him, laughing as they go.

With a groaned sigh, I stare up at the ceiling. Toby has been in a faze where he wants to color everything but paper—whether it be a coloring book or just plain paper. I thought about not allowing him to have markers anymore, but I would feel like a crappy parent for taking his creativity away. Plus, it's a lot easier to remove washable markers than crayons from almost every surface.

But now he's gone and recruited the sweet little girl down the hall. What is her mother going to think when I bring her daughter back as a delinquent?

Ellie! Shit. I lean over and grab my phone. No messages. I hope she got home okay. I know she was with some friends and not alone, but a part of me still worries.

When she looked disappointed that she had no one to watch Lilly so that she could go out with friends, I jumped at the chance to watch her. Lilly is a sweet kid, and Toby gets along really well with her.

With Ellie starting her job tonight, school, and taking care of Lilly, I know she won't have time to just get away and enjoy herself. So, if I can help give her that night off, I'm more than happy to help.

I know we've only known each other for a few weeks, but there's something about Ellie: her smile, her personality, her laugh. It draws me in.

It's been a few years since my wife has died. I never had the need to go out and find someone else. She was my whole world, the love of my life, and my high school sweetheart. During one of her final days, she crawled into my lap, taking my face into her hands and asked me not to let her death stop me from living my life. She told me she wanted me to be happy, for Toby to be happy. She said she hoped I would find a sweet woman who loved kids and could give me everything I deserved.

I didn't want to hear it at the time. It was a crazy idea because how could I love anyone else when I already had my soulmate?

Over time, I started to grow lonely. I missed her like crazy, but I knew she wasn't going to come back. I needed to move on but never forget her.

I tried dating apps, but never found anyone that caught my attention, not even making it to a first date.

On the other hand, when I saw Ellie sitting on the park bench with her face glowing in the sunlight, smiling as she watched the kids running around playing, I was completely captivated for the first time since my wife.

Something urged me to go over there and talk to her. And I'm glad I did. We easily fell into a conversation, never once feeling forced. When she laughed, I found myself wanting to do what I could to hear it over and over again, to see her smile light up her face.

From that day on, all I've wanted to do is be near her, talk to her, but this is new, for the both of us. I don't want to come on too strong, and a part of me feels guilty for being so strongly attracted to someone who isn't my wife. I know my wife would have loved Ellie, and from the short amount of time I have spent with her, they would have had a lot in common. Although, there are enough differences that make them both unique.

Knowing I need to get up, I drag myself out of bed. Toby has kindergarten this afternoon and Ellie has class in a few hours, meaning Lilly will have to go home so Ellie can get her ready for daycare.

I have another whole day free, again. I'm a teacher, but haven't been able to find a permanent job in this small town. I can leave, but this is the place I grew up, where I met my wife. My parents and hers live here. I can't take Toby away from them. I've been taking substitute jobs at the school in town as well as surrounding areas, but nothing that's consistent.

I put in my application at the university, and they told me that if they have any openings, I'd be the first they'd call. I originally went to school to become a college professor, but since I'm not willing to leave town to open myself up for job openings, it has left me with little options, forcing me with whatever I can get.

A crash from somewhere in the apartment has me moving my butt. I race into the kitchen to see a broken bowl on the floor and the jug of milk laying there, milk still flowing out. I grab the milk and toss it into the sink before looking at the kids.

"Is everyone okay?" I ask, looking at two shocked little faces.

"We wanted to make breakfast for you and Mama." Lilly pouts, looking like she's about to cry.

"Hey, it's okay. Thank you for thinking of us, but let's leave that until you're a little older, okay?" I ask, kneeling down to her level. She gives me a nod, and wipes her eyes before giving me a big grin.

"You look funny," she giggles. Crap, the marker.

"I bet I do." I smile back, giving her a little tickle before lifting her out of the way with Toby trailing behind us.

"I told her no, but she didn't listen," Toby lies, because I know for a fact this has his name written all over it.

"Did not!" she shouts back.

"Now, now," I say, putting the little one down away from the mess. "Toby, what did I say about lying?" He just blinks at me. "Toby..." I repeat in a more stern tone.

He gives me a dramatic sigh. "Fine," he whines. "I did it too. But I didn't make a mess." He points to the bowl on the table. It's filled to the brim, and consists of mostly just milk.

"I can see that. But you both did something you know you're not supposed to do. That milk is pretty heavy. Next time, you need to come and get me, okay?"

"Okay," they say in unison.

"Now, how about we get dressed and go grab some coffee from the shop down the street.

"Yay!" they cheer, running to Toby's room.

Laughing, I walk to the bathroom and see the damage that's been done to my face. "Eww," I say, looking at the really bad make-up job that they gave me. It looks like they tried to give me eyeshadow, lipstick, as well as some random scribbles.

I grab a washcloth and wet it with warm water and soap, scrubbing my face clean. After a few good rinses, I manage to get it all off, but now my face is all red. *Better than before, I guess.*

After I get changed and put on my glasses, I find the two of them by the door trying to put on their shoes.

"Mr. Theo, help please," Lilly asks, holding up her foot. I help her and Toby put them on properly, before putting my own on.

"Alright, it's still early, so it might be cold out," I tell them, getting two jackets out of the closet. I put Toby's Spiderman one on him, and go to put his Pikachu one on Lilly, because Ellie didn't bother giving me one since we didn't plan on leaving the building.

"That's for boys," Toby says, as I pull it onto Lilly's shoulders.

"Toby, clothes aren't meant for only girls or only boys. They're just clothes. If Lilly wants to wear Pokemon clothes, or play with toys you like to play with, she can." I turn to look at Lilly, "Do you want to wear this?"

She nods her head with a smile. "I love Pikachu. I have a big teddy at home."

I look back at Toby, who has a grumpy look on his face. "See, buddy? She likes it," I say, patting Lilly on the back.

"It's mine! She can't have it," he huffs.

"And she's not going to keep it. She's just gonna wear it while we go out today, okay? She has her own at home."

"Fine," he huffs, then walks up to Lilly, holding out his hand for her. She places her hand in his as I open the door for us to step outside.

Grinning to myself, I lock up and follow the two down the

hall. When we get outside, I take both their hands and walk to the shop.

I let them each pick out a donut as I grab Ellie a chocolate croissant as well as coffee and a bagel for myself.

When we get back to the apartment, the two kids have messy faces and enough energy to match the Energizer Bunny because of the sugar they just ate. Probably not the best idea I've ever had, but it was Toby's and Lilly's first sleepover, so I wanted to make it a little more special.

Knocking on the door, I wait for Ellie to answer.

"Coming!" she shouts in irritation. I don't think she's having a very good morning from the sound of it.

The door flings open wide. "What?" she snaps. I flinch at her tone, but keep a smile on my face.

"Mama!" Lilly yells, grabbing onto Ellie's leg.

Ellie's face changes into a smile as she scoops her little girl up into a hug. "I missed you, my Lillypad."

"I missed you, too, Mama. I had so much fun."

"I'm so glad," Ellie says, snuggling in close to her daughter's face.

Lilly wiggles to get down and runs into the apartment with Toby over to her little toy corner in the living room.

"Well, good morning to you, too," I chuckle, taking in her sleep outfit. My eyes linger on her perky nipples before snapping up to her face. Ellie smiles, taking the coffee from my hand and the bag of food from me.

"For me?" she asks. I give her a nod, feeling a little embarrassed for getting caught, but she's just so enticing. "My Prince Charming," she says, leaning up on her tippy toes to give me a kiss on the cheek, making it tingle at the contact.

"Of course. I thought you might need a pick-me-up. How was last night?"

Her face falls, her beautiful smile going with it. "It was fine," she mutters, turning away and taking the stuff to the kitchen.

Yeah, she's full of it. From the way her mood just changed, it sounds like it was anything but fine. I'm not going to bug her about it, but I just hope she knows I'm here to talk about it if she needs to.

# Chapter Eight

## ELLIE

DEATH. That is what I feel like this morning. I really don't understand why people enjoy drinking so much that they end up with a hangover. It's the worst feeling. Every movement makes me feel like I want to puke and my head feels like it went a few rounds with one of those cymbal-banging monkey toys. Thankfully, the breakfast and coffee that Theo brought me helps, along with some pain meds I took.

"Well, you look radiant today," Tabitha laughs, sitting down next to me and dropping her tray, letting it bang a little too loudly on the table.

"Shhhh," I groan, not lifting my head from the table.

"Someone partied hard," Val giggles, sitting down on my other side.

Rolling my head to the side, I peek up at Val and mumble, "That's one way to put it."

"We were worried about you. We tried looking for you when you ran off, but we didn't know what direction you went in," Tabitha says.

Sighing, I sit up only to slouch back down in my chair while bringing my knees up to hug, and sending my messy bun flopping back into place. "I walked for a bit, but Cooper offered me a ride."

"Cooper? As in the football player you were dancing with?" Lexie asks, sitting down at the table across from me.

"Yup." I close my eyes, wishing I am home in bed, sleeping. School is almost over for me today. I had two classes this morning, Business Administration and Business Ethics, and after lunch, I have Marketing. I plan on napping for a few hours before heading to my first day of work at 7 p.m. tonight.

I'm excited, but I'm also dreading it. I don't like big crowds, which is partly why I didn't agree right away to the party. And working at a restaurant style club, there's bound to be drunk assholes, but a job is a job. I have to take what I can get, and get over my fears one way or another.

"Oh, he's so cute! And so much nicer than most of the dick heads on the team," Lexie says.

"Yeah, like the Knights," Val inserts, rolling her eyes. "I can't fucking believe they did you dirty like that! I mean, I know they're not the nicest guys in the world, but I've never seen them be that big of jackasses! Like damn, they need to move on."

"Ellie," Tabitha says, getting my attention. I open my eyes to see her guilty ones looking back at me. "I really didn't know they would be there, I promise. I hope you know we would have found another party to go to if I did."

"I know." I give her a tired smile, and look at the others. "Do any of you know how they ended up there?"

"Someone who knew someone on the cheer team threw the party we went to. The one they were at got shut down by the cops pretty fast, so I'm guessing Rain brought them to ours," Val says with a shrug.

"I guess it was stupid to think I'd be able to avoid them forever. I guess the peace and quiet was nice while it lasted. Let the reign of terror begin!" I cheer with very fake enthusiasm.

"Look, I know we don't know the real story, but we do

believe you when you say their version of the story is false. We got your back," Tabthia says, putting her hand on my knee.

"Yeah, girl, we got you." Val fist bumps me.

Laughing, I shake my head with a smile. I really did miss having friends. As much as I love hanging out with Lilly, being around girls my own age is a nice, needed change.

"Thanks, guys."

"Oh look. It's the school bicycle," someone says, walking past me from behind. I turn around to see a few guys snicker amongst themselves. "Can we have a turn?"

"Real original, assholes!" Lexie shouts back. "And no one wants you to take them for a ride. Been there, done that, nothing to be proud of." The guy's face drops into a glower as his friends clap him on the back, yelling 'Burn!'.

Turning back around, I giggle and look at Lexie. "Did you really sleep with him?"

She shrugs, "Last year, party hook-up. And trust me when I say," she holds up her fingers maybe an inch apart as she squints her eyes.

We all burst out laughing. Maybe the hell Rain and the guys are about to put me through won't be as bad with these girls by my side.

---

"Alright Lillypad. Mama has to go to work. I won't be back before you go to bed, so I want you to listen to Katie and be a good girl, okay?" I say as I give Lilly a goodbye hug and kiss on the cheek.

"I always good, Mama," she says, rolling her eyes. *The sass is strong with this one.*

"Of course you are," I laugh. "But make sure you keep it that way."

"Okay."

"I love you, Bug."

"I love you, Mama."

"To the moon and back."

"And back!" she says, before running off to watch her show.

"Thanks again for taking the job. You have no idea how much of a big help this is," I tell Katie.

"No problem. I need the cash, and plus, this will look good on my resume once I graduate," she winks. Katie is going to school to become a preschool teacher; I was so lucky to find someone who loves kids and is amazing with Lilly.

I say goodbye to Katie and give one last hug and kiss to Lilly, who doesn't even look away from the TV. *Kids.*

As I make my way down the hallway, the door to Theo's apartment opens. "I'm glad I caught you before you left for work," he says, giving me a smile. I stop at his door, giving him a smile of my own.

"Just heading out now."

"Well, I just wanted to wish you luck on your first night," he says, a light blush taking over his cheeks. *God, he's so damn sweet!*

"Thank you," I say, leaning up on my tiptoes to give him a kiss on the cheek. "I hope things go smoothly. I'm going in early to be trained for a few hours. I guess the place doesn't really get busy until 10 p.m."

"You got this! You're sweet, funny, and fun to be around, how can they not like you?"

"You're too sweet," I say, giving him a hug. He seems startled at first, but then wraps his arms around me, holding me tight to his body and gives me a kiss on the top of my head.

Normally, I'm not so freely open when it comes to physical contact with people, but with Theo, I feel...safe. And that's rare for me.

Dancing with Cooper and Tabitha was also new for me, but I think the alcohol played a really big part in calming my nerves and getting my mind off things.

"Text me when you're done. I don't care how late," he says when I pull back.

"I will," I smile. I take off down the hall, and just as I'm about to round the corner to the stairs, I look back, finding him still there, so I wave goodbye. He smiles and waves back.

Butterflies take over my belly as I think about him the whole way to work. I'm starting to crush on Theo, *big time*. Every day with him, my worries about starting something with him become less and less. I've been having phone calls with my therapist every few days and she says I'm doing amazing, and she's proud of my progress. I'm pretty damn proud of myself, too.

Now I just hope Rain and the guys don't fuck everything up.

The place is still pretty busy, considering it's 7 p.m. A girl named Jill is helping me train. She's pretty nice and is patient with me as we go. I thought I would be getting a job as a server, and I am, but once 10 p.m. hits, I'll be working downstairs in the club. I don't know how I feel about that because the girls told me this place was a busy spot for college kids. *And how much do you wanna bet this would be a place* they *would come to.*

"Ellie!" Tony, my manager, calls.

I look up from the table I'm clearing and over at him. "What's up?" I smile, hoping the nerves go away soon. Things have been pretty good so far this shift. No real mix ups. Everyone's been patient and polite.

"It's 9:30. Take your break and get changed for your shift downstairs," he says, before taking off into the back room.

I look over at Jill who just dropped off an order to one of her tables. "We don't wear the same uniform in the club?" I ask her, brows pinched as I look down at my black t-shirt and slacks.

"No," she laughs. "Not even close. The club has a different vibe than the restaurant." *Lovely.* "There's another staff room down there, your uniform should be in the locker with your name on it."

"Thanks," I say, putting away the stuff I was using to clean the tables and heading downstairs.

The place is pretty empty, but the staff all seem to be rushing around, making sure everything is perfect. When I get to the room that says 'Staff', I hear laughter. Nerves take over at the thought of meeting all these new people, and working down here in a crowded place. I sometimes feel claustrophobic and start to panic, but I have to suck it up, because I need to do what I can for Lilly and myself. We need this money, and the tips would pay for childcare alone.

"You got this," I say to myself, taking a deep breath, and pushing the door open. All the chatter stops as I take a step inside. I give the girls a smile, and a soft 'hi' as I make my way over to the lockers at the back. They're all sitting on couches that form a square in the middle of the room.

As I reach the locker with my name on it, they pick up with their chatter again, only whispering this time. They probably recognize me from school or something. I grab my uniform without really looking at it and bring it to the changing rooms off to the side. Locking the door behind me, I take a look.

You have got to be fucking kidding me. It's a silver bra and black booty shorts. My stomach drops. Everyone is going to see me practically naked.

Sitting down, I put my head in my hands, trying to get my breathing under control. The idea of men looking at me like they want to fuck me sends chills down my spine. I know that not all men only have that one thought in mind, but this is college and I've seen the news.

*This is for Lilly,* I think to myself. Don't let your past control your future, by giving in to the fear, you let him win.

Not wanting to think of him, I push it to the back of my mind and get dressed.

"You're going to need to bring heels next time," a girl with long brown hair says, coming to stand next to me as I'm putting my things away.

"I didn't know," I say looking down at my black flats. "I thought I was just going to be working at the restaurant."

"Yeah, one of our girls quit yesterday, so you were the first choice in replacing her. Young, pretty, guaranteed to make the customers tip well."

"Or she could just fuck them. I'm sure they would pay a hell of a lot more for that than her serving them and shoving her tits in their faces," someone sniggers from the couch.

"From what I hear, no one's gonna want to use her used up, diseased pussy, anyways," another one says.

"Oh, shut up, Laura. And Kayla, you're only being a cunt because your queen bee doesn't like Ellie."

Well, I guess they do know my name, and I can only assume their 'queen bee' is Rain. So that means they are on the team with her, or are her friends.

"Look, I don't know you, or what you heard about me, but I'm just here to work and make money to pay my bills. I don't want any issues," I tell them, then look back at the nicer, brown haired girl.

"Don't mind them. They're Rain's little followers. Normally, Rain isn't so bad but she's really flipped a switch since you got here," she laughs. "I'm Aria by the way."

"Nice to meet you. Do you automatically hate me without even getting to know me?" I ask her with a grin.

"Nah," she laughs. "I like to get to know people before I go believing in all that bullshit."

"So how does this work? Do I walk around and see if people want drinks, or work behind a bar?"

"Some girls walk around with shots for sale. Others run drinks for tables. But mostly, people just go up to the bar and order drinks. The VIP section, on the other hand, gets a server assigned to them."

"How many VIP sections are there?"

"Four. They're sectioned off with three footwalls and have a few couches in the back of the room, away from the dance floor."

"She can have my section tonight," Laura offers up. "Tony asked me to run food tonight anyways. He was going to get her to do that, but I think she should be in the club tonight, getting a feel of the place."

"Thank you," I say.

"I don't think that's a good idea..." Aria looks at me with concern in her eyes.

"Why not?" I ask.

"Aria, we don't play favorites here. She doesn't get a free pass," Kayla sneers.

"Oh look, it's 10—show time," Laura says. They all get up and fly out.

"Come on, I'll give you a quick tour. People normally have champagne waiting for them in the VIP sections anyway."

We walk out into the club, and they really don't waste time. The place is already getting packed with every second that ticks by.

"The bathrooms for the club are next to the bar," Aria says, pointing them out. "They're also the easiest to get to. So if you need to pop in to use the washroom, they will be your fastest option, better than trying to make your way around to the staff room."

She takes me over to the bar and introduces me to a man behind it. "This is Tyler. He's the bartender for tonight. If you need any help with drink requests, he will put them in right away."

"Hi," I smile, giving him a small wave.

"Hi," he smiles back. "Good luck tonight."

"Thanks."

Aria gives me a pad and pen. "You're gonna need this until you can remember all the drink names."

Taking it from her, she leads me to the side. "The VIPs are back there. You have section 1 tonight. I'll be walking around with shots, so if you need anything, just look for me, okay?" She looks at me like I might actually need to take her up on that help. "And Ellie. Remember, VIP costs a lot of money, so we tend to give the customers what they want if it's within our power. Keep that in mind and they'll tip you well."

"Okay. I think I'll be good. I'll mostly just be writing things down and bringing them drinks and maybe food."

"Alright, off you go."

She takes off back to the bar, and I look in the direction of where I need to be heading. There's a little pathway along the sides of the room, so I use them to avoid the crowd."

When I get to the VIP section, I see the little '1' sign and walk over with my pen and paper in hand. "Hi, I'm Ellie. I'll be your server tonight." I put on the friendliest smile I can muster, but as they turn to look at me, my whole world spins. I forget to breathe, and I think I might just shit my pants.

"You have got to be fucking kidding me," Rain snarls, looking me up and down.

*Well fuck.* This night just turned into a nightmare.

# *Chapter Nine*

## ELLIE

**THIS CAN NOT BE HAPPENING.** Not tonight, not on my first day of work. *Why them!?*

"Hi," I repeat, keeping a friendly smile plastered on my face, trying not to make a fool of myself by puking because of the raging case of nerves I suddenly have. I swallow down my panic and continue, "Is there anything I can get you?"

"A new server would be nice," Jax drawls. They are all here with someone except Brody, who is sitting in the middle of the couch like a god, leaning back with his arms spread over the back and his legs relaxed. He's wearing a black dress shirt with the first few buttons open and dark jeans to match. He looks even more handsome now that he's a man. They all do.

Jax, Rain, and Chase all have girls in their lap, and I can't help but wonder why I haven't seen Brody with anyone yet. I haven't seen much of them since I got back, but the few times I have, he's been alone within the group. Are they all not good enough for him? Not meeting his standards?

"Hello!" Rain calls, snapping her fingers. I shake my head, looking away from Brody. "Now that you're done perving on him, can you do your job and get us our fucking drinks? Do we need to talk slowly for you to understand?"

Wow. *She really has become a bitch.* At least to me. "Nope," I force a smile. "What would you like?"

They order a ton of drinks and food, and I struggle to keep up as they all start to bombard me with requests. But I get them all down in the end. "Will that be everything?"

"For now," Chase says, giving me a once over. I can swear I see a flash of hunger in his eyes, but it's quickly gone as he turns to the girl on his lap and rams his tongue down her throat as his hand inches up her thigh.

"I'll be right back with your drinks, however, food may take a little longer." I quickly turn around to leave, but Brody stops me.

"Actually, I have one more request."

I stop, my back still toward him. Gritting my teeth as I take a deep breath, just wanting to get the hell away from here, I force my smile back on and turn to him. "Of course, what can I do for you?"

"Could you maybe change into something else? You look like a cheap hooker, and I don't think that's the vibe this club is going for," he says, giving me a smug grin.

I blink at him. *Is he for real right now?* "Umm..." I say, feeling myself starting to get hot as all the attention is on me. The girls giggle as they wait for me to answer, except for Chase's who is still too busy with him to care.

"Well?" Brody cocks his head to the side.

"It's what everyone else is wearing. I don't have a choice."

"But they don't look like trashy whores and you do." He gives me a mocking, sad smile, like he pities me. Rage builds and it's taking everything in me not to tell him to fuck off.

"Well, that must be unfortunate for me. I'll just have to deal with looking like a slut because I don't think anyone else seems to have an issue. But thanks for the concern, I really appreciate it." I bat my eyelashes. His cocky smirk turns into an angry glare as the others stop their sounds of amusement. "Right, well, I'll be right back with your drinks."

I get the fuck out of there before he can start throwing more insults. I do not look like a whore. Sure, it's revealing more than I'd like, but my hair is in long curls, and I have light natural looking makeup on.

"This is for VIP section 1," I tell Tyler, handing him the long list of requests.

His eyes widen. "Is this some kind of joke?" he asks, looking up at me.

"Umm. No?" I say, fidgeting with my pen, clicking it rapidly as I start to panic that I fucked up.

"It's just, this is a lot. How many people are in the group?"

I count them in my head. "Seven, as of right now."

He looks it over again. "Alright," he says, still not sounding sure.

He puts everything into the computer. "Give me about five minutes."

I nod my head, and look out into the crowd. The place is packed, the music is loud, and the place is getting warmer by the minute—or maybe it's just me feeling the need to escape.

When Tyler is done, he places the drinks on a tray. "Are you sure you have it?" he asks, looking at the seven drinks, and ten shots. There's almost no space for me to grab on to.

"I hope I do." I huff out a nervous laugh. I know I should be doing this in two trips, but they've already been waiting a bit and I don't want to hear them bitch. Carefully, I pick up the tray, and move around the edge of the room to avoid as many people as I can, while trying not to spill any of the drinks. "Excuse me," I shout as I dodge a few people. "Coming through." Someone bumps into me, causing the drinks to shake. I freeze, eyes wide, waiting for something to happen. When everything looks good, I make my way to their table.

"Here you go," I say, placing the tray down on the table.

"Took you long enough," Rain huffs, leaning over and grabbing a shot. She places it between her breasts, her skin tight dress holding it in place. "Here, babe." She gives the girl on her lap a seductive smile. "You have the first shot." The girl giggles as she shoves her face into Rain's tits, grabbing the shot with her mouth and tossing it back.

"Oops. Missed some." The girl bites her lip before leaning down and licking the non-existent spill from the top of Rain's tits.

My gut turns as I watch Rain groan in pleasure, taking the back of the girl's head and smashing her mouth to hers.

"Hey, that looks like fun. Here," Chase says, not bothering to grab a shot, just diving into the girl's cleavage. Her squeals turn into a moan.

"Where's our food?" Brody asks. My attention snaps to him.

"It's going to take a little longer."

"Awesome," he huffs.

"Well, we're going to dance." Rain says as the girl on her lap stands. Rain grabs her hand and leads the girl out to the dance floor, making sure to bump into me which causes me to stumble back a bit.

"Come on, babe, let's join them," Chase says, pulling the girl up. He looks sexy, his blond hair all tousled, and I can't help but think about when we had heated make out sessions. When I'd run my hands through his blond strands while kissing passionately. Holding back tears, I turn my attention away from them, over to the remaining assholes.

"If you don't need anything else, I'll be waiting by the bar for your food."

"Why are you here?" Brody asks me bluntly, taking me by surprise.

"What?" I ask, brow furrowed.

"I said. Why. Are. You. Here? Back in Silver Valley. At my school."

"It's not *your* school," I snap. "And it's one of the best schools in the country. Why wouldn't I want to go here?"

"But why four years later? We don't want you here," he growls.

"And I don't give a shit what you want. You have no right to know anything about me. So, if you don't mind, I'm done here. I'll be back with your food later." I turn and race through the club back to the bar. I need fresh air, but my break isn't for at least another hour. And my shift isn't over for another two.

It takes another fifteen minutes before the food is ready. "Here you go. Looks like the Knights and their ladies are hungry tonight," Laura grins, but it's not a nice one.

"Guess so." I force a smile.

"You know, you could save yourself the trouble and just leave."

"I can't, my shift isn't over," I say, trying to take the tray from her, but she doesn't let go.

"Not here. I meant this town, this school," she sneers, shoving the tray of food at me, causing the box of fries to fall to the ground.

"Are you kidding me?" I gasp, looking at her in shock.

"Oops, my bad. Totally an accident," she grins, turning around to head back upstairs.

"Bitch," I mutter to myself.

"I'll get that. You go bring them their food," Tyler says.

"Thank you." I give him a grateful, tired smile.

"Alright, here's your food," I say, setting the tray down, and taking the empty drink tray back.

"Next weekend, ask for a different section, because you suck at your job. It never took Laura or Kayla this long," Rain bitches as she looks over the tray. "And where the fuck are my fries!?"

Awesome, they were hers, of course they were. "I'm sorry about that. There was an accident. I will get you a replacement right away."

"Fucking useless. Don't bother. I don't have all night to wait for you to do your job right."

"Not like it's my first day or anything," I mutter to myself.

"What was that?" Brody asks.

"Nothing," I smile.

"Hey, those are mine!" Chase protests as Rain takes one of the onion rings from the tray.

"Mine now, sucker!" she grins back. Chase's face lights up before he dives on top of her, wrestling with her to get the food back. The girls they are with look at them, annoyed, as they move away.

I hate this. I hate that they are all still so close, like family. I should be there with them, joking around. A part of the group. Why did they have to trust everyone else around them, and not what we had?

*Because they never really loved you, Ellie. If they did, you would be living a totally different life. They were together before you, and will be long after you.*

"We need more drinks," Jax says, then whispers into the girl's ear. She gives him a confused look, but leaves when he responds with a death glare. She looks hurt as she rushes away. What did he say to her?

"For sure. What would you like?" Brody and Jax order drinks for the others. When I get back, the other girls are gone, including Rain. The guys sit next to each other as they all look at me with disdain.

Placing the tray down, I turn to leave. "Where are you going?" Brody's smooth voice sends shivers down my spine. I can tell he's been drinking by that glazed look in his eyes. I never liked when he drank. Brody has always been a quiet, closed off person with most people. Intimidating and scary to be around. But not with me. At least, not back then.

"I'm going for my break," I say.

"But aren't you going to clean this up?" he asks, cocking his head to the side.

"Clean what up?"

"This..." he says, tipping the glass of whiskey on the ground in front of him.

I'm vibrating now. I'm so over tonight. I walk over and kneel down in front of him and wipe up his drink with the tea towel I have tucked into my back pocket.

"You know, you look good like this," he says.

"Like what?" I ask, looking up at him.

"On your knees for me," he chuckles cruelly. His shoe makes contact with my forehead and he pushes me backward, making me fall on my ass. "Even better. On the ground like the dirt you are," he sneers.

Tears sting my eyes as I scramble to get off the ground. Chase and Jax just watch with bored expressions, like I'm not even worth their time. What happened to make them so cruel?

"Run along now. Get out of our sight," Jax says with a wave of his hand.

I can't do this. I need to go home. If this is what working here is going to be like, being subjected to this fucked up behavior, I'll find another job.

Weaving my way through the crowd, I head in the direction of the staff room. Bursting through the door, I head straight to the sink. I look at myself in the mirror. Tears run down my face, my make-up going with it.

*You're better than this, Ellie. You're better than them. Don't let them win.*

Turning on the tap, I cup some water and wash away my running make-up and cool myself down. Moaning comes from behind me. I open my eyes and meet Rain's in the mirror. My heart stops, and I choke on a breath of air logged in the throat.

There's a girl on her knees in front of Rain with her head between Rain's legs as she eats her out, drawing cries of pleasure from Rain's parted lips. Rain has a fist full of the girl's hair as she starts to ride her face.

I can't look away. I'm frozen in shock, in horror. I can feel my heart breaking into a million pieces as my stomach drops.

Rain is staring at me, daring me to look away. *Why can't I fucking look away?*

Rain's breathing is coming out in choppy breaths, and I hate that I know what's gonna happen next. She's close, and I know this because I know Rain's body better than anyone.

She locks her legs around the girl's head while arching her back, letting out a long moan as she cums.

Something in me gives, letting me finally break away from this fucked up spell I'm under. I run, needing to get out of here. I'm going to be sick.

Ripping the door open, I crash into Aria. "Wow. Are you okay? What's wrong?"

"I need to go. Please, let Tony know I'm sick. I'm sorry," my voice cracks.

"Ellie?"

"Please!" I try to hold in my sobs, but they seem to be slipping past.

She looks behind me, and stupid me, I follow her gaze. Rain steps out of the changing room, but it's not the girl she had on her lap all night. No, it's Laura behind her. Laura gives me a smug look, and I feel bile rise up my throat.

"Go," Aria says, looking back at me with fury. But it's not at me, it's for me. "I've got you covered."

"Thank you."

I don't look back as I find the exit. Bursting through the door, I find myself in the back alley.

My stomach lurches, and I puke, unable to get the image out of my head. It hurts. It hurts so fucking bad to see her like that. God. *Why?* I just want to make a better life for me and my daughter. Why can't they just let the past go and move on?

When there's nothing left in me, I strain to stand up and take a deep breath. Fuck. My purse is back in the locker—my phone, money, and car keys.

"Ellie?" Tyler's voice calls from the door I just came out of.

"Oh shit, you really are sick," he grimaces, looking down at the pile of puke.

"Sorry."

"It's okay. We're kinda used to it," he chuckles. "Perks of having a bunch of drunk people who can't hold their liquor. Here," he holds out my purse to me and I let out a sigh of relief. "Aria asked me to run this out to you. She assumed you wouldn't have gone far without it."

"Thank you. You're a lifesaver," I sigh, taking it from him.

"Just feel better, okay? And you did good for your first night. See you tomorrow." He takes off back inside.

Tomorrow. Fuck. I still have to come back here for the next few nights.

I walk to my car like a mindless zombie. I feel numb and empty as I unlock my car door. The ride home is quick and silent. When I get up to the apartment, I say goodbye to Katie and toss my purse and keys on the kitchen counter before heading to the bathroom.

I spend longer than I should in the shower, not leaving until the water is running ice cold. Wrapping a towel around me, I head into the kitchen to grab my phone. I turned it off while at work to save the battery. I hate not having it on me because I worry Katie won't be able to get a hold of me, but I gave her the number to the restaurant, too, just in case.

My phone lights up and a few missed texts pop up. Some are from the girls wishing me luck on my first night, and that they will be by tomorrow night at the club. The last few are from Theo.

**Theo:** *I know you're at work, but I just want to say I miss you, beautiful. You're going to kick ass on your first night.*

. . .

My eyes tear up again as I smile at the phone. I sink to the floor and text him back.

**Ellie**: *Hi! Just got home. Sorry, my phone was off.*
  **Theo**: *Glad you made it home safe, how was it?*

I chew on my bottom lip as I think about how to respond. Blinking tears away, they land on my phone as I type.

**Ellie**: *For the most part, good.*
  **Theo**: *Oh no. What happened?*
  **Ellie**: *Tell you tomorrow? I need to get some sleep before I gotta wake up and get Lilly ready for daycare.*
  **Theo**: *Of course. Sleep well, love.*

My heart swells as I read his text. This whole night, I was riddled with thoughts of how crappy I had it, but here is this sweet, caring man who is amazing with Lilly and me. *Fuck Rain and the guys.*

I'm going to tell Theo about them tomorrow. I'm not ready to tell him everything, but just enough for him to know what's going on. I don't want to start anything with him based on a lie or half truths. And I know I can trust Theo. There's something about him that makes me feel safe when around him.

**Ellie**: *You too xoxo. Sweet dreams. <3*

Dragging myself off the floor, I make sure everything is locked and turned off before making my way into the bedroom.

I can see Lilly in the glow of the night light. She's cuddled up to that stuffed dog she loves so much, and I have to shake my head to rid the thoughts of *them* that are trying to creep back in.

I grab a sleep top, toss it on along with some panties and crawl into bed, cuddling into Lilly. Tomorrow will be a better day. At least, that's what I tell myself.

# Chapter Ten

## JAX

"FUCK!" Brody roars, slamming the apartment door shut. He storms in and goes over to the counter, grabbing a glass and chucks it at the wall. Glass explodes all over the living room, and I know he needs to be calmed down before he destroys the whole apartment. When he's in a mood like this, there's only ever been two people who can bring him back from the edge, especially when he's drinking.

"B, you need to calm down," I say in a panic when I see him ready to pick up the lamp shade. *Fuck, I know that was the wrong thing to say.*

He slowly turns to me, chest heaving, fists clenched, eyes wild. I know he won't hurt me. He's never hit someone in one of his anger episodes, but I still take a step back when I see that unhinged look in his eyes.

"Don't fucking tell me to calm down, J. You should be just as fucking pissed off as I am." He beats his chest. "She comes back into town four years after destroying me! After ripping out my heart and crushing my soul. To *our* town, to *our* school, and acts like nothing ever happened. Like we meant nothing to her! She looks at us like we are just strangers she met in passing."

That's a lie. Because when Ellie looks at us, I see hurt, pain, and longing. But Brody is too blinded by his hate for her to see anything except what he wants to see. That night broke something in him that has never truly been fixed. The closest I've seen him to his old self is when we're all together, hanging out like a family with Chase and Rain.

Or when I'm able to get through to him during these moments, when it's just me and him.

"I'm just as mad as you are, Brody," I say, taking a step toward him with caution. "But you need to think rationally about this. Letting her control your anger like this, that's letting her win. Don't let her have that."

"You're right!" He nods as he starts to pace. "But she can't just go about her life in this school like nothing happened. Jax, she made a fool of us! She made us fall madly in love with her, only for her to fuck everyone with a damn fucking dick! We weren't good enough for Miss Priss," he says in a mocking tone. "Not smart enough. She never liked going out to parties or socializing with others. She always had her nose in a book." He stops pacing and looks at me. "So why the hell was she at a party? God, was even *that* a lie? Was it just us she didn't want to go out with? Maybe when she said she was at home studying, she was really out with other people."

Shit, he's spiraling again.

"No, no," he shakes his head. "No, she will need to leave. And if she won't go willingly, then we make her."

"Brody, we can't make her do anything. What are we going to do, kidnap her and drop her off a few hours away, a couple towns over?" I ask, laughing at how crazy that would be. He looks like he's considering it. Fuck, he really is drunk. "B, no, we can't do that." I sigh.

"We make her life hell. We make her hate this school. When she wakes up every morning, SVU will be the last place she'll want to be."

"How would we do that? There's four of us among a school of thousands. We don't even have any classes with her."

"We have the athletic teams. They would have our backs. No, we can't get the whole school to do what we want, that would take too much time and energy, but we have enough influence within the school."

"And what exactly are we going to do? Brody, as much as I can't stand her, I won't physically hurt her. We may not have meant anything to her, but at one time, she meant everything to me." *That is until I let Brody in.* "And I couldn't live with myself if I did."

"You're right. As much as I hate the bitch, I don't want to do that either." He finally stops pacing and takes a seat on the couch, gripping his hair and not caring about the glass. "I'll think of something, but we could at least start with making her a pariah at school. Everywhere she turns, she's gonna see people who want her gone. She won't feel safe or comfortable anywhere. There won't be anywhere she can hide that won't have some of our people reminding her of the trash that she is."

I walk over to him, my feet crunching on the glass with every step. "Come on. We can do more evil mastermind planning this weekend. We have class in the morning. Let's get some rest." I hold out my hand for him to take. He looks at it, then up to me. His eyes bleed with all his pain and raw emotions.

"Chase won't do it. He won't stop us, but he won't go along with it either, and I won't force him. But J, do you have my back? Are you with me on this?"

"You know I have your back, always. I will never let you down. We've been family our whole lives. You mean the world to me, B."

He grabs my hand and pulls himself up so that we're face to face. He grabs the back of my head and crushes his lips to mine in a soul consuming kiss. I moan against his mouth, opening for him, allowing his hot, wet tongue to tangle with mine. He reaches down and palms my bulge, making me arch into his touch. "Let's go shower. We can help each other work off some of this anger," he says, his forehead to mine.

I'm not as mad as he is. Over time, I learned to live my life, and leave the past in the past. I will always love Eleanor Tatum. It's programmed into my DNA. You can't love someone so wholeheartedly like that and not have them forever be embedded into your essence. With time, the pain of losing her became a numb, dull pulse in the background of my soul.

But he needs this, and I'm going to be there for him. I'll do whatever I can to help him have even the smallest ounce of closure and sanity.

He intertwines his fingers with mine and pulls me to the bathroom. He strips me out of my clothes, followed by his. In times like these, I might be his anchor keeping him grounded, but he always takes care of me.

At first, I think we're just going to have a normal shower, as much as I always hope it will be more. We wash our hair and body in silence, but just as I'm about to turn off the water, his arms wrap around me from behind. His hand glides down my slick abs, straight to my cock. It's already thick and hard for him, begging for his touch.

Brody grasps my shaft firmly before he slides his hand from its base to the tip, using his thumb to spread the bead of precum over the swollen head before gliding back down. His strokes are slow and teasing, and it's driving me wild.

"Brody," I moan his name, resting my head against his shoulder.

"Does that feel good?" His voice is low and husky, sending a shiver down my spine and making my cock twitch in his hold. He chuckles against my neck, giving it a hard suck before biting down, making me thrust into his hand. I know he's going to leave a hickey, but I don't care. People will probably think it's from some girl. Only he and I will know it's from him marking his claim on me. That's all that matters to me. "I'll take that as a yes."

He lets go, and the loss of his touch makes me whimper, which only causes him to laugh again. "Don't worry, babe, I'll take care of you. I always do." And he does. He steps away from me, and even though I hate the loss of his body against mine, it excites me to see him drop to his knees before me.

Water runs down his face, over his lashes and down his toned muscular body. His mousy brown hair is a shade darker as the wet strands stick to his face.

"What about this?" he asks, taking a hold of my cock again. He lifts it up so that he can give me one long lick from base to tip, before wrapping his plump lips around the tip, sucking as he twirls his tongue around the head of my cock. My eyes roll into the back of my head as I toss it back against the tiled wall.

My brain goes blank, tuning out everything around me so all I'm able to think about is how he's setting my body on fire.

He starts to bob his head, hollowing out his cheeks to get a better suction. He does that a few times before taking me all the way to the back so that he's deep throating me. He pauses, driving me out of my mind with anticipation. My cock twitches in his mouth as he swallows around my length, gagging a little before pulling all the way back. Spit drips down his chin, but he does nothing as he lifts my cock up and dips his head to take one of my balls into his mouth.

"Fuck," I hiss.

He does the same thing to the other one, before taking me back into his mouth. This man is going to have me blubbering like someone committed to the nut house.

He's not playing now as he grips my cock again, pumping and sucking me off. My fingers tangle in his hair as I start to jerk into his mouth.

A warning pat on my ass makes me jump. Removing my hand from his hair, I place both on the tile wall so that I'm leaning over him.

"Please," I beg, needing to cum. He looks up at me, his brown eyes less feral than before because it's been replaced with lust. "Make me cum."

He starts to bob his head faster, his grip tightening around me as he jacks me off at the same time. It doesn't take long after that until I'm cumming with a long moan, my hips jerking as Brody milks my cock for every last drop I have. Jets of cum fill his mouth and he swallows it all down before pulling away with a pop.

Standing up straight, I let him get to his feet as I fight to get my breathing under control. He grins, licking his lips before kissing me hard. I can taste myself on his lips, but I don't care.

"Dry off and get into bed," he commands, turning off the water. "I need you, now."

Knowing that he needs me makes a part of me anxious to please him.

We dry off, and I walk out of the bathroom butt naked, into my room. Chase went back to Rain's apartment, knowing we would need the place to ourselves tonight.

Brody and I don't have a label when it comes to our relationship, but we all have an understanding, and the others support us in whatever we choose to do. They give us space, every now and then, not wanting to pry into our business.

"Ass in the air." Playtime is over, and now it's all about business. With Brody, it's far from soft. When he gets going, there's no stopping him until I'm screaming his name as he brutally pounds into me. But I love it, pain and all. What he did in the shower was for me, and now, this is for him.

I do as he asks, crawling onto the bed and grabbing a pillow, hugging it to my chest for something to hold on to. He goes over to the bedside table, getting out a bottle of lube before making his way behind me.

I feel the bed dip under his weight as he gets into position. The lube noisily exits the bottle as he squeezes some out onto my ring of muscles.

"Relax," he soothes, running his hand up and down my back. He places the wet tip of his cock to my hole, teasing it, before replacing it with his fingers to rub the slickness into my skin where it needs to be. He skips using one and goes right for two, slipping them into my ass and stretching me out. I moan into the pillow as he pumps his fingers, preparing me for the thickness of his cock.

When he deems me good and ready, he pulls out his fingers and starts to push his cock inside me. My body battles with itself, wanting to resist the intrusion, but craving the feeling of being filled.

He pauses, letting out a moan of his own once he's fully seated, but I know that's the only pause I'll get. He pulls all the way back before thrusting into me, making my body push into the mattress. He starts slow but quickly picks up the pace. It doesn't take him long until he's pounding relentlessly into me, his hips slapping against my ass with every thrust.

The sounds of our grunts, moans, and slapping flesh fill the air. His grip on my hips is bruising, but the line between pain and pleasure is virtually gone when I'm with him. I know this won't last long. Brody isn't one to draw things out. It's why he always takes care of me first, making sure I get what I need—the slow, tentative care before he takes what he needs—hard, fast, and pure need propels his sex drive.

His hands on my hips shift, digging into my skin as he gets a better hold of me to fuck me within an inch of my life, and he uses the other one to claw his fingers down my back before slapping my ass, hard.

"You feel so fucking good," he growls. "I love how your tight hole strangles my cock." I moan at hearing his dirty talk, pushing my ass back into him. "You love it, don't you? You love it when I split this fine ass in two with my dick."

"Yes!" I scream. "Fuck, yes, Brody."

"Good boy," he growls, gripping my hair and pulling me up so that my back is flush with his chest. He kisses me; it's messy, wild, and full of passion. He breaks the kiss to bury his face into the crook of my neck as he wraps an arm around my stomach. He holds me close to him, fusing me to his body as he pounds into my ass harder, if that's even possible. I grab onto his thighs for support, digging my nails into his skin. He snarls against my neck, biting down hard before roaring in my ear and cumming hard, deep inside me. The feeling of his cock twitching as he fills me up has me ready to cum again.

When his balls are empty, he kisses my neck sweetly before slowly pulling out, making me hiss at the loss.

He slaps my ass before leaving the room to clean up. I fall forward, exhausted and spent from the beating my ass just took. I'm going to be feeling this in the morning, but it's the best kind of pain.

He comes back a moment later, and I feel the wet warmth of a wash cloth against my cheeks as he cleans me up. I smile into the pillow. I love when he's like this. When it's just the two of us and he shows me that just because he grew up with a cold hearted bitch of a mom, and had his heart broken into a million pieces, he's still able to care for another person the way he does with me. I'm so fucking lucky he let me in. I'll never do anything to make him regret it.

He climbs into bed with me, making my heart soar that he's choosing to spend the night. He does, at times, but it's not often. He loves his space while sleeping. He pulls me to his chest and starts to run his fingers up and down my back.

"Thank you, J." He kisses the top of my head. "Thank you for dealing with me, every fucked up piece." I don't say anything, not wanting to set him off again by getting too mushy.

It doesn't take long before his hand stops, resting on my lower back as his breathing evens out.

I lay here, thinking about everything. Ellie coming back, Brody ready to go on a rampage, Rain. Fucking Rain is about to bring hell down on this school. I've never seen her so cold toward anyone, but the way she is with Ellie...this can't be good.

No matter what happens, I'll be by Brody's side. When Ellie left, Brody went into a downward spiral. His mother started to fuck around out in the open, not even bothering to cover up the fact that she's cheating on her husband with any man who looked her way.

Brody's dad is a good man, but he's too blind to leave his wife. He has it set in his mind that the woman he fell in love with is still there deep down.

Unfortunately, he drinks because of it, a lot more than Brody. Thankfully, he's not a mean drunk, just an emotional one. Brody is left to clean up after him, making sure he doesn't stew in his own vomit.

All of that takes a toll on Brody, so he drinks. And I take his job. I take care of him, making sure he's safe and can't harm himself.

I don't mind. I love him, and even if he can't say the words, I know he loves me too. But he's too fucked up to be able to admit it, to use those words. The last person he said them to destroyed him, ruining their meaning for him.

It's not all me though. He takes care of me too. A year after Ellie left, my mother died. It wrecked me. I was an empty shell of myself for a long time. Brody kept me together, never giving up on me. The others did too, of course, but it was different with him.

My mom and I were out getting fresh veggies from the farmer's market for our Sunday family supper. We were heading back to the car when my mom remembered she forgot something, and I offered to go back. She carried on to the car, and as I was paying the vendor, the sound of tires screeching had my head snapping over just in time to see it hit her, crushing her under the weight of the car.

My whole world stopped. I screamed her name as I ran the fastest I ever have. But it was too late. She was gone. Her eyes were open, blood dripping from her nose and mouth. The sounds I made were not human.

I blacked out after that. The pain was too much to handle. The next thing I remember, I was in my room, in Brody's arms as he cried with me, Chase and Rain close by.

Then the nightmares started. I'd wake up screaming, and the last thing I'd remember was the sound of car tires echoing through my mind. Brody was always there, holding me, soothing me.

Feelings started to change, turning into something that was more than just friends. Eventually I took the chance, caught up in the moment of my nightmare, and I kissed him. When he didn't pull away, I had hope.

We took things slow, and over time, things progressed.

I might be seen with girls all the time, but it's just for show. I don't fuck them. I don't need to. I have Brody. But we are not ready to come out yet. I like what we have. I'm not ashamed of being bi, or what I have with Brody, but this works for us and I'm happy to leave things the way they are as long as they work. *Why change something that's not broken?*

As for Brody, he won't let a girl get near him except Rain. He doesn't trust anyone outside our group, and doesn't care how that might make him look.

Chase and Rain use sex as a way to deal. Over time, it just became a habit, a way to control who comes into their lives, never letting them stay longer than a night or two.

People think I'm the same, but I'm not. The last girl Brody fucked is Ellie. I messed around a bit after, but once Brody and I started our thing, I didn't want anything meaningless.

Now Ellie is back, and everything we thought we put behind us is starting to rise to the surface. Leaving us with the question, who will come out on top?

# Chapter Eleven

## ELLIE

I WAKE up the next morning with a feeling of dread at having to go back to work. I spend the whole day at school making sure to avoid everyone I can, only staying on campus for my classes. The girls message me wondering where I am for lunch, but I just need the day to myself to get my thoughts together.

Seeing Rain with Laura filled me with a sickening feeling I've never felt before. I've seen her all over girls since I've been back—and that alone has crushed me—but being caught in that moment, seeing it with my own two eyes as someone made her scream like that...that is something that will forever be engraved in my mind.

When I got back home last night, I knew I still had feelings lingering for them. With so much left unsaid, unanswered, it's hard not to. But seeing them in person, it became all too real. I don't want to feel this way. I don't want the idea of them with others to hurt so badly, but it does.

Even with Brody being so fucking cruel, a part of me still longs for the man he used to be. I know his home life is fucked up. It always has been, but other than me leaving, what happened to make him so cold, so heartless?

The way he looked at me when he pushed me to the ground, there was nothing but darkness behind his hazel eyes.

After school, I meet up with Theo. We get a coffee and take a walk in the park before we have to go pick up the kids.

I tell him that the people he asked me about at the ice cream shop aren't just people I know from my past, but that they are my exs. He looks confused but when I explain that I dated them all at the same time, for years, that we had this unique dynamic, he looks stunned.

I've never been ashamed of the type of relationship we all had, even though it was different and uncommon. It was our lives and no one else's business, but telling the guy who I am falling hard for that I was dating three guys and a girl at the same time worries me. *Will he think I'm a whore? That one person isn't good enough for me, that my needs are not able to be met?*

But he just nods his head and tells me that he appreciates that I trust him enough to tell him a little about my past. "Are you *still* in love with them?" he asks.

I look away, holding back tears. I want to be honest, but I don't want to ruin what we are building. He gently turns my face back to him. "It's alright if you are, and it doesn't change anything between us." I almost break. He's so amazing.

So I tell him. "Yes, but it's complicated. Whatever I had with them is in the past. I want to just move on and be happy with Lilly and the person who chooses to love us both."

And there it is. One half of the story out there. I can tell he knows there is more, but I'm grateful he didn't pry and it isn't a dealbreaker.

---

I go back to work at night, and it is much better than before. Rain and the guys are nowhere to be seen throughout the entire night. I get to walk around and sell shots, receiving over $300 dollars in tips. I spend my breaks with Aria, getting to know her. She's pretty cool, and I'm glad she continues to stick up for me against the others.

Laura makes sure to brag about how she is going to be the one who ends up with Rain when she is done living out her college experience. That makes my gut turn. Also, who the hell sits around and watches someone they claim to want to be with, fuck a bunch of people until they decide they are ready to settle down? It's degrading. Something tells me that she's full of shit. Aria says that Laura and Rain are not a thing and never will be. Rain doesn't do relationships and Laura is holding on to a delusion of a dream she's made up in her own mind.

I also find out that Kayla is pining after Chase. From what I overhear, they fucked once last year and she became another one of his conquests. Although, that does not stop her from following him around like a love struck puppy.

The weekend goes by calmly and on my last night of work for the weekend, Tabitha and the girls stop by, making sure to hype up my skills to anyone who will listen and tip me dollar bills every five minutes. They put a smile on my face that lasts the whole night. I'm glad I gave them a chance and let them in. They are some pretty amazing friends.

Now, I'm walking to class, heading to the cafe to grab something to eat before finding the others to meet up. As much as I don't want to go in there for fear of seeing Rain and the guys, I don't have time to run to any of the fast food places across town.

"Ellie!" a voice behind me calls out. I stop walking and look behind me to see my friends rushing toward me. The halls are still pretty empty right now with all the current classes in this wing still in session.

"Where's the fire?" I laugh as they all stop beside me, a little out of breath.

"Oh, she's making jokes. Good! That means she hasn't seen the news blast," Val says.

The humor on my face slips away. "News blast? What are you talking about?" I look to Tabitha for answers. She gives me a grim look.

"Um... So, there's this school network. It's for the students to stay connected and for the school to send out important information or notify us of events."

"I remember seeing it somewhere in the student handbook, but I don't do social media so..." After blocking everyone years ago, I never reactivated any of my accounts. I don't have any need to post photos of myself or Lilly.

"Makes sense of why she hasn't seen it yet," Lexie says.

"Seen what?" I ask, a little more forcefully than I intended, but they are starting to make me worry.

"This." Val hands over her phone. It's a photo, well more like a flyer. My face is on it, and at the top it says, 'Beware of Eleanor Tatum. Sure to spread her legs, along with other things.'

There are bullet points next to my photo.

Will sleep with anyone

Cheater

Liar

Has every STD imaginable.

Then, at the very last line it says, 'When you see her, stay six feet away at all times for your own safety.'

My stomach lurches as my heart stops. *Is this for fucking real?*

"You have got to be fucking kidding me!" I breathe, squeezing my eyes shut, trying to wrap my brain around it. I won't let this get to me. It's stupid, childish, and this is college. No one is going to go along with this. It's clearly some cruel prank from Rain and the guys.

"Sorry, babe," Lexie says, giving me a pitying look. I don't want her pity. If they want to act like children, then let them.

"Don't be. It's stupid. If people want to react to it and follow them, they can. It just means they are shitty people too."

I laugh, trying to make light of the situation when inside I'm freaking out. "Come on, I'm hungry. Let's go get something to eat," I tell them, hooking my arms with Tabitha's.

They give me skeptical looks but follow along anyways.

When we get to the cafe, I hear the chaotic chatter of the students. It sounds like it's packed, and the idea of going in there makes me lose my appetite.

I can see them through the window of the door, sitting at the head table. Brody is in the middle looking like a king—no girl with him, yet again, but Chase and Rain have girls on their laps. Brody and Jax are talking to each other, laughing about something. *Maybe they're talking about me.*

"You sure you wanna go in there? It's not too late to change your mind," Tabitha says.

I shake my head. "No, I'm not going to let them have any control over me. I go to this school too. They don't own it."

With that, I push open the door. It's like a switch slowly dims the sound of the room as everyone goes quiet. I can feel their eyes on me, like an unwanted caress from a stranger. I don't like it, but I ignore it as I hold my head high and head for the line to order. The girls follow after, and when we get there, the people paying quickly leave, giving me dirty looks.

I know the whole room is watching me now, and it's taking everything in me to hold my own and get this food. I want to run. I want to hide. I hate when all the attention is on me. But I can't.

We grab our food, and when I turn around, I bump into Rain. "Fancy seeing you here," she sneers.

"You mean the cafe, at lunch, in the school I go to? Where else would I be?" I cock a brow, all fake bravado.

"Thought you would be hiding in a corner, licking your wounds," Rain smirks.

"Or sucking a dick. You were always good at that. I wonder if it was from all the practice you had behind our backs," Brody says, giving me a look of disgust.

"Excuse me," I say, looking away and taking a step to move around them.

"Oops!" Rain says as her hand comes down, knocking my tray of food to the ground. The chicken soup I ordered splashes all over my sneakers. Rain giggles as she and Brody leave.

Taking a deep breath, I shake off the need to curl in on myself and bend down to pick up the rest of my food.

"Here," Tabitha says, handing me some napkins. We both clean up while Val and Lexie come over.

"What a bitch!" Val hisses, looking over in the direction of their table.

"Yeah, well, she seems to think that just because I'm here, we must be back in the fourth grade all of a sudden." I stand up and throw the dirty napkins in the trash.

"I got you this," Lexie says, holding out a muffin.

"Thanks." I grin, taking it from her. I take my shaken up bottle of pop and bag of chips, along with my muffin, and search for an empty table. There's one that's half full, but when we go to sit down, everyone on the other end gets up and moves. I look around to see everyone giving me dirty looks.

"You guys don't have to sit with me," I sigh, popping a chip in my mouth.

"You think this will send us running? We got you," Val smirks.

We sit and talk about this and that, but it doesn't take long before the girls have to go to their next class. "You sure you're good here?" Tabitha asks.

"Yeah," I smile up at her. "I'm almost done here. Then I have a class too. Go. I'll text you later."

She gives me a hesitant look before they all say goodbye and leave. I don't bother to look around the room. I know they're still here, watching me. So I pull my phone out and skim through Tik Tok.

I jolt in my seat when something wet smacks the back of my

head. I reach back and grab whatever it is. My nose scrunches up as I look at a slice of tomato.

Turning in my seat, I see Brody smirking as the others laugh. "I don't like tomatoes," he shrugs.

"So you felt the need to toss it at my head."

"I was throwing it in the trash," he says, giving me an evil grin. "They're gross and soggy, just like your used up cunt."

My eyes widen for a moment before they narrow into slits. I flip him off and turn back into my seat.

Something else hits the back of my head, followed by another. It takes five seconds before the whole fucking room starts tossing shit at me. I flinch and dodge things, but my body won't let me get up and move.

"Grab your stuff," a voice next to me says. I look over to see Cooper, his blond hair falling into his face. He holds out his hand and I gather my bag and phone before placing my hand in his. He tucks me under his arm. "Hold your head up. Don't let them see you break."

I blink back tears as I bite the inside of my cheek. I look forward as we head for the exit.

"Cooper!" Brody booms. "If you leave with her, you are dead to us and to the team."

I look up at Cooper with fear in my eyes. He shakes his head. "He can't kick me off the team. I don't care if they want to be my friends or not," he whispers to me.

"Cooper!" Brody repeats.

Cooper turns around. "I don't care. I don't answer to you. No loss to me if a bunch of dicks, who bully people for no reason, don't want to be my friend."

Brody is standing next to his table, his fist clenched at his side as his face becomes a mask of anger. He doesn't like to be told no, to be defied in front of all his followers. His eyes flick to mine and I can see the promise that this isn't over.

Cooper guides me out the door and away from the hell I was just in.

"Are you okay?" he asks, putting his hands on my shoulders, shielding me away from the world as I take a moment to get myself together.

"I don't know." I laugh, wiping at a stray tear. "I'm trying really hard not to be a little bitch and cry right now, but the more I talk about it, the more I have the urge to burst into tears."

"Hey." He rubs my arms. "It's okay to cry. You're not weak. What they did is fucked up. I just wish I was there sooner. I came in to grab lunch, and saw them all tossing shit at you. They are seriously a bunch of fucking children," he growls. "They have no right or reason to treat you that way. They have always thought of themselves better than everyone else, but they were still decent humans. But that..." he says, nodding his head in the direction we just came from, "that's high school bullshit."

"Well, it's just the beginning. I can tell they want me gone, but I'm not going anywhere." The need to cry is fading and pure anger slowly replaces it. I close my eyes and take a few deep breaths. If I lose my cool, they win.

"You're not alone," he grins. "I know we don't know each other very well, but I hope you're looking for a new friend, because I know I need one."

"I'd like that," I laugh. "I don't have many, and I'm okay with that because the ones I do have are amazing, but after what you just did, I think I can squeeze you into our little group," I tease.

"I'm honored," he jokes, putting his hand to his heart.

"But really, thanks for that...in there. I wanted to run, but my feet were not working," I say, picking off a piece of cheese that's stuck to my shirt.

"I don't stand with anyone who supports that. I might be on their team, but that's it."

"Shit," I sigh, looking at my phone.

"What's wrong?"

"I have class in thirty minutes, but I can't go there looking like this." I groan. "And my car is at least a fifteen minute walk on the other side of campus."

"I can give you a ride if you want. I'm parked just outside."

Worrying my lip, I think it over. Do I want him to know where I live? *He doesn't give off creeper vibes, and he did just save me in there.*

"That would be awesome. Thank you."

"No problem. I'm done for the day anyways," he grins.

We go outside to his car, but I pause before getting in. "Umm. I don't want to get your car dirty," I say, looking down at my soiled clothes.

"It's fine, really," he laughs.

We get in, and I try not to lean back against the seat. It takes only a few minutes to get to my place.

"I'll wait here if you wanna run up and take a quick shower," he says.

"Really?" I was going to call a cab, but this would save me time and money.

"Go," he smiles. "I'll just get lost down the rabbit hole that is Tik Tok." He chuckles.

I run up to my apartment, toss my dirty clothes in the hamper, and hop in to take one of the quickest showers ever. I throw on a t-shirt, sweats, and a hoodie and put my damp hair in a messy bun. I don't have time to look pretty, just human. I grab an extra change of clothes that I plan on putting in the trunk of my car. After earlier, I don't want to take any more risks.

We get back to school with five minutes to spare as he parks outside the lecture hall where my next class is being held.

"Thank you so much for this, once again," I say, grabbing my bag.

"Anytime, Ellie. I got your back," he grins. "Here." He hands over his phone. "Put your number in and I'll text you so you can add mine. If you need anything, a friend to talk to or even just an escape buddy, call me and I'll be there."

*Nope, not gonna cry. Ugh, he's just too sweet.* I smile, taking his phone and putting my number in. "See you later."

"I hope so. Maybe outside of school. I'm always looking for a study buddy. So far, all the ones I've had before just wanted to sleep with me." He scrunches up his nose like the idea grosses him out.

"Well, you are good looking, but I'm not that kind of girl," I giggle.

"And that's another reason why I want to be your friend, Ellie. I don't believe anything they say about you. I also don't judge people based on second hand knowledge. And from what I've seen so far, you're a good person. Don't let them make you think otherwise."

"Thanks," I smile, and say goodbye.

The rest of the day goes much better. I still get dirty looks, and called nasty names, but knowing I get to hang out with some of my favorite humans after class keeps me going.

Theo and Toby come over, and we make homemade pizza and watch movies. When the kids fall asleep in front of the TV, Theo stays another hour and we play cards.

"We better get going," Theo says.

I look at the time. "Yeah, I better get to bed. I've got school in the morning, yay," I cheer unenthusiastically.

"Well, maybe I can make you look forward to tomorrow a little more." He gives me a shy smile, pushing his glasses up his nose. He's so adorable and sexy. The more time I spend with him, the less I want to resist the urge to kiss him, along with other things. I want him, *badly.*

"Oh really?" I give him a playful smile.

"Come on a mini date with me. We can go get coffee and just hang out. I miss you."

"I live just down the hall. And you're here now," I point out.

"I know, but with you working and school, I just want to spend all my free time with you." His eyes widen slightly. "And now I sound creepy, great."

"Hey," I laugh, crawling into his lap. "You're not creepy. And I think it's sweet. I want to spend all my free time with you, too."

"You do?" he asks, surprised.

"Yes, silly," I grin.

That is the exact moment we both realize how close I am. Frozen in place, neither of us know what to do next. He licks his lip, his pupils growing dark as his breathing picks up.

*Screw it.* You only live once, and I won't hold myself back out of fear forever. I lean in, capturing his lips with mine. He reacts instantly, letting me take the lead, but moving his mouth against mine. I lick the seam of his lips, and he opens for me, allowing me to slip my tongue in. We swallow each other's groans as we deepen the kiss as I straddle his lap. His hands slide up my thighs and over my ass. He gives it a squeeze before rocking me into his growing erection beneath me.

My pussy pulses at the feeling of his hard length rubbing against my clit.

It doesn't take long before we're dry humping like a couple of teenagers, wrapped up in each other, in need while wanting to be with the other.

I pull back from the kiss. "We can't," I breathe, really hating myself right now.

His face falls, hurt taking over his pink, flushed face. "I understand. I'm sorry."

"No! No," I rush out, cupping his face so that he's looking at me. "I want to. Trust me, I want to, so much, it's killing me. But we are forgetting that we have an audience," I say, looking over my shoulder. Just as I do, Lilly lets out a little snore, making me laugh.

"Shit," Theo laughs, closing his eyes and leaning his head

back against the couch. "Kinda forgot about those two." He laughs again. "So, you don't regret this?"

"Absolutely not." I smile. And I don't. I want Theo more than I've wanted anyone in a very long time. I've fallen hard and fast for this man.

"Thank God," he breathes. "I was afraid I messed everything up there for a moment."

"I kissed you first," I point out with a smile.

We just stare at each other for a moment, saying nothing, before he blurts, "Will you be my girlfriend?" His eyes widen as if he can't believe he just said that.

My smile grows. *He is so friggin cute!*

"Really?"

"I mean that was not at all how I was planning on asking you, but here we are." He gives me a half grin. I can see the worry on his face, like he's waiting for me to reject him.

"I'd love to," I say softly.

His eyes light up. "Really?" It was his turn to ask.

"Yes. I like you, Theo, a lot. I don't let a lot of people in my life, and I trust even less. But with you, I feel safe. I feel wanted and cared for. You're amazing with Lilly, and she just adores you and Toby. I love spending time with you. We can talk about anything and never get bored. So, yes. I would love nothing more than to be your girlfriend."

"Nice!" His grin is so big, it has to be hurting his face.

We both burst out laughing.

I reluctantly climb off him and we sit there for a few minutes. We're smiling at each other as we rest our heads on the couch, staring, and giving ourselves some time to calm down from that hot-as-hell make out session.

"I really should be going," he sighs, getting off the couch to pick up Toby. Toby cuddles into his dad and I walk them out.

"I'll miss you," I whisper as I stand in my doorway.

"I'll miss you too." He smiles softly, giving me a sweet kiss on the lips before heading over to his place.

He unlocks his door, and before going in, he looks back and blows me a kiss.

As corny as it is, I reach out and grab it, making him chuckle before disappearing behind his door. I close mine, standing there for a moment before I start doing a happy dance, letting out an excited, but silent squeal. *I have a boyfriend!* And he is one of the best men I could have ever asked for. I may have had a shitty day, and I know whatever is going on with Rain and the guys is far from over, but knowing I have Theo at my side gives me confidence that I'll be okay.

I need to call my therapist and brag. I know she will be proud of me.

Scooping up Lilly, I tuck her into bed and head back to the living room to clean up. I'm still wound up from before with Theo, so I sneak into the room, grab my trusty vibrator and take care of myself on the couch, all while picturing it's Theo's cock thrusting deep inside me. I cum so hard, I see stars. *Next time, I need the real thing.*

# *Chapter Twelve*

## ELLIE

THIS WEEK HAS BEEN half heaven and half hell. Every day I set foot on campus, I have insults thrown my way, and dirty looks follow me everywhere I go. And then there are men. I can't count the amount of times random dudes have asked me if I'm down for a fuck and how much it would cost them.

I just ignore them, keeping my head held up and walking away like I heard nothing. But it hurts. I know it's not true, and they have all been fed lies, but it doesn't make it any less of a kick to my self confidence—having people call me a whore, a slut, a tramp, you name it, they've called me it. I go to school, blocking out everything around me and put my sole focus on my classes while spending any free time in between them in the library with the girls, studying.

When my last class is over, I'm filled with this sense of relief that I get to pick up Lilly and just go home. I love it, being a mom, spending time with my sweet little girl, laughing and playing. Lilly is my safe and happy place. Theo and Toby come over, and everything just feels right. I haven't laughed as hard, or smiled as brightly as I have since Theo and I made things official.

He finds every excuse to touch me, kiss me, or hold me.

Every time he wraps his arms around me, I feel like I can breathe and the weight of the world is off my shoulders for just a few moments.

My second weekend at work is nothing special. I have a few handsy customers trigger a panic attack—the first one in a long time. I have to go outside in the back alley to get some fresh air so that the feeling of my throat closing would go away.

I'll get over it with time, learn to read the room and avoid people like that. But for now, I'll have to deal. I hate it, but if I fought with every drunk person who got a little too close, I'd be out of a job.

And with the tips I've been making, I can't afford to lose it. One weekend and my child care for September is paid for, and this second weekend, I'm now able to pay Katie in advance. She is so grateful that she tells me she would rearrange her schedule if I needed any extra babysitting.

She's been so great. She's managed to get Lilly fully potty trained. I feel a little bad because as her mother, I should have done that, but I'm also very grateful because with all the new things added to my plate, this is one less thing I have to worry about.

I've been spending as much time at the park with Lilly as I can and on Monday in the first week of October, I invited the girls to come and meet Lilly. They don't know the entire story yet, but I trust them. I don't plan on telling them about Tim just yet. I feel like I should tell Theo first. One step at a time and this is the first step.

"Hey, girl!" Val says, her pink bob bouncing with every step.

"Why did you wanna meet at the park?" Lexie asks, looking around in confusion.

"Sit," I laugh, scooting over so that the girls can sit next to me on the bench.

"Why couldn't we meet at the coffee shop? At least there are cute guys there," Val whines, sitting down next to me.

"Do you ever not have boys on your mind?" Tabitha asks.

Val takes a moment to think about it. "Nope," she shrugs.

With a smile, I roll my eyes. "So, there's something I need to tell you," I say, biting my lip and hoping that this news doesn't send them running.

"Are you breaking up with us?" Val jokes.

"No," I laugh. "You're stuck with me." *I hope.*

"Good," Lexie grins. "So what's up?"

"See that little girl over there, the blonde one playing in the sand?" I say, pointing out Lilly who is a few feet from me playing with her sand toys.

"Yeah?" Tabitha says with a raised brow.

"That's my daughter, Lilly."

They all look at me with owlish eyes while they just blink at me. I shift in my seat as I wait for one of them to say something.

"You have a kid," Lexie says.

"Yup." I give them an awkward smile.

"Why are we just finding out now?" Tabitha asks, not sounding mad, but confused.

"Never mind that, who's the dad?" Val butts in.

"Val!" Lexie snaps.

"What?!" she screeches.

"The reason why I didn't tell you is because I don't really let a lot of people into my personal life. After everything that happened with Rain and the guys in the past, I kinda keep myself closed off. I wanted to make sure our friendship wasn't just something in passing."

"Understandable," Tabitha says.

"But again, who's the dad?" Val says, earning a smack on the arm from Lexie.

"Umm..." I don't really know how to answer that. I know who the three probabilities are, but no DNA test to prove who. "That, I don't really have an answer for." I laugh nervously, looking over at Lilly. She is the spitting image of me, never giving away any traits that could help me in the direction of one of the guys.

"Okayyyy. But like, is it one of the Knights?" Val asks.

"Oh my God, girl! Do you know how to keep your trap shut?" Lexie looks at her bestie with wide eyes.

"Sorry," Val says, looking a little guilty.

"This needs to stay between us. Please. I don't want them knowing about her. I was going to tell them when I moved back, but after how they've been acting, I don't think that's the best idea for Lilly right now." And it's not. We don't need that drama in our lives. She doesn't need to be around people who treat her mom like dirt. I want her to grow up knowing that whoever she chooses to be with, she needs to respect them and have that same level of respect in return. I hate the idea of denying Lilly the chance at having a father in her life. It makes me feel like a shitty mom, but none of them have shown that they would be ready to be a father.

"So one of them is the father?" Val asks. Lexie pushes her off the bench and on her ass. "What the fuck!?" Val shouts at Lexie.

"You're in time out until you learn to think before you speak." Lexie narrows her eyes.

Val just huffs, crossing her arms, but says nothing.

"Yes. I didn't know I was pregnant when I left. But after everything that happened, I wasn't rushing to tell them and come back."

"Wow," Tabitha whispers in awe, looking at Lilly. "You've got a kid."

"Is that going to be a problem?" I ask, hoping like hell that it's not.

"Not with me," Tabitha smiles. "I love kids. I have three little brothers and a little sister. Thankfully, all of them are much younger than me so I didn't grow up hating them." She laughs.

"I don't have any siblings, but I do have a bunch of little cousins I adore," Lexie grins.

"I like kids too," Val mumbles from the ground.

We all laugh and Lilly comes running over. "Mama, look

what I found." Lilly holds up a rock. Nothing special about it, but the look on her face tells me it is to her.

"That's so pretty, Bug! How about we bring it home?"

"Yay!" she cheers, handing it over to me. She notices the girls and looks at me. "Who they?" she points.

"Lilly, these are Mama's best friends, Tabitha, Lexie, and Val." The girls all give Lilly a hi and wave.

"Hi!" Lilly beams. "I have a friend, too! Toby."

"Toby is Theo's son," I say.

"Oh, nerdy boy has a kid too?" Val asks, getting up and dusting off her butt.

"Nope, sit back down! That just earned you another minute," Lexie says, and I can see she's loving this.

"You suck," Val mutters, but sits back down again, sticking her tongue out.

"Okay, Theo isn't nerdy. He's very sexy and sweet," I laugh.

"And a teacher," Lexie wiggles her brows.

"And her boyfriend, so leave her alone," Tabitha says. "Although, I would like to meet this mysterious neighbor who seems to have stolen your heart."

"Well, I guess that's going to happen sooner than we thought," I say, looking over their shoulders to see Theo and Toby heading toward us. The girls follow my gaze.

"Is that him?" Val gasps.

"Yes." I smile and wave to Theo. He sees me and waves back, a smile lighting up his face.

"Girl, he is fine with a capital D!" Val says.

"What does that even mean?" Lexie looks at her like she's lost her mind.

"That I would want his D. Keep up." Val rolls her eyes. Lexie looks at us for help but we just laugh.

Lilly notices Theo and Toby. "Mr. Theo! Toby!" she shouts excitedly before racing over to Theo's open arms. He scoops her up and swings her around, making her break out into a fit of giggles and making my heart swell.

"How are you not pregnant just by looking at that man?" Lexie sighs dreamily.

Honestly, if that was possible, I'd be pregnant with a whole litter by now.

"Do you mind not mentioning anything about Lilly's father? I just told Theo about them being my exes. I'm not ready to dump all that on him after we just started dating." I know I should have told him when he asked me to be his girlfriend, but I'm not ready. A part of me is afraid that it might be too much for him. He was understanding enough about me dating them in the past, but not only dealing with one baby daddy but three might be more than he bargained for.

"Well, hello there, ladies," Theo greets. The girls all blush, looking a little flustered as they shamelessly check out my man, but Theo doesn't notice. His full focus is on me. "Hello, beautiful." He pulls me up off the bench and into his arms. He places a sweet kiss on my lips, making me melt into a big, ooey-gooey puddle.

"Ewwww!" Lilly and Toby shout.

Theo and I chuckle against each other's lips before pulling back to see the two of them race off for the playground.

"I missed you today," he whispers, rubbing the tip of his nose against mine.

"I missed you too," I sigh, just enjoying the feeling of being in his arms.

I introduce the girls to Theo and we sit and talk. The girls tell him about what they want to study and what courses they are taking.

"No way!" Val gasps, looking at her phone.

"What?" Lexie asks, checking her own phone. "No way!" she repeats.

"Seriously guys, what is going on?" Tabitha asks.

"Jessica Long broke her foot. She's going to be out for the rest of the season," Lexie says, showing Tabitha something on her phone.

"Who's Jessica Long?" I ask, leaning back into Theo's arms as he wraps them around me, pulling me up into his lap. I snuggle in closer.

"She's on the cheerleading team. She's one of the flyers. Rain must be so pissed! This is going to fuck up the whole season."

"Don't they have back up team members?" I ask.

"Normally they do, but from what I heard, Rain was so picky this year that she didn't want to hold auditions. The team is only made up of people who are there on scholarship, or Rain's friends who she gave first dibs to. When she became captain last year, she made a lot of changes. I mean, so far they've been for the better. The team won more competitions last year than any of the previous years. But I guess this one is coming back to bite her in the ass," Tabitha says.

"Well, now she has to hold auditions. Look." Lexie points to something on her phone.

"How funny would it be if I tried out?" I joke, picturing the pissed off look on Rain's face when she sees me walking onto the field.

"Yes! Do it!" Lexie squeals.

"What?! I was just joking!" I say, all humor slipping away.

"You can't dance?" Val asks.

Actually, I can. You wouldn't know it from just meeting me, but I love to dance and cheer. I used to volunteer at the center back where I was living. They would let me sit in and watch, and after a while, let me practice. But then Mom and Dad weren't able to watch Lilly as much, so I had to cut back my time there. I really do miss it a lot.

"I can. I can cheer, too."

"Then why not? What's a better way of getting back at Rain than beating her at her own game, on her own turf?" Lexie grins.

"I don't know. I already have a full plate. Plus, Katie only watches Lilly when I work."

"You work Thursday through Sunday. Practices are held on Monday and Wednesday nights during football practice."

So, I would be forced to be around *all* of them. If this doesn't smell like a recipe for disaster, I don't know what does.

"If you need someone to watch Lilly on those days, I'm more than happy to. If this is something you really want to do, I think you should do it," Theo says.

Looking up at Theo, I could just kiss the face right off him. What did I do to deserve someone so amazing? "I can't ask you to do that."

"Good thing I offered then." He grins, kissing me slowly and sweetly.

"Are you sure?"

"I wouldn't have said something if I didn't want to."

I could talk to a school rep and see about getting a cheer-leading scholarship next year, saving me a ton of money.

I look at the girls. "Well, I guess Wednesday I'm trying out for the Silver Valley cheer squad."

# Chapter Thirteen

## CHASE

"WHY ARE they having tryouts during our practice? All the guys are gonna be distracted, perving on the girls. None of their focus will be where it should be," Brody grumbles as he strips out of his clothes and puts them in his locker.

"Rain said it's because it was last minute," I say, starting to undress, my candy cane clanking against my teeth as I play around with it.

"What's the big deal? They practice with us normally anyway," Jax points out, pulling his practice jersey over his head.

"Yeah, but the team has already fucked their way through the squad, except for Rain. It's fresh meat waiting to be preyed upon." Brody bends over to pick up his pants, sticking his bare ass out for Jax to get a full view. Jax checks out Brody before looking up at me, seeing he's been caught eyeing up his boy toy. I give him a wink, grinning as he flips me off, a blush taking over his cheeks.

"Move," a voice I know all too well scoffs from the other side of the locker room. "Oh please, don't bother hiding your dick. No one wants to see that anyways."

The room breaks out in chatter as they react to a girl in the men's locker room.

"You!" my best friend says as she storms over. When she gets closer and sees the others, she says, "Good, you're all here."

"Can we help you?" Brody cocks a brow. He and Jax are now dressed, but I am not.

"You will never guess who is out there right now on the bleachers waiting to audition for the team!" Rain huffs out. She's pissed, and there's only one person who has been making her steam up like a tea kettle these days.

"Dwayne 'The Rock' Johnson?" I smirk around the candy cane.

"What?" she asks, looking at me like I grew a third eye. "No, you dummy." She rolls her eyes. "Ellie."

"What?!" Brody growls. Jax sighs and shakes his head. "Just what we fucking need. Bad enough she comes to our school. Now she wants to fuck with the one thing we all love."

"Since when can Ellie cheer?" I ask with a raised brow.

"How the fuck should I know?" Rain says. "The closest thing to dancing I've seen her do was grinding her ass up against Cooper's dick."

"What about my dick?" Cooper asks, popping his head around the corner.

"None of your fucking business!" Brody snaps. Cooper rolls his eyes and walks away.

"Look, can you take your little hissy fit outside? Some of us are changing," I say, casting my eyes down to my exposed dick.

She looks down then back up to me. "No one cares about your shrimp dick, Chase."

"Oh, Rainy Poo, there's nothing shrimpy about my dick." I laugh as I start to windmill it around.

"Gross!" Rain covers her eyes. "Fine, I'm leaving. But this isn't over! She will not be joining my team!" she shouts as she walks out of the changing room.

"Does she not get that no one on these teams likes her or wants her around? It's almost like she's asking for it," Brody continues to bitch even after Rain leaves.

I turn away as Brody and Jax continue to talk about Ellie. I try not to let Brody's hateful words get to me, but it's hard. Rain and Brody loathe her. Sure, a part of them loves her still, and always will, but between love and hate, there is a very thin line. Especially with those two; it's almost non-existent. Jax goes along with Brody's bullshit because he loves him and doesn't want to piss him off.

Me, I don't share the same hate they do. That night ruined me just as much as the others, but there's always been a part of me that thought the events of that night didn't add up. Something about the whole situation didn't feel right, but we just chalked it up to being betrayed by someone we loved, who we thought loved us. So we didn't bother to find out if there is more to the story.

They seem to think our whole relationship was all a lie, but I think they are blinded by pain. I've replayed those four years' worth of memories over and over again in my mind when I lay in bed at night, waiting for sleep to take me. That kind of love can't be faked.

When one of the guys on the team mentioned Ellie's return, it was like a part of me kick started; like this little ray of hope buried deep down inside of me sparked to life. This was my chance, my opportunity to talk to her, to get the truth about what happened that night. Unfortunately, Brody didn't share my outlook regarding her reappearance in our lives. The first thing he did was get trashed, ranting about her until he passed out, and leaving Jax to clean up after his dumb ass. Rain was silent and closed off until the moment she saw Ellie in the stands during the football game.

When Rain told us she was here and then proved it by pointing her out, it was like a punch in the gut. She was no longer that 18-year-old girl who never saw the true beauty she was, but a gorgeous woman.

Her presence almost cost us the game. The others were distracted just by knowing that she was in the stands, but me, I kept stealing glances at her. That left the other team open to drop me on my ass a few times. I even took a ball to the side of the head because of it.

It was worse when I saw her at the party with her friends. I had to fight the urge to go up to her because what do you say to someone you haven't seen in four years, especially when we parted ways under such soul-crushing circumstances?

So I panicked, found the first hot drunk girl and used her for the night to take my mind off the woman I really wanted. I imagined it was *her* who was on her knees with her lips wrapped around my cock, not the fake blonde substitute.

Right away, when Brody declared war on her, I was out. I don't want anything to do with what they have planned for her. I plan on being a bystander, making sure they don't take it too far.

I'm relieved they drew the line at physically harming her because the idea of someone, let alone us, causing Ellie physical harm makes me sick.

Do I like the fact that for the foreseeable future they will be consumed with the idea of making Ellie pay for everything she did to us? No, but there's nothing I can do. Fighting with them will just cause a rip in our family, and I don't think we could survive any more loss.

I wanted to nut punch Brody for his stupid stunt at the club, and the thing in the cafe was just wrong. But I guess I'm just as bad as they are. I just sat there and acted like I couldn't care less, but that couldn't be further from the truth.

"You coming?" Brody asks, snapping me out of my inner thoughts.

"Yeah," I say, tossing the candy cane into my locker before slamming the door shut and following after the guys.

When we get out to the field, I instantly search for her. She's sitting on the bleachers with her friends. She's dressed in skin-tight athletic shorts and a sports bra. Her hair is up in a pony-tail, showing off her delicate face.

"Come on," Jax says, leaning closer to me. "Focus."

We jog over to the rest of the team to start practice. Every time a girl would take their spot to try out, I check to see if it is Ellie. We run a few plays, and by the end of practice, Ellie still hasn't tried out. Of course, Rain would leave her for last, make her sit there and sweat it out.

"You coming?" one of the team members asks.

"Nah, I'm gonna wait for Rain. I need to talk to her about something," I lie. Brody and Jax continue to run drills on their own, always getting in as much time on the field as they can.

I walk over to the bench, tucking my helmet under my arm. The breeze feels amazing on my flushed skin and my sweat soaked hair plastered to my face.

Just as I'm about to sit down, Ellie's eyes lift from her friends and lock with mine. My brain blanks at her pure beauty, and when she gives me a little smile, I panic. So instead of returning one of my own, I quickly sit down, turning around and giving her my back.

Fuck, being a dick to Ellie like the others are expecting me to be is going to be a hell of a lot harder than I thought, especially if she makes it on the team.

*Welcome to my own personal hell, party of one.*

"What are you doing?" Rain says, wrinkling her nose at me. "You stink, go shower."

"I wanted to watch." I shrug, then give Rain a mischievous grin. "And I wanted to give my bestie a hug," I say, wrapping my arms around her and enveloping her in a sweaty hug.

"Ewwww!" she shrieks as she struggles to get out of my hold. "Asshole!"

I let go of her, laughing hard as she jumps up and shivers in disgust.

"Aw, now that's not nice. I just wanted to show you my love," I pout playfully.

"I'll show you how much I love you by shoving my foot up your—"

"Last up, Eleanor Tatum," Coach Whitmore, the cheer coach, says, interrupting Rain.

Okay, she's up. *Play it cool. Don't make it obvious that all you can think about is her tits and ass and how they would feel as I rub my—.*

"Go, Ellie!" someone cheers from behind me, snapping me out of my pervy inner thoughts of my ex-girlfriend. I look over to see Ellie step onto the field. She walks about ten feet away from us and stands there, waiting for the music to begin.

"I can't wait to see her fall on her ass and make a fool of herself," Rain grins, leaning back into her chair, arms crossed with an evil smirk on her face. I don't like it; it doesn't suit her. She is normally a carefree, happy, confident person and this new Queen Bitch routine is not a good look on her.

I don't say anything as I turn my attention to the sex-on-legs in front of me. She focuses on a spot on the ground in front of her as she shakes out her arms. I can practically see her giving herself a pep talk before taking a deep breath. The corner of my lip quirks at how adorable she is. It's something she used to do whenever she had to do something she wasn't completely comfortable with. She did it right before going on stage for her valedictorian speech. Alright, I think kissing her stupid helped too, but that could just be my own ego talking.

*Hey, Mama* by David Guetta featuring Nicki Minaj and Bebe Rexha starts playing through the speakers and Rain let's out a snort.

*Why? It's a good song.*

"Oh, this has gotta be good." She shakes her head and places her feet up on the table as she gets comfortable to watch Ellie fail.

Ellie starts dancing, and she's good...really good. Right off the bat, it's easy to see that she has skills. It's like looking at a complete stranger rather than the girl I've known since fourth grade. I guess at this point she is, pretty much, a complete stranger.

The way she moves her arms, dipping and flowing with the beat of the music, she already looks better than what I've seen from half the team. Rain's feet drop to the ground as she leans forward in her chair like she can't believe the sight before her. Her face looks shocked but also like she's about to rip into Ellie. She doesn't like what she's seeing.

I'm not gonna lie, these tight pants aren't doing anything to hide the raging boner that I'm getting from watching Ellie dance like that. I cross my legs to hide it as much as I can but who am I kidding?

The song is edited to shorten down the time for tryouts and the song enters into a build up right before Nicki's part. Ellie moves far off to the side and looks forward and a look of pure concentration falls onto her face. She tilts her head from side to side before shaking out her body. *What is she doing?*

The moment Nikki starts, Ellie takes off. She gets a running start before her body goes flipping and turning in the air. I'm mesmerized at how her body glides through the movement.

I'm caught between Ellie's epicness on the field and my best friend's wide eyes and gaping mouth.

"How?" Rain whispers.

"What?" I ask, watching her flip through the air again. She pauses to dance a little more before jumping back into her ninja moves.

"How the fuck did she do that?" Rain says in disbelief.

"Do what?" I demand as Ellie finishes her dance by landing in a split. My eyes really don't want to look away from her, and from the look on Rain's face, Ellie just did some really impressive things. I mean, I don't think most of the cheer squad can do what Ellie just did.

Rain looks at me with pure venom, but not for me, for the girl on the field with a beaming smile as her friends race onto the field, jumping around as they cheer while hugging her.

"She just did a routine with a roundoff back handspring,

whips, a damn aerial cartwheel, and a mother fucking front tuck, step out, round off, back handspring full!" Rain roars.

"And that is?" *How the fuck should I know what she just said?*

"Everything you just saw, dumb ass!"

"And is that impressive or something?" I ask, looking back at Ellie. She looks over at me for a moment, the look of pride not slipping away before she goes back over to the bleachers with her friends.

"You don't understand, Chase. Those moves are not exactly easy to do, and how she just did them, that's like pro level shit! That would have taken years to perfect, hundreds of hours of practice. You can't just do what she did over fucking night."

"So what she did was good?" I ask.

"Yes! As much as it fucking burns my mouth to say it, she was fucking phenomenal. And that's a problem."

"How so?"

"Looks like we found our replacement," Coach Whitmore says.

"What? How!" Rain growls. Oh, look, that little vein over her left eye looks like it's about to pop. *This isn't going to be good.*

"Eleanor Tatum, how would you like to join the Silver Valley cheer squad?" the coach says.

Ellie smiles wide, her mouth opening to say something when Rain storms over. I'm up and out of my seat, not far behind her.

"Not fucking happening!" Rain snaps.

"Excuse me, Miss Sawyer. You might be the captain of this team, and I may have trusted your judgment last year when picking the right girls for this team, but you will not undermine my authority. Eleanor is exactly what our team needs to win nationals."

"But she's a backstabbing bitch!" Rain says through gritted teeth. Ellie's face drops, her excitement gone. I hate seeing her look like that.

"Enough. I don't want to hear talk like that. If Eleanor chooses to join, then she will be a part of this team," the coach looks back at Ellie. "So, how about it?"

"I'd love to," Ellie answers.

"Wonderful! I'll send you an email with everything you will need. We can get you fitted for an official uniform right away. Welcome to the team," Coach Whitmore says before taking off.

"You will not be joining this team," Rain seethes.

"Uhhh, I think she just did," the girl with the pink bob says —I think her name is Val. "Do you need your ears cleaned or something?"

"Shut it," Rain snaps at Val before looking at Ellie. "You will tell Coach Whitmore that you changed your mind. You will turn the fuck around and stay away from my team."

"No," Ellie says, squaring her shoulders. "I know you hate me, Rain. And I don't want to be around you as much as you don't want to be around me, but the funny thing is, I actually enjoy dancing and cheering. This is a good opportunity for me. I talked to the admissions rep and after my academic scholarship runs out at the end of the year, I can continue having financial aid with a cheerleading scholarship. I'm doing what's best for my future. So no, I won't go and tell her I've changed my mind. We're just going to have to learn how to get along with each other."

"Like fuck we will. It's never gonna happen."

"Then, I don't know what to tell you because I'm not going anywhere."

*Oh, I like this new spunky Ellie.* I know the others won't be letting up on her anytime soon, but if this is how she reacts to what's thrown at her, I think she's going to be okay. Maybe she'll even be able to come out on the other side with minimal damage.

"Mark my words, you will regret this. I will make you regret this."

"I have no doubt you will," Ellie sighs, sounding disappointed in Rain.

"How the fuck did you get that good anyways? Last time I checked, you couldn't even slow dance without stepping on someone's feet. At least your dry hump session with Cooper was a step up from that."

"You wanna know? Do you really?" Ellie asks, anger finally taking over her features as tears fill her eyes.

Rain just cocks an eyebrow at her.

"Summer before tenth grade," Ellie says.

"What?" Rain furrows her brows.

"All you could talk about was how you were so excited to try out for the school cheer team. You worked out and practiced all the time. I knew that once we got to high school, you would be spending all your free time cheering. You were so good, and you loved it so much. I also wanted to join, but only because you did. So whenever we were done hanging out and it was just me at home, I would go outside in my backyard and watch YouTube videos to learn all the basic moves and even a few dances. I worked my ass off for hours, all day long for the whole summer. That's why I was always tired. But to me it was worth it, to see the look on your face when I got to join you on that team. That way, we could do something together instead of me always being on the outside because I didn't enjoy a lot of the things that you guys did. I wanted to make you proud. But when the time came, I chickened out. I let fear ruin something that could have been so much fun, something we could have had together. So instead, I just supported you and cheered you on at every practice and every game. When I left, I started to practice more and over time, I got that good," she says, pointing to the field.

"But not anymore. I won't let fear hold me back. I won't let you hold me back. So do what you feel needs to be done, but I'm here to stay." With that, she turns around and takes off, her friends following after her. The one with the pink bob sticks her tongue out at Rain and flips me off before running after the others.

Rain lets out a scream, stomping her foot before taking off toward the locker rooms, bitching under her breath about how Ellie will regret everything she's ever done.

What Ellie just said about putting in all that time and effort into doing something for Rain, that's not something you do for someone you don't love. You don't do all that, to learn a new sport, just to be with someone you don't truly care about with your whole heart.

It also just gave me more of a reason to believe that there is a hell of a lot more to that dreadful night four years ago than we originally thought, and I intend to find out the truth. *The whole fucking truth.*

## *Chapter Fourteen*

### ELLIE

BREATHE, *Ellie, deep breaths. Did you just tell Rain something extremely personal that she had no right to know because she's now a bitch to you and is set out to ruin your life? Yes, yes, you did. But there's nothing we can do about that now, so let's try not to have a breakdown in front of your friends. Smile like you don't feel as if your heart's about to fall out of your ass.*

"Dude! That was fucking epic. I've seen that team cheer, and they are good, but fuck, none of them has ever done what you just did out there. And the way you just gave Rain a big 'fuck you'—girl, you got big ass lady balls," Val says, raising her hand to high five me.

"Ellie, are you okay?" Tabitha asks, grabbing my arms to stop me from turning away so she can get a good look at me.

"Ummm. I think so?" I blink. "My heart is beating so fast that it might explode, but I think I'll live." I huff out a laugh.

"You know she's not going to let that stand, right?" Lexie says, giving me a grim look.

"I know. But I meant what I said. When I saw that I could get a scholarship for the remainder of my schooling, it became more serious. I was planning on getting student loans, but if I can save thousands of dollars and put it toward a college fund for Lilly or toward getting a place of our own, then I have to take it."

"I totally agree," Lexie says. "And we will be there for every practice and game, so you won't have to be alone with them. If we have to do our school work from the bleachers, at least we will have a nice view, right?" Lexie wiggles her eyebrows, making me laugh and my heart starting to feel a little lighter.

"Sign me up! Watching their sweaty muscles glisten in the sunlight as they tackle each other—you think one of them might toss me around if I ask nice enough?" Val asks.

"Girl, tell your va-jay-jay to chill. You already dipped your toe in that pond." Lexie rolls her eyes.

"I mean, it was good enough to make me wanna go for a swim," Val grins.

"Okay, that's enough," Tabitha laughs. "It's getting late and we have school in the morning."

"Shit," I say, checking the time. "Sorry, I gotta go. I told Lilly I'd read her a book and sing her a song."

We say goodbye, and I spend the whole car ride wondering if that really just happened. It's been a while since I've been able to do those moves, and trust me when I say, they were not easy to learn. I spent hours practicing them, but it was worth it. Every time I do them perfectly, I get this thrill. It's addicting. Being able to do something I love again feels amazing, and I can't thank Theo enough for what he's offering to do.

I moved here thinking I was going to have to embark on this new part of my life with only Lilly by my side, but I've been blessed with some amazing friends and a man who is so sweet, understanding, and supportive. Add on the fact that he's amazing with Lilly, and it's hard to believe I could be this lucky.

I've had a few phone calls with my therapist and she's had to talk me through my freak outs and overthinking. I asked her if it's too good to be true? What if I'm not good enough? What if he doesn't want me after he finds out the truth about what happened four years ago? What if, what if, what if? She helped me see that I was starting to self sabotage and I needed to see that I did deserve it. If I keep expecting the worst, then that's what I'll drive the situation to be.

When I get to the apartment, I shut the car off and take a moment to get myself together. I just put myself in a position where I'm going to have to see the four people who owned my heart before destroying it, on a regular basis. The people who have decided that what we had meant nothing and that I'm the bad guy. The people who feel the need to belittle me and bully me. *Oh Ellie, you sure do enjoy causing yourself pain, don't you?*

With a sigh, I head up to my apartment. When I pass by Theo's door, I'm tempted to knock and tell him about making the team, but it's late and Lilly is waiting for me.

"Mama!" Lilly cheers, scrambling off the couch; a ray of sunshine rushing over to me in her pink polka-dot onesie is what greets me as I walk through the door.

"Hello, my Lillypad. I missed you!" I give her a big bear hug, holding her tight as I place a kiss on the side of her head. "I missed you."

"I missed you too, Mama. Me and Katie made cookies!"

"That's awesome, baby girl. Mama will have to try one." I place her on her feet.

"She's had her bedtime snack, brushed her teeth, and is all ready for bed," Katie says, grabbing her purse off the counter and moving to stand next to me.

"Thank you again for watching her. It was a little short notice but Theo will be watching her Mondays and Wednesdays while I have practice."

"Oh, so you made the team!" Katie smiles.

"Yup. I'm excited, but also pretty terrified." I don't do crowds well, and I just signed up to perform in front of hundreds of people on the regular. Maybe I should plead temporary insanity.

"You're gonna do awesome! But isn't that girl who sent that blast about you, the Cheer Captain or something?"

"You saw that?" I cringe.

"I don't believe a word. I get it. You had a crappy break up with some old highschool sweethearts and they are sour about it. Some people grow up, others don't. You're an amazing mom and person. Try not to let their bull—" she looks over at Lilly who is watching us with a curious expression, "poopy get to you."

"Poopy," Lilly giggles.

Katie and I grin. "I'll try my best," I say.

After I walk her out and lock up for the night, I turn back to the little monkey waiting for me.

"Alright, missy, time for books and bed."

"Story!" She races into the room. I pick out *Peter Pan*, one of Lilly's favorites, and climb into bed, snuggling up to Lilly as she cuddles with her favorite stuffed dog. *That damn dog*. Even at home, I seem to be reminded of them.

As I read Lilly her story, I can't help but wonder where's my Peter Pan, because Neverland sounds like a good place to be right about now.

"Hey! Sorry I'm running late. Class took a little bit longer than expected," I tell Lexie on the phone, who has been texting me non-stop about how I need to hurry my ass up so she can tell us all about the new guy she's been texting. She met this guy at a party, the same party that was the start of my nightmare at this school. *At least someone got something positive out of that night.*

"Fineeeee. But hurry."

"I'm coming, I'm coming," I laugh as I rush down the hall. As I turn the corner, I bump into a person, dropping my phone. "Shit!"

"Sorry about that," the person says, bending over to retrieve my phone and handing it over.

My eyes widen as I make eye contact with Theo. "What are you doing here?" I ask in surprise.

"Ellie," he smiles. "Hi. I was actually just about to call you because I knew it was your lunch break."

"Well, no need to call anymore, because here I am," I laugh. "But really, why are you here?"

"That's what I wanted to talk to you about. Do you have a minute?" he asks.

I look over his shoulder in the direction I was headed in and then down at my phone. "Yeah, sure, just give me a second." I text Lexie that something came up and to tell me about everything later before looking back up to Theo. "As much as I love seeing you, you're freaking me out a little," I say, moving to sit down on one of the benches in the hall.

"I wanted to tell you last night, but the call came in late and I knew you had tryouts. How did it go by the way?"

"I made the team."

"That's amazing! I hope to see you in action soon," he smiles.

"Theo..." I smile hesitantly.

"Yes?" he smiles back.

"You were telling me about a phone call you got last night," I chuckle nervously.

"Oh, right," he says, pushing his glasses up his nose. "So, you know I've been hoping to get a permanent teaching position for a while now, but have had no luck. Well, I originally applied to work at the university, but they had nothing to offer me, so I took a job as a substitute. Last night I got a call from the dean and she asked me to take over the Sociology department. Professor Cook has fallen ill and they asked me to fill in until he is able to return."

"So, you're working here? You're now a professor at the university I attend?" I ask.

"Well, yeah, I guess...technically," he trails off.

"What does that mean for us?" I ask.

He looks at me with a slight panicked look. "What do you mean?"

"Isn't there a rule or something about a student dating a professor?" I ask. My stomach sinks as I start to see everything good that has happened to me since I've moved here slowly fade away.

"But, but I'm not your teacher," he says. "Ellie, I want to keep seeing you. I don't want to end what we just started. I can turn the job down. You're more important," he rushes out, his voice pleading.

"Hey." I grab his hands, rubbing my thumbs on the back of them. "I don't want to end things, but I don't want you to turn this job down either. You've been wanting to work here for a while now, and I don't want to be the reason why you lose that chance."

"It's not a big deal. I can always try again when you graduate."

"Theo," I laugh. "I can't ask you to give up your dream. You're right, you're not my professor, so I think as long as we avoid each other while on campus, we should be okay."

"I didn't even think about that when I took the job," he sighs, leaning his head against the wall.

"Theo, we will be fine. It's no big deal. This place is huge. You will be teaching all day and I only have a few classes and none of them are in the building you will be working in. And if people see us outside of school, we can just say we are friends and next door neighbors."

He opens his eyes to look at me. "That could work." He visibly relaxes. "Not gonna lie, I was totally freaked out there for a moment."

"You don't say." I give him a playful smile.

"Ellie, you don't understand. I know this is new, but I have strong feelings for you. I haven't felt anything as close to this since my wife. I don't want to lose you now that I finally have you."

My heart flutters at his words. "I feel the same way about you," I whisper. "We can make this work."

"I really want to kiss you right now," he sighs.

"Probably not a good idea to do that, seeing as how we are keeping our relationship a secret as of right now," I laugh.

"Have supper with me tonight," he says, then his face drops. "Wait, you have work, don't you?" He looks disappointed.

"Actually, someone rented the place out for a private event. I have the night off." I smile, and his face brightens again. "I can call Katie so we can have some time for just the two of us. We haven't really gotten to spend time alone since we made things official." My body lights up as I remember the intense make out session on the couch.

"My mother is coming over to see Toby, why don't I see if she is alright with watching the kids at your place and I'll make you supper at mine?"

"I can't ask her to watch Lilly," I start.

"She loves kids, and she's been bugging me to bring you around more since I told her we started dating."

Oh my God. Theo is going to be at my school! Seeing how the students have made a game out of harassing me, he's probably going to find out about the lovely rumor going around about what Rain and the guys thought happened on the night of our graduation party. I need to tell him sooner than I wanted to, and this seems to be the only chance we might get to be alone to have a conversation with a topic as serious as this one.

"Alright, but there's something we need to talk about since you're going to be teaching here. I'd rather you hear it from me and not from the rumors circulating around campus," I say, biting my lip.

"Okay...see you tonight at 6?" he asks.

"Sounds perfect!" I smile.

He goes to lean in to kiss me, but stops himself only to give me an adorable smile. "I'll miss you."

I laugh. "I'll miss you too."

He squeezes my hand before getting up and leaving. I can't help but watch his ass as he walks away. The way his dress pants hug his ass makes my core clench. I need that man in every way possible and depending on how tonight works out, I'm hoping that's how our date ends.

---

There's a knock at the door making me pause as I put in my diamond studded earrings. Lilly's head snaps up from where she's sitting on the floor coloring. "Don't you dare," I warn her. She gives me a big smile before jumping up and running to the door in a fit of giggles. "You little booger!" I laugh, chasing after her. I grab her under the armpits right before she reaches the door and tuck her under my arm as I open it.

Theo's mother stands there with a bright smile as she looks down at a wiggling Lilly.

"Hello, Mrs. Monroe. Please come in," I say, placing Lilly down on the ground.

"Hi, dear, I thought I'd stop in and meet Lilly before going to grab Toby," she says, then looks down at Lilly. "And this must be the little princess I've heard so much about."

"I Lilly!" she cheers.

"Well, hello, Lilly, nice to meet you. I'm Toby's Nana. Would you like it if Toby and I came over to play with you for the night? We can watch movies and bake cookies."

"Yay!" Lilly slips past us and runs down the hall. I'm about to go after her when I see her stop at Theo's door. She pounds on it with her little fists until Theo opens the door and looks down at her with a smile.

"Look who we have here. What can I do for you, Miss Lilly?" Theo laughs.

"Hi, Mr. Theo. I have Toby please?" She looks up at him with her bright blue eyes.

"Of course," Theo says. "Toby, Lilly's here to get you. Time to go over to her place with Nana."

He looks over at us and I blush as his eyes sweep over my body. I'm not wearing anything special because we're just going to be hanging out at his place, but I did want to look nice. I'm in a pair of light blue skinny jeans and a white knitted top. My hair is curled and my makeup is natural. I wanted something cute but comfy. But with the way Theo is looking at me right now, I feel like I'm dressed in something sexy and expensive.

"He has it bad for you, missy," his mother says, leaning in to whisper. "I haven't seen him look at someone like that in a very, very long time."

I look at her, biting my lip, my blush growing hotter. "I really like him," I admit. I mean I'm borderline crazy for this man, but I don't need his mom getting a bad impression of me.

"He's a good man, and I can promise he will treat you like a queen. Just don't break his heart, please. That man has been through more pain in his life than I never hoped he would have to experience."

I can relate to that in so many different ways.

"I have no intentions of hurting your son. I'm here as long as he will have me," I smile.

She looks at me for a moment before returning one of her own. "I'm glad to hear that."

"Come on, come on, come on!" Lilly says. I look over to see her pulling Toby by the hand toward us.

"Hi, Nana!" Toby says as Lilly pulls him into the house.

We both laugh and she follows them in. "I guess I'll be going," I say looking over at Lilly who is showing Toby her new dolls.

"She will be fine, and if we need you, you're just down the hall."

She closes the door and I'm left standing in the hall.

"Fancy meeting you here," Theo says as he watches me from his position in the doorway. He's leaning back against the threshold with a sweet smile, sending butterflies to my belly... and other places.

"I could say the same about you." I laugh as I walk over, stopping next to him.

"Cute toes," he says playfully. I look down at my pink sparkly toenails and wiggle my toes.

"Thanks, I know a lady. She comes right to your house. Only she's very demanding and super picky. Also, she ends up painting the skin around it. When I think about it, I kinda over-paid with the piece of cake she got in return." I grin at him. He laughs, pulling me into his arms while I wrap mine around him and tilt my head back to look into his hazel eyes.

"Are you hungry?" he asks.

"Starving." *And it's not just for the chicken that I smell cooking in his kitchen.*

---

"That was amazing." I say, leaning back into my chair. Theo is an amazing cook and made us mango chicken tacos.

"I'm glad you liked it." He smiles and gets up, taking my empty plate to the sink.

"You're an amazing chef."

"Thank you. It's nice to cook for someone who doesn't just want dino nuggets and pizza," he chuckles.

"Ugh, tell me about it," I say. "Lilly has these phases where she will only eat certain colors, but refuses anything healthy. I have to be sneaky about it."

We move over to the couch, and a tingle runs through my body when his knee brushes mine. It's such a simple touch but I want this man so much it's slowly driving me mad. I'm hornier than a succubus who has had a hundred year long dry spell. Guess it's time to let the cat out of the bag now and hope for the best.

"So, there's something I've been wanting to tell you."

"You mentioned that earlier," he says, taking my hand in his. I instantly feel more relaxed by his comforting touch.

"This isn't easy for me to talk about. I haven't told anyone but my parents and my therapist. But I want to be honest with you about everything. I don't want you going into this relationship with me and getting blindsided or finding out things from other people that I should have told you myself."

"Ellie, you can tell me anything. I promise not to freak out and run... Wait, you're not some kind of serial killer, are you?" he jokes.

I laugh, which breaks the tension in my body, just a little. "Only if eating Coco Puffs is considered murder." *Yup, that was corny.*

"Anyways," I say, my nerves growing again. "So, I told you about my exes. And again, thank you for not judging me for having an unconventional relationship."

"Of course. Love is love." He smiles, and it warms my heart at how open he is to things like that.

"And you know that things with them ended badly. I just didn't tell you exactly what happened."

"You don't have to, Ellie. It's in the past and it's none of my business. It doesn't change the way I feel about you at all," he says, kissing the back of my hand, making me fucking melt.

"And I thank you for that," I say, smiling. "But this is something you really *should* know. It's messy and complicated but it's necessary for you to know as much about the situation as possible to understand."

"Alright."

"Four years ago, after our graduation, Rain, Chase, Jax, Brody, and I went to a party. I wasn't a fan of that kind of thing, but I went anyway because they enjoyed it. Well, they all had fun and got drunk but I only had a few drinks. I was done with the party scene but didn't want to ruin their fun, so I tried to go and find a quiet place to just read on my phone. But then I started to feel sick, and I knew something wasn't right. My brain got fuzzy and my body wasn't doing what I wanted it to do."

"You were drugged," he whispers, his eyes going wide as he picks up what I'm starting to explain.

"Yes, but at the time, I didn't know that. Someone brought me into a room. Only, they weren't there to help me," I say, my eyes starting to tear up. His face turns pale and on instinct, he pulls me into his lap, holding me close. He doesn't say anything, letting me continue at my own pace.

"I...I don't want to get into details. But, next thing I knew, my clothes were being torn off by someone who wasn't one of my partners. I couldn't speak, I couldn't move. My body just layed there, betraying me." I'm sobbing now, tears streaming down my face as I try to suck air into my lungs.

Theo pulls me to his chest, holding me as he whispers comforting words into my ear, rubbing my back in soothing motions. "I'm so sorry that happened to you," he says, his voice angry and sad. "I don't know what to say to make it better."

"You don't have to say anything," I hiccup, pulling away to look at him. His own eyes are filled with tears. He wipes my falling ones away before rubbing my thighs.

"There's more," I say.

"You don't have to tell me anything else," Theo says.

"No, I do. I want you to know everything." I take a deep breath to calm myself. "Brody found me. I didn't know until later, but he found me while it was happening. He completely misread the situation. He told the others I cheated on them and everything just went downhill from there."

"What the fuck?!" Theo growls. It's like a switch has been flipped; he goes from being sympathetic to aggressively protective in the blink of an eye. I've never seen him like this. I've never seen him lose his cool. My heart warms seeing him react like this, angry for me and not being disgusted, not seeing me as damaged goods. "Why the fuck would he think that?! Is he that fucking stupid?!"

"The guy who took advantage of me was someone who had a crush on me for a long time. I didn't see it at the time, but he was always trying to be my friend, and I was nice to him. They didn't like it, but that's just who I am. I didn't see the need for their concern at the time. So when Brody saw me with the guy, he assumed that the reason I was so nice to the guy was because I was secretly seeing him. I don't really know anything after that. I woke up the next day in that bed, alone and changed forever. I went home and after days of being a shell of myself, my parents got the truth out of me.

When I saw that Rain and the guys didn't call, text, or check in on me, I started to worry. Then I saw that I had a missed call. It was a voicemail from a drunk Brody telling me it was over, that they were done with me. So when my parents moved, I decided to go with them. I dropped out of SVU before I even started. I just wanted to leave, to go as far away from everything and everyone as possible. I was pretty messed up for a while." I huff out a laugh but there's no humor behind it.

"Ellie, you had one of the worst things that can happen to a person done to you. Of course you were affected by it," he says softly.

"I started seeing a therapist after I came to terms with everything. And when I found out that I was pregnant with Lilly, I wanted to make sure my mental health was stable."

"Oh God," Theo breathes. "Is Lilly...?"

"A result of me being raped?" The word sounds so bitter on my tongue, but it's taken me years to be able to say it out loud. "No." I smile and he relaxes again.

"Even if she was, I wouldn't see her any differently. You know that, right?" he assures me.

My eyes water again, but this time with happy tears. "Thank you," I whisper, leaning in to kiss him. "I was two months pregnant when I left. I don't know who her father is, but it's one of my exes. I'm starting to wonder if moving back here was even worth it."

"I'm glad you did. Because if you didn't, we never would have met and my life would have been pretty damn boring without you." He smiles, trying to make the mood a little lighter.

"I'm glad I did too. But, Theo," I sigh. "They still don't know what happened. They think I'm a whore, and they haven't forgotten that night. They are doing whatever they can to make my life hard. I can tell them, but why? They don't deserve the right to know because they just assumed the worst instead of talking to me."

"They don't deserve you," he says, pulling me into another kiss. "And neither do I." I go to tell him he's wrong, that it's me who isn't worthy of him, but he stops me. "But I plan on showing you every day that you mean the world to me, Ellie. I'm going to do my best to give you the world."

"So you don't hate me," I sob at his words.

"What!?" he says, gripping my thighs tighter. "Never. Ellie, you're so strong and brave. You're a survivor, an amazing woman, and the best mother. I am honored to even be in the same room with you. I'm not going anywhere, not until you make me. Even then, I still plan to do whatever I can to change your mind. You're it for me, Ellie."

He kisses me hard. It's filled with raw passion; I feel my soul mixing with his and my heart surrendering to everything I feel for this man, and all the possibilities. It's only been a little over a month since meeting him, but I am head over heels in love. He's the only other light in my very dark and fucked up world besides Lilly. A ray of hope I never allowed myself to have.

I don't care what they do to me, because at the end of the day, I have my protector at my side.

# *Chapter Fifteen*

## THEO

**THE SOUND** of Ellie's soft snores mix with the low hum of the TV. I stroke her arm lightly as I look down at her, watching her sleep in my arms. She's sitting sideways on my lap, cuddled into my chest, and I can't look away. She's so beautiful, even when she sleeps. Her lips slightly part as she breathes steadily.

I don't want to move, to wake her and have her go back home. The idea of not being around her right now makes me anxious.

When Ellie fell asleep watching the movie, I texted my mom to let her know. She told me not to worry and enjoy our night for ourselves. The kids made a blanket fort and wanted to sleep in it anyway.

My mind can't stop replaying what she told me earlier. When she told me she was raped, something inside me died. Just the thought of someone laying their hands on her like that, forcing her to do something she didn't want, while she laid there helpless...Well, it took everything in me not to demand who that disgusting waste of space was and track him down so I could kill him with my own two hands.

I'm not a violent person, I've never really been in a serious altercation, but for Ellie? I'd do anything and everything in my power to protect her, to keep her safe.

Feelings like these aren't something I'm used to. I loved my wife with all my heart. She was my best friend and lover. But with Ellie, I've never felt so alive. Every time I see her, my body starts to hum. When she laughs, my heart flutters, and when she smiles, it almost flat lines.

A part of me feels like shit for being able to feel so strongly for anyone else besides my wife, because what I have with Ellie is different than what I had with Kristen. With Kristen, it was all we knew. We grew up together, were high school sweethearts, settled down, got married, and had Toby. But with Ellie, I feel like I'm about to set out on a whole new adventure. That every day with her will be different and exciting. I don't think that will go away over time. There's something about Ellie that calls to my soul. It doesn't mean I loved Kristen any less, but even in this short amount of time with Ellie, I know we are meant to be. Maybe Kristen hand picked Ellie from heaven to brighten Toby's and my life for the better.

I'm falling hard and fast for this girl, and as terrifying as it might be, especially after thinking I'll never love again, losing what I feel for her...it would crush me.

Ellie is so strong with everything she's been through and on top of that, being a single mom. She's rare and precious and I will do everything to keep her from falling.

Now, how do I keep myself from losing my shit on those backstabbing exes of hers? Fools are what they are. Who sees something like that and automatically thinks that they are being cheated on? I'd be surprised if I don't walk right up to one of them and punch them in their pretty, preppy faces when I see them. Well, not the girl, because I would never lay my hands on a woman like that, but I'd have words!

But I can't, because then that would raise questions and I'd get fired. I won't betray Ellie's trust like that. It's her life, her story, and her kid. She's the one who gets to choose when and if they find out. Me? I'm going to stand at her side through it all.

Ellie stirs beneath me and slowly blinks open her eyes. "Hi," she smiles sleepily, her soft voice cracking with sleep, and God has nothing ever been so sexy. I hope she can't feel my cock thickening beneath her thighs.

"Hi," I smile back, brushing the hair out of her face. "You're cute when you sleep. Even if you do drool," I tease.

She laughs, and pokes my side. "Do not."

"Maybe just a little," I say, holding up my thumb and pointer finger.

She leans over and nips at my shoulder. My fingers on her thighs tighten as I hold back a groan. She looks at me with hooded eyes. Fuck, it's taking everything in me not to flip her over on this couch and fuck her until all she can do is scream my name.

I've never had the chance to be the way I wanted in the bedroom with Kristen. She was never the adventurous type. I mean, it wasn't bad sex, just not as mind-blowing as I know it could be. When it came to that aspect of our relationship, we were polar opposites.

A part of me really hopes that Ellie is not like that. Something tells me that if she's open to dating more than one person at a time, like she has in the past, then she doesn't have a vanilla sex life. But I'm not one to assume. It doesn't matter to me because as long as I have Ellie, I don't care how.

"What time is it?" she asks, looking at the window and seeing it pitch dark out. I check my phone.

"Midnight," I say.

Her eyes widen. "Crap! I gotta go." She tries to get up, but I lightly hold her back.

"It's okay. My mom is crashing on the couch. The kids made a fort and were beyond excited to sleep in it," I grin.

She relaxes against me. "Are you sure? She's already done so much."

"Ellie. We're dating now, and as long as you're comfortable with it, my mom would be more than happy to watch Lilly and Toby any time we need a night out to ourselves. She's retired and has nothing else to do," I laugh. "Also it helps that she adores kids."

She moves to straddle me and leans in to kiss me softly. "Theo," she murmurs against my lips.

"Y-yes?" I stutter, my brain short-circuiting because I haven't had sex in almost three years. I really want her. Like really, really want her.

"Take me to bed." Her eyes are shining with lust, but I need to know for sure what she wants. I don't ever want to assume or do anything she's not comfortable with.

"And by bed, you mean?" My palms are sweaty, my heart is beating against my ribs, and I need to do some deep breathing before I pass out.

"Take me to your room and make love to me. I want you, Theo. I need you."

*Fuck.* She said that, right? Like, those actual words came out of her mouth and it wasn't all in my head?

"Yes, Theo," she giggles. "I actually said that."

*Ah shit, I said that out loud.*

I give her a sheepish smile. "Sorry. It's just that I've been wanting you from the moment I saw you. Are you sure about this?" I don't know about her sexual past, or how what happened four years ago affected her in this aspect of her life. I don't want to scare her or make her feel uncomfortable.

She bites her lower lip, hesitating to answer me. "Go slow at first?" she asks in a soft voice. "I-I haven't done this in a while. And I've kinda freaked out in the past." She looks down in shame, but I cup her chin, lifting it up so she's looking at me.

"We can do whatever you're comfortable with. Don't feel like just because we're together we have to have sex. I'll wait as long as it takes for you." I give her a soft kiss as she whimpers against my lips.

"I want this. I want you," she breathes.

Gripping her hips, I walk her to my room as she starts to pepper kisses along my jaw. I have to use all my concentration not to trip and fall as each touch of her lips sends jolts of pleasure right to my dick.

When we get to the room, I lay her down in the middle of the bed. She looks up at me; her blonde hair is fanned out around her head like a halo. She's stunning and I can't believe she's all mine.

"You're so beautiful," I whisper. I lean over so that I'm hovering just above her. She gives me a shy grin. She starts taking off her pants but I place my hand over hers to stop her. "Do you mind if I unwrap my present?" I ask, fighting hard to hold back a groan at how corny that was. *I'm nervous, okay?*

She giggles and moves her hands away. "Okay."

My eyes wander over her, wondering where I should start first. I don't want to fumble around like a virgin boy who doesn't know what he's doing. I had sex for over 10 years before this. I know what I'm doing.

Yet, right here in this moment, I feel like an inexperienced virgin that just might cum the moment I put it in.

I want her to feel cared for and loved like the precious woman she is.

My hands find the edge of her sweater and I push it up, needing to get rid of it so I can touch her and feel her bare skin. She moves enough for me to get it up and over her head and I toss it to the side. She lays there in a white lace bra. Her pink, perky nipples press against the thin material, just begging for me to attend to them. I place my hands on her belly as I glide them over her warm, silky skin in a soft caress. Her eyes flutter closed when my hands meet her breasts. I give them a squeeze, making her moan as she arches into my touch. Leaning over, I take her nipple in my mouth, sucking on it through her bra before doing the same to the other. I slide my hands under her back, unlatching her bra and sliding it off to reveal her bare breasts.

They fit perfectly in my large hands as I massage them some more, plucking and pinching at her nipples. Her thighs start to rub together as she moans from my touch.

Starting between her breasts, I kiss my way down her body, over her belly, and stop at the top of her pants. Sitting back, I unbutton them before pulling down the zipper and removing them. She watches me with rapt attention, her pupils black with desire.

When I toss the pants, I do the same with her white lace panties so that she's fully naked before me.

"Theo," she says, as I become hypnotized by her already soaked pussy.

"Yeah," I say, reluctantly looking away to find her biting her lip.

"You have too many clothes on. I think you're going to need to fix that little problem." She grins.

"Right," I laugh, moving off the bed. She watches me with hungry eyes as I pull off my shirt, followed by my pants. She whimpers as she takes in my body.

"With all due respect, don't take this the wrong way. I know I'm not supposed to judge a book by its cover. I already think you're the hottest guy on the face of the planet, so I didn't think you would be small. But from just looking at you, I wasn't expecting...that." She points to my thick, bobbing cock that's pointing right at her. "Are you sure that's gonna fit?"

I bark out a laugh. It's not the reaction I was expecting, but I am not complaining.

"We'll make it fit." I give her a grin.

I crawl my way over to her, stopping between her open legs. Gripping under her thighs, I pull her closer to me so that her core is level with my mouth, and I waste no more time. The moment my tongue makes contact with her sweet pussy, I'm done for. Something inside me snaps and I eat her like a starving man. She cries out in pleasure as she starts thrashing in my grasp.

"Oh god, Theo," she cries. "Oh, oh yes!"

Her reaction just spurs me on so I insert two fingers, loving the sound her juices make as I fuck her with my fingers.

She grabs handfuls of my hair, gripping me hard as she starts to fuck my face with her pussy. It doesn't take much longer until her back arches off the bed. "Theo!" she screams as she cums all over my face until it's dripping down my chin.

She's a panting mess when I sit up, wiping my mouth with the back of my hand.

"Fuck," she breathes. "I haven't cum like that in years." She lets out a breathy laugh.

Grinning, I move my body over hers so that I'm hovering with my cock grazing her bare pussy and twitching in anticipation.

"So, was that okay?" I ask, giving her a kiss.

"Okay? Babe, I think you just broke me," she laughs.

"How about I restart you with my dick?" I wiggle my eyebrows. She bursts out laughing, and I join her, kissing her hard. She moans into my mouth and we kiss for a while. I'm just enjoying the feeling of her body against mine, molded together like two connecting pieces of a puzzle coming together. This feels so relaxing, so right and perfect with her. Nothing is awkward like I feared, and that alone already makes this night so much more amazing.

"I need you," she whimpers, pulling back from the kiss. "I need you inside me, now." *I know how you feel, sweetheart. I need to be deep inside you.* I go to move the tip of my cock to her entrance but she stops me.

"Wait!" I freeze, not moving until I know what she wants. "Condom."

Now, if she said to stop, I would have been off her in the blink of an eye, but I'd be lying if I said I wasn't so damn relieved that she doesn't want to stop.

"Right. Sorry." I give her a sheepish grin.

"I'm going to book an appointment with my doctor and get

on birth control, so it's only for now," she says. I can't wait until I can be inside her with nothing between us, but for now, I'm just happy to have her.

I fish out a condom from my side table and lean back, opening up the package.

"Should I be worried that you already had some ready?" she laughs.

"Never," I chuckle. "I haven't had sex in a long time too, but when we started dating, I bought some, just to be safe."

"Smart thinking," she giggles.

Slipping the condom in place, I position myself over her again, placing the tip of my cock at her entrance.

"Ready?" I ask, needing to make sure she knows she has the right to back out, to say no.

"Yes," she nods.

Needing to see the look in her eyes, I lock my gaze with hers as I push in. Her mouth parts as she lets out a moan and her eyes grow hooded as I feel myself inch into her slowly. The feel of her warm core wrapped around me has me gritting my teeth from the urge to thrust into her.

When I'm fully inside her, I take a moment for her to adjust to me before pulling out and thrusting back in. Fuck, she feels amazing.

We kiss as I start to do what she asked of me—I make love to her until my body is on fire and the need to cum has my balls aching.

Moving my lips from hers to the crook of her neck, I hear the sweet sounds of her pleas as I start to pick up the pace. She claws at my back, pulls at my hair, and begs me to go harder, faster. So I do.

"Ellie, fuck, you feel so amazing. I could fucking live inside you and never leave," I moan as the feeling of her consumes me.

"I'm so close, Theo, please!" she pleads as she thrusts her hips up to meet mine, needing more from me.

Moving into a different position, I sit on my knees,

spreading her thighs apart so I can watch my cock moving in and out of her as I pound her perfect pussy.

Using the pad of my thumb, I rub her clit in circles until she's shaking and her legs are trembling from the work of my cock and thumb. She tosses her head back and forth, her fingers digging into the bed sheets until the moment she shatters beneath me. Her eyes squeeze shut as her back arches off the bed. Her pussy clamps around me with a death grip as she screams the sweetest sounds. "Theo!" she cries. Her pussy quivers around me and I can't hold back anymore. With one more thrust, I cum hard, letting out a long groan as I send streams of cum into the condom, wishing I was filling her up inside.

Moving my body over hers, I'm careful not to crush her as we both come down from our climaxes. I pepper kisses all over her neck and chest as we get our breathing under control.

"Theo," she says, running her fingers up and down my arms.

"Yes, sweetheart," I murmur against her flushed skin.

"Never mind," she sighs. I move up onto my elbows so that I can see her.

"What's wrong?" I ask.

"Nothing. Just forget I said anything." She looks away. I know she wants to say something but she looks nervous.

"Ellie. If you really don't want to tell me, I won't press, but trust me when I say, you can tell me anything."

She looks at me again. "Would...would it be too soon to tell you...to tell you that I..."

"You what?" I grin, really hoping she's about to say what I hope she's going to say.

"I know we've only known each other for a little over a month, but I have never felt this way about someone before."

"I feel the same way." I give her a kiss.

"I love you," she blurts out in the middle of the kiss. I grin against her lips before moving back just enough to brush them against hers.

"I love you, too." My heart is so full right now, and as much as this freaks me out, to admit something so serious, it's not a lie. I love this woman so much that I can't imagine my life without her in it anymore.

"You do?" she asks in a wobbly voice.

"I know it might be crazy, but yeah, I do. You're it for me, Ellie. The rest we can figure out as we go."

With that, she kisses me again, and my cock hardens, ready for round two. I switch out condoms before making love to my girl again, reveling in the sweet symphony of my name falling from her swollen lips as she cums around my cock.

I'm so glad she didn't freak out like she said she had in the past, that she feels safe enough in my arms.

I don't know what will happen next, or where our lives will go from here, but I'm excited to spend it with Ellie by my side as we both take these new steps in our lives.

I'm not going anywhere until Ellie tells me to go. Even then, I won't go down without a fight, because this girl owns every piece of me, and I'm happily handing myself over to her.

# *Chapter Sixteen*

## ELLIE

IT FEELS like every nerve in my body is humming with pleasure. Theo woke me up at 6 this morning with his hard on digging into my back. I smile as I remember what happened the night before. We made love for the first time and it was incredible. I could tell he was holding back for my benefit, and I hope that with time, he will be more comfortable to voice his wants or needs in the bedroom. I was even more impressed that after we were done, I had no urge to run, cry, or freak out. I feel safe with Theo, protected in his arms like nothing bad will ever happen while I'm with him. I'm glad he doesn't see me any differently after I told him everything.

When I went to the bathroom, Theo was still sleeping, but when I got back, he was wide awake, stroking his cock and I was drenched and ready for him just at the sight. Let's just say it was a fan-friggin'-tastic wake-up call.

"Well, someone looks all bright-eyed and bushy tailed. You've got this glow to you too. Did someone get laid last night?" Val teases me, elbowing me in the side as we eat our lunch. I smile, looking down at my sandwich.

"Oh my God! You totally did," Lexie gasps with a smile.

"Soooo, how was it?" Val asks, wiggling her eyebrows. "Also, how big is his coc—" Lexie's hand covers Val's mouth, shutting her up before she can finish that sentence.

"Fuck, Val. You can't just go around asking how big your best friend's boyfriend's junk is," Lexie says, rolling her eyes as she takes her hand away from Val's mouth.

"What? It's girl talk," Val sighs.

"To answer your question, yes, Theo and I took that step last night," I smile.

"You can say it, you know. You fucked," Val grins.

"I guess, technically, yes. But it was more 'making love' than 'fucking'."

"Awe, that's so sweet! It's hard to find a guy who doesn't just want to fuck your brains out and pull your hair while slapping your ass and making you scream his name or call him Daddy," Val says as she looks off into the distance with a dreamy look on her face.

My eyes widen as I look at the other two. Tabitha and I burst out laughing, and Lexie shakes her head.

"I can't take you anywhere, can I?" Lexie scolds her best friend.

"Guys, I need to talk to you about Theo," I sigh, knowing I need to tell them about him getting a job here and, yet again, ask them to keep another secret.

"Oh God, he has a weird fetish, doesn't he? He likes feet, I bet. All the hot ones turn out to be weird." We all look at Val with bewildered looks. "What? It's true."

"Seriously, you're done talking for now," Lexie says. Val goes to talk, but Lexie puts her finger up against Val's lips and shushes her. Val narrows her eyes on Lexie and gives her a death glare before licking her finger.

"Eww!" Lexie cries, wiping her finger on her pants. "You're gross."

Val just smirks in victory.

"Anyway, what about Theo?" Tabitha asks, looking from our crazy friends to me.

"I told you he's a teacher, right?"

"Yeah, at the elementary school, right?" Lexie asks.

"Yes, as a substitute. But he's been wanting to work at SVU for a while now, and applied a long time ago. Well, he got a call and he's subbing for the Sociology professor. Professor Cook is really ill, so Theo might be here awhile."

"Wait, so your boyfriend is going to be my new professor?" Val cuts in. "Girl, that's not fair! He's so hot, but he's dating my best friend. Do you know how hard it's going to be not to stare at his ass in those form fitting dress pants he wears?" Val groans.

"I thought I told you to shush," Lexie mutters.

"Well, sorry but yes, I guess you're just going to have to deal with my man tempting you all the time. Trust me, I know it's hard not to just jump his bones every five seconds," I laugh. "But now that he works here, I don't know what the dean would do if she found out about us. I know dating your professor is against the rules, but technically he's not mine. I'm not in any of his classes and I don't intend to be. So, I'm going to have to ask you guys not to tell anyone we're dating. I won't run into him often, so it should be easy to avoid him while at school. I hate asking you to keep another secret, but I don't want to risk losing him," I say, worrying my lip as I wait for them to respond.

"Ellie, you're our best friend. Of course we don't mind keeping these things to ourselves," Tabitha smiles.

"What if she told us she killed someone, and I mean, exactly how she did it and then told us where the body was? Do we keep that a secret? Because if the cops come asking and we lie, we could get a longer sentence and I'm too pretty for jail. Also, I don't want to be anyone's bitch," Val says, sounding a little too serious.

Lexie just gives her friend a hopeless look before looking back at me. "Ignore her. We got your back, E. Soul sisters for life." She puts her fist out, and I bump mine against hers and laugh.

"You guys are amazing, you know that right?"

"Yeah, we know," Lexie says, flipping her hair over her shoulder with a smug grin. We all burst out laughing and spend the rest of our time just chatting about random things before our next class.

## JAX

"Why are we going to the club tonight?" Chase groans, throwing himself on the couch dramatically. "She's gonna be there. You know that, right?"

"That's the whole point. We still haven't gotten her fired yet," Brody says, pouring himself a drink. He's starting early tonight. This might not end too well. "But we can't make it too obvious. It needs to seem like she's just shit at her job."

"Robby is having a party at his place. It sounds like more fun than going to the club. Plus, that hot chick from the cafe is going," Chase pouts.

"There will be hot girls at the club, too. Get your dick wet there. You've never seemed to care who you were fucking and who was doing the sucking before, why now?"

"God, Brody, you make it sound like I'm some kind of whore," Chase scoffs.

Brody gives him a look. "Dude, you fuck a new chick every week, you kind of are."

"Well, I'm sorry we don't all have someone who satisfies us at their beck and call," he says, getting off the couch and going over to Rain who is coming out of the bathroom. He throws his arm around her and ruffles her hair. "We like a variety of flavors," he smirks.

"Fuck off!" Rain pushes him away. "I swear if you fucked up my hair, I'll punch you in the nuts." She huffs at a laughing Chase and turns back to the bathroom.

"Hurry up!" Brody calls after her. "We leave in five."

"B, I don't want to piss you off, but there's no way in hell

I'm letting you drive while you have any alcohol in you. That goes for any of us."

"Fine," he sighs, pulling out his phone. "I'll call us a cab, because no one drives my car, not even you."

He's been drinking a lot since Ellie came back and I'm starting to get worried. Brody has always been a drinker, thankfully nothing like his father, but he's never wanted to get trashed after every game and go out and party until he blacks out every weekend. I don't like seeing the hole he's digging for himself. I wish Ellie would just go away. It would be better for everyone if she did.

Rain comes out, and we all head down to the parking lot when we get a call that our cab is here.

"Laura booked the night off, so did Kayla. So I'll be hanging out with Laura. And Chase, do your bestie a solid—Maybe take one for the team and fuck Kayla or something? She's been talking about you non-stop and it's driving me fucking nuts. Also, I want to get laid tonight and that's not going to happen if Kayla is there with us the whole night. Love the girl but she's a... pussy blocker?"

"What the fuck, Rain?" Chase looks at her with disgust. "Pimping me out to your friends so you can get your rocks off? That's low, dude."

"Come on," Rain pouts. "You wanted some action, and she's more than willing."

"No. Not happening. The girl is a fucking crazy stalker who's been obsessed with me for far too long. I've only put up with her because she's your friend and your team member, but I know that if I show even the slightest interest in her, she will find a way to break into my room and watch me sleep." He shudders, pulling out a candy cane from his pocket. He has had an addiction to them ever since we were kids. Doesn't matter the time of year. He always has one on him. Some carry gum or mints, he has candy canes. *At least he always smells good.*

The cab pulls up, and we all get in. Chase and Rain bicker

like an old married couple while Brody looks out the window, a distant look on his face.

"Hey," I whisper, my fingers brushing against his. He turns away from the window to look at me. "Are you okay? Something's bothering you. I can tell. And it's not just Ellie."

He says nothing for a moment, his eyes tracing my tongue as I lick my lower lip. "Not here," he finally replies. I say nothing, accepting his answer as he goes back to looking out the window.

When we pull up to the club, we all get out. Chase and Rain head in before us, but Brody holds me back. Once we're alone, he sighs. "It's my dad. My mom came home last night when I was over checking on him. We got into a screaming match, and my dad got blackout drunk. It was a fucking mess."

"Hey," I say, pulling him around the corner so that we have a little bit more privacy. Everyone is already in the club, and as much as I don't care about people knowing that I'm with Brody, I don't want him to feel out of place. "I'm here for you." I rub his arms, pulling him close to place a soft kiss on his lips. He grabs the back of my head, deepening the kiss. His tongue pries my lips open and slips in to caress mine.

"Jax," he groans against my lips. "I wanna push you up against this wall and fuck you until the imprint of the brick is on your cheek."

My cock jumps at that idea. "Okay," I agree, only partly joking.

"You're a dirty boy, aren't you?" he grins against my lips, stealing another kiss.

"Only for you," I smile back.

"Good." His voice grows possessive and it's a major fucking turn on. "I don't want anyone touching what's mine." He cups my cock and gives it a squeeze. I moan, my eyes rolling into the back of my head. He gives my short curls a little tug before looking down with a smirk. "I love how easily I affect you."

"It's hard not to. But now I have to go in there with a

fucking boner. Watch me get called a creep and get kicked out," I joke.

"Naw, no one would dare kick out a Knight. And we'll hang out in the VIP section for a bit."

"Girl tonight or no?" I ask, meaning do I need to be seen dancing in public with a random lady of the night to keep up appearances or not.

"No," he growls. "People don't think you're a man whore like Chase, so it's not a big deal if you're not seen with a new girl every week. This weekend, we party as a group."

"But Rain has her friends."

"You mean her fuck buddy and the tag along?" Brody grins. "Once Rain gets her screaming 'O', she will be with us for the rest of the night."

"Don't you think it's a dick move for her to use her friends like that?" I ask. I don't like the idea of taking advantage of people for your personal wants and needs. It's not right. I know these people go in knowing that Chase and Rain are the hit and quit it type. That's different. But Laura, I'm pretty sure she's in love with Rain. I have no clue if Rain knows it or not though.

"Look, Rain has told Laura that she's not looking for anything serious and Rain said Laura is okay with keeping things *friends with benefits*. So if Rain wants to get her jollies from her friend, who are we to stop them?"

She probably only told Rain that so she can get what she really wants from her. I don't like Laura at all. I find her clingy, annoying, and a major bitch, but she's still a person.

The club is packed tonight, and when we get to the VIP section, Ellie is there with an unimpressed look on her face.

"Oh goodie, more assholes," she mutters under her breath. I smirk to myself. Luckily for her, Brody doesn't hear. He pushes past her, deliberately knocking into her as he goes to take a seat on the couch.

"Was that necessary?" Ellie asks, her voice filled with annoyance.

"What?" Brody looks up at her like he's just realized she's there. "Oh, my bad. Didn't see you there. I don't really pay attention to whores. I like my women a little more classy."

"What women? You're never with any and they all run from you as if touching you would instantly give them an STD," she snarks back. Brody's face turns red, his nostrils flaring.

"It's because all these college girls aren't mature enough for me. Like I said, I like them classy, older and more mature. Women who have their lives together. Not some scholarship student who works as a hostess."

"Hey!" Laura says, moving her face away from where she was kissing Rain's neck. "I work here too."

"Case in point," Brody deadpans.

Taking my seat next to Brody, all I can do is sit and watch the trainwreck as it happens.

"Rain..." Laura whines. "Make him be nice," she pouts.

Rain snorts out a laugh. "Girl, if I knew how, I would have tried it like seventeen years ago."

Laura scrunches up her nose with a huff.

"Fuck you," Brody laughs, flipping her off.

"Not even if you begged me," Rain purrs back. I smirk as my people joke around. But then remember someone who used to be on the receiving end of this banter is standing there watching everything and looking like she would rather be anywhere but here.

"So, can I get anything for you?" she asks, clearing her throat.

"Anyone but you, please." Rain gives her a fake sweet smile while batting her eyelashes. Laura giggles and I internally roll my eyes.

"Unfortunately, that's not possible because we are short staffed tonight. Seems like everyone has booked this weekend off or is calling in sick."

"Sorry, not sorry," Laura smirks.

"Yeah, you're a big girl. You've got this," Kayla says from her spot next to Chase. She tries to touch his arm, but he shrugs it off.

"I'm going to the bathroom," Chase announces as he gets up to leave. He stops in front of Ellie, popping a candy cane in his mouth and swirling his tongue around it as he takes a moment to stare at her. She watches the movement, and I can swear there's lust in her eyes but it's gone in a flash. "Rum and Coke," he tells Ellie before slipping past her.

"Alright, anything else?" We all order our drinks, but no one bothers with food. We all ate before coming because Rain bitched about the food taking too long last time.

Ellie leaves to get our order. Brody and I just sit and listen to the music as others chatter around us, occasionally talking to each other. Chase comes back with his hair tousled and shirt untucked.

"Seriously, you've been here for five minutes and you already got laid?"

"No," he smirks. "I was on my way back from the bathroom when I saw a hot girl. We got to talking and the next thing I knew, she was dragging me into the girls' handicap bathroom to give me a very enthusiastic blow job. What kind of person would I be if I turned that down? She was practically begging to suck my dick."

"You're crazy," I smile, shaking my head.

"You're just jelly, I be getting all the ladies," he smirks. He's joking because he knows I'm not into anyone but Brody.

"Here you go," Ellie says as she places the drinks on the table.

"Where's my beer?" Brody asks, looking at the tray.

"Beer? You didn't ask for beer," Ellie says, her brows scrunching in confusion.

"Yes I did. God, are you stupid? Or are you just deaf?" he sneers, shaking his head. "Can't even get a drink order right. I asked for a Guinness in a can." He smiles, but it's not a nice one.

Ellie grits her teeth, her face growing a light blush as the others start to snicker. "My bad. Let me go get that." She turns on her heels and storms off.

"She's right, you know," Chase says, taking his drink off the table.

"What?" Brody asks.

"About you not ordering a beer. You only ordered two shots of bourbon."

"I know that," Brody grins.

Chase just shakes his head.

"Here," Ellie says when she gets back holding out an unopened can of beer.

"Really? Seriously, you should be fired, because that's a Guinness in a can. I wanted a Heineken in a glass bottle."

"You know what..." Ellie slams the can down on the table. Brody gives her a daring look.

"What?" he challenges her.

"I'll be right back," she spits, backing down from the backlash she was about to give Brody.

"Thought so," Brody purrs, leaning back on the couch like he owns the whole place.

"Now, that's funny," Laura and Kayla giggle.

"It *is* fun to watch her run around all flustered," Rain smirks while taking one of the shots. "Alright, I'm going to dance."

"I'm coming too," Laura says, getting up to follow after Rain.

"Oh, me too!" Kayla says, jumping up after them.

Rain gives Chase a death glare for not keeping her friend entertained and letting her 'pussy block'. Chase just gives her a shit eating grin and shrugs.

"You're quiet tonight," Brody says. "You haven't said one word when it comes to Ellie. I'm starting to think you're gonna stay out of it like Chase is." The look he's giving me makes me feel like he's disappointed and pissed. I don't like it.

"No. I'm on your side. She needs to go and deserves everything coming to her. I'm just stressed with school and everything," I lie.

His face relaxes and I breathe a sigh of relief. He leans in close to talk in my ear. "Tonight, I'll help relieve some of that stress." His breath is hot against my ear and a shiver takes over my body as I bite back a groan. My cock doesn't get the memo, though. Brody looks down and smirks. "Dance with me?"

Brody gets up and I follow him. Chase sees us leaving and joins us. As we make our way to the dance floor, we pass Ellie. She gapes at us before her face twists into annoyance as she holds up the beer bottle. With a huff, she goes back to our section, leaves the beer bottle, then takes off upstairs.

We dance for a while, Chase bringing in random girls so that it doesn't look like Brody and I are dancing alone. After a few songs, Rain and the other girls join us. I find myself laughing and smiling as Chase makes a fool of himself.

A girl starts to grind herself on me and, not wanting to cause a scene, I grip her hips and dance along to the beat. Looking up, I see Brody watching us intensely, a look of pure jealousy shining bright in his eyes. My heart skips a beat knowing the idea of me with someone else affects him so strongly.

I look past Brody and see Ellie coming down the stairs with a big tray full of food. An idea pops in my head and as much as I'm not going to like this—because really, I'm not a fan of this whole plan of making Ellie's life a living hell—I need to do it to keep Brody off my back. I don't want him questioning my loyalty to him for even a second.

The girl and I dance, making our way around Brody, and just as Ellie is passing us, I back up into her, sending the tray of food flying to the ground with a big clatter. People jump back to get out of the way. "Shit!" Ellie shouts, then looks at me with wide eyes. "What the hell?!"

"Don't blame me," I sneer. "You're the one who's a fucking klutz and can't watch where they're going. First, you can't get a drink order right, and now, you're wasting hundreds of dollars worth of food. Maybe next time, watch where you're going. I'm surprised you still have a job when you're so shitty at it."

Her face fills with anger and my gut turns as I see her eyes fill with tears. She doesn't let them fall as she crouches down and starts to clean up the mess. Another person, I think her name is Aria, rushes over to help her. The girl looks up at me with pure fury for her friend before going back to cleaning the mess.

Brody and Rain laugh, then proceed to walk over the food, kicking it across the floor as they head back to our spot, the others following behind.

When Chase passes her, he looks down at her with a look of remorse, while stepping over the food, before moving on. I follow after him, not wanting to look at Ellie anymore. It was a shitty thing to do, but I did it anyway.

"There's my man," Brody cheers, putting his arm around me. "I knew you had our backs."

The others laugh and talk about Ellie like she's the butt of every joke. Chase looks pissed and I feel like a dick. I just want to go home and forget about this night.

# Chapter Seventeen

## ELLIE

"YOU HAVE GOT to be kidding me," I hiss, standing in front of the mirror in the girls' locker room. It's Monday, my first practice, and everyone else is already on the field, but I'm late because I had to finish an assignment and get everything ready that Theo might need for Lilly.

When I got here, Rain had a sour look on her face as she tossed me a bag, told me it was my uniform and that because I was late, I got the 'privilege' to wash the whole team's dirty uniforms. *Don't they have someone for that?* I feel like they do and Rain's only doing it to be a bitch.

But now, I'm standing here in a uniform that is way too small for me. The blue shorts are riding up my ass, showing off the bottom of my butt cheeks, and no matter how many times I pull the back down, they keep going back up. The silver long sleeve crop-top with blue SVU lettering across my upper chest is also way too small. It should go down to just above my belly button, but it barely covers my boobs, stopping right below. If I move the wrong way, I could give the football team a nip slip and as much as they might enjoy that, I wouldn't. I asked for a medium because my hips got wider after giving birth to Lilly, and so did my breasts. This is not a medium.

Not wanting to keep them waiting any longer, I suck it up and go out onto the field. It's only practice, so I'll talk to the coach and see about getting the proper size before the next practice or game.

"About damn time, Tatum," Rain says, her face going from a look of annoyance at my mere presence, to amusement. "You got crabs or something?" "Why are you picking at your ass?" She laughs.

"Har, har," I deadpan. "*Someone* gave me the wrong size uniform."

"Rain gave you what you asked for. Lying about your size won't work here. If you need a large, just say so. It's okay to have a little meat on your bones..." Laura says, giving me a pitying look as her eyes rake over my body. I want to slap her.

"I know my size, and I'm a medium. This isn't a medium. And even if I was a large, or an extra large, who cares? Bigger women are just as beautiful and can dance and cheer just as well."

"Seeing how you're a flyer, you don't need to be crushing the people who have to catch your lard ass," Kayla sneers.

Wow. Just wow. What is wrong with these girls? Slut shaming people, body shaming people. It's sad that they live lives with so much bitterness.

"Look girls, if you're jealous because I have bigger boobs than you—which is okay because everyone's bodies are perfect in their own way—and I can dance circles around you, it still doesn't give you the right to act like bitches. We should all be cheering each other on, not tearing each other down. Kindness goes a long way." I give them a sugary sweet smile, internally flipping them off.

"Fuck off, whore. No one is jealous of you and your used up cunt," Laura sneers.

"Says the girl who is attached to my ex like a leech. Enjoying my sloppy seconds?"

Okay, that was a little harsh, but these girls are pushing me.

I should be taking the high road. But Rain and her friends act like I sleep with every person with legs, yet Rain is with a new girl every week, as is Chase. It's not true for me, but even if it was, how is it okay for them to do it and not me? Pot calling the kettle black much?

Rain gapes at me like she can't believe I actually said that.

"At least I can make her scream until she blacks out," Laura says, taking a step forward.

"That's enough. We're not fucking talking about my sex life here," Rain says, looking around at all the girls who have gathered around to listen to the show. Even a few of the football players have stopped to listen in.

"Alright ladies, let's show our new member the routine we have been working on," Coach says, unknowingly breaking up our fight. Rain and the others give me one last death stare before taking their positions on the field.

The music starts and I watch carefully, trying to take in every move they make and commit it to memory. They're good, like really good. And Rain, dammit, it's hard not to get lost in her while I watch. She does every move and stunt perfectly, a genuine smile on her face as she does the one thing she loves. Seeing her so free and happy in the spotlight has my mind flashing back to when we were together. She was always in an amazing mood when she got to dance.

My gut clenches at the memory. *How did we go from having the world at our fingertips to hating each other?*

After they show me twice, I join in, and after the fourth run through, I've picked up most of the dance. For this routine, I'll only be dancing, no stunts. Thank God, because I know for a fact that my shirt would be showing off my boobs if I were to be flipping around the place and being tossed into the air.

"That was really good, Eleanor. Good job catching on so quickly. You should be good to go, after one more practice, for the game on Thursday," Coach says after we're done practicing.

"Thanks," I say, "and I go by Ellie."

"Well, Ellie, I'll see to getting you the proper size uniform by Wednesday," she says, then casts a glance over at Rain.

"Thanks," I say and start to do some cool down stretches after she walks away. I didn't realize how out of shape I am. After two hours of dancing, I'm sweating like crazy and my hair is probably not all that attractive.

"Yeah, baby, bend over and show me that ass," someone calls from the field as I bend over to stretch out my calves. I look over my shoulder to see a few of the guys staring at my ass. Brody and Jax are watching too, but not with lust in their eyes like the others. Brody looks disgusted while Jax looks conflicted. I look over to see that Chase is pissed, but he's not looking at me. He's looking at the guys. *What's up with that?*

Trying to ignore them, I turn around so that my ass is facing away from them and finish my stretching. Only, that isn't much better because now their eyes are on my tits as I stretch my arms above my head.

"Just a little higher sweet thing, almost there," one calls out.

I drop my arms immediately and glare at them. "How about you focus on what you're supposed to be doing and stop perving on me!" I call back. *Like seriously, get a life.*

"Nah, this is more fun," another one calls as they start to walk toward me. "So, I heard you like to have orgies. How about you give me and my friends a go? I promise we'll make it real good," he says, licking his lips as he eyes up my tits.

"No, thanks. I don't date assholes. At least, not anymore," I say, looking over their shoulders to Brody whose jaw is so tight it looks like he might crack a tooth.

"We're not talking about dating, love. We're talking about a good, hard fuck."

"Like I said, no thanks." I start to walk away when I hear Cooper call my name. I stop and smile at him as he jogs over to me, his helmet under his arm and hair plastered to his face from sweat.

"Hey, you!" I say when he reaches me. "Sorry, I haven't seen much of you. Life's been crazy with school, work, and now this," I gesture to the girls on the bench.

"Totally get it. The start of the school year is always the craziest. But I do enjoy our meme wars," he chuckles.

"Same." I smile back.

"So, I wanted to ask you..." he says, a little louder like he wants everyone around us to hear. "Are you going to Connor Phillips's Halloween party this weekend?"

Connor Philips is the captain of the baseball team, and the girls told me he always throws the best costume parties. I asked for the weekend off work and thankfully, they agreed. I would have felt like shit if I had to miss taking Lilly Trick-or-Treating. Normally, when you're so new at a job, time off right away isn't really a thing, but Lilly is my main priority, so I had to try. And now Theo, the kids, and I can go together.

"Yeah. I was gonna go with my friends," I say. Come to think of it, I feel bad for not asking him too. I figured he would have a date.

"Oh. I wanted to see if you would go with me." He gives me a stunning smile. Then he leans in to whisper in my ear, "Just go with it."

Everyone is watching us now, and I see what he's doing. "I'd love to go to the party with you, Cooper." I give him an excited smile and hug him.

The team all start to whisper and the girls give me dirty looks. "Thanks," I whisper.

"No, thank you. I got myself a hot date," he chuckles. "Meet me outside after we clean up?"

I nod my head and start in the direction of the girls' changing rooms.

Stripping off my dirty uniform, I duck under the hot spray of the shower. It feels amazing on my sore muscles. I quickly wash up and take a few extra minutes to just enjoy the feeling of the water.

"I can't believe Cooper asked her out! After everything he

was told about her," Kayla bitches from somewhere in the locker room.

"Why do you care? I thought you wanted Chase," Rain asks.

"I do! It's just, he turned on us, on his own team," she whines.

"Cooper's never really been one of us. Sure, he's on the team, but he's not friends with the other guys and he's never dated any of us." That comes from a girl on the squad, but I don't know her name.

Not wanting to hear them anymore, I turn the water off and wrap my towel around me. Slipping on my shower sandals, I pull back the curtain and see them all turn to look at me. I cock a brow as I glance at them while heading for my locker. They say nothing as they watch me pull my clothes out and place them on the bench.

"How did you do it?" Kayla asks, placing her hands on her sides and popping a hip.

"Do what?" I ask, closing the locker door.

"Get one of the guys on the team? They should know better than to slum it with trash like you." She steps up to me, blocking my way to the changing stall.

"We got to know each other. He's nice, unlike half the guys on the team. Now, excuse me, I need to get dressed." I go to step around her, but she follows my movement, repeating when I try to move back around her the other way. "Alright, we're gonna play that game I see," I sigh. "Well, if you're not going to let me get dressed in private, I'll just do it here. I have places to be." I drop my towel, exposing my body to the room. The girls all make sounds of disgust but Rain's eyes widen, lust shining bright in her eyes as they devour my body slowly.

I stand there doing nothing for longer than I should, willing my nipples not to harden because the way she's looking at me is turning me on and that's so fucking wrong. She shouldn't affect me like this anymore.

Laura looks at Rain then to me, fury passing over her face. "Cover yourself up. God! No one wants to see that. What, the guys aren't enough for you so you're going for the girls, too?"

That snaps me out of my head. I roll my eyes and start to get dressed. "Sorry, Laura, you ladies aren't my type." Lies. *There's one woman here who used to be your whole world.*

"Good because we don't want you. We have better taste than you," she says, grabbing ahold of Rain's arm in a possessive move.

"Whatever," I say, trading my sandals for my sneakers. Thankfully, the exit is behind me and I don't have to play chicken with Kayla to get out of here. Grabbing my bag, I turn around and leave as their chatter starts to pick up.

I find Cooper leaning against the wall waiting for me. When he sees me, he smiles and makes his way over.

"Sorry it took me so long. I had a little issue with the girls."

"Are you okay?" he asks, his smile dropping.

"Nothing I couldn't handle. Come on, let's hang out for a bit before I gotta get home." His smile returns and we walk to one of the coffee shops that are on campus. We laugh and talk about how our weekend went. I fill him in on my disaster of a work night with Rain and the Silver Knights. They made me look like a fool and it was so hard to hold back tears as they kicked the food around, making me crawl all over the place to clean it up. Aria stuck up for me with our boss. She told him it was a mistake and someone bumped into me. And because it was so packed, people started to kick the food around without knowing. I got off this time, thanks to her, but I'm going to lose my job if they keep up with this crap.

I can't afford to lose it. I have a bit of money saved already, but this job pays well and I'd like to have enough money in savings that I don't need to live from paycheck to paycheck anymore.

"So, I wanted to talk to you about something," Cooper says as we take a seat on a bench.

"What's up?" I ask, taking a sip of my coffee and groaning at the pumpkin spice goodness.

Cooper smiles with amusement as he continues. "I've been hearing about how the guys on campus have been treating you, and I don't like it. I don't like the things they say. So the other night, I thought up a crazy plan. It could work, but I don't know," he says, a sheepish look taking over his face.

"Well, what is it?" I laugh.

"What if...I became your boyfriend?"

My brows raise in shock. "Cooper, you're a really sweet guy, an amazing friend, and you really are hot as hell, but I already have a boyfriend," I say.

"You think I'm hot?" He smiles. "And you have a boyfriend? Okay. Does he go to this school?"

*I mean he works here, but...* "No, he doesn't attend this university."

"Then how about, just for image's sake, we let everyone believe we're dating. We can talk to your boyfriend and let him know." I just blink at him. "I told you the idea is crazy," he laughs. "But maybe if the guys around here see that you have a boyfriend, they will lessen up on the comments, maybe even the girls too."

"Aren't you worried about missing out on a real girlfriend?" I ask, actually considering the idea. Theo knows how everyone is treating me, and he's pissed he can't do anything about it.

"That won't be a problem, seeing as I'm gay and all," he says.

My brows shoot up. "You are?"

"Yup," he chuckles. "But I'm not looking to find anyone. I'm here to get my education, graduate, and then get a good job. Dating and relationships can wait. I'm not in the closet but I don't flaunt my sexuality around either. And it's not anyone's business to know my sexual preference."

"So, we are friends. But everyone thinks we're dating?" I ask.

"Yeah. Maybe a kiss here and there, holding hands when we're together, but other than that, it's just best buddies."

"I'm not saying yes, but I'm not saying no," I tell him. "But, you need to know that if you do this for me, you're getting yourself into something deeper than you're in right now. There are some things I'll have to tell you to make this work, so you will have to keep a few really big secrets."

*Am I really going to tell Cooper what the girls know?* I mean, he is willing to do this really big thing for me.

"Are you secretly a serial killer?" he asks.

"What?" I laugh. "No!"

"Then I think I can handle it," he grins.

"Okay. How about we meet this weekend before the party, and I'll tell you everything. If you're not comfortable with it, then we can just go to the party and have fun with our friends."

# Chapter Eighteen

## ELLIE

**MONDAY NIGHT,** Cooper came home with me and we talked to Theo about our possible, fake relationship, explaining everything. At first, Theo was a little apprehensive of the idea, but when Cooper told him he was gay, Theo relaxed. Theo agreed to the plan because he understands how hard it's been for me there, and if this helps in any way, he's okay with it. Another reason why I love this man so much. The idea is crazy but he agreed to it because it could make *my* life easier. He's amazing.

Then we told Cooper that Theo is now a professor at the university and that we met before he got the job. We also explained that Theo isn't my professor, but we didn't know what the school policies are regarding that, and until we do, we don't want to risk anyone knowing.

Cooper didn't care, promising to keep our relationship to himself, and seeing as how we want people to think he and I are dating, it makes it a lot easier.

Cooper's idea might have been crazy and a little out there, but the next day, the whole school was buzzing about how Cooper and I are going to the party together. He also invited me and my friends to sit with him in the cafe. No one made rude comments or anything, but if Rain and Brody's looks could kill, I'd be six feet under right now. To say they weren't happy is an understatement.

The girls are on board with the idea. Val and Lexie were a little too excited but I know they mean well. I think they're just excited to have a gay friend. Val told him she's always wanted one which earned her a smack on the arm from Lexie. They all hit it off right away and it makes me happy to see my friend group growing with true and trustworthy people.

The rest of the week went by with little to no harassment which has me honestly excited for the party tonight. Cooper is on his way to pick me up so that we can go over to Val's place and get ready. We decided to do a group costume and dress up as the Scooby-Doo gang. Cooper is Fred, I'm Daphne, Val is Velma, Lexie is Scooby, and Tabitha offered to be Shaggy.

The doorbell rings and I yell out, "I'll get it!" before handing Lilly her cup of juice. When I answer the door, Cooper flashes me a bright smile.

"Hey. You excited about tonight?" he asks.

"Actually, I am." I smile back. "Not too thrilled about seeing the assholes but I won't let them ruin my night. It's gonna be fun."

"You said a bad word," Lilly says, popping her head out the door and looking up at me.

Cooper's eyes flick from me, to Lilly, and back up to me. "Uhh... Do you know that there's a mini version of you?" he asks, pointing down at Lilly.

"Hi! I Lilly," she greets Cooper.

"Hi, Lilly. I'm Cooper."

"No, you Fred," she says, shaking her head. I stifle a giggle because Cooper is already in costume and Lilly loves Scooby-Doo.

"You're right, I am. Silly me, I forgot my own name." He smiles, making Lilly laugh.

"So, you know how I told you I had two things I needed

you to keep to yourself?" I ask, scratching the back of my neck awkwardly.

"Let me guess, she's the second one," he laughs.

"Yeah."

I invite him in and quietly tell him everything, minus what actually happened to me the night of that party, while Lilly plays with her toys. By the end of it, he is pissed, but not at me. He looks like he hates the guys more than he already did. But he agrees that it isn't his place to say anything and will keep it to himself.

"Come on, Bug. Theo and Toby are waiting for you," I say, grabbing her bag.

"Yay! Sleepover!" she cheers, dropping her dolls and taking off out the open door, right to Theo's. She pounds her little fists on the door until Theo opens it.

"Hi! I sleep over now," she says before darting past him and into his place. I laugh as I lock the door behind me.

"Here," I say, handing Theo Lilly's bag. "Thanks again for watching her."

"You don't have to thank me. I love spending time with her, and honestly, Lilly brings Toby's hyper from a ten to a seven, so *you're* actually doing *me* a favor," he laughs.

"I just wish we could do something together like this," I say as he pulls me into his arms.

"Someday." He smiles down at me and kisses me sweetly. "I love you," he whispers against my lips.

"I love you too."

"Have our girlfriend home by one," Theo tells Cooper with a fake, stern look.

"Yes, sir." Cooper laughs.

"I'm trusting you to keep her safe," Theo says, a little more seriously.

"She's in good hands. I promise."

With one more kiss goodbye, Cooper and I go to meet up with the girls. We get ready, having fun pre-partying and by the time we leave, Val is a little tipsy. I'm starting to feel the effects already. I needed something to calm me down before going into the lion's den.

When the cab pulls up to the house, we are hit with a wave of party chaos.

"Something tells me this party is going to be insane," Val says, her face alight as she takes in all the crazy costumes. Looking around, I see that most of the girls are dressed like how 'the Plastics' from *Mean Girls* were dressed at their Halloween party. *Why does it always have to be half naked bunnies or nurses?*

The guy standing on the lawn making the girls scream and run looks like he could be on the cast of *the Walking Dead* with his amazing zombie costume. There are tons of chances to dress sexy at parties throughout the year. Halloween should just be about having fun and getting lost in it all.

"You ready, Daphne?" Cooper asks, holding out his arm.

"Ready, Freddy," I grin. He snorts out a laugh, a smile taking its rightful place on his handsome face. I loop my arm with his and silently hope this night doesn't turn out to be a shit storm like all the other parties that Rain and the Silver Knights have been at that I've attended. I just want a night of fun, dancing, and drinks with my friends. A night with no drama. And as nice as this week has been with the whole school thinking Cooper and I are a thing now, I know it's not going to stop completely. But I sure as hell plan to enjoy every moment I can until shit hits the fan again.

## BRODY

"This is fucking stupid. I don't see why we had to dress up," I grumble, refusing to get out of the car.

"Don't be such a party pooper, man. It's Halloween. How about you take that dick out of your ass for one night? I mean stick. Take the stick out of your ass," Chase grins. The cocky fucker knew exactly what he was saying—he loves to get me all riled up.

"Are you just sad it's not your dick up there?" I joke back.

"Nah, bro. I like the V too much to take any D," he says. Using his fingers, he makes a V shape and wiggles his tongue between them.

I grin, flipping him off. "Fuck you," I laugh.

"Nah, I'll find me a sexy nurse or naughty doctor to take care of that for me tonight."

"Wouldn't that be bestiality?" Rain asks, pulling at the ear on Chase's costume. Rain had a fun idea to go as the cast of Scooby-Doo. She's Velma, I'm Fred, Jax is Shaggy, and Chase is Scooby. I told Rain it would be stupid to go with no Daphne, but she just told me to shut the fuck up and go with it because she wasn't going to change her mind. I suggested she be Daphne because she has red hair, and Chase be Fred, because he is blond, but Rain said she wanted to be a brunette for a night, and Chase got a little too excited about dressing up as a damn dog, so here we are.

"What the fuck?" Chase asks, looking at her with shocked disgust.

"You know, you're a dog who wants to fuck a human?" she grins.

"Dude, no, just no. Your joke has gone a little too far and that's fucked up. I'm out, see you losers later," Chase says, flipping us off before jogging into the house.

"Yeah, I'm out too. Velma wants to find someone to get 'Jinkies' with," she says before taking off.

"That doesn't even make sense!" I yell after her but she's too far away to hear me over the music.

I look at Jax and he has this amused grin on his sexy, pink lips. Lips I hope to see wrapped around my cock at some point tonight, if I have it my way.

His smile is infectious, and it doesn't take me long before

I'm sporting one of my own. "Alright, Shaggy, you ready to party with the ghosts and ghouls?" I grin.

"As long as I'm with you, always," he says softly, his hand brushing over mine before taking the lead into the house. My skin tingles where his fingers touch, and my cock responds in the worst way. I want to grab him by the arm and stop him from walking away, to push him up against this car and grind my cock against him. I want to show him just how much I want him, need him, and crave him. But I don't. And I won't. It's not that I'm ashamed of what Jax and I have. I love him, even though I have yet to say those exact words. But because of that girl, the one who took her dainty, little fingers, shoved them into my chest, wrapped them around my beating heart, yanking it out before tossing it to the ground, and stomping all the fuck over it, she's the reason I can't. I won't. I just...I just don't know how to without opening myself up to being utterly destroyed again.

I know Jax would never do what Ellie did, but if I keep living in this little protective bubble I put myself in, then I can continue to lie to myself and not take the risk.

Also, what Jax and I have, it works for us. Why fix something that's not broken?

*Because that man deserves more than being your dirty little secret, you asshole.*

The place is crowded, and I'm already over this night. I don't care much for holidays. I mean, how can I be when the only way I got to go out Trick-or-Treating was if I went with Rain or the guys' parents. On Thanksgiving or Christmas, my dad was always too drunk and my mom was always off fucking her newest sugar daddy. Every holiday, I would wake up and wish it was over the moment I opened my eyes. And even though the others would invite me to their place, I'd spend the whole time feeling like a charity case.

So, now every holiday, I order in food, buy a crap ton of alcohol, and watch the *Godfather* on repeat.

"There's a lot more people than I expected," Jax says as we weave our way through the crowd.

"Let's just find the drinks, grab a few, and go somewhere to chill out for the night," I say.

We both don't care much for parties but we go mostly because Chase and Rain love them. They go to get lost in the party scene and drink, or to hook up with people. As a Knight, we have a reputation to hold up and parties are part of the image. I prefer the club to parties, though, because we have a second to ourselves, good drinks, and tasty food.

"You find us a spot. I'll grab drinks," Jax says. I give him a nod and he takes off into the crowd, getting lost right away.

I go the opposite direction toward the living room. Unfortunately, that's where the dance floor is located, but I want a comfortable spot to sit if I'm going to be here for the next few hours.

"Move," I bark at the group of people sitting on the black leather couch. They look up at me, recognizing who I am, and one by one, they get up and leave.

*Was that a dick move?* Yes, probably. *Do I care?* Not if it means a soft place for my ass to sit tonight.

"Here," Jax says, handing me a bottle of beer. Of course, it's nothing hard. Jax doesn't like it when I drink, but he doesn't try to bitch me out about it either. He knows why I do it, and I love him for picking up my drunken pieces when I've had too much. I feel like a grade A asshole because I never acknowledge what he does for me. I always pretend I black out and don't remember. Sometimes it's true depending on how much I drank, but other times, I know he's carrying me to bed, stripping me out of my clothes and cleaning me up. Most of the time, he also leaves a bucket on the floor and a glass of water with a painkiller on the bedside table. He never leaves me and is always tired the next morning because he didn't sleep; instead, he makes sure I don't choke on my own vomit during the night.

I don't deserve him. He's too fucking good for me. Call me

a selfish bastard, but until he tells me he doesn't want me anymore, he's *mine*. Even then, he will always be mine. I've already lost one of the loves of my life. I won't survive losing the other.

"Thanks," I say, taking the beer from his hand. He takes a seat next to me, his thigh brushing against mine. *And there goes my cock again.* I don't think anywhere in the movies or shows do Fred and Shaggy...well, shag.

Bringing my foot up so that my ankle rests on my thigh, I try to hide my raging boner. For the next half hour, Jax and I alternate between talking and just fucking around on our phones.

"Hey, shit heads, how's your night going? Mine is going wonderful, thanks for asking. I just fucked some sexy firefighter while she ate out a cop," Chase says with a shit eating grin.

"We don't want to know about your sexual conquests, nor do we care. So please, do us all a favor and keep it to yourself. And please, for the love of God, tell me you wore a condom," I hiss.

"Duh." He rolls his eyes. "I'm not that stupid." Let's put some emphasis on that part, because this fucker has his idiotic moments.

"Alright, I'm taking over this playlist for a moment." Some girl, who is in a sexy version of Chase's costume, squeezes her drunk ass onto the dance floor and over to the guy with the speakers, laptop, and the playlist. I wouldn't exactly call him a DJ seeing as how all he does is press the 'next' button on his laptop.

"Oh look, it's me, but like not," Chase says. I roll my eyes at his drunk ass.

A few more people squeeze their way onto the dance floor, and my body stiffens when I see Ellie and Cooper laughing as they join the music girl and a few other people.

"Are you kidding me?" Jax says, his brow raised.

"I know," I growl. "But we expected her to be here."

"Yes, but do you see who they're here as?" Jax asks.

I take a better look, my eyes feeling a little fuzzy from my third beer. It doesn't help that I drank before coming here, but I see what he means. Cooper is dressed as the same fucking thing I am, Fred. One of the other girls is some kind of girly version of Shaggy, one is Velma and Ellie, motherfucking Ellie, is Daphne.

"Ummm, does anyone else think the universe is laughing at us because the one person who is missing from our group costume is exactly who our ex is dressed up as?" Chase asks, looking from Jax to me. I shoot him a death glare. "Just me, alright. Cool, cool," he nods his head.

"He looks fucking ridiculous," I mutter. "I make a better Fred than he does."

"Really?" Chase asks like he thinks I'm on drugs. "Because he has the proper hairstyle and color. Your wig looks like some old lady's bush." He chuckles. "Ouch!" he whines, giving me the stink eye when I smack him upside the head.

"Shut the fuck up," I snap.

"Ellie," the girl-Scooby calls when the music cuts off. "This is a shout out to my ex. Or should I say your—" she looks over at us with a grin I don't like before finishing her sentence, "exes."

"I have a feeling whatever this song is, it has now been dedicated to us," Chase says, but he has an amused look on his face. "This should be interesting."

Ellie looks over at us, her smile falling when she meets my eyes. Cooper gets her attention and within seconds, her smile is back in place. I hate that guy. *Fucking prick.*

The song starts up, and the first words are 'This is a shout out to my ex'. Lovely.

The girls all sing the song, and I don't miss the glances Ellie gives me, but her friends, the ones dressed as Velma and Scooby, stare at us like we're *their* exes or some shit.

The song says something about getting better sex and I scoff.

"Oh, I know she's totally directing that to one of you, because we all know that I'm a sex God," Chase comments. Jax and I glare at him, but he just cups his cock and thrusts his hips out at us with a grin. "No way you can fake it with me."

Turning back to the girls, the song gets to the main chorus and they are now belting out the lyrics, dancing around with their arms in the air. The smile on Ellie's face is pissing me off more than it should.

"This song is stupid," I mutter, crossing my arms as I lean back into the couch. No matter how much I don't want her in my sight, I can't look away. It's like I'm a moth drawn to her flame, like I'm desperate to get burned again.

"It's called *Shout Out To My Ex* by Little Mix. It's a good song," Chase shrugs.

"Of course you would think so." I roll my eyes.

"Anyways, I'm off to find something to eat. Or someone, if I come across a better offer than chips and dip," he says, wiggling his eyebrows before taking off.

Ellie's friends leave the dance floor, leaving behind her and Cooper. The song changes, and an uneasy flush takes over my body. I see Jax's head snap over to look at me, his eyes watching me to see how I'm going to react. This song, *Hands To Myself* by Selena Gomez used to be Ellie's favorite song. Every time it came on, she would make the guys and I get up to dance with her. She would lip sync the song, dancing around us, Rain joining in and singing the song with her. It's one of the many memories that has stuck with me even though I don't want it to.

Now, seeing her dancing to it with Cooper, a smile of affection painted on her lips as she stares up at him while singing along to the lyrics, fills me with emotions I don't want to feel. Anger, jealousy, hurt. I have no business feeling any of it. Well, anger, yes, but not at her for being with another guy. Who she is with is no business of mine. I shouldn't care. Yet, I do and I fucking hate it.

She turns around in Cooper's arms. He wraps them around her body, holding her close to him as she grinds her ass into his crotch.

Jax's hand on my thigh snaps me out of the rage building within me. He looks at me with concern. I'm vibrating right now and it's too much. I need him. I need him to ground me, to bring me back.

"Come," I tell him, my voice dangerously low.

He looks at me for a moment before nodding. Standing up, I head toward the second floor, knowing Jax is right behind me. It's blocked off to the party but no one stops us when I rip down the caution tape that was put up. I try a few doors, all locked until I get to the third one. It's dark, but I can see the basic outline of the room as the moonlight shines through the window.

Jax follows me in. After closing the door behind me, I stalk toward him, the one person who can keep me from destroying myself. I need him now before it's too late.

"On your knees."

# *Chapter Nineteen*

## BRODY

MY PULSE IS SPIKING and my cock hasn't been soft since before walking into this stupid party. I need this release before I blow the fuck up. I don't know why seeing Ellie with Cooper like that triggered me, but it took everything in me to not go over there, rip him off her, and smash in his pretty face for putting his hands on her.

*It's because you're still in love with her. No matter how much you try to tell yourself you hate her, you love her now just as much as you did before her betrayal.*

Closing my eyes, I take a deep breath, willing the thought of her to go away. When I open them, Jax is on his knees before me. I can see the lust shining brightly in his eyes as the moonlight streams through the window, bathing him in the midnight glow. He looks fucking gorgeous. He sits there like a good boy, waiting for my next command.

"Take me out, then take me deep, Jax. I need to feel your thick hand wrapped around my cock. I need to feel your hot, wet tongue lick me like the best damn popsicle you've ever tasted."

Jax shudders at my words and his hands eagerly pull down my zipper and my solid, heavy length is in his grasp in seconds.

"Fuck!" I hiss, biting my lip as he adds pressure. "Go on, be a good boy and lick it," I command, my voice deep and husky because I'm so fucking turned on.

Jax leans forward, his tongue flicking out to lick the tip of my cock, wiping away the pre-cum waiting there. He looks up at me, licking his lips, and takes me into his mouth slowly. He teases me, driving me crazy as he swirls his tongue around the head, taking me all the way to the back of his throat before pulling back and teasing my tip again.

"Look at you. So eager for my cock. I want you to choke on it. I want you to fucking gag until there's spit dripping down the corners of your mouth, and you're begging me for more," I say, gripping his black curls, and pulling his head back. His eyes are blazing with heat, his chest heaving with excitement. He wants more, and I'm gonna give it to him.

"Yes, Sir," he moans, the sound making my cock twitch. I force him back down on my dick, and he takes me in willingly.

Gripping me with one hand, he sucks and jerks me off at the same time. It feels amazing. Everything from earlier tonight disappears, and the only thing I'm able to think about is my man pleasing me.

"God, Jax. Fuck, you're taking my dick so good." I grit my teeth, resisting the urge to thrust my hips in time to the rhythm of his bobs. I can't hold back much longer. I'm going to enjoy every feeling and sensation I can as I fuck this man's throat until I'm cumming down it.

Hitting the back of his throat, I hold his head there, letting out a groan as he gags, the sound filling me with satisfaction. I know he loves it. I can see his cock thickening in his pants. If we weren't pressed for time, and worried about being caught or one of the others coming to look for us, I'd re-pay him the favor.

He hollows out his cheeks, sucking me hard. *I'm close...so close.*

"That's it," I sigh, my pace picking up. He's no longer in control of this, not that he ever really was. I take over, thrusting into his mouth and he takes it like a champ. His eyes are wild, and I can see his hands itching to touch himself. "Take out your cock, Jax. Stroke yourself while I fuck your face," I growl. Looking to my left, I see a body length mirror. I watch how perfect he looks in the glow of the light with my cock down his throat, his hand wrapped around his dick. I'm hypnotized by the beauty of it. He's watching me, his eyes on my face as I watch him, getting a full view of everything. I'm going hard and fast now, chasing my rapidly building release. My balls are tingling. My cock is throbbing and the sight of him fucking his hand is almost too much. We become in sync; me thrusting into his mouth and him into his hand. We're both moaning, chests heaving, and after a moment, his eyes roll back. His cock twitches as white jets of cum coat his hand, and I'm fucking done. I return my attention to him, locking eyes with him just in time, because with one last thrust, I cum hard down his throat, my cock spasming as he sucks and swallows down my seed.

"So fucking perfect," I breathe. "You take my cock so good. Swallowing my cum like a good boy." I praise him, stroking the side of his face as I pull out of his mouth. He beams with pride and it makes me fall in love with him all over again.

A whimper that doesn't come from the man on his knees before me has me snapping my head toward the door. My eyes lock with *hers*. Ellie stands there, door cracked open, watching with wide eyes full of shock. *And is that lust?* Doesn't matter, she just saw something that could be our undoing, and I won't let that happen.

I shove my dick back into my pants. Rage runs through my veins as I storm over to her and rip the door open. She looks at me with a stunned look like she's unable to move. I give her a bone chilling sneer, my nostrils flaring as I grab a hold of her shirt and pull her inside the room, slamming the door shut before trapping her against it.

"You're gonna regret what you just saw."

Ellie

*Ten minutes earlier...*

"I need to pee," I tell Cooper, raising my voice loud enough for him to hear me over the music.

"Alright, you want another drink?" he asks.

I nod, and he heads into the kitchen as I leave in search of a bathroom.

Tonight has been going so much better than I thought it would. I haven't seen Rain, although from what some of the people around me were saying, she's out back with a group of people.

Except for the song that Val put on and out right dedicated it to the guys, I haven't seen them either.

Heading down a hallway, I see a line of people waiting to use the bathroom. "Stop fucking and get out! We need to fucking pee," some girl yells as she bangs on the door.

There's no way I'll be able to wait that long. I haven't drunk much tonight, but the few drinks I have had are demanding to be let back out, and if I don't find a bathroom soon, I might have to go outside and pee in a bush or something.

Going back the way I came, I see a staircase. Hoping there's another bathroom up there, I make my way up to the top floor.

I try all the doors as I go, but they're all locked. Right as I'm about to try another one, I hear a sexual moan.

"Take out your cock, Jax. Stroke yourself while I fuck your face." I know that voice. *It's Brody.*

My hand stills on the door handle; my body is frozen in place. I have no idea what is going on behind this door, but I have a very good guess. Jax and Brody, huh? *Since when did they become a thing?* I know they were not together back in high school. So it must have started after I left.

Blood throbs in my ears as my head spins with all this new information. The idea of Brody and Jax together, the sounds coming from behind this door, it has me so wet. It's wrong to be turned on by this, by my exes. I have a boyfriend who I'm madly in love with. But these two men, despite how much of an asshole Brody has been, were once my lovers. And as much as I wish it wasn't true, I still love them.

Before I know what's happening, my hand is slowly twisting the door handle open. I crack the door just enough to see Jax on his knees as Brody thrusts into his mouth. Jax's back is to me, but looking to the side, I see a mirror with both of them in full view.

They look so beautiful together. Now I get why Brody is never with a woman, and when Jax has a girl around him, he looks like he wants to be anywhere but with them. Seeing the way Brody is looking at Jax as he watches him pleasure himself, I can tell it isn't just sexual, I see love there. My heart pangs with hurt. Not because of how they feel about each other, but because they used to look at me like that.

I'm entranced as I watch these two together. My breathing becomes labored, my pulse quickening as my nipples pebble against my bra. *Why is this turning me on so much?*

I rub my thighs together as my clit starts to throb. Brody is so lovingly brutal with Jax, and Jax is enjoying every moment of it. The trust Jax is showing Brody as he stares up at his lover tells me this isn't just something they do for the fun of it. They are in love with each other.

Jax lets out a moan around Brody's length, his hand moving fast over his own cock before he cums, his release coating his hand. Brody looks back at Jax as he follows after. I watch as Jax's throat bobs with every swallow as he milks Brody's cock.

My core is aching with need, and when I shift my weight to the side, I rub them in just the right way that sends sparks to my clit as I let out a little whimper. It was quiet, but not quiet enough. Brody's head snaps over to me, fury filling his once blissed out face. *Oh fuck. Oh fuck, fuck, fuck. Run, Ellie, turn around and run like your ass is on fire!*

But I don't. I can't. I'm stuck in this spot as his eyes bore into mine. He angrily puts himself away, and heads right for me like a very pissed off bull and I'm the red, waving flag.

He rips the door open, grabs a hold of my shirt, his fingers wrapping around the fabric, gripping me before pulling me into the room, and slams me back against the door.

"You're gonna regret what you just saw," he seethes.

I just blink at him, going with the first thing that comes to mind. "Maybe you should have locked the door," I say, my voice low and quivering. *Ellie, why, why are you waving yourself around for the angry bull to charge at?*

"If you tell anyone what you just saw, I will destroy you," he spits, nostrils flaring.

That causes me to snap out of my panic and my own rage to bubble to the top.

"I'm not going to tell anyone," I sneer. "Unlike you, I don't make it my life's mission to make other people's lives miserable. And despite what you think about me, I'm not a bitch. I'm not going to go tell everyone something that has nothing to do with me, and I won't be using it as blackmail even if it could help me lessen the bullshit you guys have been putting me through these past months."

"Brody," Jax says, his voice calm but I can hear the worry lacing his words. "You're hurting her." And he's right. Brody's arm is pressing into my chest. Jax places a hand on Brody's shoulder. Brody relaxes at his touch but he doesn't lessen the pressure. "Let her go."

Jax looks at me, fear in his eyes. But they have nothing to worry about.

"I don't care what you guys do with each other. It's your private life. Do what makes you happy."

"I don't fucking care if you approve of what you just saw. Hell, you're a little freak, you probably got off on it didn't you?

Was that whimper because you're so turned on watching me fuck his mouth? I bet you're just dripping, aren't you?"

"Fuck. You," I breathe. But he's right. I am wet from what I just saw. There is even a part of me that wishes I saw more. And I hate myself for it.

"You wish," he says, letting out a dark chuckle.

With everything that happened, I had forgotten the real reason I came up here. I still need to pee really badly.

"I won't tell anyone anything. I'm not trash like you make me out to be. Now, if you don't mind, I came up here looking for a bathroom. And I'd really rather not piss my pants right now." I give him a fake smile when really, I am shaking inside.

"There's a bathroom at the end of the hall," Jax says. I look over at him, his expression soft. I give him a small grateful smile.

"I mean it, Tatum, you breathe a word of this to anyone and you're fucking done," he warns before moving back.

I take a breath, rubbing the spot on my chest where his arm just was. Opening the door, I turn back, flipping Brody off with both fingers before fleeing down the hall, finding the bathroom and locking myself in.

Taking a moment to wrap my head around everything, I take a few deep breaths before going to the toilet. When I'm done, I wash my hands and use some of the water to cool my face off. What the fuck just happened? *And why does a part of me hope I get to see it again?*

I head back downstairs, my body still vibrating from nerves.

"There you are," Cooper says, coming up to me and handing me a drink. "I was about to send a search party for you," he jokes.

"Sorry." I force a smile, taking the drink. "The bathroom had a long line so I went hunting for another one."

"Well, I'm glad you're back now. Wanna dance a bit more before heading home? Gotta get you back by curfew." He winks at me, making me laugh.

"Yeah, a few more songs, then home. I'm pretty tired."

"Alright then, right this way, Daphne," he says, offering me his arm.

⬤

The rest of the weekend is fun. Theo and I take the kids out Trick-or-Treating. They get lots of candy and that's when Theo and I realize that until it's gone, they are going to be hounding us all day, every day for some candy.

When the kids go to sleep, Theo and I cuddle on his couch. We've started hanging out at his place more because we can sneak away to his room and lock the door behind us.

It feels like we are teenagers again, sneaking off and having sex any chance we get. With two kids, it isn't often, so we take what we can get and it is always amazing. Theo makes sure that I feel good, that I get my release too—not that I have any issues like that with him. Just looking at him has me soaked.

When everything is still and quiet as I lay in bed, Theo sleeping next to me, I can't help but think about what I saw last night. Their sounds of pleasure fill my ears. The looks on their faces, as if they were each other's undoing, is cemented at the front of my mind. I feel horrible for allowing myself to have any second thoughts about it, but what I saw is now imprinted on my brain. I don't think it's going to fade anytime soon.

# Chapter Twenty

## RAIN

"HURRY UP," I hiss, looking out of the locker room door to see if Ellie is coming. Giggling echoes through the locker room as the girls do their thing. Checking again, I see Ellie heading in this direction. "Guys, she's coming," I say, running over to them. They quickly finish up and shut the locker door. We all move away and start talking like nothing out of the ordinary is happening while Ellie makes her way over to her locker.

She looks over at us and we all glare back. She gives us a tight smile but says nothing as she rummages through her locker, getting what she needs for a shower.

We decided to have a last minute practice before Ellie's first game to make sure she has everything down pat so she doesn't fuck up and embarrass us. And of course, she knows the routine by heart already somehow. She's good. Too fucking good.

Leaning against the locker, I watch her every move as she strips down to her sports bra and panties. *Fuck, why does she have to be so hot?* I want her gone, never to be seen again, yet every time she's in a room, I find myself drawn to her. Flashes of our past cloud my mind and the hate takes over again.

Having her here hurts too much. It's a constant reminder of the hardest time in my life. Losing Ellie wrecked me. She wasn't just my lover. She was my best friend. We were practically attached at the hip. We knew everything about each other. We never lied, never hid things from one another. At least, that's what I thought until *that* night.

Brody wants her gone because he hates that he still loves her. Her being here reminds him that Ellie is just like his mother.

Me, I want her gone because it hurts to see her, to be around her. Since she's come back, I haven't been myself. She makes me into someone I would normally hate. I don't enjoy messing with her, not like Brody. But it's what needs to be done.

What makes it all worse is that I still love her. I thought I was over her, living my college life to the fullest, just enjoying my time before going out into the real world. But the moment I locked eyes with her at the first game of the year, it was like someone took a big pin and popped my happy bubble.

My eyes trail over her body and it takes everything in me to stop myself from going over there, pushing her against the locker, and ramming my tongue down her throat. Then I remember that she cheated on us with half the fucking swim team. So when she takes her bath products and towel into the shower, I don't feel as guilty for what's about to happen.

"I can't wait to see the look on her face. I need to get that on video," Laura whispers, enjoying this way too much.

She's jealous because Ellie is my ex. But I've made it clear to Laura, on more than one occasion, that I'm not looking for anything serious. Look what happened the last time I gave someone my heart.

Also, Laura is way too clingy. Every time I try to tell her we should just keep things friendly, she promises she's okay with just being friends with benefits. She's good with her tongue, and I've had worse, but I'm starting to think some good sex is way more trouble than it's worth at this point.

"No, you won't," I snap. She looks up at me with irritation burning bright in her eyes.

"Why not?" she huffs.

"Because, she will be humiliated enough going out there with her hair like that. We don't need to be sharing things from within the locker room. Plus, that's how people will trace it back to us. It's not that hard."

"Fine," she grumbles and puts her phone back in her locker.

The water shuts off, and Ellie comes out wrapped in a towel, her hair wrapped up on top of her head.

She looks over at us, brows pitched. "Why are you all looking at me like that?" she asks, her eyes roaming over the group of us.

"No reason," Kayla giggles.

Ellie gives us one last look before changing into her cheer uniform. She heads over to the mirror and starts to unravel the towel. Wet strands of hair fall down her back and over her shoulders. The look of pure shock and horror that fills her face has my gut turning.

Her long, almost platinum blonde locks are now full of patches of green. The girls had put green dye in her purple shampoo that helps keep blonde hair toned. Because the dye wouldn't be in there long enough for just the shampoo, they put some in the conditioner too.

In shock, she picks up pieces of her hair before letting them drop. Tears fill her eyes as she meets mine in the mirror. The others all burst out laughing, but I just stand there, watching with a blank face.

I remember when I used to be ready to tear down the world whenever she was sad or cried, to find and destroy the reason my love was hurt. Now, I'm the one to make her cry. *How fucked up is that?*

She puts on a brave face, angrily wiping her tears as she gets a brush to comb out her hair then back into a ponytail.

When she's done, she shoves everything into her locker and slams the door shut.

"You girls must be so proud of yourselves," Ellie says, her

voice low with emotion as she tries to hold it together. "Just because I don't need to spend hundreds of dollars to get my hair the way it is, doesn't mean you should sabotage it. It looks pathetic."

"Well, now your hair looks just as trashy as you are," Kayla snarls.

"You know, if you would just leave, all of this would stop," I say. Ellie's gaze flicks over to me. She walks over to us until she's toe to toe with me. I can smell the scent of her body wash— coconut. Fuck, she smells amazing, just like she used to.

"It's about time you understand I'm not going anywhere. You can keep doing these childish pranks, calling me names, laughing at me, but it's pointless. I'm here to better my future and focus on more important things. I do not need to be liked by you. I'm not going anywhere." She juts out her chin before pushing past us.

The girls all yell at her, telling her to leave the school and not come back as she pushes her way out the door and onto the field.

I watch her leave, wondering who the hell this girl is, and what happened to the shy, meek Ellie I knew most of my life. *What happened to her that made her grow a backbone?*

But she just made something clear, and by the sincerity in her voice, I know she's telling the truth. She's not going anywhere, no matter what we do.

So the question is, do we keep doing what we've been doing, or leave it be? Because there is one thing for sure, I won't ever do anything to physically harm Ellie, no matter how much I want her gone. The idea of knowing that I caused her physical harm would kill me.

"Come on." I push past the girls and they follow me. We start heading toward the field, and I see Ellie standing by the entrance from the locker rooms to the field. She's playing with her ponytail, her body shifting from side to side with nervous energy.

"Come on, slut, let's get this over with. We don't want to be near you any more than we have to. Bad enough we already have you for an extra hour," Kayla bitches before shoulder checking past her despite there being enough room for her to walk.

Kayla is best friends with Laura, so she's kind of always around by default. People might think Kayla is my friend, but there is something seriously wrong with her. The way she's obsessed with Chase is weird and it's starting to get worse, ever since going out to the club a few weeks ago.

"Let's welcome the Silver Valley cheer squad," our coach announces over the sound system. The crowd goes crazy, and my belly turns. Cheering is my life. It's an outlet and something I truly love to do. When I'm dancing, I feel free. But with Ellie here, she's all I can think about. The way her body moves, how her ass and tits look in that uniform, is so damn distracting. Mostly because I know what's under there. I've touched and tasted every inch of that body at one point, plenty of times.

We all run out onto the field jumping and waving at the hundreds of people in the stands.

"Alright girls, let's do this!" I cheer as we get in formation. The mash song we're using for this game starts to play and we start our routine. The smile on my face is genuine as I bust my ass, getting every move right. A part of me wants to look over at Ellie and see how she's doing, but I don't. I can't. It would risk me fucking up, so I push it to the back of my mind until we finish.

The crowd goes crazy and we wave, blowing kisses to them before moving to sit on the bench on the sideline. That's when I use the chance to glance over at Ellie. She's talking to her friends. They all have pissed off expressions as they gesture to Ellie's hair. The one with the black hair, Tabitha I think, looks over at me and catches me watching. She narrows her eyes at me, a look that promises something dark to come. I don't like her. She's clearly in love with Ellie, and Ellie is too blind to see it or just doesn't care. I've watched how Tabitha looks at Ellie when Ellie is talking to their other friends in the cafe. The body language when they dance together at parties. Hell, even when Ellie is at work and Tabitha and her friends are there.

It shouldn't send a spark of jealousy through me, but it does. The idea of her with other guys hits me differently than the idea of her with another woman. Ellie had always told me that she's never been attracted to girls in general, but with me, it wasn't about gender, it was *me* she fell in love with.

But who knows if that's changed since high school. Has she had other girlfriends? Has she tried having a unique relationship like she had with us, with other people?

Did we ever mean anything to her at all?

Flipping Tabitha off, I divert my attention to the field. The guys jog out and the first thing my dumbass best friends do is search for Ellie. I can tell when they spot her because their facial expressions change. Brody has a sneer that is way too unattractive for his pretty face. But that's Brody for you, as cuddly as a cactus—except when it comes to Jax. And Ellie once upon a time.

Jax looks from Ellie to Brody. His shoulders drop and a flicker of regret passes across his face before he turns away to get into their huddle.

Chase lingers for a moment as it hits him when he finally notices Ellie's hair, his face falls from this dopey, longing look that doesn't fool me, to this enraged, pissed off one. *Here we fucking go.*

Chase breaks away from the guys and storms over to me. "Why the fuck is her hair green?" he hisses, bending down so that he can be heard over the chatter of the stadium.

"How should I know?" I shrug. "If she wants to look like an ugly tie-dye shirt, who am I to stop her?"

He narrows his eyes at me. "You're full of shit, Rain. There's no way Ellie would do that to her hair of her own free will."

"I don't know what to tell you."

"Why are you all of a sudden denying it? I thought you would be bragging with a smile on your face." He shakes his head. Shit, he's right. Why am I denying it?

*Maybe because you took it a little too far.*

I mean, people threw food at her, this isn't any worse than that. Although, none of that was my doing. That was Brody who started that.

Come to think of it, other than some crude name calling and nasty looks, most of the things we've done to Ellie has been Brody's doing.

Okay, so I'm more bark than bite. Like I said before, I just want her gone.

"Fine, we thought she would look better in green. It's your favorite color. You should be happy." I grin up at him while the other girls giggle. "Why do you care?" I cock a brow.

He looks over in Ellie's direction then back to me. "I don't," he lies. "Just fuck off with the physical shit, that includes her appearance. I said I'd let you do your thing, but you know where I draw my line."

"Yeah, yeah." I roll my eyes and he shakes his head before going to join the guys.

*What has my life become?* Before Ellie came back, I'd been doing amazing—getting decent grades, hanging out with friends, loving cheer. But now, I spend most my time wondering how I'm going to fuck up Ellie's day and what we're going to do to her next. I say I hate the girl and want her gone, yet I've made my whole life about her.

Even so, I need her gone so that my life can go back to normal.

# ELLIE

I've been trying really hard to just let whatever they do roll right off my shoulders like it's no big deal. Call me names, I'll pretend I don't hear it because they are only words. Throw food at me,

I'll take a shower and put on clean clothes. But this? Dying my hair? Just thinking of how much it's going to cost me to fix this mess makes me want to cry.

I know it's just hair, but this looks so God dang awful. There's green splotches throughout it. Thankfully you can't really notice with my hair up in a ponytail.

It's not too late at night, so I call a salon and book an appointment to get this fixed after school tomorrow, but I'm pissed because I have to use my free time that was meant to be spent with Lilly before going to work. With school, work, and now cheer, any free time with my baby girl is important.

Our first dance of the night went perfectly. My smile was true and bright, and I felt so alive out there. With halftime starting, we're about to go up for our last dance of the night.

The squad stands up and moves out to the field while the two teams take their breaks. We're winning and the crowd seems to be in good spirits.

"Hey everyone, how are you doing tonight?" The crowd cheers in response to our coach. I love how involved she is and how she pumps us up. She's a good woman, and I'm very grateful she sees through Rain's crap and lets me be on the team despite Rain's efforts to get me off.

"Our lovely squad here has one more dance for you tonight."

"Before we do that," Kayla says, taking the mic from the coach. Coach gives her a funny look as Kayla continues to talk to the crowd. "We would love to give our newest squad member a warm welcome." Kayla gets behind me, and my body freezes up. Surely she wouldn't do anything to me with everyone in this stadium watching. Shit, everyone has their eyes on me.

Scanning the crowd, I see Theo sitting with some of the other teachers. He has a look of unease and concern contorting his handsome face.

I swallow hard as sweat prickles all over my body.

"But, I don't think she knows the uniform requirement.

That's okay, she's still pretty new. See, we try to all match for each performance. And tonight, we all have our hair down. You don't mind if you put your hair down, do you?" Kayla asks me, a cruel smile taking over her face. When I do nothing, just looking at her with wide panicked eyes, she reaches up and yanks out my ponytail. My hair falls down over my shoulders and back.

"Oh my!" Kayla fake gasps. "Well, looks like she's dyed her hair for the wrong team." The crowd starts to laugh. "Our colors are silver and blue, honey. Not green."

Tears fill my eyes, and I really want to turn and run off this field but I won't give them the satisfaction. "You look like a troll." Kayla looks me over with a mock sense of sympathy.

"Well," Cooper says, coming up behind me, grabbing the mic from Kayla, who tries to fight him over it. "I think she looks sexy in whatever color hair she has." Cooper leans in and whispers in my ear, "I'm going to kiss you now." It is all the warning he gives me before planting his lips on mine. It's not hot and heavy, just a sweet, hard kiss on the lips, to give them a little show. "I just want to say how proud of my girlfriend I am, and you ladies are kicking ass tonight. Keep it up."

Looking into the crowd, I see my friends and Theo cheering with the crowd, but none of them look happy about the little show Kayla just put on.

"We'll talk after the game," Cooper says before pecking a kiss on my cheek and handing the mic back to the coach.

"That's enough out of you, Kayla. Pull something like that again, and I will be replacing you next. Don't force my hand. This is college, not high school, and I don't put up with catty bullshit like this."

Okay, I want to hug that woman. She doesn't take crap from these bullies, and I admire her for it.

Kayla just huffs and moves into formation.

I try extra hard not to mess up this next dance because all I can think about is everyone watching me, all their eyes looking and judging me. But thankfully, we make it through the song, and the funny thing is, the person who messes up is Kayla. She trips over her own feet and face plants before brushing it off and acting like nothing happened. But I see her red cheeks. She's embarrassed. *Good, not such a nice feeling, is it?*

"You okay?" Lexie asks me, pulling me into a hug when the game is over. Everyone starts to file out of the stadium, and I catch Theo's eyes on his way down the stairs. We give each other a look of understanding. I know he wants to come over here and pull me into his arms and tell me everything is going to be okay, but he can't. I can tell it's killing him. That's all I want right now too, to feel safe in his arms.

"Not really." I give her a tired smile. "But it's over with. I'll have this fixed tomorrow like it didn't happen. Hopefully, not too many people took photos." I force a laugh, trying to brush it off. "I can tell you that my wallet won't be too happy about this," I groan. "This is going to cost me a few hundred to get a color corrector and dye to get it back to the way it looked."

"Those bitches should be forced to pay for it. What happened anyways?" Val asks.

"I thought it was kind of odd that they all rushed to the changing rooms after practice without cooling down, but I just thought they wanted extra time to get ready for the game and relax. Nope, they were putting dye in my purple shampoo and conditioner bottles. Because the soap also rinses out purple, I didn't realize anything was wrong. That is, until I took the towel off my head and saw my hair." I force another smile.

"Seriously, what are they, thirteen? What happened to just avoiding someone you don't like as if they are the plague and be a fucking adult? Who has time for this shit?" Tabitha says. She's clearly upset for me. I put my hand on her shoulder, giving it a little squeeze. She smiles up at me.

"It's mostly Kayla and Laura. Rain likes to use her words, but she gets her little minions to do the dirty work," I sigh.

We part ways, and I see Cooper waiting for me at my car.

"Are you okay?" he asks, pulling me into a hug. I close my eyes and relax into my best friend's arms.

"Better now that I have all you guys here for me," I mutter.

"I thought us dating would help, but clearly it's not going to stop the girls."

"It's done enough and I can't begin to thank you," I say, pulling back to look at him.

He gives me a cheeky grin. "It's honestly not that hard. You're fun to be around, beautiful, and you smell good, too."

"I do not," I laugh.

"Do too, like coconuts."

Coconut is my favorite scent. I love anything that tastes or smells like it.

"Guess it's better than smelling like BO," I grin.

"Or roses."

"Roses?" I ask with amused curiosity.

"Yeah. Never liked the smell," he shrugs.

Shaking my head, we say goodbye. I promise to keep him updated and he will check on me tomorrow at school.

I'm ready to break down after everything. I hate all the attention that was on me tonight. Being on the cheer squad is a big step out of my comfort zone, and what happened would have set me back if I didn't have amazing people at my side.

Normally, Theo watches Lilly for me while I'm at practice but he wanted to be there for my first game, and teachers attend games all the time, so he saw this as a perfect opportunity to watch me dance. He had asked his mom to watch the kids, and she was more than happy to do it. I really like his mother. She reminds me of mine. Little did we know it would turn out this way. At least I wasn't the one to mess up the routine and add to my humiliation.

When I get out of my car, Theo is waiting on the steps outside our apartment.

"Hey," he says, saying nothing else as he pulls me into his

arms. I sigh as I melt into his embrace. I always feel better with him around.

"Hi," I say, pulling back a little to look up into his eyes. "Guess you didn't think you would end up dating a troll."

His eyes are filled with pure fury. "What they did was messed up," he growls. I shiver and not because it's cold. I like protective Theo. It adds to his sexy factor.

"I know. But, what's done is done. I just hate that I have to go and spend a ton of money I didn't budget for," I sigh.

"Let me pay," he says.

My eyes widen and I shake my head. "No. I won't use you for money. You already do enough for me. I don't want you to think I'm some kind of gold digger."

"You aren't using me. I'm offering. And you're far from a gold digger," he chuckles.

"It's not funny." I try not to smile.

"Ellie, you are one of the most hard working and selfless people I know. You are an amazing girlfriend and an even better mother. I just want to help the woman I love. I don't like what they are doing to you. I wish I could say something," he says.

"It's too much to ask for." I shake my head. "And I won't let them win. I'll get my hair fixed and just make sure not to keep any of my stuff accessible to them. Maybe I'll keep it in my car, get a better lock, or just wait until I get home to shower."

"You shouldn't have to do that," he points out.

"No, but what am I going to do? Go to the dean and say some girls pulled a stupid prank? The name calling and weird looks have pretty much stopped since I started fake dating Cooper. It's just these catty girls I have to worry about now. They're not too happy that I'm on the team."

"Well, they should be grateful. I saw you out there, sweetheart. You were really amazing." He beams down at me.

"Really?" I smile back.

"Heck yes! The way you move, I had to make sure I wasn't

paying too close attention and have the other teachers think I'm perving."

That makes me giggle. "I'm just glad that part of the night went well."

"So, you're pretty flexible, huh?" His eyes turn from playful to hungry.

My breath catches and my body flushes. "Yeah, I can bend in ways most people can't." It comes out breathier than I intended. "If your mom doesn't mind watching the kids a little longer, I can show you."

Theo growls again, and fuck, my lady bits sure do enjoy that sound. He picks me up and I wrap my legs around him with a giggle, biting my lip when I feel his hard length against my core.

We head up to his place, and I follow through with showing him just how flexible I am before having to part ways for the night.

I go to bed with a smile on my face and positive thoughts that just because I had something unfortunate happen to me, I won't lose any sleep over it.

## Chapter Twenty-One

### CHASE

"WAIT UP!" I call out to Rain when I spot her getting out of her car as I shut off the engine to my bike. Taking my helmet off, I shake out my sweaty hair, and am thankful for the slight breeze to cool me down. It might be November but it's fucking hot outside today.

She stops and looks over her shoulder. When she sees me, she rolls her eyes but waits for me to catch up.

"So, you're really doing this?" she asks as I reach her side.

"Yup." I beam at her, just slightly out of breath.

"Do you even like kids?" She cocks a brow, putting her hand on her hip.

"They can't be that bad. We volunteer for a week, it looks good on our job applications and school record. It's either this or helping out at the retirement home. And as much as I respect my elders, I don't want to be washing out bedpans or yelling all the time because the ones that are hard of hearing can't understand me. Also, they kinda smell funny." I wrinkle my nose. "The one that my 'nana' lives in always smells like death. Like literally, someone has always *just* died when I go to visit."

"Maybe you're just bad luck," Rain smirks.

I grin at her while flipping her off. She leans forward and

bites my finger. "Ouch," I hiss, rubbing the bite mark, but she just giggles throwing me a cocky smirk. "You really are a bitch sometimes."

"Only to you." She bats her eyes.

"And Ellie." I narrow mine. Her smile drops and her face goes blank.

"Whatever, she deserved it," Rain mutters as she turns and heads toward the building that the university's daycare is located in.

"We're gonna have a blast. Me and you, besties hanging out. We're like two balls in a banana hammock," I say, throwing my arm over her shoulder.

"You have issues," she says, shaking her head with a laugh.

"But you looooove me anyways," I sing-song back at her.

"Sure..." She rolls her eyes.

"And about Ellie, I know we all want her gone and shit, but this is a big school. Can't we just move on with our lives? You only have to see her, like, what? Two times a week and at games, right?" I've always loved football, but I love practices even more now that she's joined the cheer team. Although, it's really hard to focus when she's prancing around in her skin tight uniform. All I can think about is ripping her shirt off and burying my face in her round tits.

"Hello!" Rain says, waving her hand in front of my face.

"Sorry, spaced out there for a moment, what did you say?" I blink.

She huffs, sounding annoyed with me. "I said, it's not that simple. She's not only at cheer, she also works at the club we always go to, and she and her friends have started going to the same parties as us. She's everywhere!"

"Well, that first party was our fault. We could have gone to any one of the twenty other parties going on that night. And I think Brody is picking parties that he knows she might be at just so he can fuck with her." I shrug as we keep walking.

"Still. Like I said, she's everywhere."

Not gonna lie, I like it. This school is so big that I probably would never get to see her if she wasn't on the team or working at a place we frequent.

"Anyways, you didn't answer me, do you even like kids?"

"I mean, they're okay. Some are really fucking annoying. It depends on the kid, too. Some are cool and just play with their toys, while some are like my little cousin, Bentley. He reminds me of that character, Stewart from MAD TV. For every little thing he does, he needs your attention and be all 'look what I can do'. Then all he does is make some spazzy move like this," I say, contouring my body weirdly. Rain bursts out laughing.

"Well, you might get some kids like that here. You're just going to have to deal with it and be nice."

"I'm the nicest person I fucking know, baby." I grin, holding out my arms wide.

"And you can't swear, you dummy," she says, shaking her head.

"God, that's going to be hard. Like, every second word out of my mouth is 'fuck'. Maybe I should have picked the retirement home. At least if I'm quiet enough, they wouldn't be able to hear it."

We get to the daycare and sounds of children screaming and playing make their way through the door.

"Great," I mutter. "I'm probably gonna leave here with a major migraine."

"Quit your whining. You sound almost as bad as they do," Rain laughs. "If you can handle the bass at a party and the sounds of the crowd during games, then you can do this. We're only here for an hour anyways," Rain says, knocking on the door.

A lady comes out with a bright smile. "Hello," she greets us. "You two must be our student volunteers."

"Hi." Rain shakes her hand. "I'm Rain Sawyer."

"Chase River." I take her hand with a light shake.

"I'm Miss Macy, the daycare director. Please come in. I'll explain and go over a few things."

She opens the door wide enough to let us in before closing and locking it behind us.

"We are so excited to have you here for the next week. The kids love having visitors." She brings us over to some little chairs against the wall. "Please have a seat."

Rain sits down, and I look at my chair for an extra second, hoping my ass doesn't break it. *It looks like it's meant for an elf or something.* Or, well, I guess small children. I'm not built like a bodybuilder but I do have some muscle to me, and I don't think these are meant for people as big as me. But I sit anyway, making sure not to put all my weight on it.

"Basically, all you have to do is play with the kids and help them out if they need anything. We still have our trained workers around if you need any help and aren't sure what to do. Pretty much, you get to be a kid again for a few days," she smiles brightly.

That doesn't sound too bad.

She goes over the rules—when we should be getting one of the workers to do something and when we are able to do it ourselves, the safety precautions, and any health issues certain children have. We're not allowed to know any personal information except for their name and age.

"Children, can I get your attention please?" Miss Macy calls out to the room. One by one, kids stop what they are doing and look over at us. "We have two very special guests this week that will be around to hang out with you all. This is Rain and Chase. Please be sure to be nice and respectful, okay?"

As soon as Miss Macy is done, the kids go back to doing whatever they were doing before as if we aren't here.

"Feel free to mingle with the children. Today, we can just meet and greet. Tomorrow, I'll get you two to help with a few activities," she says before leaving us standing in the middle of the room.

"Give us those." The voice of a little boy has me looking over at the corner of the room where two boys and a little girl are. "They are cars. Cars are for boys," the little brown-haired boy, who is much bigger than the girl, says. I grab a mini candy cane out of my pocket, unwrap the end, pop it into my mouth, and watch the interaction. The little boy goes to grab the car from the little, blonde girl. I'm about to step in because like hell if I'm going to just sit and watch him bully a little girl, but she opens her mouth which stops me in my tracks.

"I play first!" She stomps her foot, holding her ground. "You have later."

"I want it now. Cars are not for girls," the little boy goes to take it again, but the little girl holds it to her chest.

"Are too! I play cars with Toby." I don't know who this Toby kid is, but she's right. Cars are cars. They're not meant for any specific gender. "Me play, you go," she says, turning her back to the boys. She takes the two cars in her hand and makes them drive up and down a play slide, ignoring the boys completely. The boys go to grab it again, and that's when I decide it's time to step in.

"Hey, little dudes. She had the cars first," I say, crouching down to their level. "You can have them when she's done, okay?"

"But she's a girl! Cars are for boys." *Really, dude, what are your parents teaching you?*

"That's not true," Rain says, stepping around the kids to take a seat at the reading nook on the window sill. "I'm a girl and I used to play with cars all the time with my best friends. They are guys, and we all played together."

"Really?" the other little boy with the black hair asks.

"Yup. Boys and girls can play with any toys. If you want to play with dolls, go for it. If she wants to play with cars and dinosaurs, that's cool too."

"Oh," he says, looking at the little girl then back to us. "Fine," he says, then looks at his friend. "Let's play with the sand." The two kids take off, and I take a seat by Rain at her feet on the floor.

I watch the little girl play, a big smile on her face as she makes the little car noises. After a few minutes, she notices us still there. "You play with me?" she asks, holding up one of the cars. I grin, taking the red car.

"I'd love to."

She looks at Rain. "You too?" she asks, handing out a yellow car to Rain.

"Sounds like fun," Rain smiles, taking the car. We all sit down and play for a while.

"We forgot to ask your name," Rain says when the little girl switches cars with her.

"I Lilly," she beams. "I three."

"Lilly. I love that name." Rain smiles back.

"What's your name?" she asks, cocking her head to the side.

"I'm Rain."

Lilly shakes her head, her little blonde curls bouncing with the movement. "No, you're Fire." Lilly plays with Rain's hair. Rain watches as Lilly becomes fascinated with her hair, fluffing it up. Rain laughs and Lilly smiles back.

"Who are you?" Lilly asks. Guess she was one of the kids that weren't paying attention. But she's three, so I won't hold it against her.

"I'm Chase," I grin.

"Ace," she nods, and I chuckle at my new name. She looks at the candy cane in my mouth. A smile lights up her face. "I like candy cane too!"

"You do?"

"I have one?" she asks, giving me bright blue puppy-dog eyes.

Looking around I see if anyone is watching, I reach into my pocket and grab another one. Taking the wrapper off, I offer it to her. I don't think I should be giving it to her, but a little candy won't hurt, and I'll watch her. Plus, look at her, she's friggin' adorable.

"Thank you," she says, popping it into her mouth then goes back to playing. She does this little happy dance while humming and enjoying her candy.

I look over at Rain, and she is smiling from ear to ear. "I like her," she whispers.

"Me too. Favorite kid here." I grin back.

Rain laughs. "We haven't even met most of them."

I shrug. "I don't care if we do or not. I call dibs on her this week. She seems like a good kid, and she's pretty cool for a three year old."

"You can't just call dibs on a kid," Rain scoffs. "Plus, I want to hang out with her too. Like you said, she's cool."

"Are we really arguing over who gets to be besties with a toddler?" I laugh.

"You were right, kids can be annoying as heck. If we stick with this one, we will have an easy week."

Rain and I stick with Lilly for the rest of the hour. No other kids seem to care that we're here, and no one tries to play with us, but I'm okay with that. We play tea party while Lilly talks all about this stuffed dog she sleeps with every night. She says it's her best friend, and that Toby kid she mentioned earlier.

When snack time rolls around, even Rain and I get one and I get all excited. *Like I'd turn down chocolate pudding.* "Uh oh," Lilly says, looking at her hair that somehow got into her pudding cup.

"That's okay. Just give me a second, and we will get that cleaned up," Rain says, getting up and going over to the teacher. The teacher hands her a few things before she comes back over. "Here," Rain says, taking a wipe out of the baby wipe bag. She pulls the hair out of the pudding and cleans it off the best she can. "Miss Macy gave me a hair tie to pull your hair back. Is it okay if I put it in a ponytail so it's not in the way?"

Lilly nods and puts her pudding down. Rain smiles and

gathers up Lilly's hair, putting it up and out of the way. Something on Lilly's neck catches my attention. She has a little brown birthmark behind her left ear. My hand automatically covers the one that looks way too similar to hers but mine is behind my right ear. Talk about a freaky coincidence.

"There you go," Rain says.

"Thank you, Fire," Lilly says before digging back into her pudding. She gets most of it on her face, but when she grins at me, she has chocolate covered teeth. I burst out laughing and Lilly follows into a fit of musical giggles with Rain right behind her.

After how today went, I'm glad I didn't go hang out with the old people. Little people are more fun.

## Chapter Twenty-Two

### BRODY

"DUDE, you have no idea how excited I am to have the next week off," Chase says, flopping down on the couch and putting his feet up on my lap, almost knocking the Xbox controller out of my hands. "Rub my feet for me, will you? It's been a long week running after kids."

Ignoring him, I focus on the game, getting my last two kills in and winning the game. "Fuck, yes!" I shout, fist pumping the air with one arm then turn to Jax who has a grin on his plump, pink lips. "Suck on that, baby. I won three games in a row."

"We're on the same team," he chuckles. My eyes trace the curves of his lips and before I know what I'm doing, I pull him into a kiss. It's slow and sweet which coaxes a moan out of him.

"Now, now, let's not suck on that right here for my virgin eyes. You were about to rub my feet. You can rub something *of his* later." Chase's voice is filled with amusement as he wiggles his toes.

"Fuck off. There's nothing virgin about you," I laugh, pushing his feet off me with a hard shove, making his whole body go with them.

"Ouch!" Chase says, pouting as he gets off the floor. "Fine."

He turns to Rain who comes out of our bathroom dressed in her cheer uniform. "Rain, come rub my feet. Please, bestie? I'll love you forever." He gets on his knees and raises his hands in a praying position.

"I'm not touching your crusty feet even if you paid me a million dollars," Rain says laughing as she flicks him on the forehead. "Plus, you're gonna love me until the day you die anyways. No other woman would put up with your crazy ass."

There was one woman who put up with all of us. But now, she's the enemy. Life works out wonderfully. *Not.*

"Shut this shit off," Rain says, gesturing to the TV. "The game starts in an hour. It's the Thanksgiving game, and you know it's going to be crazy."

She's right. There are two things this town goes nuts for. Thanksgiving and football. Add them together and it's almost as bad as the Superbowl.

"You girls ready? How is that new routine coming along?" Jax asks, getting up from the couch and stretching. His shirt rides up, showing a small patch of dark hair that leads down to a place I sure do love to explore.

"Unfortunately, it's going just fine," Rain scowls.

"Why would you be pissed about that?" Chase asks, grabbing his duffle bag full of football gear from the closet. "I thought you wanted to do well."

"We do," Rain says. "But we were hoping that a quick change in routine would fuck Ellie up. But nope, she picked it up just as fast as the others."

"Maybe you should focus more on cheer and less on messing with Ellie," Jax says.

Both mine and Rain's heads turn in his direction.

"What?" he shrugs, his face not giving anything away. "I know you want to bring her down and get her gone, but is it worth it if it risks your teams?"

"He has a point," Chase says.

"Oh, shut up," I scoff. "You would love it if we just left her alone and pretended she didn't fuck us over, betraying us."

"I was over the petty bullshit you two have been doing to her since the first stunt. It's not who I am. I don't like making people cry, or fucking with their lives. What she did was pretty fucking shitty and it hurt like hell. But, are you really going to let it take over your whole life?"

"So what, you're taking her side now?" I growl, my anger rising as I hear him defend her.

"No. I'm on your side, always," Chase defends. "But we also had lives before she came back, pretty good ones. Now, all you two do is find ways to fuck with Ellie. For people who say they hate her, you're pretty obsessed with her." He turns around, grabs his bike helmet off the entrance table, and storms out of the apartment, slamming the door shut behind him.

"Do you feel the same way?" I ask, turning to Jax, irritated with this whole conversation.

"I'm with you on whatever you want to do," he says, his face softening, pulling me into a hug. I grind my teeth, knowing he wants to say something similar to what Chase did, but keeps quiet. I know what Rain and I have been doing is not really his thing. Jax is quiet, and keeps to himself when it comes to anyone outside our group. He doesn't like confrontation but he's been putting up with all of this because he loves me and doesn't want to see me mad.

But I'm only doing what needs to be done. I hope they both see that once we get rid of Ellie, life will go back to normal and everything will be fine again.

*Or you're just lying to yourself, telling your heart anything it needs to hear to keep from accepting the knowledge that Ellie has never left you. She's a part of your soul and after coming back, it just solidified that feeling.*

Jax, Rain, and I grab our things and head down to my car. The drive to the football field is quiet. Rain plays music to drown out the thoughts that we know, for sure, are running through all of our minds.

When we pull up to the parking lot, the place is packed. Thank God for student parking or we wouldn't have a place to park.

"See you after the game," Rain says before taking off to the girls' locker room.

"Come on," Jax says, giving me a squeeze on the shoulder. "Forget about all that, and let's just focus on beating the other team's ass." He grins. His smile alone helps melt away my shitty mood.

"Alright, let's go." I clap him on the back before we break apart, hands brushing as we walk. I want to grab hold of him, thread my fingers through his, and kiss the back of his hand.

"Hey, Brody!" some guys cheer as we make our way into the locker room. "Sup, Jax," others greet. We give a few 'heys' and head nods, agreeing with how we'll take another win as we gear up.

I love home games. Being on our own turf always gives me an extra rush when we win. We wait to be announced, my adrenaline spiking as I get my mind set focused on the game. Nothing else matters at this moment, only winning.

But when they call out for our team, we burst through that banner, jog out onto the field, the first thing I do is look for her. She's standing on the sidelines, cheering with the rest of the squad. She looks happy, her hair back to regular blonde from that God awful green. I thought Rain would have been bragging about that, but she hadn't said anything when I asked her about it. The hair only lasted a day before she got it fixed and it was like nothing happened.

Ellie's eyes follow in my direction, her face lighting up. For a second, I think she's watching me, but then Cooper jogs ahead of me, her eyes following him. I feel like an idiot for thinking she was looking at me. Of course she's not. She hates me. Thinks I'm a fucking monster. Good, I want her to.

*Lies. All lies.*

I scowl as I watch Cooper run over to Ellie and scoop her up into a hug. She laughs, a full, toothy kind of laugh as he spins her around before kissing her quickly and running over to our coach.

Seeing her with someone else shouldn't make me want to go over there and clock him, but it does.

Shaking off the treacherous feelings, I join the others and get this game started.

I force my attention on the game and not on the blonde beauty who haunts my dreams.

We make it through the first half of the game on top. We're up by ten. Alright, I almost got tackled by some meathead but managed to dodge him, sending him face first into the ground. The team made sure I was wide open and watching that ball sail through the air was a beautiful sight.

We spend halftime in the locker room while the cheer-leaders do their thing before heading back to the bench.

I brush my sweaty hair out of my face then squirt some cold water from my bottle over my head before I have to put that stuffy helmet back on. Some water slides down my back and fuck, the cool liquid on my skin feels amazing.

Shaking out my wet hair, water droplets hit Jax in the face by accident. He laughs, grabbing the bottle from me and wraps his lips around the tip of it. He doesn't look away as he gulps down big mouthfuls of water. I watch his throat bob with every swallow and my dick twitches, wishing it was something else that he was swallowing. I force myself to look away, not needing a fucking boner in these skin tight pants.

Coach tells us it's going to be a minute, saying something about an issue the other team is having. Grabbing a football from the ball bag next to the bench, I head over to Jax. I have too much energy to sit still, and Jax can see it. We start to toss the ball back and forth, but my eyes keep drifting to Ellie standing as she talks to her coach. My gaze slowly trails up her long toned legs, over her tight ass, and linger on her tits as she turns to face in my direction with a smile.

*Look at her all happy and shit.* My hand flexes and I find myself filling with the urge to toss the football at Ellie, wiping that grin off her face.

But Chase would have a cow if I did something to her that caused bodily harm, and honestly, the idea of hurting her like that doesn't sit well with me.

*But, no one said I couldn't do anything to Cooper.* When he steps into view, just behind Jax, I see him take a drink from his water bottle. Tossing the ball to Jax, I purposely miss him, throwing it with a little too much force in Cooper's direction.

The ball goes flying through the air and hits him right in his face. The bottle explodes, water splashing all over him and sending it to the ground.

"What the fuck?!" Cooper roars, his hands flying to his nose. *Shit.* Blood starts to seep through his fingers. "You broke my fucking nose!"

"Sorry. I missed," I grunt.

"You're the fucking quarterback! You don't miss throwing a ball to someone who's five feet away," Ellie snaps after rushing over to Cooper's side. Of course she would come over here to baby him.

"It's just a little blood. He's gonna be fine."

"Fine?! You broke his nose," Ellie says. She's livid, and if looks could kill, I'd be on fire right now. She grabs one of the towels from the bench, holding it to Cooper's nose. Cooper hisses and Ellie cringes. "Sorry," she says sweetly, making me swell with jealousy I don't want or need.

"You have nothing to be sorry about," he mumbles through the towel giving her a gentle look, but then turns to me. "I get it. You don't like me. I'm dating your ex, whom you have some fucked up obsession with and want to get revenge for something that happened when you were in fucking high school. But I'm also your teammate and you need to take your petty shit and save it for another time. Now I'm out of the game and if we lose, it's on you."

Ellie shoots me one last death glare before she and Cooper leave. The coach starts to lose his shit at me, but that's nothing new. This dickhead always likes to blame me for anything that goes wrong despite being the one who's responsible for every fucking win.

Gritting my teeth, I let him bitch me out before it's time to go finish the game. "Shitty that he broke his nose, but I thought it was funny," Chase says, grinning, before going over to the huddle.

Jax just gives me a half smile and a shrug before joining him.

Knowing that Cooper is being taken care of by Ellie, that she's probably all over him, babying him, and loving up on him is causing me to be so distracted that we end up losing the fucking game. The team isn't happy with me and I'm fucking pissed off at myself.

Jax is right. No more shit when it involves football or cheer. It's not worth fucking up our wins. We still have a few more games before the season is over and I intend to win every last one. This is my last year on the team and I plan to go out with a fucking bang.

Looks like I'll have to find other ways to get rid of Ellie.

———

"Fuck, this tastes like heaven," Chase moans around a mouth full of fries, stuffing more in.

"Dude, breathe and slow down before you choke," Rain laughs.

We're all having supper at Bill's Diner in Spring Meadows, the next town over. We might have one of the best and biggest universities in the country, but the town of Silver Valley only has a grocery store, schools, a few convenience stores, and that's about it. The good thing is that Spring Meadows is only a fifteen minute drive.

We decided to go see *The Conjuring: The Devil Made Me Do It* before we all go to our parents' houses for Thanksgiving tomorrow. We've spent most of the break just relaxing at home playing video games.

I have nothing special planned except to go home and make sure my dad doesn't drink himself into an early grave.

We're going to a party tomorrow night after supper then enjoying the last free weekend before it's back to school on Monday. It's been nice not having to see Ellie everywhere I look and having my mind clear of her. Well, at least when I'm a half pint in of Jack Daniels it is.

"I think it's sexy that you can eat all that and still look as good as you do," Kayla purrs, stroking Chase's arm. Chase looks at her with a scowl, and I snort a laugh because he looks fucking ridiculous with his cheeks full of food like a chipmunk.

He shrugs her off and Kayla frowns.

"Why did you bring dumb and dumber with you?" I ask Rain, leaning back in my chair. Chase chokes on his food before grabbing his drink to wash it down. Jax snorts a laugh next to me.

"Excuse you," Laura gapes at me as Kayla glares. "You can't talk to us like that."

"I'm a Silver fucking Knight. I can do what ever the fuck I want to do. Seeing how Ellie is an outcast at this school, do you really want to be next on my list?"

Laura says nothing, shrinking back into her seat.

"Brody, you don't have to be such an ass all the time," Rain sighs.

"Yes he does," Chase chuckles. "He's Brody, Asshole Supreme. King of the Asses. Fitting, seeing how he is an ass man." Chase wiggles his eyebrows. I shoot a glower at him, seeing Jax's body tense up out of the corner of my eye.

"Well, he doesn't have to be so rude to us. I'm friends with

Rain and Laura is her girlfriend. You should treat us with a little more respect, " Kayla says.

Rain's eyes go wide as she looks at Kayla. "Laura is not my girlfriend. We're friends and fuck buddies, that's it."

I almost feel bad for Laura when her face turns red and her body slumps. Rain's words hurt her, but what does she expect? Rain makes it clear all the time that that's all they will ever be. She's in love with Rain, and Rain needs to cut her loose before she becomes more trouble than she's worth. Poor Chase already has his own little stalker by default.

We sit and chat about some upcoming assignments and the girls gossip about people I don't care enough about to learn their names. I order myself some onion rings and a smoothie when I hear the bell over the door chime.

The place has been pretty dead tonight, most people already home with their families for tomorrow, so when it opens, I have the urge to look. And when I do, I wish I didn't.

Ellie walks in the door looking good with her hair in a high ponytail, light make-up on, and a hoodie over some leggings. Very casual.

At first, I think she's here with Cooper but when no one else follows her in and she takes a seat at the table by herself, I just assume she's here for something to eat.

The rest of table notices she's here as well, but she doesn't notice us.

"What the fuck is she doing here?" Laura sneers as she leans into Rain in a possessive way.

"Eating like everyone else," Chase says, cocking a brow. Laura just makes a stink eye at him and goes back to watching her.

A few minutes later, she orders a drink and some fries. The door dings again and in walks my Sociology professor, Mr. Munro.

Our old professor, Mr. White, was a racist and a homophobe. I was happy to be rid of him when he got sick and Mr.

Munro replaced him. He's a little nerdy and young, but he's kinda cool. He makes learning fun, and I no longer have the urge to fall asleep during that class.

I'm about to say hi but stop when I see him looking around. When his gaze lands on Ellie, his face breaks out into a huge smile. Ellie gets up from the table and gives him a hug before he joins her at her table.

"Why is our professor having lunch with Ellie?" Chase growls next to me. Chill dude, your jealousy is showing.

*Like yours is much better.*

Even though he's not fighting me on what we've been doing to Ellie, I know he hates it and he's clearly still in love with her.

*And you're not?*

"She's probably fucking him and cheating on Cooper. He deserves so much better than that slutty trash," Kayla snipes. "Also, that man is way too hot for her."

*What the fuck does that mean?*

"Probably doing it for a better grade," Laura adds.

"She's not in his class," I say, at least, not the one I'm in. And I know because I made it my job to know what classes she is in. I might not fuck around like Chase and Rain, but I do know how to flirt and it can get me far when I need information.

"Still. He's like what, forty? He shouldn't be hanging out with twenty-two year old girls," Chase huffs.

"What do you care?" Rain asks, her lip twitching.

"I don't!" he snaps.

Rain just smirks as she drinks her milkshake.

Taking my phone out of my pocket, I discreetly take a few photos of the two. You never know when you're going to need blackmail material. She might need a reminder to keep her mouth shut about what she saw at the Halloween party. I don't trust that she won't say shit. *Why wouldn't she?* She has every reason to tell—not that people will believe *her* over *us*, but it's not something we want floating around. Maybe I'll show it to

Cooper, get the idea that Ellie is cheating on him in his head, and maybe he will break up with her, leaving her heart broken like she should be. It's what she deserves.

As for Mr. Munro, I officially hate him. I don't care how nice he is, how good of a teacher he is, he's now the enemy. Side with her, you're against us.

## ELLIE

"Thank you so much for having us over," I say as we sit around a table in the middle of Theo's parents' restaurant. They invited us to Thanksgiving dinner. I'm sad that I can't spend it with my parents, but it would cost way too much and this break isn't as long as the Christmas one. When I called them last night to catch up, I realized that they have no idea about what's going on with Rain and the guys. If they did, they would probably try to get me to move back to their place or something.

I'm not going anywhere. I love school, my friends are amazing, and I have the sweetest man standing by my side. As long as I have that, Rain and the guys can go fuck themselves.

"We are so glad to have you and Lilly here," Theo's mother beams. "You two are family now."

"Mom," Theo groans.

"No, it's okay." I smile at Theo, placing my hand over his. "I like the sound of that."

"You do?" he asks, perking up.

"I do. That is, if you feel the same way," I say, feeling a little insecure about how quickly I came to feel like this. Plus, I feel bad putting him on the spot like that.

"Toby, you, and Lilly are my whole world. You are my family," he says softly, bringing my hand up to his lips and kissing the back of it. I swoon like I'm in a historical romance novel or something. My pulse skips a beat and my belly fills with butterflies at the way he's looking at me. It's like I'm the only woman in the world worth his time. Like a man in love. I've never felt so adored in my life.

"I love you," I say, my words barely a whisper.

"I love you more," he says, leaning in and kissing me.

"Ewww," Lilly says. "Mommy's kissing Mr. Theo!"

"Ewwww! Your mommy is kissing my daddy," Toby says. They both look at each other. "Ewww," they say at the same time, bursting out into fits of giggles.

The whole table joins in as we sit to eat the amazing food. By the end of the night, I've smiled and laughed so much that I have completely forgotten about everything bad going on in my life because there's so much good to cancel it out, even if it's just for tonight.

"Did you do something with your hair?" Theo's mom asks. "It's a little darker blonde than normal."

"Ah, yeah," I say, looking at Theo. His mouth is in a thin line as he tries to hold back his anger on the topic. "I wanted to change things up," I lie, forcing a smile.

"I think it looks beautiful," she smiles.

I hope so, it cost me around $500 with tip. Thankfully, I only had to go around with the troll-like hair for a day. The girls and Cooper came with me to get it fixed, but I had some weird looks from a lot of people on campus.

When Lilly saw it, she asked me if I was trying to look like Cosmo from *Fairly Odd Parents*, and said she wanted to change her hair to be pink so she can be Wanda. I laughed at that, making the crappy day just a little brighter. But she was not a happy toddler when I said no to pink hair, and we compromised on just the tips with wash-out kid's dye.

"Thank you," I say with a smile. "And thank you again for having us," I look over to see Lilly and Toby asleep in one of the booths, "but I think it's about time we get going home."

"Of course." She laughs looking at the sight of the little ones. "Let me get some leftovers done up for you to take home."

"It's crazy that even after all the meals we delivered today, you still have enough to give to us after our own supper."

Theo's mom cooks a Thanksgiving meal for people who can't afford much. Everyone deserves to have a home-cooked meal for the holidays. She does it for Christmas as well.

When I heard this, I jumped at the chance to help her. It makes all the hard work worth it to see the smile on everyone's faces.

"I always make sure to make extra. Perks of having my own restaurant," she laughs, heading back into the kitchen.

We get the kids loaded in the car, and his mother brings the food out to us. We thank her again before saying goodbye and driving home.

"This break has been a lot of fun," Theo says as he drives.

"It has. It was nice to go out, just me and you." And my ex's in the back corner. I saw them as I was coming into the restaurant and forced myself not to pay them any mind. I also didn't tell Theo when he didn't notice. It didn't take long before I forgot all about them and just got lost in the attention of my sexy boyfriend and his soulful eyes.

"I just wish we could act like ourselves and not have to focus on keeping things friendly," he sighs.

"I know, but other than being out in public, we have it pretty good. Lots of perks for being neighbors." I wiggle my eyebrows, and he looks away from the road for a moment, giving me bedroom eyes, making my joking mood turn to something more than playful.

"Sleepover at my place tonight," he says, looking back at the road. I shiver at the sound of his deep and husky voice. Clenching my thighs together, I try to focus on answering him and not the throbbing between my legs.

"Okay," I whimper.

"There's something else I want for dessert, and I'll give you a hint, it's not the leftover pumpkin pie," he growls. Fuck, my cheeks flush as my panties flood. Even if he did want the pie, I'd cover myself in whipped cream and become the pie if that's what it took.

I've never wanted to get home as fast as I do right now. I know what I'm thankful for on this bountiful day, and that's my hot as hell boyfriend's very talented mouth, hands, and cock.

# Chapter Twenty-Three

## CHASE

"FUCK," I hiss with a cringe, using a wet paper towel to clean this stupid nose ring. Well, at least I try to. It's so swollen and red. *Fuck, it hurts like a bitch.*

When a group of drunk girls tell you that you would look totally hot and sexy with a nose ring and they bring out a fucking needle—that they pulled out of God knows where— don't let your equally-as-drunk ass let them pierce it at a house party in a basement.

The guys wasted no time giving me a hard time about it. They both laughed when they took one look at my reddened nose, and then proceeded to call me an idiot.

I was going to take it out, but Rain told me it's infected, and that if I take it out before it's cleared up, the infection would close over and my nose would get worse. I don't know if she was serious or just fucking with me, but I'm not taking any chances.

The most annoying thing about it is that the stud in my nose isn't even a nose ring, it's a fucking earring.

"Ugh," I sigh, slamming my hands down on the counter and leaning in closer to examine it. *Guess it's good for now.* I throw out the dirty paper towel and wash my hands before leaving the bathroom. Just as I open the door and step out, I bump into someone.

"Sorry," I grunt, grabbing a hold of the person's shoulders to steady them. Looking down, I see the person I stumbled upon is the girl who has taken up residency in my mind, body, and soul. "Ellie," I breathe.

She looks up at me, shocked. Her pink lips part as she sucks in a little breath, her bright blue eyes widening in surprise. My heart starts beating faster knowing that I'm touching her. My hands are on her bare shoulders, the spaghetti strap of her dress just a few millimeters from my thumbs.

"Chase," she says, her voice oh so low. It's as if we're caught in this time warp, neither of us wanting to move or speak, we're both just consumed by the other's presence. Then she blinks, her eyes clearing of whatever shocked state she was in, before shaking her head and stepping back.

"Sorry about that," I say, clearing my throat and hoping like hell she doesn't look down and notice the massive hard on I have. I'm sure my sweatpants aren't doing a good job at hiding it, either, but I don't want to adjust myself and draw attention to it. I also don't want to do nothing and have her think that I'm some kind of perv.

"That's okay. I wasn't looking where I was going," she huffs out a laugh, holding up her phone. "Was a little distracted by a photo Val sent. That girl shares way too much. I'm all for being there for my friends, but I could have lived without being asked if the thing on her ass is a pimple or a mole. I mean there's dermatologists for that. I don't need to see a photo of it, you know?"

I bite my lip, holding back a smile. She's so fucking adorable.

"Oh God," she says, slapping a hand over her mouth. "I'm sorry. I tend to—"

"Ramble when you're nervous? I remember." I smile softly.

"Right," she says slowly, then her nose scrunches up. "What on earth happened to your nose? It looks gross."

"Gee, thanks," I laugh.

She smiles, and my heart soars because I'm the one who did that. *I* made her smile. "I just mean, whoever pierced your nose, you really should get a refund because they did a horrible job."

"Makes sense. I didn't go to a professional," I say, scratching the back of my neck.

"Did it yourself?" she asks, a smile playing on her lips as she raises a brow in question.

"Not exactly," I cringe. "I got drunk, and let some equally-as-drunk girls do it for me."

The sudden burst of laughter from her is nice to hear. "Yup, that would do it. It looks pretty infected."

"I know," I groan. "I'm going to the store to get everything to clean it after school."

She looks at her phone, then the brown paper bag in her hand like she's debating her inner thoughts. "Come with me," she says, letting out a little sigh.

"What?" I ask, shocked that she's even still standing here talking to me instead of telling me to fuck off and avoiding me like the plague.

"You need to get some peroxide and some antibiotic cream on that before it gets worse." She turns around and starts heading in the direction that she was coming from.

I stand there, dumbfounded for a moment before my feet catch up with my brain and I race after her like a puppy.

"You know, you really shouldn't make these kinds of decisions when you're drunk," she tells me as we walk down the path to one of the student parking lots.

"Trust me, I know. They told me I'd look hot with a nose piercing. My drunk ass wanted to impress..." I look over at her, and she glances up at me. "To impress someone I like."

She looks away, her shoulders tensing up. "Since when do

you have to impress anyone? From what I've seen and heard, you've had almost every girl here."

"You make me sound like a player or something."

She cocks a brow. "Aren't you?"

"Okay, point taken. But those days are behind me. I haven't fucked anyone in like two weeks."

She snorts out a laugh that sounds more irritated than joking. "Well, we should get you a gold medal and a lollipop then."

If I didn't know better, I'd think she sounds pissed off...and is that a bit of jealousy I sense? *Why would she care about what I do and who I do it with?*

My heart fills with hope that maybe, just maybe, she still cares about me.

"Nah, no need, I already have this," I say, pulling a candy cane out of my pocket, taking the bottom off, and sucking it into my mouth with a grin.

She chuckles. "You still eat those?" she asks as we come to a stop next to a little white beat up car.

"Yup. All day, every day," I grin.

"I never understood how you didn't end up feeling sick. That's a lot of sugar."

I shrug. "It's just a habit now. As long as I eat other things, I'm good."

She nods. "Sit." She points to the bench before heading over to the car. I do as she says, and sit there, waiting, as she rummages around in the trunk of her car.

My legs bounce as I bite on my lower lip while nervous energy thrums through my body. This is the most time I've spent near Ellie in four years. I've been craving to be near her since she's come back. I want to ask her so many things, but I don't want to upset her or scare her away. So I just keep quiet.

"Here we go," she says, closing the trunk of her car. "I always have a first aid kit in my car." She sits next to me on the bench and places a really fancy first aid kit on her lap. She opens it and the thing is full of pretty much everything you would need to treat something that you wouldn't need to go to a hospital for.

"Well, aren't you prepared," I laugh as she gets out a few Q-tips, a bottle of peroxide, and a tube of cream before slipping on a glove.

"It's better to be safe than sorry." She shrugs with a grin. She puts some disinfectant on the Q-tip. "Lean in closer," she instructs. My breathing starts to pick up, and the moment her soft delicate hand cradles the side of my face to hold me still, my cock twitches. Fuck, I am a perv, but I'm her perv. *I mean, I'm only a perv for her.* Fuck. Never mind.

"This might sting," she whispers, her eyes meeting mine. Her tongue flicks out, licking her bottom lip before she presses the tip of the swab to the nose ring.

I let out a moan of pain, and she pulls back. "Sorry," she says with a grimace.

"It's okay. I've had worse, like a football to the head," I grin.

"Speaking of football. Your friend broke my boyfriend's nose." She glares at me.

"Hey, that was Brody, not me. I had no part in that," I defend and it's true. I laughed because he's the man who is with the woman I yearn for, but Brody went too far and really needs to chill the fuck out because all of this is getting out of hand.

"Mhhmm," she hums, adding the cream now. "You're just the one who sits in the background while the others do the shitty things."

I purse my lips. "Yeah, you're right."

"All done," she says, any form of friendliness gone as she cleans up, putting everything away. "You should get a proper nose ring. There's a little shop in Spring Meadows that sells jewellery."

"I don't like what they're doing to you," I blurt out. She looks up at me, brows creasing.

"Then why don't you say anything? Why do you just sit there and watch?" she asks, hurt filling her words.

Fuck. *Why did I go and open my big mouth?* "Because they are my best friends. They're my family. I don't want to go against them."

"But you will sit back and let them fuck up my life for no reason."

"No reason? Ellie, do you not remember what happened on graduation night?" I scoff.

Her face drops and goes pale. "Yeah. I do. Every single minute of every single day," she whispers before getting up. She quickly heads over to her car, tossing the kit in, and slamming the door shut. That brown paper bag is clutched in her hands once again. She leaves, not bothering to spare me a look as she heads back into the school.

I sit here, pissed off with myself. Things were going so good then I had to go and fuck it up. But I will find out her side of the story one way or another. I need to know. It's been nagging in the back of my mind everyday since. I need to hear it from her own mouth.

## ELLIE

I must be in some alternate universe or something. I just spent a good fifteen minutes with Chase, and he *didn't* insult me like the others. He was actually...nice. A little charming and funny. It's like when Chase is alone without the others' influence, he's a completely different person than what I've been seeing. He's still the guy who sits in the background and watches his best friends torment their ex though. His ex. He's not all that better because he does nothing to stop it. He allows it to happen, but he, himself, hasn't really said or done anything. That's the only reason why I didn't just walk past him and continue on to Theo's office after I bumped into him.

When I saw his nose, I guess the caring and nurturing side

of me wanted to help. His nose looked pretty awful, and he looked like he was in some pain.

I'd be lying to myself if I said I didn't enjoy that small bit of time with him. It was nice to talk, to see the Chase that I grew up with. And those candy canes. He still eats them. I always used to tease him about it. He never had bad breath, that's for sure, and his kisses were always sweet.

In the end, we are not friends, and I haven't forgotten about all the shit the others have put me through. He's with them, on their side. I get it and he's right. They are his family. It just seems to slip his mind that I was once a part of that family too.

I needed to get out of there. The more time I spent with Chase, the more old feelings started to creep back in, reminding me that I'm not over him and I may very well never be.

It felt wrong. I'm with Theo. I love *him,* and he's my whole world. Knowing I still love Chase, love them all, despite all the nasty things they've done to me, makes me feel like a shitty human. Like I'm cheating on Theo.

Theo says he understands my feelings. That what Rain, the guys, and I had isn't something that one just puts to the back of their mind and forgets about. It sticks with you forever, but it's about what you do about it that counts. And I'm choosing to do nothing. I'm leaving them in the past. The only thing I'll have to do is tolerate them while I'm at cheer or if we happen to run into each other at a party.

I love my life. I love my job, my friends, and my boyfriend. But most of all, I love my daughter, the light of my life.

It hasn't slipped my mind that her father was once my lover and is now my bully. I just don't know what level of bully he is.

Is he the one who stands by and watches?

The one who is too in love to go against his lover's wishes?

Or is he the worst one of them all?

Doesn't matter because at this point, with the way they all have treated me, none of them deserve to be in her life. She doesn't need that toxicity.

Plus, I can't risk them rejecting her and crushing her little heart when they find out who the father is, because it can't be all of them.

Not wanting to let them ruin another good thing in my life, I focus on what I'm here to do.

Theo's mom gave us some leftover turkey, and when I was done with my class, I slipped home to make Theo a hot turkey sandwich. He told me how excited he was to have one so why make him wait?

I know going to his office is a risk, but if anyone asks, I'm just being a good neighbor and bringing him some lunch. *There's no harm in that, right?*

"Come in," his smooth voice makes its way through the door after I knock. And just like that, any bad mood I was in vanishes solely at the sound of him.

I open the door and find him deep into whatever he's working on. His fingers tap away at the keys on his laptop, brows furrowed in concentration. I want to go over there and run my thumb over the wrinkle in his brow to smooth it out.

"Working hard or hardly working?" I ask playfully.

His head snaps up, shocked at first before a loving smile appears that has my heart fluttering, as well other places.

"Hi," he says, closing his laptop. "What are you doing here?"

"Well, when you texted me that you might not be home until late tonight because you had to grade papers, I thought I'd bring you something to eat. Can't have my man going hungry, now can I?"

"Nope," he laughs. "Can't have that. That would be a terrible thing to allow."

I giggle and place the brown paper bag on the table.

He opens it and inhales with a groan. "Is this what I think it is?" he asks.

"Check and see." I shrug, playing coy.

He takes out the plastic sandwich container and opens it up. "No gravy?" he asks.

"Look in the bag." He digs around, retrieving a little container. "I didn't want it to get soggy."

"Hell yes," he sighs happily, opening up the gravy and smothering his sandwich in it. "You are truly a goddess. I love you," he says before sitting down and taking a massive bite. "Fuckkkkk."

"Careful," I warn. "You keep making those noises and I'm gonna be a little jealous that it's a sandwich making you moan like you're cumming in your pants and not me," I giggle.

He looks up at me, his eyes turning to molten lava as he looks me over in a Summer dress, despite it being almost Christmas. I bite my lip, loving the look of love and desire that he's giving me.

It's like, ever since the first time we had sex, I'm constantly horny. I mean, look at the man, he's hot as sin and sweet as can be. And God, those hands, that tongue, and that cock. It's enough to make a woman go mad. But in a very, *very* good way.

"Trust me, sweetheart, no one can make me moan like you can," he says, his voice growing deep and husky. My core clenches and I find myself leaning forward, over his desk with my tits eye level to him.

"Maybe I need a little reminding, just a little reassurance," I purr, my voice dropping low and seductive as I make my way around his desk. He drops the sandwich back into the container, pushing it aside and moving back, allowing me enough room to hop up onto the desk. "How about a little dessert?" I open my thighs, loving the way Theo's pupils expand, turning his eyes dark, almost completely black. His throat bobs as he swallows hard, shifting in his seat.

I know this is a bad idea. We are in his office. *What if someone walks in on us?*

But, his office is the only one on this floor. This floor is mostly used for storage, and the school gave Theo the office up here temporarily until they know if the professor he's filling in for is going to come back or not. We should be fine.

I mean to ask him if he's expecting anyone when his large, warm hands make contact with my skin, and I lose all train of thought. I suck in a breath as he pulls his chair forward, sliding his hands up my thighs, and pushing the dress higher as he goes.

"A tasty sandwich and a delicious treat to go with it. You spoil me, sweetheart. Now let me spoil you," he growls.

I sigh as his lips press a light kiss on the inside of my leg. My body gives in, and I lean back on my forearms, opening my thighs wider and granting him access to my core.

"Theo," I breathe. My breaths are starting to come out in tiny pants as he leaves a trail of kisses closer and closer to where I desperately want him to be.

"You're soaked sweetheart, right through your panties," Theo groans, nudging my swollen clit with the tip of his nose. "And it's all for me."

"Yes, only you," I whimper as he grazes my clit through the thin fabric.

"I need to taste you. It's all I've been able to think about since I fucked you into a sobbing, sweaty mess the other night. Just like now, you were so fucking beautiful. Always a vision."

Fuck, I love when he talks like this. He's been slowly breaking out of his shell, exploring his desires with me. I love being the one to help him figure out what works for him. Theo has an inner dom, and I've been starting to see glimpses of him. I fucking *love* it.

"Well, sometimes it's okay to have dessert first," I breathe, my body already trembling beneath his touch.

"I think that sounds like a wonderful idea." His grin turns feral, and a little moan slips past my lips. I'm beyond ready for him, needing him more than I've ever needed anything before.

"Lie back," he says, and I quickly obey.

His fingers find the waistband of my panties, lightly caressing the sensitive skin there. He starts to pull them down, leaving open mouth kisses on my lower stomach, then my mound, and finally on my clit.

"Oh," I breathe softly as he sucks the bundle of nerves into his mouth, giving it a little nip.

Once I'm free and bare to him, he lifts my legs, and places them over his shoulders. When his tongue makes contact with my core again in one long lick, a shiver travels through my entire body, and I need to grip the edge of the desk.

"You taste divine," he moans against my pussy, sending vibrations through me. "I need more." And he takes more. He gets to work, sucking and swirling around my nub. Somehow, he simultaneously uses his tongue to lap up all of my liquid desire, being very thorough as he cleans any prior juices from before. Then he lets out a snarl, unable to hold back anymore.

Theo eats me out like a man presented with his last meal. He's slow yet consuming. He switches back and forth between flicking or slurping at my clit to dipping that sinful tongue into me.

"Oh, God!" I sob, tangling my fingers through his hair, needing something to hold on to and wanting to hold him as close to me as he can be while he works me over. I feel like a spring being twisted, coiling tighter and tighter, just waiting to bust from the pleasure.

"That's it, sweet girl, just give in. Cum for me, gorgeous. Coat my tongue with your sweet cream. Soak my beard until it's running down my chin."

Sweet mother of God, this man and his mouth are a dangerous thing. But in the best possible way.

When he slips two thick fingers into my pussy, pumping them in and out as his mouth continues to ravish my clit, I have no other option but to clamp my thighs over his head. All the sensations are too much, but it feels so fucking good.

Without moving his mouth away, he opens my thighs wider using one arm to hold a leg down as he uses his fingers inside me to rub against G-spot.

"Oh, oh God. Theo, please," I cry.

"Just give in," he murmurs before sucking hard on my sensitive bud, making my hips buck against his mouth. "Give it all to me. I'll catch you when you fall. Always."

His voice is sweet but full of need.

I grind against his face, chasing the orgasm that's right out of reach.

He works his mouth and fingers faster, matching the pace of my hips, and then I dive over the edge, giving in to my body's needs.

I bite my lip so hard I think I can taste blood as I try to muffle my scream while one of the most powerful orgasms I've ever had rips through my body like a tidal wave. Theo continues to lick, suck, and pump as he helps me ride my release, holding on to me as I shake and twitch.

"You did so good, my love," he soothes, rubbing my thighs as he stands up.

My mind is a hazy mess and for a moment, I don't know where I am. I blink up at him as he towers over me. His glasses are fogged from the heat of my core and his thin beard glistens with my release. I whimper at the sight, needing that thick cock of his inside me now.

He wipes his mouth off with the back of his hand and grins down at me. My chest is heaving, my breasts almost spilling out the top of my dress as I lay there with my legs draped over the edge and my dripping pussy exposed.

"You know, I've had a certain fantasy ever since I got my own office," Theo says. He licks his lips, savoring my taste. *So hot.*

"Yeah?" I ask, my breathing starting to even out. "What is it?"

"To have you bent over this desk as I fuck you into it."

Oh, I want that, I *really* want that.

"It doesn't have to be a fantasy." I bite my lip, seeing his eyes heavy with need, and his nostrils flaring.

"You'd like that, wouldn't you?" he growls.

I nod frantically.

He leans over and kisses the hell out of me, leaving me breathless again before pulling me to my feet and spinning me around.

I let out a little squeak as my breasts get pushed against his desk as he holds me down, his hand firm on my back. I immediately let out another one, this one a little more from shock because his hand came down on my ass in a light slap.

"You're a naughty girl, aren't you? Do you need to be punished?" His voice is as smooth as a hundred year old whisky and makes me rub my thighs together, wishing for just a little bit of friction.

"Yes, Sir," I moan, and he lets out another growl of approval.

"Then try to be a good girl and don't move." He moves his hand down my back. Then I hear the sound of his zipper before the soft tip of his cock rubs against my pussy lips. Slipping in between them, he slides back and forth so that he can coat his shaft, driving me wild. *More like to the brink of insanity!*

"Theo," I moan. "Sir, please, I need you."

"I got what you need, baby girl. Shhh," he soothes as he runs his hand up and down my back before thrusting inside me with no warning, making me cry out at the sudden intrusion.

It's a tight fit, but my orgasm from before helps him glide in, right to the hilt. It feels so good. Just what I needed.

"Fuck," he hisses. "You feel so damn good on my cock." He pulls back. "I can never get enough of you, Ellie." He thrusts in, making me moan and my eyes roll into the back of my head as he starts to pick up speed.

I'm just along for the ride, enjoying how my man makes me feel, controlling my pleasure as he takes his own. He makes me feel loved, sexy, and cherished.

"You are my everything," he grunts as he pounds into me, his hips slapping against my ass cheeks. "God, you're so perfectly imperfect. The missing piece I've been looking for. You bring out parts of me I've kept locked away. Freeing me, allowing me to be who I am."

"Fuck me, Sir. Take what you need. My body is yours." Tears fill my eyes at his words, happy ones. Theo treats me like a queen. Not once have I felt unloved, worthless, or broken when I'm with him.

He sucks in a breath, slowing his movements. "No, sweet girl. Your body is yours. And I'm so fucking lucky you share it with me. I will worship it, take care of it, and adore it like it should be. But thank you for offering this part of you. I'm so proud."

Fuck, now I'm crying. He's so perfect. I thought that night had ruined me. And for the longest time, it did. But this man, my guardian angel, is putting me back together one broken piece at a time.

He leans over me, leaving kisses across my shoulder blades and spine as he fucks me into ecstasy. I don't care if we're in his office, on his desk, it's beyond a perfect moment.

"I know, baby," he says as I turn into a babbling mess from the intensity of the physical pleasure mixed with internal happiness. I feel another orgasm building, my pussy begging to milk him dry. "I feel it too. It's so fucking good. You make me feel amazing."

"Theo," I cry.

"That's it, love. Give it to me. Let it all out."

I cry out his name as I clamp down on his cock, my core pulsing around him. He curses at my grip, thrusting a few more times before finding his own release and spilling himself deep inside me. I feel his cock twitch as streams of cum coat my insides.

"I love you," he breathes, kissing my cheek as I lay there, slowly coming back to reality.

"I love you too," I croak, still full of emotions I'm not used to.

He pulls out of me, giving my ass a rub before grabbing a box of tissues and cleaning me up. He helps me off the desk and back into my panties. Taking a seat and pulling me down onto his lap, we just sit there cuddled together in comfortable silence, enjoying the buzz of everything.

I feel safe and protected in his arms, like nothing bad can ever happen to me again. As long as I'm here with him, the outside world can't get me. If I ever lose Theo, I don't think I would survive. He's branded himself into my heart and soul. He has me now and I won't let him go. No matter what life throws at me, Theo is here to stay.

# Chapter Twenty-Four

## BRODY

"DONE," I sigh, tossing the assignment I was working on to the side and relaxing back into the couch. "I hate papers."

"Well, it's kind of a big part of going to a university," Jax chuckles. I crack a grin, loving the sound of him as I close my eyes and just take in the moment. "You should get that in to Mr. Munro before he marks it as a late assignment. If we go now, we should be able to make it to his office before his next class. Then we can head to lunch."

"Yeah," I say, opening my eyes. I grab my paper and shove it into my backpack. "I just need to put this book back and we can go." I would just leave it here, but last time I did, the librarian bitched me out for it. She's a scary old lady, and part of me thinks she's a witch.

Grabbing the book, I head down toward the back of the library, looking around as I try to remember which bookshelf I got it from. That's when I realize I'm on the wrong side of the right one.

Just as I'm about to round the corner, I hear a moan. *Looks like someone is getting a 'little library' action,* I think, grinning like a mad man.

Peaking my head around, I see two people going at it like

they are under some kind of horny spell. Two guys to be exact. A guy with brown hair fists the blond headed guy, whose back is to me, as they grind against each other. My mind goes to Jax and how I wouldn't mind doing something like this back here. Sure beats using this place to study.

I watch for a little bit, telling myself it's because I need to put the book away in the same aisle they're in, but really, it's just fucking hot to watch.

That is until I see the guy with blond hair shift his body a little, breaking apart from the kiss and coming up for some air. I know that guy. *That guy* is on my team. *That guy* is mother fucking Cooper.

My eyes go wide, and I just stand there in shock. It takes my mind a moment to process what I'm witnessing. Before I know it, I'm caught between blinding rage that he has the fucking balls to cheat on Ellie, and satisfaction because I just stumbled upon the best ticket for a little revenge. This might not get rid of Ellie on its own, but getting a little payback by breaking her heart like she did ours sounds good right about now. My heart is struggling with the conflicting feelings.

Guess my idea to plant false information into Cooper's mind about Ellie cheating on him is out the window. Not that he would listen to me anyways after I broke his nose. His face is still pretty swollen and bruised. Cooper must be good at whatever the hell he's doing with this guy for him to want to make out with his beat up face like that.

Quickly, I slip my phone out of my pocket and snap a few photos, making sure to get a view of Cooper's face. Now I need to get out of here before they catch me watching. Putting the book on a random shelf, I turn and leave.

"Ready to go?" I ask Jax when I get back to where I left him.

"Yup. Chase just texted. He's waiting outside the library."

I nod, so we grab our bags and leave.

"I'm fucking starving. Let's drop this off so we can eat. Rain said she will meet us at the cafe."

"I just hate that we have to go all the way to the other side of the campus to get to his office," I huff as we head out to my car.

## CHASE

"I really fucking wished I knew you needed to come here because I just walked fifteen minutes to meet you guys when I could have just stayed here in the first place," I complain as we get out of the car. My legs hurt like a bitch, and I just want some food! I get 'hangry' too, it's not just women.

"What were you doing here?" Brody asks.

"I had a class, duh." I roll my eyes.

"Yeah, but it ended over an hour ago. Why were you still here?"

"I spent most of my time in the bathroom cleaning this stupid fucking nose ring," I grumble. "Then I ran into..." I stop talking, not wanting to give away the fact that I was with Ellie. I don't think Jax would care all that much. He doesn't seem to be affected by her return like we are. I know he still loves her, but he already lost Ellie once. Then having to lose his mother too, in a more permanent way, I don't think he's allowing himself to open up old wounds. He's actually the most realistic one out of all of us. He's more mature about everything that's happened. He has Brody, so I think that is a big reason why he's not pining after her like I am, or consumed like Brody is. Rain just can't stand the sight of her, a consistent reminder of the past and what we lost. "Anyways, after cleaning it up a bit, I came to meet you guys. This is my cardio for the day. You guys can chauffeur my ass around for the rest of the day. It's the least you can do."

"You're twenty-two not eighty-five. And you're on the fucking football team. Having to walk fifteen minutes isn't like climbing a damn mountain. Stop being a baby," Brody laughs.

"Fine, but I'm still expecting that foot rub you owe me," I grin.

"I don't owe you shit," Brody says.

"Nah bro, that's nasty. You can keep it."

Jax snorts a laugh. "Your mind is a messed up place, isn't it?"

"I think you mean fun," I wink and he shakes his head.

We ride the elevator up to the top floor and walk down a long hall to where Mr. Munro's office is. I just want to get this done quickly. There's a burger and fries in the cafe calling my name.

Brody raises his hand to knock on the door when we hear someone moaning, "Theo."

My face lights up. "Well, looks like our professor forgot all about little ol' Ellie and found himself a fuck buddy. I bet he has her bent over the desk right now," I say, moving to open the door but Jax stops me.

"What the fuck are you doing?" Jax hisses.

"Watching," I say, looking at Jax like I don't understand how it's not the obvious thing to do.

"You really are fucked in the head," Brody mutters. "I just hope he gets his rocks off soon so I can hand this in. If he's not done in the next minute, I'll slip it under the door. If he doesn't get it, then he can kiss my ass. It's his fault for fucking around when he should be thinking of his students."

"I mean, we did come all this way. Why not get a little show for our troubles?" I say with a mischievous grin, cracking the door open just enough for me to peak in.

My grin slips away as my stomach drops. Fury fills my veins as I watch the scene before me.

Turns out Mr. Munro did not forget all about Ellie. *At all.* The complete opposite actually because he sure does have a person in his office, bent over his desk as he rails her from behind, and that person just so happens to be Ellie, herself.

My heart cracks as I watch my professor fuck my ex-girlfriend. She's pressed against the desk, her breasts spilling out of her dress as her face contorts with ecstasy. And the most painful part of watching the girl I still love get fucked by another man, is the look on his face. He stares down at her like she's the most precious thing in the world. He's in love with her.

I know that look all too fucking well because it's how I feel about her too. No, this isn't happening. *She's supposed to be mine!* The thing between her and Cooper is bullshit, and all too fucking convenient if you ask me. Even if they kiss or hold hands, and even if they are actually dating, there's nothing there. I can tell when they look at each other, it's only friendship.

But this, this is my worst fucking nightmare. I'm completely and utterly crushed.

Looking over at the guys, I see that Brody is livid. His face is red from anger as his nostrils flair. Jax watches, a pained look taking over his face showing that he is clearly affected by this too.

We say nothing, not wanting to give away our position but unable to look away as we watch the one woman who we all loved—love—more than anything in this world, be with another man. We knew she's been with other people, but actually seeing it with our own eyes breaks something inside me that I had thought was already shattered.

"What are you doing?" Jax whispers to Brody. I don't look, still caught in the web of this soul crushing sight. I want to look away, but I can't. The way he's fucking her...*that should be me!* I should have grown a fucking pair and talked to her sooner. Hell, at this point, I don't even care about the past. We were kids, shit happens. I just want her back. I want my Ellie-Belly back. I'm going to kill that man. I'm going to wrap my hands around his fucking neck and squeeze while I watch the life drain from his eyes for putting his fucking hands on my girl.

"What do you think?" he hisses. "Recording it. This is prime information right here. A teacher fucking a student. It's gotta be worth something if we need it." He's trying really hard to play this off like he is watching a stranger that he has a grudge against, instead of a part of his soul.

The idea of anyone seeing this makes me want to grab Brody's phone and smash the shit out of it.

"You can't do that," Jax says, but does nothing to stop him, looking back at what's going on inside the office as he records. He fucks her for a few more seconds before they both finish. The sounds coming from them are too much.

"I love you," Mr. Munro tells her, leaning over to kiss her cheek while he's still fucking buried inside her. I'm vibrating right now, and it takes everything in me not to go in there and rip him off of her.

Then she speaks and my world goes still. "I love you too," she says, her voice cracking with so much raw emotion. Her voice is filled with something so much more real than it had ever sounded when she says those three words to me.

I need to get out of here. I can't breathe. It feels like the air in the room is slowly being sucked out. Everything is spinning and I feel like I'm going to pass out.

I lost my chance to be with her again. I sat there for months and let my friends treat her like trash. Sure, it made me sick to watch. To see the pain, embarrassment, and humiliation on her face. There were even a few times I wanted to kick Brody's ass and bitch out Rain. But the simple fact is, I didn't. I sat back, watching, and it makes me just as bad as them. Maybe this is for the best. She deserves better than me, than us. She made a mistake back then, but we have no right to keep punishing her. People can grow and change. But sometimes, we're too damaged and fucked up to even bother trying.

I don't wait for the elevator, taking the stairs two steps at a time. When I get to the exit, I burst through the door, and suck in lungs full of fresh air, trying to get this sick feeling in the pit of my stomach to ease.

"I saw Cooper sucking face with some guy in the library," Brody says after ten minutes of silence with us just sitting in his car. I try to get the image of *him* fucking her like a crazed man out of my mind. I can still hear her moans and see the pure euphoric look on her face as she came around his cock.

"What?" I shout, snapping out of my own thoughts. "What the fuck are you talking about?"

"When I went to put a book away, I saw him. And trust me, it was him. Here." He hands me his phone. Jax leans over to see the screen too. I flick through different photos of Cooper and some guy I don't think I've ever seen. Yup, no denying what's happening there.

"I was going to show Ellie, and tell her that her boyfriend is cheating on her to fuck with her some more. But seeing as how she's fucking our professor, it doesn't seem like she would care too much," Brody growls.

"So what are you going to do with the photos and what we just saw up there?" Jax asks.

"I don't know yet," he mutters, but something tells me he already has a plan.

I don't get it. Why is she with Cooper anyways if she's also with Mr. Munro? Why be with both? Is one not good enough? Do they have something like we used to have? Do they know about each other?

This is all too fucking much for my brain to wrap around right now. I need to drink. A part of me wants to go to a party tonight, find a willing girl, and fuck Ellie out of my brain. That's what I've done for the past few years, drink and fuck, making it so that the only thing on my mind is the pleasure in that moment.

But the idea of doing that now makes me sick. My dick has no interest in being put into any woman that's not her. It's always been her and just that short fifteen minute talk earlier solidified it. She still has the same effect on me now that she did back then.

But what the fuck do I do now after what I just saw? Until

this moment, I thought I probably stood a chance. Her and Cooper do not look serious from what I've seen.

*Maybe she hasn't changed after all.*

Nope. No. I'm not going to allow my mind to go there. I know nothing about what I just saw, what her and Cooper's relationship limits are, none of it. I won't be jumping to conclusions this time.

Right now, I'm gonna go about my life and try like fuck to forget what I just saw. I need to talk to her, get her alone, and hear the words from her mouth. Not others, no more second hand knowledge.

But I do know one thing for sure. There's no way in hell Brody won't do something about Cooper and Ellie. I can see it in his eyes. He's lying because he damn well knows exactly what he's going to do with this bit of information, at least what he has on Cooper.

# Chapter Twenty-Five

## ELLIE

THE FIRST PRACTICE back after Thanksgiving is a little odd. The girls make snide comments of course, but Rain is oddly quiet. I keep looking over to find her watching me with an unreadable expression.

The guys, however, are not as subtle. Brody keeps sneering at me with looks of disgust. Jax looks like he has a million things he wants to say to me, but can't and Chase...Fuck, Chase. Every time we lock eyes, he looks like a kicked puppy. A look of pain mixed with longing. It's weird if you ask me. *What does he have to be so upset about?* I'm the one who's being treated badly.

This whole mood shift is weird, and makes me feel like it's the calm before the storm. It has me on edge and lost in my thoughts.

"Hey, you want a bite?" Cooper asks me, holding out a spoon full of ice cream. I look up at him and smile.

"Sure." I force a smile, taking the bite.

"You okay? You look a little lost in your own mind," he asks, his brow pinching with concern but then he cringes from the pain of his busted up face.

I still want to clock Brody a good one and have him feel the same pain he's putting Cooper through. The poor thing has a broken nose and two black eyes. All because he chose to be my friend and help me reduce the harassment of the sleazy men on campus, men who only came after me because they follow the Silver Knights.

"Sorry, just thinking," I say.

"About what?" Val asks, giving me a naughty grin. "About your sexy, nerdy man fucking you over his desk? I bet you're still sore."

I gape at her and Cooper chokes on his ice cream.

"For fuck's sake, Val," Lexie hisses. "We're at a park full of kids. Watch your mouth. We are not discussing our bestie's s-e-x life around little, innocent ears who could overhear." Then she looks at me. "That's for girl time later." She winks, making me laugh.

"Do I wanna know what the heck she's talking about?" Cooper asks, looking between me and Val.

"Nope," I say, shaking my head. "I told them something in confidence, and Val hasn't learned the meaning of that word yet." I cock a criticizing brow at Val.

"Sorry," she grimaces. "You know me and juicy topics. I just love them. Just like I'm sure Theo loved *your* juicy pus—"

"Alright, that's enough from you," Lexie says, putting her hand over Val's mouth. Val argues against Lexie's hand, it coming out as muffled mumbling. "We're gonna go. Tell Lilly 'bye' for us, and we will make cupcakes like I promised soon." She removes her hand from Val's mouth and grabs her arm, pulling her off the bench to drag her away.

"See you later, you sexy bit—" Val starts, and Lexie slaps her hand over her best friend's mouth again, tossing me an apologetic look over her shoulder. I giggle as she mouths 'sorry' to me, then hurries Val away, scolding her on their way out of the park.

"Okay, come on, girl. Tell Boyfriend Cooper what you and Boyfriend Theo did." Cooper grins, the sun making his blue eyes sparkle with amusement.

"Well, let's just say I brought Theo some lunch, and then he had some dessert," I grin.

"You're bad," Cooper laughs. "But you're not the only one who got a little TLC."

My eyes go wide. "You didn't!"

He just smirks and shrugs. "It was just a hookup. I know I said that wasn't my thing, but God, he was so hot! And he knows how to use his hands, and that mouth," Cooper groans. I slap him on the arm with a laugh. "It was just a little library hookup, no biggie."

"But, don't people know you're dating me?" I ask, not really upset about it, but if he starts messing around with people, it will start to look like he's cheating on me. Cooper is too nice of a person for me to allow him to have that kind of reputation. He's a caring, loyal person and would never cheat on me if we were actually dating.

"Not everyone knows what's going on with you, the Silver Knights, and Lady Rain."

"Well, I'm glad you're getting what you need. God knows I am," I grin.

"I'm so jealous. He's so hot and nerdy," Cooper sighs, sounding just like the girls.

"I know. I'm the luckiest girl alive." My smile turns soft.

What Theo and I did in his office, although really risky and something we don't plan on doing again, was amazing. I've never felt so alive, so loved and cherished. Just when I didn't think I could love Theo any more than I already do, he does something that has me falling harder.

"Mama," Lilly says, running over with a big smile on her face. "Look!" She holds up a flower. "Can I give to Ace and Fire?"

Here we go again with this 'Ace and Fire'. I have no idea who she's talking about and when I ask her, she keeps telling me they're her friends from daycare.

"Sure, Lillypad. But I don't know if it will still be bright and beautiful by tomorrow when I bring you to daycare."

"Oh," Lilly says, her face falling. "Okay." Her face lights up again and she looks at Cooper with a big smile. "Pooper have it," she says.

I snort a laugh at how she mispronounces Cooper's name, and he smiles wide at my little girl, the name not bothering him one bit.

"Here, Pooper." Lilly climbs up onto the bench and on his lap. She takes the flower and tries to stick it behind his ear. With his help, they get it to stay in place, and then she squishes his cheeks between her little hands. "Oh, no," she says, her voice changing, sounding sad. "You hurt. I make better." She leans over and kisses Cooper lightly on the nose. "All better." She gives him a big grin before climbing off and running back to the playground.

"Alright, that's it," he says, turning to me with watery eyes. "I'm kidnapping that kid."

I smile wide. *That was so stinkin' cute!* I love that my little girl is so caring and loving.

"Sorry, dude, I think I'm gonna keep her."

"Lucky," he fake pouts.

"Excuse me," a lady says as she approaches us.

"Hi."

"Sorry to bother you but I just wanted to give you this and let you know, seeing as you have a kid who plays here."

I take the paper from her, my brow pinching in confusion. "What's this?"

"It's a flyer some of the other mothers and I made up. We've been seeing the same man in a red car hanging around here a lot lately. We've called the police but because the man is on public property and hasn't actually done anything wrong, there's nothing they can do. But you can never be too careful when it comes to our little ones."

An uneasy feeling takes over me, and I look around with the sudden feeling that I'm being watched. "Thank you."

She smiles and nods before taking off to the next parent. I look down at the flyer. It pretty much says the same thing she did with the make and model of the car listed, and recommends everyone to be on the lookout for it. Come to think of it, I've seen that car around.

"I think it's time to go," I say to Cooper and he nods, looking concerned. Knowing there's some creep out there watching kids, *my* kid possibly, makes me panic. I hate to take Lilly away from this park because it's her favorite one around, and it's the closest to our house, but I'm not going to risk her safety.

"Come on, Lilly!" I call out. She runs back over to me as I gather up our things.

"I don't want to go home," she whines, looking like she's about to cry.

"I know, sweetie, but Theo is going to be home with Toby soon. You can play with him then."

"And you can have my ice cream," Cooper says, holding out the bowl. Her face lights up and she starts to dig into what's left.

I cock a brow with a grin. "What? You might be able to say no to that face but there's no hope for me," he chuckles.

"Trust me, it's not that easy," I laugh.

## CHASE

I try to drown out the chatter of the cafe around me as my foot taps in anticipation. I'm watching, waiting for her to walk through those doors. We don't have any classes together so I only get to see her at practice and here. She hasn't been to any parties lately, probably too busy with work. And when we do go to the club, she's never taking care of our section—hasn't in a while.

Kayla said that Aria got Ellie switched to running food to the bar, so at best, I get glimpses of her.

I meant what I said before. I haven't touched a girl in weeks and fuck, does my cock hate me for it. But he's the one who can't seem to get it up unless I'm thinking of Ellie. I'm sick of fucking other girls with Ellie in mind. They aren't her, they could never come close. I want the real thing, and I'm willing to wait while I fight for it.

When I see her blonde hair moving through the crowd as she makes her way over to her friends, a smile slowly creeps onto my lips and I'm finally able to relax. My leg stops bouncing. I lean back in my chair, and pop a candy cane into my mouth. I've already eaten my food so I just sit back and watch Ellie.

She greets her friends, her face lighting up with a smile as she talks to them, making my heart flutter. She heads over to grab food before sitting back down with her friends.

Sucking on the candy cane, my eyes trace her face as she laughs. I can't hear her from where she's sitting, but it's like a phantom sound, my mind replaying the sound in my head that I had heard every day for years.

She's so sexy, the way her nose scrunches up when her friend offers her something she doesn't like. She hates peaches, and cringes at the smell of them.

I watch how her eyes go wide, her blue eyes sparkling as she talks to her friends.

"If you stare any harder, your eyes are gonna fall out," Jax whispers, leaning in close so no one else hears.

My head snaps over to his and we are so close our lips are almost touching. He cracks a grin and backs away as I glare at him.

"I don't know what you're talking about," I mutter, picking up my phone and pretending to check social media. I stalk Ellie. Or at least try to. I've checked every day to see if she finally got her Facebook page back, made a Tik Tok account, or even got Instagram, but there's still nothing.

SILVER VALLEY UNIVERSITY: HIDDEN SECRETS

"Mhm," Jax says, not believing a word from my mouth.

"Whatever. She's hot and I'm not blind." That might be a believable statement to anyone else if she was dressed a little more revealing. But she's in a maroon sweater with no skin in sight, light blue ripped jeans, while her hair is down and curly. It's darker than her original color thanks to Rain and her little bitches. I love my bestie but I hate what she did to Ellie. I hate when she calls her a slut, a whore, or trash. It's not the Rain I know and love. I don't like seeing this hateful side of her.

"So, Kayla wants to know if you will go to the party this weekend as her date," Rain asks me from my other side. I turn to look at her, a look of pure horror on my face.

"Fuck no," I scoff. Kayla is a few seats down from me, listening in. I can tell because she slides down in her seat. God, give me a break.

This girl has been obsessed with me for years. We fucked around one time, a long, long time ago. And since then, she has never left me alone. I try to be as nice as I can because she's on the cheer team and friends with Rain, but ever since Ellie has come back, she's kicked it up a notch.

She was texting me nonstop and when I blocked her number, she just got one of those text apps. I have her blocked on all social media, but she's been making new accounts, pretending to be someone else and hitting up my inbox to flirt with me. She's not that smart about it because it only takes a few messages for me to realize it's her.

I honestly fear that she's going to find a way to sneak into our dorm and watch me sleep or some shit.

"Dude, could you be any more of a dick about it?" Rain sighs. "I had to ask."

"No you didn't. You need to tell your little friend to fuck off and leave me alone. I've put up with enough shit because she's your friend but I'm done."

Rain studies my face, seeing how genuinely pissed off I am. She doesn't know half of what Kayla does because I don't tell her. I don't want to cause drama where it's not needed. She knows enough just from watching, seeing how bad Kayla has it for me, but that's about it.

"Okay," she says softly. "You need to tell me everything, okay?"

"Yeah," I sigh, looking away as I lean back in my seat again. "Soon."

Rain turns back to her friends, sternly telling Kayla 'no' and not to ask again or she will be pissed. I can hear her sniffles from here and roll my eyes.

"You boys ready for the show?" Brody asks. I look over at him with a raised brow.

"What show?" From the look on his face, I don't think I'm going to like whatever is about to happen.

He looks over at the entrance to the cafe, and I follow his gaze. "Just wait for it."

The moment Cooper walks in, buzzing and beeping starts to ring out throughout the room. Everyone takes out their phones, checking whatever that's being sent around. Gasps and whispers start making their way around the room. I watch as Cooper's face pales like he's going to be sick with a panicked look as he looks up and over to Ellie. She's looking at him with sympathetic eyes.

Needing to know what the fuck is going on, I look at my phone and see what has everyone losing their minds.

Brody sent the photos, the photos of Cooper going at it in the library with someone who isn't his girlfriend. Someone who happens to be a guy.

"Can I have your attention please?" Brody raises his voice to be heard over the fast growing gossip as he stands and addresses the room. "As you can see from the text you have all been sent, Cooper, the all American boy, the sweet chill guy everyone seems to love, has been cheating on his girlfriend." He turns to Ellie, a cruel grin spreading over his lips. "How does it feel to be the one who's been cheated on this time?" he chuckles.

We all know she doesn't care because she's seeing someone behind Cooper's back too. But the look that Ellie just gave Cooper tells me there is way more to this story that we don't know.

*I can't believe he's doing this here.*

Ellie's chair scrapes against the floor as she gets up and starts heading over in our direction. She's fuming, her face contorting into a murderous look. But it's not at Cooper. No. She's looking right at my asshole of a best friend who's making a spectacle of himself, unable to just let shit go.

"Looks like you're not the only slu—" *Crack.* Ellie slaps Brody across the face.

"How fucking dare you!" she seethes, her body shaking with anger. Brody's grin slips, replaced by his own look of murder. "You just don't know when to leave well enough alone. What the fuck is wrong with you? I have put up with enough of your bullshit, Brody. I've let you throw your little tantrums, not stooping to your level of petty crap while you get whatever revenge you *think* you're owed, but this..." She holds up the phone. "This is one step too far." She leans in so that only Brody, Jax, and I can hear. "You saw a way to get back at me and didn't think of the consequences. Do you realize you just outed a gay man to the whole fucking school?"

Brody's face drops. I can tell he didn't think of that. Only the need to get back at Ellie was on his mind when he made those decisions.

"You of all people should know what that might feel like. You asked me to keep your little secret, and I did. I would never, and I mean NEVER, do something as cruel as this."

Wait. He did? When? What the hell is he not telling me?

"It's not worth it, Ellie, come on," Cooper says, coming up behind her, gently trying to turn her away from us.

"No," she says, shaking her head. "He can't just do something like this and get away with it." She looks up at him, and I can see how much she cares for him.

He smiles down at her with a sad smile. "Thank you for caring. You're such an amazing friend but, really, it's okay." He turns to the crowd. "So...I guess it's out. I'm gay. Who fucking cares?" He turns to Brody. "It was never a secret. I just don't make it public knowledge what my sexual preference is. I like guys, and I'm proud of it. There's nothing wrong with it."

"Then why were you dating her?" Brody snaps, his face flush with embarrassment that his plan is going down the drain fast but refuses to accept it.

"Because," Ellie answers the question. "You declared me an outcast, free for all to pick on and bully, and the perverts came out of the woodwork. Everyday, I had pigs asking me for gang bangs and how much an hour with me would cost!" Ellie yells, tears falling from her eyes.

"He was doing it to protect me. He saw what was happening. He couldn't just stand there and do nothing because he's a real friend. An amazing friend. So yeah, we decided to 'fake date'. You happy now?" Ellie turns to look at the room. "Cooper and I were never dating. It was all an act because I didn't feel safe in this school. You all blindly follow the Silver Knights because why? They're rich? They're the head of the football team? You're all just as bad as they are. When you graduate from this place and go off into the real world, when is any of this social bullshit gonna prove useful? These people will mean nothing to you later in life."

She turns back to Brody. "Leave me the fuck alone," she snaps before turning around and storming out of the cafe, her friends getting up from their table to follow.

"You need to just stop, man. Ellie is a good person, and whatever shit you had with her in the past, it's not worth it. Move on because this is just pathetic," Cooper says with a shake of his head, turning and leaving.

The room breaks out in chatter again as Brody stands there, vibrating with rage, his hands clenched at his side.

My brain is trying to comprehend what the fuck just happened.

"You took it too far," I say. He looks down at me and blinks.

"Excuse me?'

"I love you, man. You're my best friend and brother, but since she's come back, you've gotten this unhealthy obsession with getting back at her. And I've just sat here and let it happen. But no fucking more. I'm done. I won't just sit here while you call the girl we all loved more than life itself degrading names, making her out to be some low life, worthless piece of trash. It's over. Or I'm done."

I leave him standing there in shock. I jump over the table, shooting a glance at a stunned Rain. "I know it hurts to look at her, and that's why you've been such a grade A bitch since she's been back, hoping it would send her running. But Rain, she's stronger than that, stronger than we had all anticipated. She's not going anywhere, so please, stop making it worse on yourself."

"She's a fucking cunt and needs to leave this school!" Laura sneers.

"And you're a pathetic leech who can't accept that Rain will never be more than your fuck buddy. You have no room to talk," I scoff, before turning on my heel and running after Ellie.

I make it out into the courtyard, my heart pounding as I search the grounds. I spot her standing by her car, talking to the others.

"Ellie!" I call out as I run over to her. She looks up, her face shocked at the sight of me.

"What do you want, Chase?" she asks, her voice tired.

"I want you to know that I didn't know he was going to do that. I mean, I knew he had the photos but I didn't think he would share them like that with the whole school."

"Bravo, do you want a pat on the back and for me to tell you that you're a good boy?"

"What?" My brows scrunch together in confusion.

"Like I said before Chase, you may not have been behind any of the crap they've thrown at me, but you didn't do anything to stop it."

"I know," I sigh, hating that it's true. She looks taken back by my admission. "And I told him I'm done. I won't sit back and watch them hurt you anymore, Ellie. I hate it. I've hated everything they've done to you." I step close to her, cupping her face in my hands. "And I'm so fucking sorry." She looks up at me, her eyes wide and a million different emotions playing on her gorgeous face.

"I might not be with Cooper, but I do have a boyfriend," she whispers, as if she's trying to remind herself while we stare at each other like we're in our own little bubble.

"I know." I smile down at her as the reminder of what I saw sends a jolt of pain through my heart. Her face fills with fear and she starts to panic. "It's okay. I won't tell anyone." And I sure as fuck hope Brody won't. I know Jax won't say a word, and Rain doesn't know yet.

"How do you know?" she asks, her voice shaky.

I grimace. "I think, next time, making sure the door is locked would be a very good idea."

Her face pales and fills with horror. "Fuck," she lets out a soft whisper, a little cry leaving her beautiful lips.

"I know you are with someone. And I'm glad you have someone who loves you and makes you happy. I know I don't deserve you. But please. Someday, can we just sit down and talk about everything? We never got your side of what happened that night. I'd like to hear the whole story."

Whatever I said was the wrong thing to say. Her body shuts down, face going blank as she takes a step back. "You should have taken the time to ask back then before assuming you knew what happened because of what you think you saw. Thank you for admitting you were wrong but it's too late. The damage is done," she says, turning around and getting into her car. Her friends stay silent as they follow after her.

I stand there, my heart breaking all over again. What does she mean? *What we think we saw?* "Fuck!" I roar, punching the pole next to me as I watch the car drive away.

I refuse to believe this is it. I'm not giving up until I know everything. I'll give her some time and space from whatever just went down, but I'm not done. I'll never be done. Eleanor Tatum is a part of my heart and soul. There's no getting rid of her even if I want to. Which I don't and never will.

# Chapter Twenty-Six

"ARE you sure you don't want me to come with you?" Theo asks, pressing a kiss to the top of my head.

"I would love it if you could, but I don't think it would be a good idea." I give him a forced smile. He strokes my cheek with his thumb, his eyes swimming with unease. I lean into his hand, closing my eyes and revelling in his touch.

Since that bastard outed Cooper to the whole school, everyone thinks I'm single. So the asshole college guys are back at it again. I've gotten suggestive offers daily, been called degrading names, and it's all becoming too much for me. I can't go to school and enjoy learning anymore without someone coming up to me, asking if I'm down to fuck him and his buddies.

"Please, let me talk to the dean. What they've done is wrong, messed up, and immoral. The dean is a sweet lady. I know she would not stand for this if she knew what is going on."

"It's okay." I smile up at him, putting on my brave face. "It's the last game of the year. After today, I won't have to see the guys around as much. As for Rain, I won't have to work with her until the competitive cheer try-outs and practice start up in the spring."

"But that doesn't stop the assholes from disrespecting my lady," he growls, my body tingling at the sound.

"I'm a big girl, Theo. I've come this far. I won't let them get to me. It's nothing I can't handle." I pull him in for a heated kiss. He moans into my mouth, pushing me against the door. His strong hand creeps up my side, cupping my breast to give it a squeeze.

I really want to say 'fuck it' and drag him over to the couch to ride him until the Sun sets. It sounds like a much better idea than going to the game. But I can't let my team down, even if that's all they've done to me.

As for telling the dean about Brody and Rain, I would love to so everything would stop. But that's not me. The guilt of ruining their school careers or any other plans they have is strong. I'm too nice, and I don't do the best job at putting myself first. It can be a blessing, like loving and caring for my friends and daughter, but it can also be a curse which causes me to get bullied for months on end over a stupid grudge that they don't fully understand.

I want to tell them so badly, to yell at them that they are stupid and pathetic for causing so much hate and pain. I wish I could tell them that I didn't cheat, that I had no choice in what happened, but they would call me a liar and tell me I was only saying it to get them to stop. Most likely, it would just make things worse.

I've been having more and more calls with my therapist. I don't know if it's what they are doing to me, or the overall stress from school and work, but I feel all the progress I've made since coming back is slowly slipping away. I can feel myself back tracking, once again, allowing my past to dictate my future, closing myself up, and walking away from all the new challenges that had me opening up since coming back.

Honestly, if it wasn't for Theo, I would have packed up our stuff, grabbed Lilly, and ran a while ago.

I would have given up a good education and the best life for my daughter because they drove me away.

But when I come home and he wraps me in his arms, kissing me and telling me how much he loves me, it all drifts away. It all becomes bearable and worth it because I have my warrior at my side, ready to fight my demons for me, if I would let him.

"Theo," I whisper, blinking back the tears in my eyes from the intense emotion swirling through my body.

"Yes, sweetheart?" he smiles.

"I love you." My voice cracks. "Thank you for sticking by my side when all I've offered has been pointless drama."

"Enough," he growls lightly. "Don't ever think for a moment that you're not worth it. I don't care what kind of past you have. I don't care what kind of bullshit is sticking with you because it's not your fault. You didn't ask for any of it. You did nothing wrong, and I'm not going anywhere, Ellie. You are my life."

"You deserve so much better than me," I cry. "I'm so fucked up in the head." I let out a humorless laugh wiping at the tears that have fallen. "After all they have done, after all the pain they've put me through, a part of me still loves them and will probably always love them. How fucked up is that?"

"Ellie," he says, his voice strong and fierce. He cups my face, forcing me to look at him. "I am the one who doesn't deserve you. You are a strong, loving, amazing woman. You're the best mother to Lilly and a fan-fucking-tastic girlfriend. I don't care if you love a thousand men and women. As long as I get to be one of them, that's more than I could ever ask for."

He holds me while I cry, rubbing my back. After I've calmed down, I step out of his arms and wipe my eyes. "Well, that was a little dramatic," I laugh trying to make light of the situation.

"Nah. You have every right to feel however you want. You're stressed."

"Come on, we better get going," I say. I run into the bathroom and touch up my makeup. Thank God, most of it is waterproof. We say goodbye to the kids and leave. Giving each other one last lingering kiss that leaves me breathless and wanting more, we get into our own cars and head to the school.

Since Chase chased after me when all that bullshit with Brody went down, I've been so confused. Not about how I feel about Theo, never with him. I'm madly in love with that man and I never want to be without him.

But Chase. Fuck, I knew I was still in love with him. I've never stopped. But the way he looked at me, how sincere his words were, something inside me started to stir.

When he told me he wanted to hear my side, I shut down. They shouldn't get to hear my side. The facts are, I was raped and they didn't bother to look deeper to see it for what it really was. They let Brody and his fucked up home life convince them it was something it wasn't.

It's not something I can just forgive, and that night sure as hell isn't something I can forget. It's something that lives with me every second of every day. A dark mark to my soul that can only be managed through healthy relationships with my friends and family along with a ton of therapy sessions over the phone.

My therapist suggested I go to a support group with other survivors. I've been meaning to but my life has been so crazy and finding the time is hard.

I'm stressed, and a little depressed. I haven't been able to sleep since Chase told me they pretty much saw Theo fucking me in his office. I knew I should have checked the locks. It was stupid and reckless. As amazing as it was, it's not worth the trouble it could cause. Now, the people who have been making my life hell can hold that over my head. I've been waiting for Brody to do something like he did when he outed Cooper and our fake relationship, but nothing has happened. Yet.

Getting out of the car, I leave my bag and lock it up. I'm already in my cheer uniform and ready to go. After what they did to my hair, I don't trust them not to pull another stupid stunt.

The place is packed. Everyone is here to support the Silver Knights on their last game of the year. We've had a lot of home games and they always seem to be the craziest.

"Fuck," I hiss when I hear the sound of the marching band playing. We're up next and I really have to pee.

Weaving my way through the crowd, I make my way over to the locker rooms. I slip in only to see that everyone is already out on the field. Damn it. I pee quickly and wash my hands. When I get outside, I almost trip over my shoelaces. "If it's not one thing, it's another." I let out an annoyed sigh and bend down to tie it.

A hard slap on my ass has me falling forward. My hands shoot out to catch myself from face planting.

"Look who we have here," someone says, sending a chill of unease down my spine. I quickly scramble to my feet and see who has the nerve to put their hands on me without my permission.

My eyes widen and I'm frozen in fear.

"Did you miss us, pretty girl?" Ricky asks, taking a step toward me. My brain kicks into gear, allowing my feet to move. I take a step back, my eyes quickly flicking around to find an escape, but there's none. Behind me is a fence and they are blocking my only way out.

"I think she remembers us," Vin says, stepping up to flank his friend.

"Look how her eyes light up at the sight of us. You remember that night, sugar tits?" Luke questions.

These three. These fucking three. *How are they here?* I made sure that none of them attended this school when I applied for the scholarship.

"Maybe we should call Tim. He's sitting in the stands

right now. We can recreate that night four years ago," Ricky says, giving me a nasty grin. The same grin he gave me as I laid there unable to move while his friend raped me. I can still feel their hands on my skin, groping and pawing at me. They may not have gone as far as Tim did, but they still assaulted me, and I know they would have taken their turn if they had more time.

"I'll scream," I say, my voice shaky as they start to back me toward the fence. It's dark and the light outside the locker room casts a shadow over their faces, making them look as evil as their black souls.

"Go ahead," Vin taunts. "No one will hear you." He's right. The crowd is roaring as they answer the cheer squad.

"They will notice when I'm not there. They are probably already coming to look for me," I lie. No one will care that I'm not there. Sure, they might be pissed but they will pick a different song to dance to, compensating for my absence.

They ignore me and keep talking. "When we found out our school was up against yours, we ran a search on the cheer squad, you know, to see if there was some fresh pussy. It was a pleasant surprise to find out you're on the squad. We thought you disappeared into thin air."

I need to get out of here. I need to run. But my body isn't letting me move, caught in a loop as my mind replays that night over and over, their sick smiles being the last thing I saw before passing out.

"Shh," Luke coos, his hand coming up to touch my face. I'm hyperventilating and I think I'm going to be sick. "We'll make it good."

"What the fuck is going on?" a voice booms. Luke's hand snaps away from my face as if it's being burnt and they all step away. I look behind them, my eyes wide with terror. When my eyes lock with two bright and enraged ones, I almost break down, sobbing as I realize who it is. Jax stands there in his football gear, looking like a dark knight. We might not be on good terms, but I know Jax would never stand there and allow someone to get abused.

"Jax, my man. Long time no see," Ricky says.

"Fuck you. I asked you a question." His eyes flick from mine to theirs. "What the fuck is going on?"

"Look, we were just having a little fun. No harm."

"Sure as hell doesn't look like she's having fun," Jax sneers.

"We were just catching up," Vin says. "Isn't that right?" he asks me.

"I want to leave," I say, looking at Jax, my eyes pleading, holding back the sob lodged in my throat.

"Go," he says. And it's like the magic word to my spell. My feet start working and I take off running, getting one last glimpse of Jax's eyes, filled with so much anger and concern.

I run in the opposite direction of the field. I need to get out of here, to get away from them.

"Ellie?" I hear Theo's voice call out. It pains me to do so, but I ignore him, his face a mask of worry and confusion. I run past him, heading right to my car.

My hands shake as I try to get the key into the ignition. I'm numb the whole ride home and as I walk up my steps, into my apartment. The moment I shut the door behind me, I fall apart. Everything from the past few months, all my past trauma, comes crashing into me like a tidal wave.

## JAX

I watch Ellie disappear into the crowd before turning back to the assholes. Fury I haven't felt in a long time has my whole body fucking vibrating. It's like something I've kept locked up is now being let out. The look in her eyes was pure terror. Something they said or did really affected her.

"Someone wanna tell me what the fuck that was about?" I growl, looking at the cocky fuckers' smug faces.

"We were just talking," Ricky shrugs.

"I don't think the lady wanted to talk to you," I snap.

"Why do you care? Shouldn't you hate her or something? From what we hear, you and your friends have been riding her tail hard since she came back from wherever the hell she took off to in the first place."

"How the hell do you know that?" I narrow my eyes.

"Really?" Vin laughs. "Dude, we might not go to the same school anymore but people talk. It's all over social media. From that flyer Rain made up about Ellie to all the things people have been doing to her in an effort to please their 'Kings'," he says, making finger quotes. "To her recent break up with some Cooper guy."

"So when we walked by her, we saw the perfect opportunity to catch up with an old friend," Luke says.

"She's never been your fucking friend," I say, my voice low and deadly.

"No, but she was a friend we were fucking." Ricky gives me a cocky smirk. I step into him, pushing him against the wall, my hand flying to his neck.

"Shut the fuck up," I roar, my fingers flexing, gripping him tighter.

"Still butt hurt she fucked us all while she was fucking you too," he rasps, letting out a laugh that ends up with him coughing to breathe.

"I'll fucking kill you," I warn, my voice low. "Say one more fucking word. I dare you."

"Let go of him, man. You don't want to get kicked off your team for getting into a fight, do you?" Luke says, his voice panicked. There might be three of them and one of me, but I'm bigger than them. They could probably take me but not without some broken bones.

Although, he has a point.

"Get the fuck out of here," I warn. "You stay away from Ellie. If I find out you so much as looked in her direction, I will destroy you."

He says nothing and I let him go. He drops to the ground. "Come on, man," Vin says, helping his friend off the ground. They all take off like scared little mice. *Not so fucking tough now, are you?*

I can see now why she and Cooper faked a relationship. Some of the guys at this school are fucking dogs. Brody and Rain made her a target and vulnerable to the vultures of this world.

But after what I just saw, the fear in her eyes, I can't just sit back and do nothing anymore. I love Brody, and the last thing I want to do is have him feel like I'm going against him, but this has gone way too far. I couldn't live with myself if I hadn't gotten here in time. If they took advantage of her. Despite everything we've been through, that woman is still one of the loves of my life. The idea of someone forcing themselves on her makes me sick to my stomach and fills me with the urge to kill.

Still vibrating, I storm into the locker room. Chase is glaring at Brody as he laces up his shoes. The other guys leave the locker room to get ready for kick off.

"Revenge on Ellie stops now," I say when I reach them.

"What?" Brody asks, brows pinched.

"I'm done. I can't do this anymore." I look around, making sure the guys are all gone before turning back to him. "I love you, Brody, I do, but this has gone too far. What she did to us fucked us all up in different ways, and it hurt, but I think she's had enough. It brings me no happiness to see her in pain, to see her hurt. Hell, every time someone's done something mean or said something degrading to her, it's pissed me off. Including what you and Rain have done."

"So what, you're just gonna forget that she fucked us over?" Brody growls.

"No. But I'm also not going to stand by and let you bully her anymore. I. Am. Done." I try to make my words firm but soft, to lessen the blow.

His eyes flash with hurt. "So you're on her side."

"No. Damn it, Brody!" I shout, my fist pounding into the locker in frustration. "I just stopped a group of guys from tormenting Ellie and possibly raping her."

"What?" Chase roars.

"You didn't see the look in her eyes, man. She was truly terrified. We said no physical harm. Not just by us, but by anyone."

Brody's jaw ticks. He wants to argue, but thankfully, he doesn't. "Fine. I was going to call it off anyway. That bitch isn't worth my time anymore anyway."

"That bitch, as you so kindly put it, is my fucking girlfriend." Our heads whip around to see Mr. Munro. He doesn't look like the awkward nerdy professor we normally see in class. No, he looks like a hulked out version of himself. "I've had enough of your shit and it stops now."

# Chapter Twenty-Seven

## THEO

I STAND THERE, unsure what to do as Ellie hops in her car and drives away. I want to run back to my own car and follow her, but something happened, something that caused her to freak out like that, and I'm not leaving until I find out.

I was sitting in the stands, waiting for the cheer squad to do their thing, excited to see my sexy girlfriend in her element, but when they were called out and Ellie wasn't with them, I went to go look for her. I just made it out of the stands when I saw her running past me, fear filling her eyes.

If those assholes laid a fucking hand on her, I'll kill them.

The music from the cheer squad is still playing, so I know the guys haven't gone out yet. Wanting to catch them before the game starts, I head over to the men's locker room in determined strides.

Passing the tunnel, I notice that the three stooges aren't there. *Good.* They must still be in the locker room, making this easier. I'm just about to open the door when I hear a bang. "No. Damn it, Brody!" Jax shouts. "I just stopped a group of guys from tormenting Ellie and possibly raping her."

My blood turns cold. My body starts to tremble in pure rage. Someone fucked with MY woman. Someone tried to hurt the love of my life. My heart, my fucking soul, and it's all because of these three cock suckers. *They* are the reason why my love hurts, cries, stays awake at night, and is afraid to go to school.

I've felt hopeless, unsure what I can do for her. I want to help. I want to save her from any pain life throws at her, but I don't want to take away her choice. As much as it hurts me to do so, when she asks me to leave things alone, I do. She's a strong, fearless woman who is so brave and independent.

So I hope she forgives me for getting involved right now. But I can't just hold back anymore. I won't be like Chase and allow that pathetic excuse of a man to hurt her anymore.

Brody speaks, "Fine. I was going to call it off anyways. That bitch isn't worth my time anymore anyway."

*Alright, fuck this shit.*

I hulk smash through the fucking door and all three of their heads snap over in my direction. "That bitch, as you so kindly put it, is my fucking girlfriend. I've had enough of your shit and it stops now."

"What the fuck do you want?" Brody sneers. "Come to prey on another student?"

"Oh, fuck you," I sneer right back while walking toward them. "I'm not preying on anyone. Are you jealous she came to a real man who loves, adores, and cares for her? Someone who treats her like the queen she is because clearly the little boys she had before me don't seem to know how to treat a lady."

"Please," he scoffs. "We gave her everything. She was our whole damn world. But it wasn't good enough for her. *We* weren't enough for her! Your girlfriend is a whore because three cocks weren't enough to please her greedy pussy."

"Watch what you say about her," I warn, my voice low and dangerous. It's taking everything in me not to knock him on his ass. He's not worth getting fired over. I turn to the others. "Who was it? Who tried to put their hands on my woman?"

Jax answers with, "It was some guys who we used to go to school with."

"Who?!" Chase demands. At least he has the decency to be upset about the whole thing.

"Why do you care all of a sudden? You've stood by and watched this jackass and your lady friend make Ellie's life a living hell. Why do you care now?"

Chase looks at me, eyes filled with anger. "I was wrong." His jaw clenches. "I let my friendship cloud my better judgement. I sat there like a fucking pussy and let them fuck with her. I know, I'm just as bad as they are."

"Are you fucking kidding me?" Brody snaps at his friend.

"Don't think I don't know that you're trying to weasel your way back into her life." Chase looks at me, slight shock showing on his face. I let out a laugh. "What? Didn't think I'd know? Ellie tells me everything. We keep no secrets, including her telling me that her ex all but confessed his love for her."

"So what? So what if I still love her?" He puffs out his chest. "Love like that doesn't just fade." *Trust me, dude, I know.* "Maybe I realised I made a mistake in judging her too harshly, and now I want a second chance. Or to at least be her friend."

I snort a laugh. "Wow, you're a real piece of work." I shake my head. "You think you deserve her? After everything you did, you think you deserve another chance? To even have the privilege to have someone as amazing as her be your friend?"

"No," he says, sounding defeated and turns to Jax. "Which guys were they?"

Jax scratches the back of his head and grimaces. "It was Ricky, Vin, and Luke."

"Fuck's sake," Chase growls.

Why do those names sound so familiar?

"Just fucking perfect," Brody laughs. "You find her with the guys she cheated on us with. All she was missing was Tim."

*Tim.* Tim is a name I know all too fucking well. Before I know what I'm doing, I have Brody's jersey wrapped around my fist, slamming him back against the lockers. My face is an inch from his, my eyes feral, and my body begging to rip into him.

"You are a coward, a fucking poor excuse for a man. You use your shitty family life to justify your crappy choices. Boo *fucking* who. Just because your mother likes to fuck around, doesn't mean all women do," I growl. Was that a low blow bringing his mom into it, yes, but I'm past caring about hurting people at this point. Not after everything he did to Ellie. "So, how about you grow the fuck up and stop trying to make yourself feel better by making others feel worse. You're a bully, Brody. No one likes a bully. Next time you set out to destroy someone's life, maybe get all the facts straight beforehand," I growl, slamming him against the locker again. "You're lucky I don't go to the dean and tell her everything. Ellie is too nice when it comes to the lot of you. Even after everything you've done, she won't say anything, not wanting to affect your future and shit—even when you don't give two fucks about hers. But me? I might not be so nice. Do something else. I dare you, and we'll see how fast I bring my fucking wrath down on you."

My chest is heaving, my fingers itching to get Ellie's pound of flesh with this loser when my phone rings. Needing to answer in case it's about Toby, I let go of Brody, pushing him into the locker as I do.

"Hello?" I answer my mother's phone call.

"Theo, hunny. You need to get home right now." My mom's voice is filled with worry.

"Is Toby okay?" I ask, my mind conjuring up the worst.

"He's fine. So is Lilly. But there's a lot of commotion going on at Ellie's apartment. Just get home before someone calls the cops."

"I'm on my way." I hang up and look back at Brody. "Remember this, if those useless sacks of shit did rape her tonight, it would have been your fault."

With that, I leave them and race to my car, ignoring the

sounds of the cheering crowd as the football game goes on as planned.

"MOVE!" I shout at the car in front of me who doesn't go at the green light fast enough for my liking. I pound on the horn. I need to get to Ellie. I need to make sure she's okay. God, I should have gone after her right away, but the need to defend her was too strong in that moment.

I barely have the car parked before I'm slamming the door shut, clicking the lock button of the key fob, and racing up the apartment stairs two at a time. When I get to my floor, I look down the hall and see all the neighbors in their doorways. A crash and scream has me racing down the hall. My mom is standing in my doorway, a look of pain on her face. She's crying.

"It's okay. I have them. Go take care of your woman." I nod and go to Ellie's door.

Walking in, my heart sinks at the sight before me. Ellie is tossing things around the room, screaming between sobs. Glass shards cover the floor. The TV is smashed and there are cups and plates scattered around the room.

It takes a moment for my brain to process before I make my way over to her, pulling her into my arms. "Ellie. Ellie, baby, it's okay, I got you," I try to say softly, my voice breaking alongside my heart. "I have you, baby." I hold her tightly in my arms, her body trembling. Her sobs cause her whole body to shake.

"Why?" she blubbers. "Why do they hate me so much? All I ever did was love them. Where were they when I needed them the most? Where were they when I laid there helpless? As I was being RAPED!" She screams the last word before breaking down into another fit of sobs. I pull her to the floor with me, gathering her in my arms. I rock her, whispering loving words, letting her get it all out.

I thought my wife passing away was the worst pain I could ever feel. But I had time to process the reality of that situation. We knew it was coming for a while. It didn't make it any better but it did help.

But this? Watching the woman who brought me back to life, the woman who helped me love again when I thought I never would, be so defeated, so destroyed is fucking unbearable. The pain I feel for her feels like someone is ripping my heart out and crushing it in their hands before my eyes.

"Whyyyy," she cries, body shaking. "Why didn't they check on me? Why didn't they see what was right in front of their faces? They didn't love me enough to see?"

We sit there until she falls asleep, her body giving in to exhaustion. When I know she's not going to wake, I pick her up and tuck her into bed.

"How's she doing?" my mother asks, walking into the apartment.

"Not good," I whisper, unable to look at her as I wipe the tears from my eyes while still trying to sweep up the broken glass. I wanted to cry with her, but I wanted to be strong for her too. Now that I've had time to wrap my head around it, I break. A sob rips from my throat, and I feel my mother's arms around me. I drop the broom, letting it clatter to the floor before I wrap my arms around her, holding onto her like she's my only saving grace.

"She's the best damn human to ever come into my life," I sniff. "Why do shitty things keep happening to her? She deserves so much more than what life is giving her."

"I know, hunny." She rubs my back. "But she has you. And I know you will always help her see her worth. She has us. She's family and we take care of our family. I don't know what happened tonight, and that's okay. That's between you two. But I'm always here for you both."

"Thank you. Fuck. I just love her so much and I feel so useless. All I want to do is take away her pain and make life perfect for her. She's suffered enough. She has so much to worry about with school, work, and Lilly. She's gonna freak out when she realizes what she did to the house."

"I know you want to swoop in and take it all away, but

you're only human too. As for Lilly, you know I love that little girl and I will always be here. Whenever you need help, just ask. You're doing an amazing job, and I see how much that girl loves you. Don't think I don't notice that she's taking care of you just as much as you are her. Seeing you happy again, it's all a mother could ever want. And I owe her so much for doing that for my son."

"She really is the best, Mom. I loved Kristen, and a part of me always will. But Ellie, there's just something about her spark, her light that draws you in and makes you feel alive. Makes you feel things you never knew you could. She's good for me, Mom. She's perfect for me."

"One day at a time, hunny. That's all you can do."

She's right. We will take whatever life throws at us and fight it together, standing side by side.

Every single thing with her exes is like one big fucked up tangled web. I know she loves them. All I know is that no matter what she decides, I'll be right there alongside her.

# Chapter Twenty-Eight

## ELLIE

I JOLT AWAKE, startled by a dream or nightmare. I don't know which because by the time I blink my eyes open, I thankfully forget what it was about.

"Shh." Strong arms pull me against a warm hard chest. I smile at the feeling of waking up in the arms of the man that I love. "You're okay." He kisses the back of my neck. I sigh at the feeling, so safe and protected.

"You stayed." My voice comes out hoarse, then I remember why. I squeeze my eyes shut hard, trying to force last night out of my mind.

"Of course I did." His thumb caresses my lower belly, sending a shiver of pleasure through my body, providing the perfect distraction. I won't try anything because I share this bed with my daughter, but it doesn't mean I can't enjoy just laying here with him.

"Thank you," I say softly, snuggling into him deeper. "For last night. Sorry you had to see me like that. I promise I'm not crazy. I've never done anything like that before, but last night, it was..."

"Too much. Ellie, I know you're not crazy. You're a little bit of an odd-ball but not crazy." I giggle, smiling against his arm.

"You were faced with a traumatic part of your past and your response was valid. I would have been worried if you *didn't* react like that. I'm just sorry you had to go through it in the first place."

I roll over and drape myself over him, needing to feel as close to him as I can.

"I think I'm gonna go to one of those meetings," I murmur against his chest. He squeezes me tighter.

"Whatever you think is best, sweetheart. I'm by your side no matter what."

"I love you," I say, trying to hold back tears. I cried enough last night. I needed that. After everything that's been happening, there's only so much I can hold in.

"I love you too." We lay there for a while just enjoying each other's embrace before Theo speaks again. "I know it's none of my business, and I won't ask again after this, but are you sure you don't want to go to the authorities? Those monsters should not be able to get away with what they have done."

"I want to..." I say, moving to sit up on the bed, crossing my legs. "I do. But Theo, they have money. It's been years, and I have no proof." I sigh.

"I hate how spoiled, little rich brats get away with so many sick things because daddy has money," he growls.

"Me too. I could try but I don't think I could mentally do it. I work so hard every day to get through school, work, and parenting Lilly, even though it haunts me in the back of my mind. I don't want to risk bringing it all back and somehow affecting her negatively. I need to be strong and healthy. That's why I think going to that meeting and talking to other survivors could help." I give him a forced smile.

"Okay," he says, sitting up and pulling me in for a kiss. "Whatever you think is best."

"We should get ready for the day." I climb out of bed and leave the room to go to the bathroom. I freeze. I was expecting this place to be a mess. But it's not. "You cleaned it all?" I ask, looking back at Theo. "You didn't have to."

"I wanted to," he says, giving me another kiss. "Now, we just need to replace everything that broke."

I groan. "Damn it. Why did I go for the TV?"

"You can use the one from my room for now until we replace it."

"Thank you, baby."

"Anything for my queen." He spins me around in twirls, making me giggle. "How are you feeling?"

"Better," I smile up at him, "because of you."

"Good." He smiles back. "Mom took Lilly to daycare and Toby to school, so we're good until your first class."

A cell phone rings. I look around, not sure where it is. I follow the sound and find it sitting in the corner, the screen smashed.

"I can't answer it," I sigh, holding up the phone to show Theo.

"We can take it to the shop and get you a replacement phone after classes. We both have the afternoon free."

"Yeah, okay." I toss the broken phone on the counter. "I'm gonna go grab a quick shower."

"Okay. I'll run over to my place to shower and change."

Once I'm showered and dressed, I throw my hair into a messy bun, not having the energy to do any hair or makeup today when I hear Theo talking. Opening the door to the bathroom, I see him in clean clothes, hair damp from his own shower. He's pacing back and forth as he talks to whoever is on the other end of his phone call.

"I'll let her know. Alright, thank you. We'll be there right away." He hangs up. "Fuck!" he says, shoving his phone in his pocket.

"What's wrong?" I ask, stepping out of the bathroom. He turns to me with a look of dread on his face. "Theo. What's wrong?" He has me freaking out inside. I don't like that look.

"That was Dean McNeil," he says, his voice tight.

My stomach drops. "They showed her?" I croak.

He nods. "I think so. She says she needs us both in her office right away to discuss some important matters."

"Fuck!" I shout. "Can't they just leave me the hell alone?"

"Look, let's not get too worked up. We will go and talk to her first." He pulls me into his arms. "They won't kick you out. If anything, they would just fire me."

"But you love your job," I mutter into his warm chest.

"I love you more. So much more." He kisses the top of my head. "I can find another job, Ellie, but there will never be another you."

"You're so corny," I giggle. " I love it."

"Damn right you do," he chuckles, making me laugh harder.

"Alright. Let's go get this over with. We knew it was going to come to this eventually. Just didn't expect it to be like this."

The car ride is quiet, filled with nervous energy. My hand is clasped with his the whole time, his thumb rubbing back and forth in a soothing caress.

When we get to her office, none other than Brody Creed is sitting there in one of the chairs outside her door.

He looks up at me, his eyes swimming with pain, regret, and something else I can't quite make out. But that can't be right. This man made my life hell. Why would he suddenly feel bad about it? But when he looks over to Theo, he gives him a murderous look. *What's that about?*

"Mr. Munro, Miss Tatum, please come into my office," Dean McNeil says from the doorway to her office, snapping Theo and Brody out of their stare off.

We take a seat in the chairs in front of her desk as she takes her seat.

"Sorry to have you both come down here on such short notice, but I wanted to get this resolved as quickly as possible. Do either of you know why I've asked you here today?"

I look at Theo, my stomach threatening to bring back last night's supper. "I think so," I say, looking back at the dean.

"It's come to my attention that the two of you are involved in some kind of relationship. Is that correct?"

I'm not going to lie. There's no point, and I'm not hiding. I clear my throat. "Yes."

"I assumed as much. I was shown a very...graphic video of the both of you taken in your office, Mr. Munro." My cheeks heat as sweat starts to form on my brow. God, this is embarrassing. "As soon as I could identify who was in the video, I shut it off. I have a few questions I'd like to ask you."

"Of course," I nod.

"How long have you been involved with Mr. Munro?"

"For about three months now. We met at the beginning of the school year before he started working here. We live in the same apartment, and..." I look back at the door.

"No one can hear you, Miss Tatum," the dean says.

"We met at the park. My daughter and his son became friends. We started talking and then we started dating." I smile over at Theo before returning my attention back to the dean.

"I know I should have said something when I took this job, but I was afraid that it wouldn't be allowed. I love this woman more than anything in the world. I would give up my job, my dream job, for her if I have to." The dean smiles at Theo and I really hope that's a good sign.

"That sounds like a man truly in love," she laughs lightly. "Well, from all the information I've gathered, I think we can all leave here happy."

My heart almost stops, and I hold back a sob of relief.

"Really?"

"Yes. Our university doesn't have an issue with a student dating a professor but there are a few things that are required. You will have to fill out these forms. It's to help us with liability." She hands us both a set of papers. "You have to be over the age of twenty-one and from your records, you're almost twenty-three so that isn't a problem. Also, you will not be allowed to take any classes taught by Mr. Munro."

"That won't be a problem," I smile.

"I can tell this is a serious relationship with two consenting adults that started before Mr. Munro was employed. We do, however, ask you to keep your relationship professional, meaning no PDA while on school property." She looks at Theo. "Your office is for working and nothing else. Am I understood?"

Theo's cheeks turn an adorable shade of pink. He pushes his glasses up and nods. "Of course. I am very sorry about that. It will never happen again. We will leave anything personal for our private life."

"Alright then. Thank you for coming in. I'm glad we got this cleared up. Please, have those filled out and sent in as soon as possible."

We say our goodbyes, giving our thanks and apologies once again before leaving the office. I'm so happy and relieved this didn't go how I thought it would. I really want to squeal and jump for joy right now. But it's not the time, nor the place.

Brody is still outside when we leave the office. He stands up, staring at me like he's not sure which way his plan went. He's about to find out it failed, yet again. I'm pissed. I'm done with it all. "I'm only going to say this once. Leave me alone. If you try to fuck with me again, I will get a restraining order on you as well as tell the dean everything you and Rain have done to me this year." I shake my head. "What happened to you, Brody? The man I knew would have never gone this far."

"I guess it shows that we never really knew each other at all then," he says, his jaw clenched and nostrils flaring. "You don't have to worry anymore. I told everyone you're off limits. You won't have any more issues with me or the others."

"About time," I scoff. "It just took months of hell for no damn reason. I'm not your enemy, Brody, and I hope someday, you'll realize that."

I turn away from him, not giving him any more of my attention. Theo's hand slips into mine and we leave the office.

Once we are in the car, I turn to Theo.

"It's over." I grin and start to laugh like a crazy woman. "No more secrets! We can be together, and go out, and do things like a real couple."

I kiss Theo hard, making him moan that turns into a chuckle. "I'm so glad." He puts his forehead to mine. "Do you think he was telling the truth?"

"Yeah. Surprisingly, I do."

## BRODY

I knew the moment she walked out of that office that my stupid plan failed. I was so pissed off with how that pompous dick talked to me, putting his fucking hands on me, I wasn't thinking clearly.

As soon as he left the locker room, we all went out and played in the second half. I was so angry that it actually helped us win. I put all my focus and energy into the game. And it paid off.

As soon as it ended, I didn't even bother staying to celebrate with everyone. I knew the dean was at the game, so I searched her out, showed her the video, and then it was done. But as soon as I showed her, I regretted it.

I know once the guys and Rain find out about it, they're going to be pissed. On my way home, I sent out a mass text telling everyone that Ellie was off limits. That anyone who fucked with her would have to deal with the Silver Knights.

I'm done. She's not going anywhere, and after a long talk with Jax last night, where he mostly yelled at me, I realized that I can't do this anymore.

All I wanted was her gone so I didn't have to see her beautiful face or hear her musical laugh. But I got so wrapped up in my own pain, I let it take control. It made me into someone I had never wanted to be.

There was a time I would have killed anyone who treated Ellie the way I have. I'm a fucking monster.

It might not have looked like it, but when Jax told me about the guys who were harassing Ellie, I was ready to hunt them down and end them myself. I felt sick at the idea of someone laying their hands on her or forcing themselves on her.

As much as I hate what Ellie did to us in the past, I would never, ever wish that on her.

But then that stupid teacher, her stupid *boyfriend*, had to come in and fuck everything up. I was ready to leave it alone. But God, just the way he talked about her, the love just oozing off them while he fucked her in his office. I was jealous, so fucking jealous that all I could think about was getting rid of him.

But it was pointless and stupid because the dean told me how they are both adults who started dating before he took this job at school, and as long as she's not in any of his classes, it doesn't go against their rules.

I'm exhausted and drained. I got up early for that meeting and didn't have a good night's sleep on top of that.

"You wanna tell me what the fuck this is about?" Chase demands, on my ass the moment I get into the apartment.

"What the fuck are you talking about?" I mumble, tossing my keys on the counter. I sit on the stool of the island in our kitchen, my face in my hands as I lean against my arms, my head throbbing.

"This." He thrusts his phone in my face. I look down, seeing a text from an unsaved number. *Keep a leash on your bestie or I'll be getting restraining orders on all of you.*

"Who sent that?" I ask, although I already know the answer.

"I'm pretty sure it's Ellie. I don't have her number, but it's easy to get ours. So what did you do now? Where did you just come from, this early in the morning?"

I knew it. Time to fess up because lying will only make it worse.

"I was at the dean's office."

"What?!" he asks. "Why?"

"I was pissed off after Theo paid us a little visit last night, and showed Dean McNeil the video."

"You what?" Jax's voice comes from behind me. I turn around to see his face bright red with anger. "Why would you do that? For fuck's sake, Brody," he growls, fisting his hair. "You lied! You told me you were done fucking with her. She's had enough. You got your fucked up revenge."

"Well, technically, I didn't lie. I showed her the video before I told you I was done." Yeah, that's not helping anything.

"I love you, so fucking much, but there's only so many times I can stick up for you and turn a blind eye to your behavior before I start questioning my own morals. Do you know how hard it is to watch you hurt the girl I love? The girl we all fucking love! I kept telling myself I had to because I shouldn't do anything to make you mad. Because all I have left is you. That I'm so in love with you nothing else matters. But I was wrong and I can't do this anymore. If this is the Brody you really are, then I'm not sure I want to know him," he says, his voice breaking before he takes off, leaving the apartment.

"Fuck!" I bang my hand down on the table. Pain shoots up my arm, causing me to grit my teeth.

"You only have yourself to blame." Chase shakes his head. "I'm telling you this now, I plan on making it up to Ellie. I want to talk to her and let her tell me her side of the story, the one you didn't let us get all those years ago. There's something that's not right. I always thought that night was messed up, especially after what happened with the guys we all think she cheated on us with." He runs a hand down his face. "Shit just doesn't add up."

I don't want to admit that I was wrong. Even if I was hurt by what happened, the way I went about it was all wrong. Hell, it was fucked up. And now I may have lost another person I love. Chase is right. This is on me.

Going to the cabinet, I grab a bottle of Jack and lock myself in my room. If there's one thing I know, it's drowning myself in liquor.

## RAIN

I've been keeping my distance from the guys. Mostly because Brody has still been so set on getting revenge. But me, I'm done. I hate seeing her upset, the broken look on her face every time we do something.

She's so strong, never letting anything we do beat her down. As much as it hurts to see her everywhere, knowing she's not mine anymore, it's not worth the feeling I get when we hurt her.

It didn't help to find out about her and Brody's professor though. I have no idea why I insisted on watching the video Brody took, but it broke me all over again seeing how in love she is with him.

And God, when Brody outed her and Cooper to the whole school, I wanted to kick his ass. As a gay woman, what my best friend did to Cooper was completely wrong, especially when Brody himself is bi-sexual and pretty much in the closet. I've lost a little respect for him.

Brody says it's Ellie who's changed us for the worse, but he's wrong. We did that to ourselves because while we're over here being hateful assholes, Ellie is happy outside of this school. So really, who are the losers in this stupid game?

"Knock, knock," I say, peeking my head into Chase's room.

"So, you are alive. I thought you must have died because you've never been away from us that long." He grins, taking off his headphones and tossing them to the side.

"I know," I sigh, inviting myself into the room. "I just needed some space."

"From me?" he asks, his brow pinched in worry.

"Not just you, from everyone."

"Is this about Ellie?"

I plop down next to him, curling my body into his, my red curly hair covering my face. "Yeah."

"I told her I was sorry," he says softly, "after the whole Cooper thing. I told her I was stupid for standing by and doing nothing and that I regret everything."

Wow... "I still love her," I say, my eyes growing blurry with tears. "I love her so much, it fucking hurts. Seeing her so happy with her friends, with that guy. I want that. With her. Hell, at this point, I don't even care about the past. I just want her again, Chase." I don't cry much, but when I do, it's with him.

"I do too," he says, rubbing my back. "I love her and haven't stopped. I want her back too."

"But we ruined any chance we had at that. God."

"We had a chance to talk to her, you know. At that party, we should have talked to her and asked her about that night. But then Brody, and you..."

I groan. "I know. It was all a shock seeing her after so long. My anger was feeding off Brody's, and well...we fucked it up before we even had a chance."

"Brody is family. And I love that man. But don't you think that a lot of this could have been avoided if we hadn't listened to him? Maybe if we made our own decisions on how to handle that night, we could have saved ourselves a lot of heartache."

"Yeah." I let out a humorless laugh. "I'm starting to see that now."

"So, what do we do now?" he asks, playing with my hair.

"Well, I guess we can start with leaving her alone for a bit. I don't think she wants anything to do with us. And it's too soon to try and talk to her."

"Yeah, I may have chosen a bad time to tell her all that."

"Yeah?" I laugh. "I'm gonna have to suck it up, put my big girl panties on, and kiss ass, aren't I?"

"Probably," he chuckles. "But I'll be right alongside you."

"She's never gonna take us back."

"No, maybe not. But we owe it to her to hear her side if she's willing to tell it, even though she doesn't owe us anything at this point. Not after everything. But we have to try."

"Yeah."

"So, what are you going to do about Laura?"

My nose scrunches up as I sit up to look at him. "I don't know. She's becoming more clingy than ever. And since we stopped messing around, she's been blowing up my phone."

"Well, it can't be as bad as Kayla," he scoffs.

"You wanna tell me about that?" I ask. I know she's been crazy about him, but how crazy is what I need to know.

"Well, to put it simply, she's a stalker. I've had to block her number way too many times. She's always following me, always trying to get me to ask her out. I've put up with it because you're friends with her. But Rain, if we're going to try to get on Ellie's good side to get her to at least talk to us, being friends with those two won't get us there."

"I know," I sigh. "They get way too much enjoyment out of tormenting Ellie. I hate it. The things they say about her, ugh! Makes me wanna tell them to fuck off."

"Well, now you can." He gives me a big, goofy grin.

"True," I laugh. "But I do have to try to keep things as civil as I can. We might be done cheering on the school's team but we still have the competition team in the Spring."

"Well, I guess you're just gonna have to hang out with me all the time then." He grabs me by the arm, pulling me down to him before putting me in a head lock and giving me a noogie.

"Fuck off," I laugh. "You're going to mess up my hair." I pull away from him with a huff.

"Too late, Fire." He grins, using the nickname that sweet, little girl, Lilly, gave me.

"I miss that kid."

"Me too." He lets out a sad sigh. "Is it sad that the most fun I've had in years is with a three-year-old?"

"Nah. She's a cool kid. Easy to love."

"Well, maybe we can look into volunteering there again. For like field trips or something."

"Maybe. Wouldn't hurt to try," I shrug.

"Fix your shirt," Chase groans. I look down and my tits are almost hanging out.

"Since when does this bother you?" I laugh.

"Since I haven't gotten laid in weeks and have only had the company of my hand with Ellie's name on my lips as I cum." His grin is suggestive. "I'm still a man who loves boobs and I'm not blind."

"Eww." I smack his leg with one hand while fixing my shirt with the other. "I don't need to know that."

"Like you're not doing the same thing."

He's got me there.

# Chapter Twenty-Nine

## ELLIE

CHRISTMAS EVE ROLLS AROUND MUCH TOO QUICKLY. The kids are in bed and I have so much to do!

"Ellie, sweetheart, calm down," Theo says, coming out of the bedroom. I stop and look over, a cookie in my hand frozen midair as I put some out for Santa and his reindeer.

"Well, I wasn't expecting to see you so soon," I grin. "This is for you, I guess," I say, straightening up as Theo walks toward me. He's dressed in a Santa suit, and fuck does he look sexy.

"Thank you, Mrs. Claus. But, I have something much sweeter and tastier in mind that I'd like for a snack instead," he says, his voice low and husky, causing my breath to hitch and my panties to dampen.

"Oh, would you look at that," I breathe, looking up at the mistletoe. "Looks like you're going to have to kiss me," I say, biting my lip. He gives me a sexy smile before pulling me into his arms and kissing me hard. I moan, wrapping my arms around him, holding him tighter to me.

"Get off my mama!" The yell has me jumping back from Theo. Lilly is pulling on the Santa coat.

"Lilly, baby, it's okay!" I try to reason with her. The little turkey should be sleeping right now. But before I can say anything else, Theo groans in pain.

"Miss Ellie is Daddy's girlfriend!" Toby says, punching Theo in the private parts. I'm shocked, taking in the scene before me. Just as Toby is about to kick his father while he's down, I grab him from under the shoulders and pull him away.

"It's okay, buddy!" I say, not sure how to explain what just happened without telling them that Santa is really Theo in a costume. Although, I don't think we're going to win them over that easily.

"You kissed Mama!" Lilly screams.

"Lilly, Toby, calm down!" Theo scrambles to stand and avoid any more damage to his manhood. "It was just a friendly kiss. See?" I say pointing up at the mistletoe. "When two people are under the mistletoe, it's tradition to give them a kiss."

They both look up, then Lilly looks at me. "I kiss Toby?"

My eyes go wide. "Little kid kisses are okay, on the cheek," I say, tapping my index finger against my cheek.

Lilly giggles and goes to give Toby a kiss but he takes off down the hall screaming "Eww! Girl cooties!"

"Are you okay?" I ask, trying not to laugh. What a night.

"Overall, yes. My pride and junk, not so much." He grimaces, adjusting himself.

"I'll kiss it better later," I wink.

"Deal," he growls.

"Mama," Lilly says, running back into the living room.

"Yes, Lillypad?"

"Why is Santa here?" she asks, looking Theo over.

"To bring you presents of course." I smile. "But, you're up. And Santa doesn't bring gifts when little kids are up. So, you're gonna have to go to bed, and go back to sleep, so Santa can come back later. Only then will he leave the presents under the tree."

"Okay," she says sadly, "Come on Toby, we gotta sleep."

Toby gives Theo the stink eye before asking, "Where's my dad?"

Shit. I hate lying to them. "He went out to get more milk since Santa drank all of ours."

"Okay..." he says. "Night."

"Night, buddy."

When we are sure the two of them are in Toby's room, I sigh with relief. "Sooo, role-playing was a bust," I giggle.

"You think?" he laughs. "Now I remember why we wait until we have no kids for the night before we get freaky."

"Get freaky?" I smirk, cocking a brow.

"Oh, you know you love it, my dirty girl." Fuck, the look he's giving me is pure torture. I can't do anything about it right now though.

"Only for you, Sir." I bite my lip, hoping like hell I look seductive.

Christmas Day is amazing. We wake up and open gifts. The kids seem to not be too scarred from last night. They're just so excited and grateful for everything. I'm all smiles and proud of their reactions. No one complains and wishes they got something different.

We spend the day in Spring Meadows, and man, is it nice not to pretend we are just friends. We hold hands and act like a real couple, but a part of me is always worried that Rain and the guys are nearby. After everything that's happened, it's hard to feel like it's really over. I just pray that Brody was telling the truth. I just want to be able to enjoy going to school instead of constantly worried about being harassed.

I know it's stupid of me, but I get where they are coming from. In their minds, they think I cheated. Sure, they didn't trust me enough to know I would never do something like that, but in their minds, that's what I did. They still went way too far.

Even if we had been together for years, and this didn't diminish the love I had, and still have, for them, we were only teenagers. No matter the heartache, it didn't call for years of grudges to come out later on in life. They should have tried to move on, and be happy, not hold onto the hate inside.

That's what I did. Like I've said time and time again, I love them, always have, always will, but I didn't let what they did to me that night dictate my whole life. I didn't hold a grudge. How could I? I had a daughter to take care of. She is more important than anything else in the world.

Chase seems like he's sorry and wants to make it up to me. Maybe someday I'll hear what he has to say, maybe even have another civil conversation with him. I don't think he was involved in showing that video. That was all Brody. But the fact is, as much as I'd love to think better of Chase, he sat back and watched.

But, should I punish Chase for his friend's actions? Should I keep him away from my little girl when he could possibly be her father?

I don't know. There's so much going on right now, I just need some time to breathe, clear my head, and get my life back on track.

There's a support meeting in the new year that I plan on attending, and hopefully by talking to fellow survivors, I'll be able to find some peace.

Theo's parents have us over for supper, and it is just as fun and yummy as Thanksgiving was.

They offer to watch the kids for a few hours after supper, so Theo and I could go back to Spring Meadows for a mini date. We got some hot cocoa, and are now at the indoor skating rink. I told Theo I love to skate, and he insisted we come here. He failed to mention that he has no idea how to skate.

"Babe," I laugh, "give me your hands."

He looks so terrified as he clings to the side of the rink, trying not to fall. He makes *Bambi on Ice* look easy. But he's so cute.

"Can't," he says. "Need to hold on."

"Want me to get one of the skate trainers?"

He looks at me with a scowl, making me giggle. "What, one of those things the kids are using?" he asks with a scoff. "They look like something an old person would use."

"Then maybe you should use it, old man. You look like you could use the help," a teenage girl says as she skates by like a professional.

"That's it," he says. "I'll show you! Old man, my butt. I'm only thirty," he grumbles, letting go of the sides and shuffling his feet toward me. I stifle a giggle as he wobbles his way over to me while holding out my hands for him.

When he gets to me, he goes to grab them but slips just as his hands make it to mine, pulling me onto him, and I burst out into a fit of giggles.

"I vote we just hang out down here," he says, wrapping his arms around me. "I like this better."

"Me too. But I think the group of kids and their parents would think otherwise," I say looking up and finding we have an audience.

"Fine," he huffs. "Get me a walker. This old man needs some help."

We skate for an hour, and by the end of it, Theo is able to move without any help. He slips a few more times, but overall, he does well. It's the perfect ending to an overall amazing day. I'm so excited for this new year and new adventures with my new little family.

Even if my life has had its hellish moments the past few months, it's also had some of the best ones I could have asked for.

And I'm excited to see what else life has in store for me. Let's just hope it's more good than bad.

## BRODY

"Hello!" I call out as I open the front door to the house—my father's house. I might live here on school breaks, but this place doesn't feel like home. For as long as I can remember, I've hated being here. But I keep coming back because of him, my dad. He might be a wreck, but it is only because that bitch who gave birth to me made him that way.

Shouting from within the house has me picking up my pace.

"It's Christmas!" my father roars. At first, I don't see who he's talking to until I step into the kitchen. "Can't you just think about someone other than yourself for one fucking minute?" He has a bottle of rum in his hand. He's drunk. It's the only time he has the balls to stick up to my mother. That's who he's yelling at.

"Oh, please. Why would I want to stay here in this bum fuck, middle of nowhere, town when I can go to Mexico with the girls?" she scoffs. She might be wearing designer clothes, looking like a millionaire's wife, but under all that money, she's a selfish, trashy bitch.

"And let me guess, you want me to fund this little trip?" my dad scoffs.

"Come on! You're my husband. All the other husbands are paying for them."

"I'm only your fucking husband when it pleases you. Why don't you go ask one of the twenty other guys who you're opening your legs for?"

My mother's face drops as she gapes at my dad. "How dare you talk to me like that!" She raises her hand to slap my dad.

"Enough of that," I growl. My mother's head snaps in my direction and I can see the shift in her persona as she goes into 'fake as fuck' mode.

"Brody, darling, my sweet boy." She rushes over to give me a hug, but I take a step back.

"What are you doing here?" I ask.

"It's Christmas, of course. I want to be with my family."

I scoff. "Don't bullshit me. I heard everything. Why do you keep on insisting on putting on this act? We all know you're here to shake Dad down for money so you can go party and fuck whoever you want."

"I am your mother!" Her nostrils flare.

"All you did was give birth to me. That's it. There's nothing motherly about you. Do mothers pass off their children to the nanny? Do mothers miss their kid's birthdays because she's getting laid, and THEN has the nerve to bring her little fuck buddy to the party? Do mothers call him her 'friend' while this 'friend' eats all the fucking food?! You're trashy. There are no other words for it. You had a chance to live this amazing life, but you go and fuck around on Dad with these low life thugs and drug dealers."

"Well, maybe if your father's dick wasn't so damn small, I wouldn't have to go to someone else for my physical needs!" she shouts back.

My dad curses and takes a long swig from the bottle.

"You're a real class act. How about you fuck off. No one wants you here anyways."

"You can't mean that! I'm family. This is my house too. This is my husband."

"No, that is a man you had a child with and left him to do his best at raising me. You might be married, but you're no wife to him. So, go find someone else to fund your shitty life and leave us the fuck alone!" I roar in her face.

With everything that's happened with Ellie, and Jax not talking to me, while Chase and Rain can't even look at me, I'm just fucking done.

She turns to look at my dad, but I step in front of his view. "GO!" I say in a dangerously low tone.

"I could call the cops, you know." She juts out her chin. "This is legally my house too."

"You could. But you won't because once your boyfriends find out you've been dealing with the cops, you will lose all that dirty cock you're so hungry for."

"You ungrateful little bastard! I should have aborted you like I wanted to! You think I'm a waste of space? You're just as bad," she tsks.

"Maggie!" my dad shouts. "That's enough. It's one thing to come in here and insult and harass me, but I will not allow you to talk to my son like that in my home!"

"Fine! Fuck you, fuck both of you," she screeches, turning around and storming out of the house, slamming the door behind her.

"Got any more of that?" I ask, looking at the bottle in his hand as I let out a harsh sigh.

"Don't I always?" he murmurs, tossing me the keys to the liquor cabinet before heading somewhere in the house, most likely the theater room.

I despise that woman more than words can explain. She's never been a mother, and I'm used to it. It's all I've ever known, but seeing how she treats my dad hurts.

She only married him for his money. But my dad, for God knows what reason, fell head over heels for her. My dad isn't what most women would call gorgeous or sexy, but he isn't an unattractive man either. So, she saw a meal ticket and someone she could play. They got married and had me.

What she said earlier, about aborting me, is something she throws at me to remind me how much she regrets not doing it.

She got pregnant with me the first year they were married. She didn't want to be a mother, just wanted to be a gold digging whore and free to do what she pleased. But my dad begged her, bribed her, gave her a crap ton of money, not to end her pregnancy because a child was all my dad had ever wanted. He wanted a wife and kids but instead, he ended up with an ungrateful cheating bitch, and was forced to pretty much be a single dad.

Want to know why I'm so fucked up and I can't trust anyone? Well, she's a good place to start.

Grabbing my own bottle of Jack, I head up to my room. Flicking on the lights, I see that nothing's changed. The place is just how I left it when I was last here during the Summer. I didn't bother coming home for Thanksgiving except to quickly check on my dad. I knew this holiday would hit him the hardest, so I needed to be here to pick up the pieces at the end of the night.

Tossing my bag to the floor, I flop down onto my bed, grab the remote to the TV on my bed stand, and put on *Home Alone*. Cracking open the new bottle, I take a swig and settle in for a long fucking night.

## JAX

Christmas used to be one of my favorite times of the year. But since my mom passed away, it hasn't been the same. My dad tried to keep up with the traditions, but it just didn't feel right without Mom. We used to bake all Christmas Eve, go caroling, then watch Christmas movies by the fire while eating the cookies we made. It was something we did for as long as I can remember. Then we would wake up early, open gifts, eat pancakes, and spend all day in the kitchen cooking. I loved to help her with everything. She would try to get me to go and have fun, but I told her that doing that with her was fun for me.

Now, pretty much all we do is just go over to my grandparents' house for supper, then come home and do our own thing. This year is harder than the last few. My dad has started seeing a new girl, Wendy. She's a sweet lady, has a kid a few years older than me. He invited her to Christmas dinner and it just felt wrong, like I was betraying my mom somehow. So I ate supper, then told my dad I was going to check on Brody. My dad knows all about Brody's home life, the whole town does. His mother doesn't exactly try to hide what she does.

I know how he gets on this day, and I might be pissed at Brody, but I would hate myself if I didn't check in on him. And after everything that's happened, I feel like today might be a little harder than normal.

I press in the security code to the gate and head up to the house. From what I can see, there's no lights on. Maybe Brody stayed back at the apartment? I can't leave without checking first, though.

Parking the car, I press the key fob to lock the doors. The beep sounds so loud on this quiet night.

I don't bother knocking, knowing his dad will already be drunk and fast asleep. Brody could be the same by this point. Letting myself in, I check the whole house. I was right about his dad. He's drunk, passed out in his theater room with a movie playing. Turning off the TV, I take the bottle of liquor hanging loosely in his hand, and check to make sure he's still breathing. When he lets out a loud snore, I know he's fine.

After that, I go up to Brody's room. He's not there, but his bag is so I know he's been here at some point since school break started. Looking at his bedside table, I see an empty bottle of Jack. Fuck. I need to find him. The idea of him wandering around wasted has me fearing for his safety.

Where could he be if he's not in the house?

Then I remember the meadow between his house and the woods. It's a place that holds significance to him and I've found him there a few times in the past.

Making sure to lock up behind me, I head toward the clearing.

It's dark, only the moonlight's glow helping me navigate my way. I keep walking, looking around, trying to see if I can spot him when I trip over something hard.

"Hey," a voice slurs. "Watch where you're going, Mr. Deer."

Getting up off the ground, I dust off my hands and knees. "No deer here, just me," I say looking down at Brody who's sprawled out on the ground, looking back up at me.

"Jax?" he asks, squinting.

"Yup," I sigh, taking a seat next to him.

"What are you doing here? Thought you hated me," he mumbles.

"I don't hate you, Brody," I admit.

He lets out a huffed laugh. "Sure, and there are no dancing polar bears in the sky. You're not fooling me!"

*What?* I look up on instinct, but then I remember he's drunk and probably seeing things.

Shaking my head, I look down at my drunk boyfriend. "I don't hate you, Brody. Am I happy with how things are right now? No. But I don't hate you. I just don't like who you've become."

"No one likes who I've become," he says. "Not you, not the others, not my mom, and not Ellie."

My blood starts to boil at the mention of his toxic mother. "You should know by now not to listen to anything that horrible woman has to say. It's all lies and bullshit."

"I hate her, you know," he says, lulling his head to the side, but not opening his eyes.

"Who, Ellie?"

He snorts. "No, not Ellie. I love her," he whispers. That much, I know. He may have been a grade A dick to her these past few months but he's never stopped loving her. "My mother. She says things. Things that stick with me."

"I know. I wish you could see past her bullshit," I say, brushing his brown locks out of his face. He sighs at the contact.

"You know. The day we saw Ellie, before the first football game, I saw my mom." He blinks open his eyes. "I ran into her in town. She told me she heard Ellie was back. She laughed at me, told me no wonder Ellie cheated on me, that I'm a sorry excuse of a man, that no one would ever love me, and that I'm nothing but a disappointment."

My heart breaks. I had no idea he saw his mother that day.

"So when we went to that party, I saw Ellie all...happy and I lost it. I let my mother's words get to me. Ellie being there, reminding me how I will never have her, that she never wanted me. It hurt so much, and all I knew how to do was lash out."

His words are soft and slow. I just sit there and listen. This is the most I've heard him admit his feelings about anything.

"After that first night, it was like a domino effect, one thing after another. But Jax..." He reaches out and grabs my hand. "I don't want to be like that anymore. I don't want to be who my mom thinks I am."

"You're not," I insist.

"But I am. I fucked with the girl I love, all because I didn't think I was good enough. And I just proved everyone right."

"You were hurt and you went about it the wrong way. Just like Rain did. It hurt to see Ellie around, so she wanted to make Ellie leave. Having her back stung. It brought back old feelings we thought we could get past." Well, I thought I could. Since my mom died, I've kept my heart closed, much like Brody but only letting him in. I tried to block out anything that could cause me pain. It's why, at first, I was so okay with just letting Brody do what he thought he needed to do to make himself feel better.

But seeing Ellie like that, thinking about what those pieces of shit might have done to her, it broke that barrier down. The idea of someone hurting her like that makes me enraged and sick.

"I love her, Jax," he says, his voice breaking. "I love her so much, it fucking hurts. And seeing her with him..." he spits. Mr. Munro. Watching her with him, seeing the raw emotions in their eyes as they had sex, it fucking hurt.

"God. I can't get the image out of my head. Him being behind her, his hips slapping into her ass as he fucked her like an animal." He takes his hands and starts pounding them together, mimicking fucking. I bite my lips, trying to hold back a laugh because now is not the time for it.

"It broke something inside me all over again. Seeing her so happy and in love with someone else who isn't us just reminded me of how we will never have her again. Maybe that's why I did it. Why I did all of it. By making her hate me, it helped me hurt a little less. Well, I thought it would," he scoffs. "Now, I just feel like a big bag of dicks who made the only people who care about me hate me."

"Brody," I say, leaning over him, my face right into his. "We don't hate you," I tell him again, and I'll keep telling him until he gets it. "But we do have the right to be mad at you. Chase is obsessed with her, Rain now too. But in the way we should have been. I think we need to rethink everything."

"What do you mean?" he asks, his face looking panicked. "You mean us? Jax, please, no." He sounds so desperate. "Just because I love her doesn't mean I love you any less." He grabs my hand. "Please don't leave me, Jax. I love you so fucking much. If I lost you too, then fuck, I don't think I could survive."

"Shhh," I soothe, leaning in to kiss him deeply, ignoring the taste of whiskey on his tongue. My heart is fucking soaring out of my chest right now. He finally said the words. Fuck, it feels good. "I'm not gonna leave you." I kiss him again. "Never. I love you so much. And you're forgetting something." I smirk when I pull away.

"What?" he breathes.

"We kinda love the same woman." He blinks and gives me a shy smile that looks so foreign but adorable on him.

"Right."

"What I was going to say was, we need to re-think some things. I have no hope that we will ever get another chance with Ellie." His face drops. "But we do owe it to her to apologize for everything that we did."

"She's never going to talk to me," he groans. "I was so fucking horrible to her, Jax. A fucking monster! It pained me to

337

see the embarrassment, the hurt, and the sadness I was causing her but I couldn't fucking stop!"

"Well, I know we definitely have to give her some space. Let her be free from all the bullshit. And when things have calmed down, we can send Chase in to ask her to talk to us."

"Send in the golden retriever...smart," he says with a serious nod that has me smiling.

"We never got the chance to hear her side, Brody. You saw what you saw and we went along with it, not bothering to hear her speak. She deserves to tell her side of things."

"I know," he says, squinting his eyes.

"One step at a time."

I lie there with him and we talk about how he and Ellie used to come here all the time to watch the stars. It hurts to think about the good times, the times we missed out on, and the times we might never get, but it also feels amazing to think of them without having so much hate in our hearts.

I feel like a big weight has been lifted off my shoulders. I never want to cause Ellie pain again. I never want to see the broken look on her face or the sounds of her cries.

I might have Brody, and I'm so blessed to call him mine, but there's always been a piece of my heart that's been missing. She owns it, and without her, I don't think we'll ever be complete.

When it starts to get cold, I nudge Brody, who fell asleep, to wake up enough so that I'm not dragging dead weight back to the house. I manage to get him into his house and into his bed. I take off his shoes then his pants, getting a mumble from him that I think is him telling me he's gonna rock my world before he passes out again. I chuckle as I tuck him in. Normally, I leave after I'm done picking him up, cleaning him off, and putting him to bed, but not tonight. I think we both need to wake up next to each other and remember that we're not alone.

## Chapter Thirty

### ELLIE

"THIS IS SO EXCITING!" Val says, bouncing on the balls of her feet with excitement.

"I know! I haven't had time to come here when I'm not working, and any days I did have off, we went to parties," I laugh.

"Well, I'm glad we get to party here tonight! And on New Years. Girl, I hope your babysitter is good with watching the little buggers all night because we are getting SMASHED!" Val cheers.

"Lexie." Tabitha looks at the person in question.

"Yeah," she sighs. "I'm on Val duty, what else is new?" She rolls her eyes.

"Girl, you're the only one who can tame her ass when she's drunk," Tabitha laughs.

"Guys, I'm not that bad," Val pouts. Lexie and Tabitha look at each other then burst out laughing. Val gives them the stink eye while flipping them off. That just has them laughing harder.

"And how awesome is it that you get to bring your man with you?" Lexie asks. "Must be nice to finally be able to go out as a couple."

"It is," I smile, tilting my head back to look at Theo. He's holding me in his arms, just letting me and the girls do our own thing, enjoying the simple fact that he gets to be with us.

Theo looks down at me, his smile leaving these cute, little dimples as he gives me a peck on the lips.

"Don't worry about me. I don't plan on stepping on anyone's toes. Just do as you normally would. I'm just here to ring in the new year with my love, and have an early birthday celebration with her." He gives me a little squeeze.

My real birthday is next weekend but the girls and I are going to a big party to celebrate the football season win. Everyone left for Christmas break right after, so they didn't get a chance to.

"Love, awww!" Val says. "You two are adorable. So, Theo, got any hot professor friends looking to rob the cradle?" My mouth opens in shock as Theo makes a choked sound.

"For fuck's sake, Val!" Lexie snaps. "The night hasn't even started, and you're already blurting out stupid things."

"What! I'm serious. I'm sick of boys at this school. I need a real man. And from what Ellie has told us, men Theo's age sure do know what they are doing, sir." Val wiggles her eyebrows.

My cheeks heat as I let out an embarrassed groan, moving my hands to cover my face.

"Well, Miss Tatum, have you been spilling our dirty secrets?" Theo asks, sounding like he's getting way too much enjoyment out of this.

I peek up at him. "Yeah? I'm sorry, but when Val hounds you for juicy details, it's hard for her to take no for an answer."

"It's true. Val is a hornball and gets off on everyone else's sex life because her mouth prevents her from having her own," Lexie shrugs.

"Rude! My mouth can do many wonderful things. Just ask Tabitha," Val says.

Tabitha's eyes go wide. "That was one time," she squeaks. "And we were drunk."

"Still counts," Val says, giving her a naughty smirk. "I might prefer the D, but the V isn't too bad either."

"Alright, that's enough talk from you," Lexie says. "Look, we're up next!" Lexie starts to drag Val into the club.

I could have gone in without waiting in line because I work here, but tonight, I just wanted to be like everyone else so we waited in line like everyone else.

Clasping my hand with Theo's, we follow after the girls.

The place is packed, the music loud, and the energy of the whole place has a fun, carefree feel to it. Normally, a crowd like this would have me in panic mode, but being here with Theo right beside me, I feel safe.

"Hey, you!" Aria says, coming up and giving me a hug.

"Hey!"

"Weird seeing you here and in something a little more modest than what they make us wear," she laughs. "Looking good, Tatum."

"Thank you." I smile. I'm in a little black, sparkly dress that cuts off just above the knee and shows enough boob without it being too revealing.

"Happy early birthday! Boss man booked one of the VIP spots just for you. And, I get to be your lucky server," she bows.

"What, really?" I ask. VIP is normally an extra hundred on top of the admission fee and it's first come first serve. For me to have one of the spots is exciting, especially for my first time here as a guest.

"Of course. You've been good for business, and you're a hard worker."

"This is fucking awesome!" Val's eyes light up. "Is your boss hot? I'd like to tell him thanks for the VIP."

"Seriously?" Lexie stares blankly at her best friend. "You haven't even had a drink yet!"

"Ha! Jokes on you. I pre-gamed at home." She sticks her tongue out.

"Come on." Aria laughs at my crazy friend and guides us over to the VIP section.

I'm laughing and feeding off the vibe of this place as we walk through the club but when we make it over to our spot, all happy feelings slip away in the blink of an eye.

They're here. I should have known that they would be here on a night like this. It is their regular spot. So much for hoping for one night to myself and friends to just be happy.

"Here you go," Aria says and the others take a seat on the couches, me being the last one to enter.

These sections are blocked off with about six foot walls that wrap around into a semi circle for privacy, but just as I'm about to disappear into our space, I get the feeling of being watched.

The urge to look over takes my better judgement, and I find both Brody and Rain looking at me with a mix of emotions. It's so weird not seeing hatred and disgust in their eyes after seeing it for months. No, they look miserable. Brody has dark circles under his eyes like he hasn't slept in weeks, and Rain is missing her carefree energy that normally radiates off her.

"Ellie, sweetheart," Theo's voice has me looking away and over to him. "You okay, love?"

"Perfect!" I say, plastering on a big smile with a little too much cheer in my voice. Hopefully, the music drowns it out.

Taking a seat on Theo's lap, I settle in and we give Aria our orders. We made sure to eat before coming here so that all we had to worry about was drinking and having fun.

When Aria gets back, we down a few shots and just enjoy the music.

"Having fun so far, sweetheart?" Theo whispers into my ear, sending a shiver through my body causing my skin to prickle in pleasure.

"Yeah," I sigh dreamily, leaning back into him and feeling the effects of the alcohol. I'm not much of a drinker. I'm a super lightweight, so I'm already enjoying the buzz.

He chuckles and gives my neck a kiss. "Wanna dance?" he asks.

"You dance?" I giggle, turning my head so that I can see his face. He gives me a mock wounded look.

"Listen here, young lady, I might be older, but I'm not old."

"Alright then, Sir," I purr, running one of my fingers along his lower lip. He bites it, giving me a soft growl that has me squirming on his lap.

We stand up and Val is the first to notice. "We're dancing now?"

"Yeah, let's go dance and you can make all the boys jelly," I wink.

"Hell, yeah!" Val woops, moving past us and taking off into the crowd.

"On it," Lexie says, following after her.

"Meet you out there," Tabitha says, giving me a peck on the cheek.

"Ready to grind that toned ass against me?" Theo nips at my ear. I'm too turned on to talk while holding back a whimper, so I just nod. "You're the one who's going to make all the guys AND girls jealous. And I'll be smiling the whole time knowing I have the most amazing, sexy, and beautiful girl coming home with me tonight."

I really love it when he says things like that.

## CHASE

"Whose bright idea was it to come here tonight?" I mutter, watching Ellie and Professor Ugly Face get hot and heavy on the dance floor. *Okay, so he's not ugly.* He's actually quite attractive. You know, if I was into guys. But he has my girl in his arms, so I'm going to be a bit petty. *Do I have the right to be?* No, but I am. "Now we get to watch *that* all night and be reminded how we're a bunch of fuck-ups." They just so happen to be in view

343

of the doorway to our VIP section. Out of the whole crowded place, why do they have to be in that spot?

"We overheard Ellie's friends talking about coming here at the mall yesterday when they were shopping, and had the same idea of being stalkers and showing up so that we can make ourselves miserable as we watch the girl we love be happy with someone else," Rain says in a bitter tone before downing a shot.

"Well, aren't you a ray of sunshine?" I cock a brow.

"Bite me, blondie," she snipes.

I just kiss the air at her and she flips me off.

"So we're just gonna sit here all night?" Jax asks, looking over at Brody who looks like he's passed out.

He responds with, "What else would we do?" *Nope, not asleep.*

"I'm not dancing," Jax says.

"Me either," Brody comments.

"I have no friends to go out there with and I'm not really in the party mood," Rain says.

"Well I'm not going out there alone." I down a shot by myself.

"So we sit here all night and get trashed?" Rain asks.

"Sounds good to me," I shrug, raising a shot glass. She clinks hers with mine and we both down the strong liquid.

*A few hours later...*

"I don't know how much more I can take," I whine. No, I'm not talking about the alcohol. I mean watching Ellie have the time of her life and that buttface looking at her with his dopey eyes.

"We deserve it all," Brody mutters. "Every bit of pain we feel. We should drown in it."

"Dude, chill. You sound suicidal or some shit," I say, resting my head back against the couch.

"Well, I feel like death, so maybe I'm already there."

"So fucking dramatic. And you say girls are bad," Rain scoffs. "You know what pisses me off? The way that black haired friend keeps looking at Ellie like the sun shines out her ass," she snarls.

"Wait? Tabitha likes Ellie?" I ask, squinting my eyes as I try to see, but there's nothing there. *Fuck, I'm drunk.*

"How do you not see it? She's practically a dog with its tongue hanging out as she pants over her when she's not looking," Rain says way too loudly, causing people to turn and look.

The song switches over and my eyes narrow. What a blow to the nuts. *Guys My Age* by Hey Violet starts to play. Rain, for some reason, loves this song, and I've listened to it way too many times, so I know all the lyrics.

Sensing we're watching, Ellie turns around in Theo's arms. Her hands come up behind Theo's neck as she starts to sway her body in time with his while his hands skim her body. His face is tucked into her neck, but she's locked eyes with me.

"She never complained about how I touched her before," Brody mutters in response to a part of the lyrics.

"I did love her good!" I defend. I think she can read my lips because hers crooks up at the side like she's enjoying this whole thing.

Okay, so maybe dating an older guy has its benefits. She has someone who has a job, his own place, his own money, can provide for her...yeah, maybe older guys do, do it better.

But I can still offer her things. Like loving her and being there for her. Making her my whole world again.

*Yeah, you did such a fantastic job with that already, asshole.*

The song continues on, and we all mutter things back and forth, but it's not until the last words of the song that it hits me hard.

'Never going back.' Fuck, I hope that's not true.

I will do whatever I can to make it up to her. Whether we ever get back together again or not, I still owe it to her to try to make things right.

The song ends and Ellie whispers something to Theo. They break apart and Theo makes his way back over to their VIP section while Ellie heads toward the bathroom.

"I gotta take a piss," Brody says, his eyes following her. He gets up, stumbling a bit before leaving and disappearing into the crowd.

"Oh, boy." I look at Jax.

Snagging a bottle of beer from the table, I twist off the cap and chug it. Watching her with someone else is like someone taking a hot poker and piercing my heart over and over. I need to dull the pain even though I know I deserve to feel every ounce of it.

## ELLIE

Tonight has been the most fun I've had in a long time. All night, I've been taking turns dancing with the girls and Theo. They have been so awesome about sharing me, knowing this is exactly what I've needed.

We hardly spend any time in the VIP section, our feet never leaving the dance floor.

For the most part, I forget who is here, lurking in the shadows. I've been too busy enjoying myself and having a few drinks has helped too.

They haven't said or done anything to me tonight, and I can't help but think that maybe they just want me to let my guard down before striking again.

I saw them watching me while I was dancing with Theo just now, and couldn't help but direct the song toward them. I mean, the song isn't completely true. They were amazing partners once upon a time...until they weren't.

Needing to pee like crazy and take a small break, I excuse

myself from Theo and head toward the staff room to use the bathroom.

"Hey!" Aria greets me from the couch in the staff room with a big smile.

"Hey, sorry. I know I'm here as a guest tonight, but I really gotta pee and that line is crazy," I laugh.

"Perks of working here, you never have to wait to use the bathroom. Guest or no," she giggles.

Bee-lining for a stall, I let out a sigh of relief at the fact that I won't get in trouble for coming back here off the clock. Once I'm done, I wash my hands and look myself over in the mirror.

I see a broken, tired girl who's fighting tooth and nail to heal. I had a setback, but I won't let it take me down. I have the best support system at my side. Theo is more than I could have ever imagined. He's so selfless, loving, kind, and patient. I have no idea what I did to deserve such an amazing man like him but I am so fucking grateful.

"Better get back out there," I say, fixing my hair and lipstick quickly.

"Happy birthday again!" Aria says. "We need to chill some time outside of work."

"Yes, we do. Next year, I'll have some more free time," I smile.

I've spread out my classes over the next few years because I have to manage school, home life, and work. But even if it might take me a little bit longer to get where I need to be, the point is, I'm still giving Lilly the best life I can. So, next semester, I will take fewer classes to spend more time with her.

Aria and I hug goodbye and I head back out toward the dance floor.

"Ellie."

I jump back, surprised by being cut off so abruptly. It takes a moment for my brain to realize who it is.

"Brody," I say with caution as I go to move around him. I don't need this right now.

"Ellie, please, wait." He moves with me, blocking me from leaving.

"Move." I grit my teeth, my eyes flashing with anger.

"I will, but please just talk to me for a second," he pleads. He looks so broken and tired. Good, serves him right after everything he's done to me. I hope karma kicks him around a few times.

"What do you want?" I give a frustrated sigh, hoping he just says what he has to say and lets me go.

"Look, I just wanted to say..." He bites his lip like he's thinking of what to say next. "I know no amount of apologies can make up for everything I've done to you this year."

"You think?!" I let out a sarcastic laugh.

"But..." he continues, ignoring my interruption, "I need to try anyway. I'm sorry for what I did to you, Ellie. It was wrong. I'm so fucked up. My mother. God. My mother," he growls, gripping his hair.

"Brody, you're a big boy. You can't use her as an excuse your whole life. I know she's a horrible person, and you deserve better than her for a mother, but she didn't put a gun to your head and tell you to make my life hell over something that happened four years ago."

"No, I know," he sighs. He's drunk. I can tell from his bloodshot eyes and the way his body is swaying. "But she just has a way of getting in here, you know." He thumps his head with the heel of his hand.

"I know," I find myself saying, my voice softer than I expected. "But she's wrong, you know. Everything that comes out of her mouth are hateful lies. Always have been, always will be."

I don't like the way he's looking at me right now. Like I'm the best thing on Earth. *What the fuck is happening right now?*

"You were always the one to talk me down after she put me in this mindset. You knew me better than I knew myself."

Before I know what's happening, he leans in and kisses me. Fucking kisses me!

I'm too stunned to react right away. My eyes widen in shock, and body is as stiff as a board while his lips press against mine. I can smell the whisky on his breath.

Thankfully, my brain kicks in and I push him away. He staggers back a bit, a look of hurt taking over his face.

Now that I can think clearly and assess the situation, I rear back my arm and punch him right in the face.

"Fuck!" he hisses, his back meeting the wall.

"Don't you ever put your hands on me again," I spit. "You lost the right to do that years ago. What the fuck is wrong with you? You bully me for months, try to break me, and now you're confessing you're sorry and...and...you kissed me!"

He glares at me, wiping the blood from his lip with the back of his hand. "I deserved that," he grumbles.

"You deserve this too." He looks at me with confusion for a moment before I step closer and bring my knee up as hard as I can into his junk. I'm vibrating from my fight or flight instinct, and honestly, I just really wanted to do that. Fucker had it coming.

He lets out a pained groan as he drops to the floor.

Turning around, I leave to storm off and find the others watching. Chase is holding back a laugh, Rain's brows are hitting the roof, and Jax is just giving me a sad look.

"Like I said before, keep him on a fucking leash," I snap. "What has gotten into all of you? Am I in the fucking *Twilight Zone* or something?" I say before pushing past them and storming over to Theo.

"We're leaving," I say a little too harshly. Theo jumps up when he sees the state I'm in.

"Ellie, what's wrong?" he asks, putting his hands on my arms and giving them a comforting, calming rub.

"What's wrong? What's wrong is that my exes are fucking crazy, the whole lot of them." Okay, so maybe I'm being over dramatic but I'm still a little shocked at what the heck happened. I'm also a bit pissed at myself because I can still feel his soft lips on mine.

"What did they do?" Theo growls.

"He kissed me!" I blurt, and the girls look at me with wide eyes.

"Who?" Lexie asks.

"Yeah, who? I'll beat his ass!" Val slurs, trying to stand up but loses her balance and falls back onto the couch.

"Sit down, woman, you're drunk," Lexie snaps.

"I can still fight," Val mutters before...did she just fall asleep?

Shaking my head, I look back at a furious Theo.

"Was it him who kissed you?" Theo points to Brody, his voice is so low and furious that I forget what we're talking about and my core starts to tingle. *Fuck's sake, Ellie, no sexy boyfriend right now!*

"Yes. Then I punched him in the face and kneed him in the balls." I raise my chin, feeling pretty proud of myself.

Theo's face lightens a little, and I think I see a hint of a smile. "Look at you. My baby girl is defending herself. I'm so proud."

The way he's looking at me does nothing to get rid of the feeling between my legs. Needing to forget the lingering feeling of Brody's lips on mine, I pull Theo into a kiss.

He wraps his arms around me, holding me close. I moan into his mouth as he slips his tongue in and over mine.

When he's done, we pull apart, leaving me panting. "These lips are mine," he growls softly.

"Yours," I breathe back, my head spinning.

"If I wasn't worried about losing my job, I'd go over and give him a few more kicks."

A laugh bubbles up and slips free, earning a grin from Theo.

"Ready to go home?" Theo asks.

I nod and look over at the girls. "We're gonna head out. Thank you so much for spending the night with us."

"We're going to wait until the ball drops, then we're gonna head out," Lexie says, then looks down at Val.

"Well, I guess just Lexie and I will, seeing how this one has passed the fuck out," Tabitha laughs.

Smiling, I shake my head and wave goodbye before Theo and I make our way through the crowd.

When we get outside, Theo pulls me to the side. "Wait." He pushes me up against the wall and just stares at me with a smile.

"What?" I laugh.

"Just wait," he says, his grin growing wider.

We just stare at each other for what feels like forever. I feel his love for me radiating off of him, washing away any negative feelings from earlier. I love the way he looks at me like I'm the only girl in the world.

Fireworks start to go off, and we hear the whole club scream, "Happy New Year!"

"Happy New Year, my love," Theo says. "I love you more than the sun, the moon, and the stars combined. I can't wait to see what this new year brings for us." He then kisses me with so much love and passion, I'm jelly in his arms.

No matter what this new year brings, as long as Theo is by my side, and we have the little ones, nothing else matters.

# Chapter Thirty-One

## ELLIE

**"I'M EXCITED AND SLIGHTLY TERRIFIED,"** Val says, looking out the window of the car at the packed parking lot.

"Have you ever played before?" I ask with a slight laugh.

"Umm, no? Look, my hair might be pink, and I do crazy things, but going onto a field with a bunch of people whose sole purpose is to shoot balls of paint at me has never appealed to me. I've seen some of the welts they leave on my cousins who play. I'm too pretty for *those* types of bruises." Val gives us a mischievous grin.

"And what kind of bruises would you prefer?" I cock a brow.

"Ones left by sexy men and their big meaty hands." She wiggles her brows.

"I should have guessed." I smile, shaking my head. "It's not that bad. Plus, it's going to be fun. We can make sure we're on the same team."

When the girls told me the students have a tradition of going paintballing every year before going back to school after Christmas break, I begged them to go. They have never taken part in this tradition, but I love to play.

Unfortunately, it also brings back memories of *them*. It's something we always used to do together. Jax and I were the most competitive. We were always the last two standing, but he always won and came out on top. At least we were on the same team.

"Sorry, we can't all be like you. You have your own paintball gun and everything," Lexie giggles.

"Marker," I smile, correcting her.

"What?" She cocks a brow.

"The gun is called a marker," I laugh.

"Whatever." She rolls her eyes playfully.

"I used to have all the equipment, but sold most of it years ago." I would have sold the gun if I needed to as well, but I'm glad I didn't have to.

"Well, let's get this done and over with," Tabitha sighs dramatically.

"You guys are acting like I'm bringing you to your execution or something. It's just some fun. Get over it, you big babies." I giggle as I climb out of the car and to the trunk to get my marker.

"Alright, alright," Val mutters as she gets out of the car and the others follow.

"We need to go rent, like everything," Lexie says, looking around at everyone who's already geared up. "We must be the only people who don't own anything."

"Unlike someone," Val says and all three of them look at me.

"What?" I blink. "I still gotta rent the goggles, mask, and buy the paintballs."

"Says the girl who's wearing a teal sweater and pants with a matching gun," Tabitha says.

"Jersey," I correct her as I slam the trunk shut, and start toward the building where we can get the rest of what we need.

"What?" Val asks, as they all start to follow.

"It's not a sweater, it's a jersey. And I like to match," I shrug. "And it's my favorite color."

"Tabby, who is this woman, and what happened to the book nerd we call our bestie?" Val not so quietly whispers.

We get everything we need and head toward the field where we will be playing. The previous group of people come out dripping in paint. You can easily tell who won and who lost by the energy each person is giving off. But to me, it doesn't matter if we win or lose overall, I'm just excited to get out and have a good time.

That is until I see two girls coming out of the field, also covered in paint. Laura and Kayla, lovely. They notice me and give me a set of matching sneers.

"Pity you weren't on our opposing team just now. That would have been so much fun," Kayla says.

"I'm sorry? What was that? I didn't hear anything you just said over that God awful noise you call your voice. Sounds more like a cat in a blender. You should get that checked out, or you know, just not talk. Save everyone from having their ears bleed," Val sneers back. I hold back a snort of laughter at the ugly scowl she gives Val.

"Fuck you, you talking bubble-gum-stick."

Val grins and turns to us. "Is that supposed to be an insult or something?"

"What did you say to her?" Laura demands randomly, her face flushed with anger as she steps into my personal space.

"What?" I look at her with confusion, taking a step back and bumping into Tabitha.

"Rain, what did you say to her to make her leave me?" She looks like she's three seconds away from gouging my eyes out.

"N-nothing," I stutter. *What the heck is going on?*

"Back away from her, Laura." Rain's voice comes from the left side of our group. Laura's face snaps up to look at Rain. A flash of pain paints her face before it morphs into jealousy and anger.

"Why? Why are you defending her all of a sudden?" Laura shrieks. I mean, I kind of want to know too.

I look over at Rain, stunned. Chase has been the only one who has shown any shame in how they have treated me. I don't count Brody's drunken actions. I'm going to say that was temporary insanity.

"Because, I'm done being a bitch to her." Rain's eyes flick to mine quickly before looking back at Laura. "It was stupid to start shit with her anyways. I'm over it. It's done. I already told you this."

"You're still in love with her, aren't you?" Laura cries.

"Stop, just stop," Rain sighs, running a hand over her face in frustration. "It doesn't matter if I am or not. It's none of your business. I told you that whatever you and I had is over. I'm done being a catty bitch. It's not who I am."

"Please, Rain. Don't do this," Laura begs, and I start to become uncomfortable. Looking at the others, they just give me a shrug. Well, not Val, she's eating this up like it's her favorite dessert, her grin wide as she takes it all in.

"Can we not do this here?" Rain asks, taking a step back but Laura goes to grab her arm.

"I'll do anything, please. I'm okay with just being friends with benefits. I just don't want to lose you." Laura is in tears now. Rain looks way more uncomfortable than I am. A part of me is loving this. The part of me that will always love Rain wants to say 'fuck you bitch, she doesn't want you' to Laura.

"Okay, this is just getting pathetic," Brody growls, pulling Laura's hand off Rain. "She says she doesn't want to fuck you anymore and she can't stand your stalking ways. So take you and your equally nutty friend and get lost."

"Ohhh," Val whispers, her tone sounding giddy.

Kayla doesn't hear what Brody just said. She's too busy perving on Chase. Chase notices and cringes back from her.

"Shoo," Chase says, flicking his hand at her. "Bad dog. Shoo."

Okay, I can't help but smile at that.

"This is all your fault," Laura snaps at me before she grabs Kayla's arm and drags the pouting girl away, storming off.

Chase turns to me and gives me a wink that has my belly fluttering and my heart pumping faster.

"Sorry about her," Rain says, watching the girls leave before turning to me. "Look, I know this is shitty timing, but..." She bites her bottom lip, looking nervous. My eyes are drawn to the movement as she licks her bottom lip before speaking again. "Look, I'm sorry for being a bitch this year, okay? It was shitty of me and yeah."

My eyes flick up to hers and I just blink at her, stunned, before huffing out a laugh. "You call that an apology? After all the shit you did? Costing me hundreds of dollars on my hair? Calling me nasty names, and other lovely things? Sure, it was that dickhead who did most of it, but you're not any better." I look at Brody. "Nice fat lip," I grin. "Matches your big ego. Also, a little cover up might hide that bit of a black eye." He says nothing, cringing lightly.

"To be fair, the girls did the color to your hair, not me," Rain says sheepishly.

I turn to her with a death glare. Saying nothing, I start heading closer to the field entrance, waiting for the referee to tell us what's up. The girls follow behind knowingly.

"Alright, everyone. Groups of ten please."

"Ten," Lexie groans. "We gotta play with strangers."

"Well, not totally," a voice I know well says.

"Cooper!" I shout with excitement. I launch myself at him and he catches me with a chuckle, spinning me around.

"How's my favorite girl?" he says, kissing me on the cheek.

"Better." I give him a reassuring smile. He looks over his shoulder at Rain and the guys. Brody gives him a dirty look while Chase glares. Jax just watches and Rain is looking at the field.

"You sure? Looks like we're up against them," Cooper asks, looking back at me.

"Perfect." I give him a playful grin. "Shooting my exes with paintballs sounds like a fun afternoon to me."

⸻

"Go, go, go!" the referee shouts and the horn blares.

"Come on!" I call to my team. Half of them break apart, but my friends follow me. I lead them behind a big beat up school bus covered in paint.

"What do we do?" Val asks breathlessly, looking around.

"Well, at first, I'd say we try to win. But now, since the Silver Knights and Lady Rain are here, change of plans. Try to stay in the game until they are out," I say.

"Or, we say fuck it and just hunt them down and shoot them up," Coop says. I can't see his face behind his mask but I can hear it in his voice. He's dying to take a crack at them.

"I like this idea," Val says. "Mostly because I have no idea how to play, but also because I wanna make them bleed!" She lets out an evil villain kind of laugh. "Well, at least with paint," she shrugs.

"So, we what, just wait here until the rest of them get out?" Tabitha asks. "I'm okay with that plan."

"We need to move from this spot because people are going to check here." I wave them to follow me, and we all pile into a wooden hut.

"We have a window over here that we can watch and shoot if necessary, but I say give them a good ten minutes, and the rest of our team will be down and out," I say, crouching down by the window. I watch a few people get taken out. I have no idea whose team it is. I'm not paying attention. This is all for fun, so I really don't care if we win or lose. I only care about getting *them* out before they get me.

We sit there in silence for a while, just listening to the

sounds of paint balls hitting their targets, the cheers of the winning team, and shouts of protest from the others.

"I think we're good to move out," I say.

"Finally!" Val groans, standing up and stretching, raising her arms above her head. "My ass is sore as fuck, and it's gonna hurt to sit for a few days. AND it wasn't even from anal."

"Sweet fuck, Val," Cooper chokes out a laugh.

"No, I prefer it a little rough," she grins.

Cooper smiles, shaking his head.

"Enough sex talk, you hornball, let's go," Lexie says, giving Val a little push.

With our markers raised, we scan the area. One of the other's gun goes off and Tabitha lets out a little shriek that has me quick to check on her.

"I'm on your team!" a guy with a pink paint splat in the middle of his chest shouts. His shoulders drop in defeat as he turns around and walks away.

"Sorry!" Tabitha whisper-shouts, and she turns around to look at us. "I thought it was one of them," she shrugs.

I get them down into a trench, and just as luck has it, Rain and the guys are a few feet from us.

Looking over at the others, I put my finger up to my lips, signaling them to be quiet. They all look over to see who I'm warning them about, and grins break out on all their faces. Val goes to speak but Lexie slaps her hand over Val's mouth. I mouth 'thank you' to Lexie, and she gives me a nod.

They're distracted, arguing about something. This is my chance to give the others their instructions.

"Okay," I whisper. "They are all fair game. We don't care about rules, just hit them. More than once. Hell, use all your balls if you want. But leave the Silver asshole to me." I smirk, not that anyone can see me. "I'll go first."

Raising the gun up onto my shoulder like I'm some kind of badass sniper, I squint my eyes and aim for Brody. Once I know I have a clear shot, I open fire...right at his dick.

Multiple balls hit him in the privates in rapid succession. "Fuck!" Brody lets out a loud roar, clutching his balls, and as soon as he spins around to drop to the ground, I let off another set of shots, hitting him in the ass and propelling him forward. He lands face first into the dirt screaming like a little bitch.

"Bullseye," I say to myself with a satisfied sinister grin. I don't feel bad at all, and I hope he feels this for weeks. It's not even close to what he deserves after everything he's put me through, but it will have to do for now.

Shots ring out again, and I look over at Rain. She lets out a scream and I see her chest covered in paint.

"That was my boob!" Rain yells.

"Tittie hit!" Lexie cheers. "Alright guys, let it rain paint balls."

"This is Sparta!" Val shouts, and they all start firing at the others. Chase is cursing, jumping around as he tries to dodge the paint balls. "Dance, monkey, dance!" Val cheers and cackles with glee. I'm glad she's on my team.

As my friends start chasing after Rain, Brody, and Chase, shooting them as they go and not giving two fucks that they already got them out, I see Jax slip away in the other direction. *Not so fast J-Man. You're mine.*

## JAX

Before Ellie's friends opened fire on us, we were arguing about how to handle the rest of the game. We knew they were still playing because none of them had gone to the dead box, an area where eliminated players go.

Once Ellie's friends started chasing after the others, not caring that they already got my friends out, I noticed Ellie was among them.

See, that's what we were arguing about. They wanted to take it easy on her, let her win. None of them wanted to be the ones to shoot her, because of the bullshit we put her through already, but I knew Ellie a little more than they did when it comes to this game. Ellie would never want anyone to let her win. She would rather go down fighting.

Ellie and I had always loved this game. She was my second in command. You would think Rain and Brody would have led the team every time we played but no, this game brought the two quiet ones out of our shell. We always worked perfectly together. She was almost always the second to the last one to get out, which gave me the chance to make the winning shot. She never got to make it, but always still gave me her gorgeous smile as she cheered at every victory.

I try my hardest to be quiet as I make my way around a few obstacles, heading in her direction. It's quiet, the voices of people in the distance are a whisper in my ears. The only thing I can hear are the birds in the trees, and the sound of dirt crunching under my feet.

I have no plans to go easy on her, so at least she will be the second to the last one to make it out of here.

Standing by a tree, I scan the area. Nothing but the sounds of nature to be heard. *Where is she?*

Just as I back up, ready to move somewhere else, my back is met with something hard. Spinning around, I come face to face with Ellie. My gun is half cocked, ready to end this game when I find myself locked in place, her wide, shocked, bright blue eyes putting me under some kind of spell.

This is the first time I've seen her clearly up close. The club is always too dark to truly appreciate her beauty.

But now, the sun is shining down on her making her face radiant and her blonde locks glowing like an angel's halo. Fuck. My dick is getting hard as I look at her plump pink lips, and my mind flashes back to when she would suck me into her mouth, blowing my fucking mind every time. Her eyes swim with the brightest blue like the Caribbean ocean waters. She's a fucking vision.

A thump rings in my ears, followed by a sharp pain. Slowly, I look down and see a bright teal splatter on my chest.

"I won," she says in disbelief, pulling off her mask. "I actually mother fucking won!" Her stunned face splits into a giant smile, and she starts to do this adorable victory dance. "I won. I won and you lost. After all these years, I finally get to win!"

I can't help but smile. Seeing her so happy after all the misery we caused her warms me to my core and makes my heart squeeze. I love seeing her like this. This is the Ellie I remember. This is the Ellie I miss.

"Good game," I say, taking off my mask.

She stops and looks at me, chest heaving a bit from her excitement. We just look at each other for a few moments, not saying or doing anything. I can feel the air thicken around us.

A part of me just wants to push her up against this tree and claim her mouth as mine. But that's not my right. I don't deserve her anymore.

"Thanks," she finally says, clearing her throat and taking a step back. "Never thought I'd see the day where I'd beat the mighty Jax Hunter."

I'm tempted to say the only reason she won was because I was too distracted by her beauty. But that sounds both corny and a surefire way to make things even more awkward.

"You earned it."

She gives me a forced smile. "Well, I better go tell the others." She stands there for a moment longer, biting her lower lip. She looks away and back to me. "Thanks. For the night of the football game."

My smile slips a little, and a fury fills my veins as I remember those creeps cornering her.

"Things between us all may not be good right now but I would never let something bad like that happen to you, Ellie. I wanted to rip them to shreds, I still do." My voice is hard and my fist clenches.

"Boy, do I wish that were true." She gives me a sad smile before taking off in the direction of her friends.

*What the fuck does that mean?*

Not sure what to make of her words, I start heading in the same direction as she is, seeing how that's where her friends chased mine like an angry mob.

"All that arguing and you still let her win?" Chase asks with a raised brow and a grin.

"Actually," I say, looking over at my blonde angel celebrating with her friends. Her smile from before that still has my heart racing is plastered on her face again. "She won all on her own."

"Nice." Chase nods, beaming as he watches her too.

"Can we go now?" Brody groans as he lays on the bench in the fetal position, clutching his balls.

"You okay, babe?" I say softly, kneeling down next to him.

"No," he squeaks. "It feels like my nuts are going to pop like balloons. And I don't think we will be having sex anytime soon." Biting my lip while holding back a smile, I help him stand. He groans in pain, leaning his weight against me. "I think my dick is broken."

"Oh, you deserve every bit of pain you're in and more." Chase laughs, then slaps Brody's ass as he dances away, racing toward the parking lot.

I don't like seeing Brody in pain...but Chase has a point.

Brody lets out a curse, his knees almost buckling as he bites back a scream.

"My tits hurt," Rain mutters, rubbing her boobs. "My nipples are totally going to bruise."

We start heading to the car, passing Ellie and her friends as we go. She looks up at me, giving me a small smile. I return it before she brings her attention back to her friends.

The whole ride home, it's like a silent video plays in my head as I relive all the perfect moments we had together. Alone, and as a group.

As crazy as Rain and Chase's plan is to get her back, or at least talking to them, a part of me wants to join in on their crazy scheme. Because my heart and soul really likes the idea of potentially being in Ellie's life again. Or at least have her not hate us anymore. Not that any of us deserves that.

# *Chapter Thirty-Two*

## ELLIE

**"YOU GOT EVERYTHING YOU NEED?"** Theo asks as I shove some clothes into my bag.

"Yup," I smile up at him.

"Be safe, okay? Drink, have fun, enjoy yourself because we both know you deserve it. But just please, be safe." He pulls me into his arms, wrapping me in a blanket of warmth and safety. A sick feeling of guilt takes over, and my body tenses. He pulls back just enough to look at my face. "Enough of that, sweetheart."

"I'm sorry. I just feel...well, you know." I snuggle back into his chest.

The past week has been a mindfuck, not one that I totally hate. After what happened at paintball, Rain and the guys have made a complete 180°. Rain has started saying 'hi' when we pass in the halls, and giving me a smile that always catches me off guard. On Tuesday, Jax found me struggling with a pile of books I borrowed from the library and helped me bring them to my car. We even reminisced about past paintball games.

Brody, well, he's been keeping his distance. And honestly, I'm glad. He's the one who's hurt me the most, and he's the last person I want to talk to right now. I don't know what made them change their ways in only a few short weeks, but I'd rather have this—whatever *this* is—than how it was before.

The one that I can't seem to get rid of, and kind of don't mind having around, is Chase. He's found any reason he can to be around me—walking me to classes, to my car, helping himself to a spot at our lunch table. My friends were not overly happy about that, but he is the one they hate the least and can actually stand to be around.

Wednesday night, Chase found me in the library, took a seat, and watched me study. *Not that I got much studying done.* I could feel his heated gaze all over my body.

When I asked what he was looking at, we talked.

*"You. Did you know you look sexy with reading glasses? Totally gives me naughty librarian vibes. Nothing like that batty witch over there."* I looked behind him to see the very old, creepy librarian glaring at us.

*"I seriously think she's a real witch," I giggled.*

*"She totally is, no debating that." He gave me this grin that had me shifting in my seat. "So, I need to tell you something," he said, leaning forward on his arms.*

*"Okay?" I sat up and crossed my legs. The look in his eyes told me this wasn't just a casual conversation that we were about to have.*

*"Look, you know me. And before you say 'no, you don't and it's been years', yes, that's true, but some things never change. Like me being a determined, stubborn man; when I want something, I go hard until I get it."*

*Oh boy. Yup. Totally not prepared for this.*

*"First, I'm going to apologize to you again. Yes, I know I already did, but I will continue to do it until I'm blue in the face. I was a dick, an ass, a stupid idiot for standing by while Rain and Brody made your life hell. I was too worried about pissing off my best friends and losing them after I had already lost one of the*

*most important things in the world. So, I chose wrong. I was wrong. And I hope you know that I hated everything they did to you, and all of it made me sick to my stomach to watch."*

*I bit my lip as I played with my fingers, needing something to do with my hands. My stomach felt like it was going to drop out of my ass, as sweat prickled my body.*

*"Second, I know you have a boyfriend, and I do respect that, but I'm going to say this anyways. I love you, Ellie. I always have and always will. What happened in the past...I don't know the full story. You were gone and had us blocked before we could all cool down enough to talk about it. It was wrong of us to react that way, and we should have heard you out. I'd like to hear your side now, if it's not too late. If not now, then whenever you feel it is the right time to talk about it. I am ready to listen. Please, believe me, I'm done letting the pain of my past ruin my future. I want you, Ellie. I want to be with you. To love you. To care for you, and to be a better man than I have been. I know I don't deserve you, but this is me, shooting my shot."*

*I gaped at him, too stunned by his words to make any of my own. He got up from the couch and walked over to me. Closing my mouth, I looked up at him as he towered over me. I just stared at him, still unable to speak as he tucked a piece of hair behind my ear.*

*"I'll give you some time to think about it. See you at the party this weekend." He leaned over, placed a lingering kiss on my forehead before turning around and leaving.*

I sat there for the longest time, my brain swimming with so many thoughts, and my heart drowning in too many emotions. Then, I cried. I cried as I left the library, cried in the car on my way home, and then cried in Theo's arms as I told him everything like I always do. It was hard, but Theo and I, we don't keep secrets, no matter how tough or awkward things might be.

. . .

"Ellie, love, you okay?" he asks, dragging me from my thoughts of the night before.

"Yeah. Sorry, just thinking about..." I take a step back. "Doesn't matter."

"You were thinking about Chase." It isn't a question.

Biting my lip, I try to hold back my tears. "I'm sorry," my voice cracks with uncertainty.

"Hey," he says, taking a step closer, filling in the gap I just put between us. "You have nothing to be sorry for."

"I'm thinking of another man, Theo. How can you be so... okay with that?"

"Because you have every right to feel anything you do. This is your life, your mind, your heart. I have no say in what you do. If you love him, it's not my right to be mad or tell you not to. Ellie, baby, I don't control you. I love you. I will stand with you. I'm going to care for you in any way you need me to. You can love anyone you want to, and as long as I'm one of them, then that's all I can ask for." He cups my face, bringing his lips down to mine, giving me a kiss filled with so much love, it has my tears breaking free. "And even if someday you no longer feel this way, I'm just honored you've loved me at all."

"Fuck's sake, Theo," I sob. "Why do you have to be so perfect? I don't deserve you. There will never be a day that I ever stop loving you. You're stuck with me for life."

"No, it's me who doesn't deserve you, my love. I'm not perfect, just a man madly in love. And I'd gladly be stuck to your side for all of eternity." He gives me a heart stopping grin. "Life is short. Finding one person who loves you unconditionally is a gift, but if you can get that from more than one person, then why deny the love you deserve? I don't agree with what any of them did, not for a moment, and honestly, I don't think I'd be so agreeable if it was Brody we were talking about."

I huff out a laugh as I wipe away the stray tears. "You don't have to worry about that. He's last on the list of people I want to talk to, let alone feel anything for." I might still love them all, but after that talk with Chase, my feelings for him are a lot less contained. I can no longer keep them buried deep down inside with how they hit me like a freight train. I find myself wanting to get a piece of the past back, and really get to know this new Chase.

"But Chase, as cowardly of a thing as it was for him to just sit back and watch what Rain and Brody did, from what you said, he didn't actually say or do anything to you."

"No." I shake my head. "He didn't. He didn't stop them, but he didn't help either," I admit.

"You have a long history with them, sweetheart. I'm not saying how they reacted to what happened to you was right because it wasn't at all. They were morons and need a good ass beating for thinking the worst and not trusting in what you had, but they don't know the whole truth. Do you think they would have treated you like this if they did?"

"I don't know," I sigh, running my hands through my loose strands. "I want to say no. All of them always acted like they would start a war for me if anyone hurt me. But well, you know how that ended up."

"If you want to hear Chase out, get to know him better and possibly something more, I won't stand in your way and I won't leave if that's what you're worried about. I'm with you, Ellie, for as long as you want me, I'm yours. All I ask for is open communication. Nothing behind my back. But remember, if you do choose to spend more time with Chase, getting to know him better, you have to remember Lilly; you'll need to decide what you want to do about telling him, or them. It's your choice of course, but can you become friends with him and not tell him something so big?"

"I don't know what I want, Theo. But I can promise I will never hide things from you. If something were to happen with Chase, or anyone, I'd tell you, always. As for Lilly, I'll tell him. I have to. He has the right to know, and as much as I can't stand Brody, they should all know. Brody showed me that he can do the right thing by leaving me alone. But before I tell them anything, I need to know that's going to stick. I can't bring Lilly into that bullshit and end up with her getting hurt."

"Thank you. And you do whatever you feel is right, at your own pace." He kisses me again, this time, it's more rated R than PG-13. I let out a lustful moan as I fist his shirt, desperate to take him back to his place and never leave the bed.

"Knock, knock, bitches!" Val's voice comes from the other side of the door and harsh whispering follows. "Oh chill, I know none of the kids are here."

"Have fun," Theo tells me as I give him one more peck before grabbing my bag. "Enjoy celebrating with your team and their win. You kicked ass this year, baby. You deserve this."

"I love you," I tell him, meaning it with my entire heart.

He smiles, brushing his thumb against my cheek bone. "I love you too, sweetheart." He leans over, placing a kiss on the top of my head before spinning me around and giving me a hard slap on the ass. "Now, shoo. I have *Lord of the Rings* to watch."

I crinkle my nose. "Have fun with that."

"There's our main bitch!" Val cheers when I open the door, and she pulls me out into the hall and into a hug.

Cocking a brow, I look at Lexie over my shoulder silently asking *'what the heck?'*

She mimics drinking something, telling me Val has already had a few drinks.

"Hey, babe. Ready to party before drowning in school work again?" I ask her as we head down the hall.

"Hell yes! I'm on the hunt tonight, and my prey is dick, all the dick I can handle," she says with enthusiasm.

"Rico ghosted her," Lexie tells me.

"Ohhh," I grimace and she nods.

"Well, fuck him anyways. We were only fuck buddies for a few weeks, I can find someone better. I'll find ten someones better. Hell, I'll fuck the whole damn party!"

"Woah there, let's dial this back a bit, babe. No way in hell am I letting you do that."

"Fine," she pouts. "But I'm still riding a dick before the night is over."

"Of course, sweetie," Lexie says, patting Val's arm. We both bite our lip trying to hold back our laughter.

We go downstairs, climbing into Cooper's car where he and Tabitha are waiting for us.

We don't go far, just to Spring Meadows which is the next town over. The parents of one of the guys on the football team has a massive mansion with an indoor pool. So, of course, the party is at his place, if they win.

"Man, this place is like five times bigger than my place," Val says, looking at an enormous structure that belongs in a home design magazine as she shuts the car door.

"Well, who cares? We're here to drink, dance, and swim. Let's go," Lexie says with a big smile cresting her face as she starts to race toward the already crowded house. Laughing, we follow her.

"Pool is straight through the main floor at the back of the house. It's hard to miss," a guy I recognize as someone from the football team says to the group of people who came in before us.

When he sees me, he nods, "Hey, Ellie." He looks at the others behind me. "Hey, Coop and friends."

"Hey there, big boy. You got a date for the night?" Val asks, biting her lip as she starts to flirt with the first guy she sees here.

"She's hopeless," Lexie sighs, and I giggle.

"Umm. No, not really, but I could." The guy grins, looking my bestie up and down like she's a meal he really wants to have.

"Well, you're in good hands. Stay out of trouble," Lexie says before pulling me toward the back of the house.

"Should we just be leaving her there alone like that?" I ask, looking back to see them already making out. *Damn.*

"She's fine. And a big girl. I can't always be her keeper."

"You're right." I nod, praying Val will be okay for the night. But there's no reason for me to worry yet, so I won't.

We find the drink table and grab a few coolers. This place is amazing. They have a slide, a rope, and a friggin' rock waterfall on the other end. From the looks of it, this pool can open up to be an outdoor pool also.

We find some spare chairs to sit and drink. "I thought there would be more people here," I say, looking around and finding that there are a lot of people, but not as many as most of the parties I've been to have had.

"It's just the sport teams and cheerleaders and whoever they invite. Still a ton of people, but not open to just anyone," she explains.

"Oh, makes sense, I guess."

A squeal of laughter catches my attention, and I see the guy who we left Val with throwing her into the pool before jumping in after her.

"Come on, let's swim!" Tabitha says, standing up and taking off her shirt and pants before running and diving into the pool.

"Hell yes!" Lexie follows.

"Ready for some fun?" Cooper asks.

"With you guys? Always," I grin. We strip down to our swimsuits. Cooper takes the slide while I go for the rope. With a scream of excitement, I swing on the rope before letting go and splashing into the pool.

"The water is so warm," I tell Cooper as I wipe the droplets away from my face and smooth my hair back.

"It's the perfect temperature," Cooper agrees before grinning. He stalks toward me.

"What are you doing?" I laugh, taking a step back.

He says nothing before grabbing me under the arms, picking me up, and tossing me into the deeper water a few feet away from him.

Over the next hour, Cooper tosses me and the girls into the

water. We take turns using the rope or slide, and just enjoy our night. After my third cooler, I start to feel too warm and need to take a break.

"I'm going to go use the washroom and just sit down for a bit," I tell Cooper and the girls.

"You okay?" Cooper asks with concern.

"I'm fine, promise." I give him a reassuring smile. And I am. This night has been amazing. No one has looked at me funny. No one has called me names. Rain and the guys haven't shown up yet. Kayla and Laura are nowhere to be found. It's been a perfect night.

Getting out of the water, I go over to my chair and dry off a bit before going to the washroom. When I'm done, I wash my hands and splash some cold water onto my face.

As I make my way back to the pool, I take a moment, not quite ready to go back in there yet.

The bass vibrates through my body as I lean against the wall of the dark corner I've escaped to.

They haven't arrived yet. Maybe that's why I've been able to let loose and relax for once. But I know they won't miss one of the biggest parties of the year.

Closing my eyes, I listen to the music, singing along under my breath. Arms wrap around me, pulling me into a warm, hard chest. I freeze, eyes snapping open as my body tenses up. I wait for my fight or flight instinct to kick in, but the contact is so sudden, I'm taken by surprise and my stupid body won't move.

Then the scent of peppermint invades my nose, and I feel a hot breath of air hit my neck. My whole body shivers in fear of the situation or because of the man who has me in his hold; I honestly don't know. Maybe both.

"What are you doing?" I breathe, wondering where Chase came from, and how long he has been here. With him here, I know the others can't be far.

"Dance with me," he requests with his mouth against my

neck, making my eyes flutter shut again. It's like my body remembers his touch, his lips.

"Why?" I ask. My heart is beating harder and harder, banging against my rib cage every second I stay wrapped into his arms. "Why, after all these months, do you want me now? I thought for the longest time you hated me."

"I've never hated you, Ellie-Belly." He kisses my neck, causing me to bite back a whimper. Even though I was just swimming, I feel like I'm overheating. "Even if a part of me wanted to or thought I should, I could never hate you."

"Where are the others?" I whisper. *Can anyone see us right now?*

"Shhh. Let's not talk about them. They don't matter right now. Be with me, Ellie, in this moment, just me and you."

*Never Forget You* by Zara Larsson and MNEK starts playing through the speakers, and Chase takes my lack of protest to his proposal as a yes. He grips my hips, but not too tightly, as he starts to sway our bodies to the beat. I lean back into him, my body molding with his, not ready to lose his touch. I never knew how much I've missed him, and how much my body craves his, until now.

We get lost in the music, my head lying back against his shoulder, tilted to the side, his face pressed against my neck as our bodies fuse together and move as one. I know this is wrong. I know I shouldn't be doing this. I'm with Theo now. I know he said he would love and support me no matter what I choose to do, or who to love, but I still feel guilty.

*Then why am I still here, in this moment, with Chase? Why haven't I pulled away and left?*

MNEK's part starts and Chase sings the lyrics against my neck and shoulder. I tune out the music, focusing on the lyrics spilling from Chase's lips. Every word he sings causes something inside me to stir—feelings I thought I put to rest a long time ago. But I'm fooling myself because even though I've had more bad times with the guys and Rain than good since I've been back, it's hard not to be reminded of how things used to be every time I lay eyes on one of them. Flashes of past memories pop up when it's not wanted.

Tears start to well in my eyes as my heart breaks and puts itself back together. *Does he mean the words he's singing?* Because it feels like so much more than just singing along to the song that's playing. It's like he's stealing these lyrics and using them to tell me how he really feels because he can't find the right words himself. Every word hits me hard, making me even more confused.

Trying to blink away the tears, one escapes as I hold back a sob. So many bewildering emotions are running through my mind.

Chase spins me around in his arms, backing me up into the corner. He puts his forehead to mine. "Fuck!" he breathes. "How the fuck did everything get so messed up?"

I don't say anything. I know the answer, but right now is not the time for that.

"I miss you so fucking much, Ellie. So much it hurts. Seeing you everywhere, at school, at the club, parties. Every time I lay eyes on you, something inside me shifts. The feeling to hold you close, even just for a second, consumes me. I wanted to hate you so fucking bad," he growls.

*Gee, thanks.*

"But I don't. I can't," he breathes, pulling back to look into my eyes. What I see hits me hard and fast, sucker punching me, and makes my breathing become erratic. My gaze flicks between his eyes as I feel the energy shift between us. I lick my lips and Chase devours the movement with his eyes. Before I can have a moment to think, his lips are on mine.

I'm stunned for a moment, but as if it's muscle memory, my lips greet his, kissing him back. He moans against my lips like a starved man having his first taste of food in weeks.

My arms wrap around his shoulders as he lifts me up, my legs locking in place around his waist. I expect fear to take over, flash backs to start up, but nothing. I'm lost in his touch, his lips, his hands. It shouldn't, but it feels so right.

He kisses me like he's trying to suck out my soul. He holds me like he's trying to blend his body into mine. It's raw love, and fuck, it's causing all logical thoughts to leave my mind. I want him. Oh boy, do I ever fucking want him. And I know I'm going to hate myself after. But right now, I don't seem to care.

"I need you," he pants, pulling back from our kiss. I get lost in his ocean blue eyes before his lips are back on mine. I feel his hard cock grinding against my core. I rock into him, chasing the friction I so desperately need.

"Chase," I murmur against his lips with a desperate need as he shifts around a bit, taking the thin fabric of my bikini bottom and moving it to the side.

Pulling back, his eyes bore into mine. The only warning I get is the feeling of the tip of his cock before he thrusts up into me. His eyes roll into the back of his head as he lets out an animalistic noise. Mine go wide as I suck in a gasp at the sudden intrusion, nails digging into his back, and my legs tighten around his waist.

He takes a moment before he opens his eyes again. He gives me a determined look like a man on a mission as he pulls back only to thrust into me again. My body automatically reacts, my core constricts around his cock, pulling a groan out of him. He wastes no time as he starts to rut into me like a beast, all while his attention is still on my face, watching me as he withdraws pleasure from my body.

The feeling of his cock inside me is amazing.

"You feel so fucking amazing around my cock," he grunts, "like your pussy was made for me. You are mine, Ellie, I had you before him, remember that."

I say nothing, my mouth parted as I pant while heat builds in my lower belly.

His hand slips between us, his fingers finding my clit. When he adds pressure, I get lost in the new sensation. My body feels like it's been set on fire, the need for release hovering on edge.

He tucks his face back into my neck, sucking and nipping, marking me as his. But I'm not his, not anymore.

He grips my hip with one hand as he plays with my clit with the other. "There it is," he groans against my neck. "I feel your pussy pulsing around me. I know you're about to cum. I know your body better than you. Cum for me, Ellie. Cream on my cock," he growls, his dick hitting my sweet spot deep inside, and that's all it takes.

My orgasm explodes. "Chase!" is all I manage to get out before he quickly captures my lips again, swallowing my scream as my body shakes in his hold. My core locks around him, demanding his cum.

"Ellie," he growls against my lips before locking his hips in place, his own release following mine. He lets out a long groan as I feel his cock twitch inside me as jets of hot cum coat my insides. Knowing his seed is inside me again after all these years sends a tremor down my spine.

"Chase," someone barks from behind me, causing us both to go stiff.

"Fuck," Chase hisses, looking at me with slight panic. My eyes slowly move from him to find Jax standing in the doorway with a hungry expression.

"Seriously, man? This was not a part of the plan. I knew you declared your love for her again, but you couldn't last more than twenty-four hours?"

Chase looks at me with a guilty expression. Is it because of what we just did? Or is it because we got caught?

He pulls out of me, putting my bottoms back in place, and I feel his cum dripping out of me. He tucks himself away, looking over his shoulder at his best friend, then back at me.

"This isn't over," he says with pleading eyes before turning around and pushing past Jax. Jax looks back, giving me a look like he wishes it was him who was just inside me. He gives me a half smile. "See you later, Ellie. I hope that asshole being so forward didn't just fuck everything up."

I stand there with my head spinning and my brain working in overdrive. What the fuck just happened? Why did I let him fuck me? Why didn't I say no?

*I liked it.*

God, I fucking loved it, so much it hurts my soul. The sudden craving of need lingers. Old feelings finding a spot in my heart, that have no business being there.

Theo. Fuck. Fuck, fuck, fuck! I was supposed to tell him if anything was going to happen with Chase. Damn it! But I didn't know we were going to do that. It kind of just happened.

But this isn't just some meaningless hook up. Theo is amazing. He makes me laugh, and smile, while also giving me the feelings of being loved and cherished. He's everything I have been needing. But that doesn't take away from the feelings I still have for my first loves.

I knew I was still in love with them all when I came back here, but their horrible treatment toward me helped to dull those feelings.

I need to tell Theo, like now. I won't keep any secrets, not ones like this. I made a mistake, and I need to own up to it.

But was what just happened really a mistake? Or was it something else entirely?

# Chapter Thirty-Three

## ELLIE

**TEARS STING** my eyes as my belly flushes with a sick feeling. Not because of what Chase and I just did. That was everything I didn't know I needed. But because just a few hours ago, Theo and I had that conversation of me needing to tell him if anything was going to happen, and yet here I am, jumping on my ex's dick the moment he gets to the party. *What is wrong with me?*

Needing to call him now, I take a few deep breaths to get myself under control and wipe the tears from my eyes before heading back into the room with everyone.

"Hey, babe, you good?" Lexie asks, grabbing her towel to wipe her face.

"Yeah, just want to call and check in," I lie, hoping my voice doesn't shake as I dig around in my bag for my phone.

"Umm, what's on your leg?" Lexie asks the moment my hand makes contact with the phone. I freeze and look between my legs. *Fuck! Why didn't I go to the bathroom before coming back out here?*

With my phone in hand, I grab the towel on the chair next to me and quickly stand, wrapping it around my waste.

Turning to look at her, I can't help the look of horror on my face as my cheeks flush with embarrassment.

"Is that...?" she asks with wide eyes while mine start to burn with tears again.

"Don't," I say, my voice cracking.

Her face slips into a look of understanding. "Chase?" she asks, her voice softer, no judgment and fuck, if I'm not grateful for that right now.

Not trusting my voice, I bite my lip to hold back a sob as I nod my head.

She looks at the phone in my hand then back to me. "Go. I'll tell them you are checking in on the little one if they ask where you went."

"Thank you," I whisper. Without another word, I rush back to the bathroom I was in. With shaking hands, I press Theo's name in my contact list and raise the phone to my ear. I'm shaking right now as I try to fight off the urge to puke, listening to the ringing, and waiting for him to pick up.

"Ellie, sweetheart. Are you okay?" At the sound of his voice, I almost fall completely apart. "Ellie?" he asks again, more urgently this time.

"I'm here," I croak.

"What's wrong?" he asks. "I can tell something is wrong."

"I'm so sorry," I whimper. My back hits the door, and I slide down to the floor, tucking my face into my knees.

"Baby. It's okay," he says, and I know, I just know he has an idea of what this phone call is about.

"It just happened. He said all these things that had my head so fucked up. Ah!" I cry, grabbing a fist full of my hair.

"Did he force you?" he asks, his voice hard.

"No," I rush out. "No, he didn't. As fucked up as my head was in that moment, I...I wanted it." I let a sob slip. "I'm so sorry."

"Hey." His voice is too calm and soothing. *Is this man even human?* "It's okay. We talked about this. Did I think something would happen so fast? No, but you did exactly what you told me you would do."

"What?" I ask, raising my head from my knees.

"You said if anything were to happen, you would tell me and not keep secrets. You did just that. Ellie, what you have with them, it's deep. It's branded into your soul. They were your whole world for ten years, baby. You had this unique bond that no one but you guys can understand. That's not something that just goes away. I saw how you looked at them that day in the ice cream shop. The look of pain and longing. When you told me they were your exes, I knew that it wasn't over with you all. But I knew I wanted you too, so I went for it. And I'm so glad I did because I got the most amazing, brave, strong, and beautiful woman to love."

"Theo." I'm in tears now, like ugly crying. Thank God, I'm alone. I hope no one is in line waiting to get in and hearing this little break down.

"Go have fun. Enjoy your night. We can talk about this more when you get back. But baby, all I ask is communication. If you want him too, just talk to me, okay?"

"Okay," is all I can say. He's not giving me room to argue. I need time to think. I need to get fucking smashed, stay away from the sexy, blond man, who still owns a piece of my heart and just blew my fucking mind, and party with my friends.

"I love you," he says, and I let another sniffle break free because I can hear how true his words are.

"I love you too," my voice cracks. "So much, Theo. Please know that I never want to be without you, no matter what happens with Chase."

"I know, sweet girl, I know. I trust you and our love. You're mine, baby girl. And I'm yours, always. Now go enjoy your night and if you need me to come get you, I'm just a phone call away."

"Okay, bye," I say, my voice sounding so small. I hang up, place my phone on the ground before putting my face in my hands and cry. After getting everything out, I get up, take a deep breath, and clean myself of any evidence from what Chase and I did before heading back to the pool area. I don't bother checking over my appearance, I can't stand to look at myself right now. I can't change what happened. And I don't think I really want to.

I need to trust Theo and his words. I know I don't deserve such a loving, understanding, and supportive man, but God, thank you for giving him to me.

Going back to my bag, I put my phone away and slip my shorts on. I'm not in the mood to swim anymore.

"Hey! There you are," Val cheers. "Most of the party had enough with swimming, so we are taking the party into the living room! Come on, let's go get our drink on."

"You know what? That sounds perfect," I say, forcing a smile.

Val hooks arms with me, dragging me to the main part of the house. The room starts to fill up fast, and someone plugs in their phone and starts up a playlist. The first song that comes on is *Abcdefu* by GAYLE.

"Fuck yes!" Val whoops. "I love this song."

"You okay?" Lexie says leaning in so that only I can hear.

"Yeah. Or at least I will be. Right now, I say we drink, dance, and forget about everything other than us." I force a smile.

"Sounds good to me," Tabitha says, handing me a cooler. She gives one to the girls and Cooper too. "To us!"

"To us!" we all cheer, clinking our bottles and drinking.

The main chorus of the song comes on and I get lost in the music, screaming out the lyrics. The others do the same, and I can't stop the smile that takes over my face as I just enjoy being in this moment with my friends. I don't know where Chase and the others are right now, but I know they are nearby, watching. Although I'm not worried about them right now.

I don't even know how long we've been dancing or what time it is. All I know is that I feel amazing. I have a nice buzz going on and I'm enjoying myself.

Val has skipped out on us for the football player she hooked up with when we first got here while Lexie is in the corner making out with someone she started dancing with not too long ago. Cooper is hanging out with his teammates and Tabitha is off getting more drinks.

A slower song comes on and I close my eyes, just swaying with the music. Arms wrap around my waist as they start to move their hips with mine. I don't freak out because I can smell the scent of peppermint. I just lean back into Chase as the music plays on.

"I knew you loved my touch," he whispers into my ear.

My eyes fly open, my brain suddenly becomes more critical. This isn't Chase. Jumping forward, the stranger's arms drop from my body, and I spin around to see who was touching me.

Frozen. I can't move, I can't breathe as I look into the eyes of the monster who tried to destroy me. His pale gray eyes haunt my dreams every night.

He gives me a twisted grin as he blows a bubble of his gum and pops it. A burst of peppermint meets my nose. Fuck, how could I ever mistake this sick man for Chase?

"I-I gotta go," I say, before turning around and running. Pushing through the crowd, all I can think about is getting outside and away from him. *Tim.* What the fuck is Tim doing here? *Why, why the fuck is this happening to me now?* I feel like my chest is caving in, my heart is pounding too fast, and my head is spinning.

Bursting through the doors outside, I run over to the bushes and puke up everything from tonight. He had his hands on me. I fucking leaned into his touch. The more I think about it, the more I heave into the bush.

"You know, that's a bit of a hit to my ego. You try to dance with a girl, but she runs away and gets sick. I hope it's because of all the shit you've been drinking and not because of me."

I stand up, and spin around to find that Tim has followed me outside. Fuck. Looking around, I see that I just trapped myself. There's a big stone fence in the backyard, and the only way out that I can see are the doors I just came out from. But I'd have to get past Tim first.

"Let me go," I say as I wipe my mouth with the back of my hand. My head is pounding and my stomach is turning in on itself. I just want to go home. I want to be in Theo's arms. Is this my punishment for what Chase and I did? Is this the universe's way of reminding me that I'm not allowed to be happy and that I always fuck it up?

"Why so soon? We were just catching up." He takes a step forward, his black hair shining in the moonlight covering one of his eyes.

"I have nothing to say to you." *Come on, Ellie. He took advantage of you before, don't let him win. Don't let him take any more away from you. He's already taken enough. Fight. Stand your ground. You're not drugged like last time. And you didn't drink enough to not be able to function, not yet meeting the 'get smashed' goal of the night. Thank God.*

"Well, I have a lot to say to you." He gives me a sleazy grin. Why is no one else outside? How can not one person be back here?! "When my guys told me they ran into you at the game, I was disappointed I wasn't with them. To find out you were back in town, going to school with your exes, was a nice surprise. Heard it has been pretty rough for you though. Guess they still see you as the whore you are."

"I'm not a whore," I snap.

"No? Then why did you cheat on them with me?" He cocks his head to the side.

"I didn't cheat and you know it. You...you..." *Come on, Ellie. You can do it.* "You raped me." That word comes out on a hushed sob, but I did it. Saying it out loud to him, confronting him, it's not what I want to be doing, but here we are.

His smile turns to one of pure evil. "Oh sugar, you know you loved it."

"No, no, I didn't. I didn't want any of it. I was in a loving relationship. I would never have cheated on them. You drugged me. You raped me!" This time I say it a little louder with more strength behind it.

"Yeah, yeah, I did rape you. You were a fucking tease. Always flirting with me, leading me on then treating me like I was nothing!"

"I never flirted with you," I insist. "I was just trying to be nice."

"You're a stupid, selfish whore. You got what you deserved. And you know what? It's all I've thought about. Every time I'm alone, I replay that night. The way you looked up at me with fear in your eyes, unable to move while you just laid there, and I got to take everything I was owed. When I'm with another girl, I pretend it's you. Best fuck of my life."

"You're sick!" I shout.

"Nah, babe, I just know what I want. And now that you're here in front of me, I'm gonna have it again. No one's going to save you, just like they didn't save you last time."

No, no this can't be happening. Not again.

I turn my head to look for help, but he's there in front of me in a flash, gripping my face with his hand so hard it hurts. "Look at me you little—" before he can finish what he was saying, he is yanked away from me.

## RAIN

God, my tits still fucking hurt and it's been a week. The bruise on them is excruciating. At first, it was a blueish purple, now it's an ugly yellow.

Adjusting my bikini top, I leave the bathroom. I've been

drinking since the moment I got here. Knowing she's here and I can't be near her, fucking sucks.

As I head back to the kitchen to grab another drink, I'm almost knocked over as Ellie pushes past me.

"What the hell?" I mutter as I watch her while she pushes through the rest of the crowd and out the back doors to the yard.

Turning to the direction she just came from, my blood fucking boils when I see Tim standing there. He starts to head this way, moving past me like he doesn't even recognize me, and follows after Ellie.

I get this feeling, this sick inkling that something isn't right. Looking around, I spot Chase in the next room talking to the guys.

This fucker didn't take long to brag about fucking Ellie the first moment he got here or how mind blowing, Earth shattering, and world changing it was. Chase was quick to rub it in our faces. *Lucky fucker.* Saying I'm jealous is an understatement. I would kill to be able to hold her in my arms again.

"Come with me," I tell them, breaking up their conversation.

"What, why?" Chase asks with pinched brows.

"I just saw Ellie run out of here like a bat out of hell. And guess who was right behind her looking like a predator stalking his prey?"

They all just look at me, and I roll my eyes with a huff. "Tim is here, and guys, I'm not getting a good feeling. Something isn't right."

Brody's face morphs into fury and he's up and out of his seat.

"What direction?" he snaps as we all follow after him.

"Backyard." He pulls out his phone and I look down at it, wondering what the hell he is doing. "What's that for?"

"Insurance," he growls.

"Seriously, dude, haven't you learned?" Chase barks. "Stop being a fucking asshole."

We get to the door, Brody presses record, and just as we step outside, we hear their voices. Rounding the little corner of the back porch, I spot them by the back wall, over by the bushes. We come to a stop, and Brody raises his phone. Giving him a death glare, I turn to Ellie and Tim.

"No, no, I didn't. I didn't want any of it. I was in a loving relationship. I would never have cheated on them. You drugged me, you raped me!" she shouts.

My eyes go wide, and I let out a gasp as my brain tries to process what she just said.

"Yeah, yeah, I did rape you..."

I do not hear anything else after that. A loud ringing in my heart becomes deafening as my mind plays those words on repeat. Rape. She was raped. When we came up into the room after Brody told us what was going on, we saw her lying there and we just left her there after he forced himself on her. We left her there like discarded trash and went home thinking she cheated on us. We let Brody get into our heads and assumed the worst.

Something warm runs down my cheeks. I touch my face and look at my wet fingers. *Am I crying? I must be crying. I think I'm going to be sick.*

Like an elastic band snapping back into place, I come back to reality as Brody shoves his phone into my chest and stalks off like a pissed off bull toward Tim. Looking over at Ellie's face, all I see is terror as Tim grabs her face in a painful looking grip. But it doesn't last long because Brody pulls him off of her and onto the ground in a second.

Bending over, I throw up as my mind conjures up images of Tim forcing himself on her, and her being put through the worst thing anyone can go through. She must have been so scared.

We spent years hating her, all for nothing. Now I hate myself.

## CHASE

Rape. The word plays on an endless loop as everything starts to click into place. She never cheated on us. That fucking pig raped her. *He raped my girl!* No, no! This can't be happening. But it is. No matter how much I wish I heard those words wrong, I didn't.

I feel like my soul is being ripped from my body, or an arrow is tearing apart my heart. I want to cry, scream, kill at the idea of her petrified as that vile waste of space took what wasn't his.

Flashes of memories play before my eyes. What she said to me when she helped me clean my nose ring. When I mentioned graduation night, she looked ready to cry and a little sick. Now I know why. All this time, we brought up that night to her, telling her she cheated. Forcing her to remember it. She didn't cheat. She was raped. And for years, we thought the worst while she was suffering in pain. Alone.

And he fucking admitted it too! I'm going to fucking kill him. But before I have time to react, Brody is already racing toward him.

## JAX

All this time, we were wrong. So fucking wrong. What she said at paintball, it makes sense now. I told her I would destroy anyone who tried to force themselves on her. But I failed her. We failed to protect what was ours. Our love, our heart, our girl. As much as I love Brody, right now, I really fucking hate him too. I hate that he was so dead set on what he thought he saw and I hate myself for trusting his words. We should have known better, trusted that she would have never done something like that to us, never cheat. We were wrong this whole time. She never cheated on us. He took her, touched her, and *raped* her.

I feel sick. My heart is shattering as my brain processes everything. And when that sack of shit puts his hands on Ellie, I do nothing to stop Brody as he storms over to Tim.

## BRODY

Pure mother fucking fury courses through my veins right now. Murder. I'm going to fucking murder him. He touched her. He touched her with his filthy fucking hands and forced himself on her.

He fucking raped her. Right now, I can't think about how much of an imbecile I was for thinking she cheated. I'll beat myself up over that later. Right now, I only have one thing on my mind and that's feeling my fists pounding into his flesh while I watch the light drain from his eyes.

And when he puts his fucking hands on her, I lose it. With my chest heaving, body vibrating, I charge at Tim. Grabbing the back of his shirt, I yank him away with all of my newfound strength and throw him to the ground. I'm on him in an instant, straddling his chest with one hand on his throat as I choke him, and the other pounding into this putrid face.

I ignore the pain radiating through my hand as I relentlessly smash his face in. I ignore the crying behind me, the sounds of the party goers making their way into the backyard. I ignore Jax as he tries to get my attention. My tunnel vision only sees one thing: This fucker dying.

"He needs to stop or he's going to kill him," I hear Jax through the ringing in my ears.

"Good, that bastard doesn't deserve to live for what he did," Chase roars.

"I know!" Jax shouts back. "But it's no fucking good if he's in prison for murder!"

"FUCK!" Chase curses.

Then I feel two sets of hands wrestling me away, pulling me off of Tim.

"Let go," I bellow. "I'm not done with him!" I roar, spit spraying from my mouth like a rabid dog.

"I know. I know, Brody. I know you want him to pay. We all do. But you're no use to Ellie, to us, if you're locked up behind bars for killing him."

I fight against their grip, desperate to get back down there and finish the job.

"Cops!" someone yells and the whole party starts to erupt into chaos.

"Damn it," Jax sighs. Chase grabs a hold of me from behind, and Jax moves to face me. "There's no way of getting out of this. They're going to arrest you for assault but we will get you out and tell them the truth, okay? Brody, that's enough for tonight. Don't make it worse. I love you." His eyes are red with tears, his face broken and pained, a total opposite of my red and feral one.

Looking over my shoulder, I see Ellie in Cooper's arms, her friends crowded around her. She's crying as they hold her up and my heart fucking breaks. This is all my fault. I walked in on her being raped, and my damaged, screwed up mind thought the worst. My mind went to cheating and not the truth. Looks like Tim isn't the only monster.

The cops make their way into the backyard and over to me. They talk to the guys, but I don't pay any mind to them. My attention is on the girl I was supposed to protect, but failed to do so.

Hands roughly grab me, forcing my arms behind my back. "You're under arrest. Anything you say can and will be used against you in the court of law," the officer says, reading me my Miranda rights. I don't struggle.

The cop pushes me forward, telling me to move. As we make our way to the back door, I look over at Ellie one last time. Her eyes are wide and blood shot.

"I'm sorry, Star. So fucking sorry." My voice cracks when I use the nickname I haven't used in years. My little falling star. She bursts into tears again at hearing that name, and I feel like shit for leaving her like this.

They guide me through the house and out to their waiting squad cars. Red and blue lights light up the dark night. The door closes behind me, and I sit in the backseat, waiting to be taken in.

A big secret has been unravelled tonight. I don't know what's going to happen now. But what I do know is that I plan on doing everything I can to help Rain, Chase, and Jax get back the love of their lives—the one that I so stupidly took away from them. I don't deserve her. I probably never did, but they do.

Only question is, will she be willing to let us back in after everything we did?


To be continued...


What's going to happen next? Find out in
Secrets Revealed: Silver Valley University Book Two.

# Books By Alisha

**Emerald Lake Prep – Series:**

Book One: Second Chances (February 2021)

Book Two: Into The Unknown (May 2021)

Book Three: Shattered Pieces (September 2021)

Book Four: Redemption Found (Early 2022)

**Blood Empire – Series:**

Book One: Rising Queen (July 2021)

Book Two: Crowned Queen (December 2021)

Book Three: Savage Queen (Coming 2022)

**Silver Valley University – Series:**

Book One: Hidden Secrets (January 2022)

Book Two: Secrets Revealed (Coming 2022)

**Standalones**

We Are Worthy- A sweet and steamy omegaverse. (2022)

# *Thank You*

I would love to give a big thank you to anyone who has supported me on this journey. A big thank you to every single person who helped bring Ellie's story to life. Without each one of you, this book would not be possible.

I'm also beyond grateful for Jessica, Jennifer, and Amy. You ladies are more than just my Alphas, you're family now! Thank you for all the time and energy you put into Hidden Secrets and for helping it become the awesome book that it is! I don't think I would have had as much fun writing it without you three! Can't wait to make way more books with you! And a big shout out to Tamara. Thanks for being there for me, and helping me with everything you do, you're the best wifey!

Many thanks to my Beta and ARC teams. You all helped me make my book even better, and I look forward to sending you way more work in the future.

And finally, thank you to all my readers. It was an honor to write this book for you. Thank you for giving my new book series a chance.

*About the Author*

Writer, Alisha Williams, lives in Alberta, Canada, with her husband and her two headstrong kids, and three kitties. When she isn't writing or creating her own gorgeous graphic content, she loves to read books by her favorite authors.

Writing has been a lifelong dream of hers, and this book was made despite the people who prayed for it to fail, but because Alisha is not afraid to go for what she wants, she has proven that dreams do come true.

Wanna see what all her characters look like, hear all the latest gossip about her new books or even get a chance to become a part of one of her teams? Join her readers group on Facebook here - Naughty Queens. Or find her author's page here - Alisha Williams Author

Of course, she also has an Instagram account to show all her cool graphics, videos and more book related goodies - alishawilliamsauthor

Sign up for Alisha's Newsletter

Got TikTok? Follow alishawilliamsauthor

Made in USA - North Chelmsford, MA
1310429_9798444632635
04.05.2022 0903